A
PLAIN
MAN

OTHER BOOKS BY MARY ELLIS

Standalone Novels
Sarah's Christmas Miracle
An Amish Family Reunion

The New Beginnings Series
Living in Harmony
Love Comes to Paradise
A Little Bit of Charm

The Miller Family Series
A Widow's Hope
Never Far from Home
The Way to a Man's Heart

The Wayne County Series
Abigail's New Hope
A Marriage for Meghan

The Civil War Heroines Series
The Quaker and the Rebel
The Lady and the Officer
Angel of Mercy

A PLAIN MAN

MARY ELLIS

HARVEST HOUSE PUBLISHERS
EUGENE, OREGON

A PLAIN MAN
Copyright © 2014 by Mary Ellis
Published by Harvest House Publishers
Eugene, Oregon 97402
www.harvesthousepublishers.com

Library of Congress Cataloging-in-Publication Data
Ellis, Mary
A plain man / Mary Ellis.
    pages cm
ISBN 978-0-7369-4980-4 (pbk.)
ISBN 978-0-7369-4982-8 (eBook)
1. Amish—Fiction. 2. Bachelors—Fiction. I. Title.
PS3626.E36P53 2014
813'.6—dc23
                                                                2013031966

ACKNOWLEDGMENTS

Thanks to Carol Lee Shevlin for providing my home away from home, Simple Pleasures Bed and Breakfast in Winesburg, and for opening many doors in the Amish community. I will be forever grateful.

Thanks to Joanna, Kathryn, Rosanna, Esther, and members of the Old Order Amish districts of Wayne and Holmes Counties. A special thanks to Rosanna Coblentz for her delicious recipes.

Thanks to my agent, Mary Sue Seymour; my lovely proofreader, Joycelyn Sullivan; my publicist Jeane Wynn of Wynn-Wynn Media; my editor, Kim Moore, and the wonderful staff at Harvest House Publishers.

Thanks to my husband, Ken, construction superintendent extraordinaire, for building the house that shelters me and answering my endless questions about construction and labor disputes.

Thanks to my former pastor, Reverend Bob Petruccio, for leading me into a reedy, fish-infested, muddy-bottomed lake to baptize me. You changed my life forever.

Finally, thanks be to God. All things in this world are by His hand.

The boots of the warrior
and the uniforms bloodstained by war
will all be burned.
They will be fuel for the fire.
For a child is born to us,
a son is given to us.
The government will rest on his shoulders.
And he will be called:
Wonderful Counselor, Mighty God,
Everlasting Father, Prince of Peace.
His government and its peace
will never end.
He will rule with fairness and justice from
the throne of his ancestor David for all eternity.

Isaiah 9:5-7

COME, THOU FOUNT OF EVERY BLESSING

Come, Thou Fount of every blessing,
Tune my heart to sing Thy grace;
Streams of mercy, never ceasing,
Call for songs of loudest praise.
Teach me some melodious sonnet,
Sung by flaming tongues above.
Praise the mount! I'm fixed upon it,
Mount of Thy redeeming love.

Sorrowing I shall be in spirit,
Till released from flesh and sin,
Yet from what I do inherit,
Here Thy praises I'll begin;
Here I raise my Ebenezer;
Here by Thy great help I've come;
And I hope, by Thy good pleasure,
Safely to arrive at home.

Jesus sought me when a stranger,
Wandering from the fold of God;
He, to rescue me from danger,
Interposed His precious blood;
How His kindness yet pursues me
Mortal tongue can never tell,
Clothed in flesh, till death shall loose me
I cannot proclaim it well.

O to grace how great a debtor
Daily I'm constrained to be!
Let Thy goodness, like a fetter,
Bind my wandering heart to Thee.
Prone to wander, Lord, I feel it,
Prone to leave the God I love;

Here's my heart, O take and seal it,
  Seal it for Thy courts above.

O that day when freed from sinning,
  I shall see Thy lovely face;
Clothed then in blood washed linen
  How I'll sing Thy sovereign grace;
Come, my Lord, no longer tarry,
  Take my ransomed soul away;
Send thine angels now to carry
  Me to realms of endless day.

1

Come, Thou Fount of every blessing,
Tune my heart to sing Thy grace

FREDERICKSBURG, OHIO
MARCH

Caleb Beachy pulled the wagon up to the door and carried two buckets brimming with sap into the barn. Careful not to spill the sticky liquid, he struggled up the stepladder and dumped one and then the other into the sap evaporator.

"How many does that make, Cal?" Pushing up the brim of his hat, James Weaver peered up from his crouched position in front of the woodburner.

"These are seventy-seven and seventy-eight for today, one-forty-two including yesterday's for the weekend. But who's counting?" Caleb winked to let his friend know he was teasing. Then he returned to the wagon for the rest of the sap—his eighth load of the day and by no means his last. Other friends and neighbors were collecting buckets from Weaver maple trees spread over two hundred acres of wooded hills. The trees had been planted by James's *grossdawdi* many years ago. The other workers would combine half-buckets together and set them in rows at the collection point on the trail. Caleb and James's *daed* each drove a team of Belgian draft horses to the Weaver sugarhouse, a veritable beehive of activity every January, February, and March.

Maple syrup, along with sugar candy in a variety of shapes, was the cash crop for the Weaver family. Plenty of people preferred real maple syrup on their pancakes and waffles instead of the less expensive cane syrup. And judging by the joyous expression on his face, James would still enjoy producing syrup when he was a *grossdawdi* himself.

As for Caleb, he couldn't wait to take a hot shower and wash away any remaining amber goop. "How many trees did you tap this year?" he asked good-naturedly. As much as he disliked the work, he liked James. And friends within the district were few in number since he'd moved back from Cleveland.

"Over two thousand." James straightened to his full height of barely five and a half feet. "That's a record for us." Tugging off his gloves, he drained his water bottle in a few swallows. "If prices stay as high as last year's, we should have plenty to pay taxes and fatten the medical expense fund." His bright pink cheeks and curly red hair gave him a boyish appearance. James couldn't wait to find a wife so he could grow a beard, insisting he would then look his age of twenty-five.

"Well, I plan to stay until your last tree runs dry." Caleb offered his most authentic smile. "Without a job, working here for free was the best offer I got." They both chuckled.

"Don't forget we give you lunch. Plus you'll take home a year's supply of syrup." James followed Caleb out to the wagon instead of feeding more wood into the evaporator. "Say, are you going to the big pancake breakfast in Shreve in two weeks? They hold it on both Saturday and Sunday, so it won't interfere with preaching services."

Caleb fastened the top button on his coat before the wind cut him in half. "I hadn't planned on it. My *mamm* fixes pancakes all the time. Why would I pay money for them? Besides, it'll be nothing but a bunch of *Englisch* tourists there." He lifted two buckets from the wagon, spilling some on his leather boots.

"Nope, lots of Amish folk attend the annual event, especially if it's a nice day." James stepped closer to whisper conspiratorially. "Plenty of Plain *women* will be there too."

Caleb almost swallowed his tongue trying not to laugh. From his inflection, it sounded like James considered females as rare as gold or silver. "Gosh, I'm not sure I've seen one of *them* before." He strode toward the barn, trying to keep his buckets evenly weighted.

James followed at his heels and took no offense from Caleb's teasing.

"Will you get serious? Here we are—almost a quarter of a century old and still no wives. If we don't get moving, all the young and pretty ones will be snatched up."

Caleb climbed the stepladder, thinking his friend might climb up behind him. "What will that leave us—bald-headed grannies in their seventies? At least they should be great cooks by that age." He leaned back from the heat while emptying his sap into the evaporator.

James peered up from ground level. "Maybe Emma Wengard will come, or Dot Raber. Then we could—"

"Are you allowing this fire to go out?" Ben Weaver appeared in the doorway of the sugarhouse, abruptly curtailing his son's romantic plans. Although his father sounded stern, his blue eyes twinkled with amusement.

"*Nein,* I'm just discussing something with our best employee." James sprinted to the wagon for an armload of split firewood.

"Employee implies a person gets a paycheck. I've only got ham sandwiches with hot coffee for you boys." Ben set down a cloth-covered basket and thermos and returned to his own tasks. No idle hands during sugar season.

James washed his hands in a bucket of soapy water. "At least think about going to the breakfast. You need to get off the farm more. Aren't you bored since coming back from the city?"

Caleb rolled up his sleeves, picked up the bar of soap, and scrubbed off the dried-on sap. Seldom did anyone bring up his five-year venture into the *Englisch* world. Most Amish people preferred to forget the life he led since leaving home. "Bored? Nah, I'm not bored. I have a roof over my head without a rent payment to worry about. I eat three square meals a day from the *second* best cook in Wayne County. I have clothes on my back and not one, but two hats to my name." Caleb pulled on his suspenders. "And I get to barrel down the road at eight miles an hour as long as it's not snowing or raining too hard."

James wasn't sure how to take the sarcasm. "Are you thinking about moving back to the city?"

Caleb met James's eye. "Absolutely not. The *Englisch* world isn't all it's cracked up to be. When my car broke down, I couldn't afford to repair the junk-heap. After I could finally afford to buy a truck, it got towed because I parked in the wrong spot. By the time I figured out where they towed it, the impound fees and fines were more than the truck was worth. Without a vehicle I couldn't get to work on time, so I got fired."

James seemed to sort the details in his mind. "Wasn't there public transportation or a coworker to give you a lift?"

"Even if I caught a ride to the union hall, I usually sat around twiddling my thumbs. Construction was slow, and I'm not just talking about winter. Without a paycheck a man doesn't eat. I don't know if you ever tried it, but going hungry is no fun."

James dried his hands and dug their lunch from the basket. "There must have been something you liked up north. You stayed away for five years." He handed Caleb two sandwiches.

Caleb slouched down against a post. "Plenty at first, when I had wheels and a good job. But money management didn't turn out to be my strong suit."

His friend's confusion only seemed to deepen.

Caleb didn't know how much to reveal about his past. Could he admit he'd hung out in bars until closing time and bought drinks for people he'd never met before? Should he talk about sleeping with women who were little more than acquaintances? How about the fact that he'd attended church only once during his entire time in Cleveland? Unless he counted church basements that operated as free soup kitchens. No, none of that would help him reconnect with his few friends in the district.

"Let's just say it's harder to be successful in the *Englisch* world. And if a man's not successful, he's not going to be happy." Caleb lifted the top slice of homemade bread to inspect the sandwich. It was almost an inch of honey-smoked ham and Swiss cheese with fresh lettuce, tomatoes, red onions, and bread-and-butter pickles. "Do you know how much a sandwich like this would cost in the city?"

Shaking his head, James took another bite of lunch.

"Eight or nine dollars. All I have to do here is put in ten hours of hard labor."

The two laughed in camaraderie before returning to their assigned tasks—James tending the evaporator and stoking the fire; Caleb ferrying endless buckets of sap to the sugarhouse. But when Caleb climbed into his buggy to head home that night, he felt tired but content. He had helped a neighbor and filled his hours with muscle-building work instead of spirit-draining mental activity. Each day the sun grew warmer and the hours of daylight longer. Caleb had even spotted a robin that morning—a sure sign that spring was around the corner.

Spring would definitely help his disposition. He needed to get out of the house. A man could only sweep the barn or restack hay bales so many times. Once the land dried out, they could start plowing and planting. Outdoors with the sun on his face and the wind in his hair, he felt free.

And less like a prisoner.

His homecoming on Christmas Eve had been sweeter than he imagined it would be, surely better than any prodigal son deserved. His mother had fawned over him for days—cooking his favorite foods and baking extra sweets. His three sisters welcomed him with unabashed affection. Sarah made no mention of his empty refrigerator in a deplorable apartment. She greeted him with a smile each morning, always ready to help smooth his transition from *Englisch* back to Plain.

Caleb didn't mind owning few clothes. Or the fact that his *mamm* cut his hair to look like every other Amish man in town. He didn't even mind his slow mode of transportation. But must his father watch his every move like a prowling dog near the henhouse? Couldn't he give him the benefit of the doubt? Why did Eli Beachy treat him like a shirttail relative dropping by on his way to a family reunion?

He had come home, but his father refused to believe it.

❧

Eli watched his firstborn kick off his boots from the kitchen window. His face looked smudged with soot and raw from the wind while his chore coat was dirty beyond belief. It would take Elizabeth every trick in her laundry book to get the coat clean again.

As Caleb swept open the door, Eli let the curtain drop back in place. "Leave that jacket on the porch, son. It's filthy. What's the matter with you?" An icy blast filled the room.

"Nothing is wrong with me. It's cold outside." Shrugging off the garment, Caleb tossed it onto the glider. Once inside, he headed straight for the bathroom.

"Your *mamm's* been holding supper for you. The rest of us are starving. Do you know what time it is?"

Caleb halted halfway across the kitchen and peered at the battery wall clock. "It's six thirty. Sorry, *Mamm.* James wanted all the buckets down to the sugarhouse before dark." Caleb spoke to Elizabeth over his shoulder. "You've got no idea what critters come down from the hills to make a feast…or a mess if we leave them out. Animals can smell something sweet a mile away. Mind if I shower before I eat?"

"I can just imagine." Elizabeth lifted pans from the oven with her mitts. "No problem. Nothing bad will happen if the meat loaf, mashed potatoes, and butter beans sit for ten more minutes. You go ahead."

Caleb shut the bathroom door behind him without acknowledging his father. *A sign of disrespect*, thought Eli, joining his *fraa* at the stove. "That boy spends more time down the road than he does at home. It's as though we don't have enough chores to keep him busy."

"I heard him ask if you needed help with milking last evening and you told him no." She carried the double meat loaf to the table's center trivet.

"Well, I didn't, not last night." Eli frowned as she returned to the stove.

"And he asked if you needed help ordering seeds. Sometimes the fine print in those catalogs is hard to decipher, even with reading glasses." She slipped her soiled apron over her head.

"The boy could see I had my magnifier out. How many people does it take to order a few packets of radish, carrot, and turnip seeds?" Eli carried his mug of coffee to the head of the table and eased into his chair. "Besides, I don't like anybody to hover over my shoulder."

Holding a pot of beans aloft, Elizabeth stared at him over her half-moon glasses. "If you want or need Caleb's assistance, tell him what you wish done and when. Give him a list of chores, *ehemann*. Stop waiting for him to read your mind." She placed the pot on another trivet and walked to the bottom of the steps. "Sarah, Rebekah, Katie, come downstairs. It's time to eat."

Eli clamped down on his molars and dropped his voice to a whisper. "I haven't needed help since he came home. January and February aren't exactly the busy season around a farm. If the Weavers could use him with sugaring, I don't mind sending him over. They gave me a hand last October with the corn harvest."

Elizabeth removed a huge bowl of salad from the refrigerator. "Now you've got me confused, Eli. What exactly is the matter?" She also spoke softly as she slipped into her chair.

"He barely pays me any mind at all since coming back. He seems to go out of his way to avoid me. And I'm his pa."

"*Jah,* but he's twenty-four years old, not fourteen. He's a grown man, accustomed to living on his own. You can't expect him to ask for help with his homework or for you to take him fishing down by the river. You said yourself not much is happening this time of year, so maybe there's not much to talk about." She pinched the bridge of her nose as though to stem a headache.

"I watched him from the corner of my eye at preaching last Sunday. He was practically dozing off."

Much to Eli's dismay, Elizabeth burst out laughing. "Goodness, he wouldn't be the first man—or woman—to fall asleep during the younger minister's sermon. The man does tend to get long-winded."

"It's not funny. The boy should show me some respect."

Elizabeth stretched out a hand to pat his arm. "Like I said—he's not a boy; he's a man. Please be patient with him," she pleaded. "He was gone a long time and his shift back to Amish life will not occur overnight."

He nodded, knowing she was right, but something still niggled in the back of his mind. "We don't know what his life had been like. Who were his people up in the city? What kind of nasty business did he get involved in?" Eli felt a frisson of anxiety run up his spine, not for his son's physical safety, but for his eternal soul.

"You're right. We don't know and we never will. It's not our concern. He hadn't joined the church yet, so all can be forgiven and forgotten once he does. Let the past go, Eli. It's causing you much grief." Again she patted his arm as though he were a child.

"Then the sooner he gets baptized the better." When he lifted the lid from the meat loaf pan, the pungent aroma of garlic and onions filled the room, whetting his appetite.

"Give him a chance. And while you're at it, why not give him a job?"

"Work for *me* again?" His anxiety didn't diminish.

"You said yourself it's almost spring. Soon the roofing contracts will pick up, along with barn building. Couldn't you use an extra pair of hands?"

"*Jah*, but—"

"With so small a herd of cows, the girls and I can manage most farm chores. We won't need Caleb home all day."

"But I thought—"

His *fraa* interrupted a second time—a rare occurrence. "Caleb is an accomplished carpenter. Sarah told us he'd been an apprentice for three years and had made journeyman. He was a member of the carpenters' union in Cleveland, so it's not like you're hiring a man without skills. The two of you working together makes perfect sense to me."

"Mind if I put in my two cents' worth? Or do you prefer to handle both sides of the conversation?" Eli glowered at his beloved wife.

She laughed at his distress. "Sorry, *mei liewi*. I got carried away. I grant you the floor." Elizabeth flourished her hand over the table just as his three daughters sauntered into the kitchen, carefree as a picnic on a warm summer day. Their youngest walked straight to the chocolate cake on the counter and stuck her finger in the frosting.

"Leave the cake alone and sit down," Eli thundered. "Why must your *mamm* fix supper alone while her three *dochders* laze around their bedroom like *Englischers*?"

Sarah's jaw dropped while the younger two slinked to their seats like chastised hound dogs. "I baked the cake as soon as I got home from work," Sarah said. "Then I ironed every shirt and dress in *Mamm's* laundry basket. I was sewing in my room until Cal got home."

Rebekah looked annoyed. "And I fixed the salad along with the mashed potatoes."

"I set the table." Katie sounded like she was on the verge of tears.

"I can vouch for truthful statements all around." Elizabeth appeared to be biting her tongue.

"In that case, *danki.*" Eli couldn't quite bring himself to apologize to his *kinner.* "Sit down, Sarah. As soon as your *bruder* finishes—"

"I'm here." Caleb stood in the bathroom doorway. It seemed to be the night for interruptions. His wet hair was plastered to his forehead and his feet were bare, but at least he wore clean trousers and a fresh shirt. "I hurried as fast as I could." On his way to the table, Caleb pulled both suspenders up to his broad shoulders.

"Let's bow our heads." Eli didn't close his eyes until every family member shut theirs. Then he waited long after his prayer before announcing, "All right. Let's eat." Faster than a person could draw a breath, bowls started flying around the table, silverware clattered, and female tongues began to wag.

"How's James?" Rebekah asked her brother. "What's he been up to?"

"Does anybody want to see Mrs. Pratt's new puppy after supper?" asked Katie.

"*Mamm*, did you remember to buy shampoo on your last trip to town? I'm practically out." Sarah's question was the calmest and most reserved. However, since all three had been asked simultaneously, none were answered.

Instead Elizabeth pivoted toward her son. "Sounds like sugaring is in full swing, *jah*? As soon as the Weavers no longer need you, your *daed* would like you to work for him."

Eli choked on a mouthful of salad. Sarah jumped up to pound on his back, while Caleb turned his dark brown gaze toward Eli. "Is that true?" he asked.

Eli wiped his mouth once his coughing stopped. "It is, but I don't seem to talk fast enough for the Beachy household."

His son neither laughed nor smiled. "Work for you for money?"

"Of course, for money. I pay all the men on my crew." Eli tossed down his napkin.

"How much?"

Rolling his eyes, Eli quoted the hourly rate for his most experienced employee.

Caleb considered for a long moment. "All right, I'll take the job once James no longer needs me." Then he devoured his three slices of meat loaf as though they would disappear if he didn't wolf them down.

No *"I'm glad to be able to put my carpentry skills to good use."*

No *"I would love a dependable paycheck so I can save for the future."*

Not even so much as a *"Danki, Daed."*

The next words out of Caleb's mouth had something to do with mashed potatoes. But Eli was concentrating on his own meal so he wouldn't say something he would regret. He had already questioned the wisdom of Elizabeth's suggestion, doubting their son would ever come back to the fold.

❧

Sarah stood next to her boss on the front porch of Country Pleasures Bed-and-Breakfast. The requisite morning meal was finished. Every fresh strawberry swimming in whipped cream was gone, while the four groups of guests had put a healthy dent in the cheese soufflé with crisp Canadian bacon. She'd even seen one elderly woman fill a bag with the remaining blueberry muffins and iced cinnamon buns. Not that she needed to be clandestine. Lee Ann Pratt happily sent leftovers home with departing guests, along with the recipes.

All you had to do was ask.

Lee Ann would give the shirt off her back as long as it was warm outside. That had been Sarah's favorite quip since she started working here four years ago. People kinder or more generous than the Pratts would be hard to find in Amish Country, Ohio…or anyplace else.

Amish Country—she and her Christian sect were the reason tourists poured into Wayne, Holmes, and Tuscarawas counties nine months out of the year. A few brave souls even traveled during the dead of winter to snap photos of shaggy draft horses creating clouds of white vapor with each exhalation, or of farm fields blanketed in snow. Or they came to relax by the fire in a cozy inn, sipping tea or cocoa while reading a good book. The countryside was nothing if not peaceful during cold months. Some guests came to buy handmade quilts, oak or walnut furniture, local cheese, or free-range beef without the crowds and heavy traffic like in fair weather. Sarah enjoyed this time of year, especially since the B&B was seldom at full capacity. But their quiet weekends were rapidly drawing to a close.

"Thanks so much, Lee Ann!" A well-dressed woman in her forties hugged the innkeeper for the third time. "As always, everything was perfect. We can't wait to come back, maybe in June. I'll check my calendar." Waving, she carried a small makeup case to their sleek sedan while her husband lugged three large suitcases—one for each day of their short stay.

Within a few minutes, the seven-member, multigenerational group from Medina trudged out the door. They too were effusive with their praise and grateful for Mrs. Pratt's hospitality. Pausing in front of Sarah, the matriarch studied her one last time. "It was a treat to meet someone Amish while we were sightseeing. We really got our money's worth." The woman pinched Sarah's cheek as though she were a toddler and followed her family to the parking lot. The last to depart were two young couples—one on their honeymoon. Both pledged to return to Country Pleasures each year for their anniversary. One husband added that it was much cheaper than Florida, considering the price of gasoline. Sarah and Lee Ann released matching sighs of relief when the final car tooted and drove off in search of their next bargain…or headed home and back to work.

"Goodness, that was a lively bunch." Lee Ann slipped an arm around Sarah's waist. "Let's go inside. It's not as warm as the sun would lead one to believe."

Sarah pranced ahead to open the door. "Is there anything left for our breakfast and Mr. Pratt's? That was a hungry group of people."

"I saved some in the kitchen just to make sure. With the work we have ahead of us, I'm in no mood for cold cereal or white toast with jam."

As usual, the innkeeper and employee ignored four messy guest rooms, plenty of towels and linens to wash, a dining room of dirty dishes, and a cyclone-hit kitchen until they ate their own meal. Sarah loved chatting with Lee Ann. The woman had enough stories about her missionary days in Africa to keep breakfast interesting for years. But today she had another topic in mind. "How's Caleb doing? You never talk about your brother much. And I seldom see him on the lane."

Dividing the remaining food onto three plates, Sarah gave Lee Ann's husband the largest portion. She delivered his breakfast to the private family room where Roy watched morning talk shows and then settled down to eat by the front window. Their little table had a perfect view of the flower garden, birdfeeders, and busy street down the sloping lawn. "There's not much to tell, I guess." Sarah picked up the coffee cup Lee Ann had filled.

"Oh no you don't. You always say that. Then I pry out all kinds of tasty tidbits. Has he joined the Amish church yet? Did he find a job? What about a girlfriend? Has he found someone new or rekindled an old flame?" Mrs. Pratt's brown eyes almost danced out of her head.

"I truly think you should write books in your spare time with your vivid imagination." Sarah chewed a piece of bacon. "Let's see…no, no, and no. Any more questions?"

"Only one—how come?" Lee Ann crossed her arms over her full apron.

"It's hard to find carpentry work in the winter, especially since he doesn't want to work for *Englischers*. And he can't join the Amish church without taking the classes to prepare for baptism. And baptism is only once a year, usually in the fall. I'm sure he'll join the next class that will start in summer." Sarah swallowed some delicious egg and cheese soufflé.

"*And?*" Lee Ann drained her cup and refilled from the carafe. "He needs a nice woman to settle down with."

Sarah felt odd discussing Caleb with Mrs. Pratt, but her boss had only his best interest at heart. And she wasn't a gossip. "I couldn't agree more, but he keeps to himself when he's not helping one of our neighbors. In the three months he's been home, he's gone nowhere other than preaching services. And if the rest of us remain to socialize, he walks home—no matter how far or how nasty the weather. When we go visiting on Sunday afternoon, he stays in his room. He tells my parents that he's not ready. I don't know how a person *readies* himself for eating pie and drinking coffee with folks you've known your whole life." Sarah's exasperation with her older brother slipped out.

Lee Ann reflected quietly while finishing her eggs. "He must be ashamed to face people—afraid they'll ask too many questions."

Sarah shrugged, setting down her fork. "He can't hide in his room or the barn forever."

Mrs. Pratt pinched her arm. "*You* need to do something, young lady. Before he decides coming back to Fredericksburg was a mistake."

"What can I do? Cal never asks me for advice."

"Think of something. What about those singings on Sunday nights? I'll bet plenty of single girls attend them." She leaned across the table as though in anticipation.

"True, but he says he's too old. He's not, but that's his excuse. Lots of men his age are there."

"What else is going on, social-wise?"

"He won't go ice skating with Rebekah, Katie, and me because he hates being cold and it reminds him of his last apartment. So that rules out sleigh rides, tobogganing, and ice fishing." Sarah finished her last bite of breakfast. "I'll have more success when the weather warms up. Cal always enjoyed volleyball and softball. And who doesn't love picnics, hayrides, and bonfires under the stars?"

Her boss clucked her tongue. "Nope, you can't wait that long. Come up with something soon, before your brother disappears as mysteriously as he arrived on Christmas Eve. I know you love Cal, so put your imagination to work. Seek him out and get him talking. Don't let him hide from the world. He needs a confidant he can trust." She rose to her feet and stacked their dirty dishes. "Now, speaking of Rebekah, I think it's time your sister came back to work for me. If the recent reservations are any indication, spring seems to have arrived early in Wayne County. We can use your sister's help making up rooms and in the kitchen."

Sarah scrambled up to start her chores, but her former good mood had soured. Not due to Mrs. Pratt's suggestion about Caleb. She had been worried that his return wouldn't be permanent and agreed that he needed someone to confide in. No, her bout of depression had everything to do her sister coming back to Country Pleasures Bed-and-Breakfast. A morning spent working with Rebekah all but guaranteed a splitting headache by noon.

2

Streams of mercy, never ceasing,
Call for songs of loudest praise.

END OF MARCH

Caleb wasted more time than he would have thought possible in the Country Pleasures barn and backyard. Roy Pratt had shown him their new Haflinger draft horse along with two new ponies that would be used with children in the summertime. Roy pointed out every nuance and characteristic of the animals as though Caleb were a tourist down for the weekend instead of an Amish man who had been around horses his entire life.

But Caleb didn't mind since it helped pass the time. And he had plenty of time lately since the maple sugar season was finished. He'd enjoyed spending his days at the Weaver farm, but he couldn't follow James around as he went about his chores. It would look like he had no life…even though at the moment he didn't. The Beachy farm was miniscule compared to the Weavers'. And his father had become so accustomed to plowing and planting alone while he'd been gone that Caleb only felt in his way.

Roy Pratt took him to their small apple orchard where he explained in detail how he pruned each tree limb to assure maximum fruit production. Caleb stifled a yawn during the innkeeper's account of natural bug deterrents along with limited spraying. With customers so worried about pesticide residue the Pratts were committed to growing safe apples for their pies, cobblers, and breakfast compotes.

Caleb thought he would fall asleep upright if he didn't separate himself from his overly detail-oriented neighbor. Fortunately his sister exited the inn's back door just as his eyelids began to droop. "Thanks, Roy, for making time for me during your busy day." Caleb pumped the older man's hand. "There's Sarah, and I need to speak with her before she sneaks away." The moment Roy released his hand Caleb sprinted across the lawn to head Sarah off at the gate.

"Goodness, Cal. You scared the daylights out of me." Sarah carried a huge picnic hamper along with her tote bag. "You are the last person I expected to see lurking in the Pratt's garden."

Caleb joined her on the path from the inn's back entrance to the private lane connecting their properties. Other than their families, no one used this road except for the UPS man and an occasional lost tourist.

"Who would be the first person?" Caleb pulled the basket from her hand.

"That would be Rebekah." Frowning, Sarah glanced over her shoulder. "She's always sneaking up on me as though trying to catch me in something naughty. What does she think I do behind her back? You would think we were still little girls."

He offered no advice, having learned to steer clear of sisterly squabbles long ago.

"Anyway, to what do I owe this rare honor? Did you have business with Roy?" Hefting her tote to her shoulder, she turned her pretty honey-brown eyes up to him.

"Not business, just killing time till you got off work."

"Are you finished at the Weavers?" Sarah glanced back toward the inn once more.

"*Jah.* Mainly I want to stay out of *Daed*'s way."

Her young forehead creased into deep furrows. "But I thought you planned to work for him in construction."

"I suppose I will, but no projects have started yet. He hasn't said anything since supper that night."

"*You* could broach the subject, Cal. He's not going to bite your head off."

"Okay, but right now I came to ask about a pancake breakfast in

Shreve this weekend." He kicked a stone down the leaf-strewn path. It landed in a mud puddle with a satisfying plop.

Sarah stopped short and grabbed his jacket sleeve. "Why, are you thinking you might go? Actually mingle with other live human beings? You do realize you'd be forced to leave Beachy land, don't you?"

Caleb shrugged from her grasp. "Very funny, but I haven't made up my mind yet. James Weaver keeps bugging me to attend. He says it's a great place to meet single women." He rolled his eyes.

"Oh, this is good news. Lee Ann said I should help you get back into the flow."

"Mrs. Pratt is worried about my social life?"

"In a perfectly harmless way." Sarah picked up their pace as though the breakfast was today and they were already late. "James is correct. There'll be plenty of single women in Shreve that day. You'll have a great time."

"Not if all the women are *Englisch*. I don't need to meet more of them." Briefly the image of dark-haired Kristen flitted through his mind, with her tight blue jeans and figure-hugging sweaters. He had behaved shamefully with her and done things he would regret for the rest of his life. All because he'd thought they were in love. But when his fat paychecks dried up and he had no money to spend, Kristen started dating someone else. Caleb shook his head to rid himself of the painful memory.

"Not to worry. Probably half the people attending will be Plain," she said. "Adam took me once and I bought ten different kinds of maple sugar candy. I ate so much in one day I got a bellyache."

"Do you think you and Adam would like to go too?" Caleb tried to make the question sound a little less desperate. "If we are in a group, I might be able to relax. Otherwise, I'm afraid James will attempt to have us both seriously courting by sundown, if not engaged."

She chuckled. "Sure, Adam and I would love to go. It will be fun. He's always begging me to go more places with him. And who doesn't love pancakes swimming in real maple syrup?" Sarah ran to the pasture fence. One of their Holsteins had wandered up to the rails with her newborn calf. Just as Sarah's fingers almost reached the downy head, the calf scampered between his mother's legs while the cow issued a loud *moo* in protest.

"How long will you keep trying to pet new calves?" Caleb laughed at his sibling. "That is never going to happen."

"One of these days, I'll catch a pair off-guard. It will be worth the wait." She linked her arm through his elbow. "I'm so glad you want to meet Amish girls. It's a step in the right direction."

"I've come home, Sarah. You don't suppose I want to live with our parents forever, do you?"

"I don't know what your plans are, but you can confide in me. I won't tell anyone and I won't judge you."

Because you have no idea what I have done. Caleb gazed down on her fresh, innocent face. "I don't have many plans other than get a job, join the church, and I suppose settle down with the right girl. As long as she's not too picky about my checkered past." He forced a laugh.

"You were on *rumschpringe,*" she said very softly.

"Not for five years I wasn't."

"Everybody has a fair share of problems in life. If not while they're young, maybe when they're older."

"How about you, little sister? You got problems?" Caleb was eager to turn the topic away from him.

"Other than Adam Troyer nagging me to get married? No, I'm good." Her laughter could have awakened hibernating bears.

"I thought that decision was behind you."

"It is, but he wishes I had joined the church last year. Now I can't be baptized until the fall."

"If I remember correctly, Adam is a good man. He'll wait far longer than fall if necessary." As they rounded a curve, Caleb halted as the Beachy farmhouse loomed into view—the house in which he'd been born; the house where he spent his entire life except for five years; the house in which he would probably die. With sunlight reflecting off the roof and upstairs windows, it seemed to glow from within.

"Adam is a good man, and I will happily become his bride when the time comes." Sarah sounded wistful, yet her lips pulled into a thin grimace.

"Then why are you upset? Did some nosy *Englischer* ask one too many questions?"

"No, I love it when they ask questions. Then I can ask some nosy questions of my own. It's Rebekah who upsets me. She got on my last nerve at work. She always criticizes me in front of Mrs. Pratt. Today she accused me of watering down the orange juice and leaving spots on the glassware." Sarah released a huff of breath. "Only one week back on the job but Rebekah thinks she's an expert on everything."

"Lee Ann Pratt is your friend besides your employer. Whatever our sister says probably goes in one of her ears and out the other. Rebekah has followed you around since she learned to walk. Take her constant attention as high compliment. I think she admires you but is too prideful to admit it."

"I really don't think that's the reason. But just the same, could we *forget* to mention we're going to the pancake breakfast on Saturday?" Sarah latched onto his sleeve.

"She bothers you that much?" Caleb stared, amazed by the thin skin of the female half of the world.

"I'll ask Mrs. Pratt for Saturday morning off, but she can't spare both of us. Country Pleasures is usually full on Friday nights, as well as Saturdays. If Rebekah hears James is going, she might leave Mrs. Pratt high and dry."

"As you wish. According to you, I seldom say two words to my family. So I guess I can avoid a heart-to-heart with Rebekah during the next couple of days."

"Good, then I'll call Adam at work from Mrs. Pratt's. You can count on him to hire a van to take us back and forth. He's still got money from his last paycheck burning a hole in his pocket."

Caleb watched as Sarah slipped into the house and headed straight for the refrigerator. He remained on the porch, however, pondering how to spend the remaining afternoon. Releasing a weary sigh, he strode down the steps in search of his father. It was time to get the inevitable showdown with his new boss over with.

Eli scratched his earlobe with one hand while swatting a pesky mosquito with the other. Not even April and already the biting insects were out in full force. How did that bode for mid-summer? Pushing his reading glasses back up his nose, he pored over the standard blueprint for a new banked barn. Even though he'd used these drawings to erect dozens of barns across three counties, plans would always change due to the terrain of the site, the number of anticipated helpers, and the pocketbook of the perspective owner. On his left sat a battery lantern. On his right waited a yellow tablet and pen to jot down his list of required materials.

His office, carved years ago out of a corner of the barn, was a haven from the rest of his family. Not that Eli didn't love his *fraa* and three daughters. But being the sole male member of the Beachy household, he needed somewhere to work without constant questions like, *Daed, is it all right if I stay at my friend's house Saturday night, then ride to preaching with them?*

Or, *Take a look at this fabric I bought in town. Won't this make the prettiest dress you've ever seen?*

Or, on the rare occasions when none of his daughters were home, Eli could count on Elizabeth to break his train of thought: *What would you like for supper tonight?* No matter how many times he answered, "Whatever you feel like cooking," she never stopped asking the question. Here in his office he could orchestrate the next barn project in their district, schedule the roofing jobs, which were his crew's main source of income nine months out of the year, do payroll for his employees, and balance checking accounts for his family and the business without constant interruptions. And then there were his duties as bishop—a responsibility he took very seriously since drawing the lot many years ago. He would serve the Lord and his district for the rest of his life.

But he wasn't the sole male Beachy any longer. His prodigal son had returned—a shock to his system last December and a continual surprise each day he walked into a room and saw Caleb. Eli had expected an occasional visit after his son left to take up a new lifestyle. Most youths who refuse to join the church usually kept in touch with their families on a limited basis. But after five years without a single phone call or letter, Eli thought he'd seen the last of his firstborn. Although he never forgot Caleb in his prayers, he'd stopped praying for his return long ago. Lately Eli prayed for his health, safety, and for him to someday find the Christian path to salvation.

Never in a million years would he have imagined his son would become Amish again. Of course, although Caleb regularly attended services with the family, he had yet to get baptized or take the kneeling vow of commitment.

I'll believe it when I see it. Eli reached for his thermos, hoping strong coffee would wash away his doubt and negativity. However, after a full mug he still felt just as mean-spirited. For distraction, Eli picked up the contract for a replacement roof for a warehouse complex. Since this would be paid commercial work, he would be obliged to hire Caleb— courtesy of his wife. At least his son wouldn't stand around twiddling his thumbs. If there was a certain road to trouble it was idleness.

Before Eli finished the second page outlining specifications and the anticipated timetable for completion, the scrape of a boot heel nearly stopped his heart.

"Could I have a word with you?" Caleb asked over Eli's shoulder.

"Sure, I didn't hear you come in." Eli swept off his hat to scratch his prickly scalp. "You erased a few years from my life."

"Sorry, I cleared my throat in the doorway, but you must have been concentrating." Caleb leaned over to peruse the roofing contract.

"Sit, sit. You know I don't like it when people hover." Eli pointed at a metal chair used as a storage place for county trade periodicals.

Gathering them up, Caleb dumped the pile unceremoniously on a low shelf. "Do you have a job ready to start? Somebody needs a new roof?" He rubbed his clean-shaven jawline.

"*Jah*, I was awarded the contract to reroof a warehouse in Millersburg. I'm calling every man on my crew to tell them to be ready to start Monday. Looks like it will be a four-week job between the demo, replacing most of the rafters and supports, and then installing the new roof on three buildings in the complex."

His son narrowed his gaze. "Does this crew of yours include me?"

"Of course it does. I agreed to hire you and I keep my word. But like any other employee, you will be on probation for the first three months."

"Fair enough." Caleb leaned his head against the office wall. "How will we get to Millersburg? Will everybody drive their own rig?" He fiddled with a pile of paperclips on the desk.

"No, I want to start work promptly at first light, or eight at the latest. It would take too long if we drove our buggies. One of my *Englisch* carpenters owns a large van. I pay him an extra stipend to pick us up, plus each man chips in for gasoline."

This information had little effect on Caleb. He continued to line up clips into rows of five.

"Are those terms okay with you, son?" Eli spoke a bit louder than necessary.

Caleb peered up. "Fine and dandy. Hopefully your driver can wait until my first check for my portion of the gas." He focused on the barn blueprints. "We have a barn to build too? That will be a lot more fun than a commercial reroofing."

"Work isn't supposed to be fun. But *jah*, the Yoders need a new barn. The old relic on their property from when the first Yoder moved in fell down. The weight of snow on the roof finally collapsed the support beams."

Caleb straightened in the chair. "Were any livestock injured or killed?"

"*Nein*, their livestock stalls were on the lowest level. It was the loft that fell. He lost his hay storage, along with some equipment, but his cows and horses came through the ordeal fine. They're stabled in a neighbor's barn for now."

"Josie Yoder's family?" asked Caleb.

"I believe one of his daughters is named Josie."

"When will this be scheduled?" He tapped the blueprints with his finger.

"Time will tell. Let's concentrate on the Millersburg project first." Eli experienced an odd spike of irritation with Caleb's interest in a community barn-building over regular, paid employment. Hopefully, his son hadn't lost every ounce of ambition and initiative he'd once possessed.

Caleb stood, slowly stretching out his back muscles. "I'll be ready first thing Monday morning. I brought home my tools. They were the only things worth moving from my last apartment on Davenport Drive." He headed toward the office door as though their meeting had concluded.

"Hold up," demanded Eli. "I've got a few questions before you start work."

Caleb glanced back but held his position. "You want me to fill out an application, or maybe supply a list of Cleveland references?" He laughed as though amused.

Eli pointed at the metal chair. "No, but I am entitled to know what kind of construction you did for those *Englischers*. It would be useful when I start assigning tasks." He kept his voice level while inside his irritation continued to build.

Caleb slouched back to the chair. "My friend Pete helped me get into the carpenters' union."

"The same Pete who worked on that big tourist hotel and restaurant in Wilmot?" Eli interrupted—a trait he abhorred in other people.

"Yes, Pete Taylor—one and the same. Pete was already in the union. When I moved north, he helped me obtain my union card. I was an apprentice for four years. I would have made journeyman but the housing bubble burst and work dried up."

"So you built big fancy homes for *Englischers*?" Eli pictured those mansions he saw in magazines at the dentist's office.

"No, we did commercial work—office buildings, restaurants, and public government housing for the low-income elderly. When the mortgage crisis hit, construction of every type ground to a halt." Caleb lifted his hand. "Don't ask me to explain. I'm only repeating what the stewards rammed down my throat for years."

"Go on." Eli fought the impulse to ask, *So why didn't you come home?*

"That's pretty much the whole story. I had a good-paying job for two years. After that I mainly sat around the union hall. Occasionally I got day work to keep the lights and heat turned on."

"Did you familiarize yourself with the Cuyahoga County building codes?"

"No." Caleb's eyes could have bored holes through Eli's forehead.

"Did you learn to read blueprints and schematics?"

"No. Pete told me to sign up for classes, but they were offered at night at the downtown community college campus. A man gets tired after putting in a full day of work."

"What about the three slow years, when you sat around the hall?"

Caleb flushed. "Those classes ain't free. They cost money and a man needs a reliable set of wheels to get there."

Eli saw no reason to back down. "Sarah said she used public transportation almost to your doorstep when she visited. She only walked two blocks."

His son's face darkened as he gripped the edge of the desk. "Is this an interrogation about my past or an assessment of my skills? I thought my years in Cleveland were to be forgotten. I know how to use every tool to do any carpentry project out there. I can do the job, *Daed.*" Caleb lifted his chin with defiance.

Strangely, Eli took no solace from his *Deutsch* term for father. "I know you can, and eventually I will teach you how to read blueprints. For now it won't be necessary, but I can't make you a foreman." He began stacking his papers. "Let's go into the house and check how supper is coming. I need a cup of coffee to tide me over." Briefly, he considered offering his hand, but his son had already reached the door before the idea jelled. Eli swallowed hard. *Take it one day at a time. After all, you promised your wife.*

⁂

Sarah set her wicker basket on the kitchen counter and headed to the fridge for a soft drink. She didn't notice her mother half-buried in the pantry.

"What's in the hamper?" The voice sounded echo-y and far away until Elizabeth rose to her feet. Her arms were filled with empty Mason jars which she placed in a packing crate.

"Cleaning cupboards?" Sarah took a large gulp of Pepsi.

"*Jah*, good day for it. Let's see what you brought me." Her mother flipped the lid on the basket.

"Mrs. Pratt and I baked all day after the guests left. This morning I took several jars of canned pumpkin, zucchini, and blueberries from the cellar. Lee Ann bought every overripe banana at the IGA along with chopped walnuts on sale. We made a dozen loaves of pumpkin bread, zucchini bread, and banana-walnut and blueberry muffins, far more than Country Pleasures needs. So she insisted I bring some home."

Elizabeth leaned over the hamper and inhaled deeply. "Smells *wundabaar*, but why didn't you stick them in the inn's freezer? All of these freeze nicely."

"Because there's not an inch of space from the last time we baked."

"They surely won't go to waste here, not with your *bruder* home. Have you ever seen so thin a man eat so much? A person could think he never ate his entire time in Cleveland."

That's not far from the truth, she thought. Sarah had tried to forget Caleb's depressing apartment with strange odors emanating from the hallway and his kitchen, the threadbare carpet, and his stained and broken furniture. She had found only a couple Cokes, a six-pack of beer, a half-eaten pizza, and bottles of suspicious-looking catsup and mustard in his refrigerator. "He won't stay skinny with you in charge of his meals." Sarah grinned at her mother, grateful her parents never witnessed their son's former existence. "Cal met me at the Pratts' and walked me home."

"Whatever for? Was he worried you would lose your way?" Elizabeth unloaded the basket into their propane freezer.

"He plans to attend an event in Shreve on Saturday. James Weaver wishes to meet Amish women not from our district, and Cal agreed to go with him."

"Great news." Elizabeth clapped her hands as though at a horse show or theater performance. "But why did he meet you at Country Pleasures?"

"He wants Adam and me to join them, believing there's safety in numbers. Please don't tell Rebekah. If she stalks James like a serial killer, he'll be unable to make new friends."

"Sarah Beachy," *Mamm* scolded. "A serial killer? Have you been watching TV at Mrs. Pratt's? I suggest you limit yourself to the Hallmark Channel so you don't put such nasty ideas into your head." Elizabeth made that clucking sound with her tongue—a gesture every mother masters eventually. "Rebekah likes James in a perfectly normal way."

"Just the same, let's give James a chance to see some new faces."

Begrudgingly, her mother nodded.

"Would you mind if I walked to Josie's? I'd like to take the Yoders a loaf or two of these sweet breads."

"Of course not. Why would I mind?" Her mother placed the last two tightly wrapped loaves by the door.

"*Daed* gets mad when he comes inside and finds you fixing supper alone. He thinks I work too hard for Mrs. Pratt and not hard enough at home."

She laughed from the belly. "Eli is so old-fashioned. Don't be surprised if he insists you quit your job the moment you and Adam announce your engagement. Run along. I'll tell your father I ordered you to go, because that's what I'm doing. Tell Margaret Yoder I'll see her at quilting." She transferred the breads into a smaller basket. "Are you up to something, sweet girl?" Elizabeth Beachy couldn't be fooled for long; she could sniff out a sly plan while standing in a garden of summer roses.

"Maybe. I'll let you know if I'm remotely successful." Shrugging into her cloak, Sarah grabbed the basket and headed for the door, kissing her mother's cheek on the way out. "In the meantime, say a prayer that the love-bug bites not one, but two people in our neighborhood."

"The love-bug? First serial killers, now romantic insects?"

Sarah closed the door behind her and headed around the barn with energy that belied her long workday. The Yoders lived on a different township road, but a well-trodden path connected the two farms. The trail wound between fenced pastures, through the orchard, around the woodlot that stretched into the hills, and past an abandoned gristmill. Seldom did a trip to Josie's not include a five-minute break at the piece of history from a bygone age of agriculture. Sarah would stand on the ivy-covered stone wall and peer down into the cascading water far below. The mill itself was beyond repair, yet the grapevines and rampant wildflowers softened its decrepit appearance. A rusty waterwheel had locked into position for all eternity, but Sarah loved it here—so peaceful, so quiet. She could still her mind and listen to God prodding her in one direction or another. Right now, He told her to get a move on or there wouldn't be time for her errand.

Josie was outdoors when Sarah rounded the corner and approached the house. Josie Yoder—petite, small-boned, with sparkling green eyes and hair so dark it looked black. Since Sarah was tall, blonde, freckled, and brown-eyed, the two were polar opposites physically. But in other ways, they were sisters under the skin. They often guessed what the other was thinking with amazing accuracy.

"Hi, Josie," Sarah called while still yards away.

Her friend turned at the clothesline, a billowy white sheet in hand. "What are you doing here? Didn't you work at the B&B today?"

"I'm pleased to see you too." Sarah wrinkled her nose. "Of course I did, but it's after three o'clock."

"Time flies." Josie concentrated on folding the bed linen before it dragged on the grass. "*Mamm* made me wash things that were perfectly clean." She snuffled to emulate her favorite barnyard animal. "When she gets the spring-cleaning bug, look out. Soon she'll have me dusting in between the windows and the screens." Josie dropped the folded sheet atop her laundry basket. "What's up? Did you hear gossip that won't wait until Sunday?"

Breathing hard, Sarah reached the triple clothesline. "I don't gossip, but my mother and I were just discussing bug bites an hour ago. What are you doing the day after tomorrow?" She asked without preamble.

Josie blinked her cat eyes. "Saturday? I haven't thought that far ahead. I'll probably help cook food for the Sabbath. You have something better in mind?"

"Let's go to the pancake breakfast in Shreve. They purchased Weaver maple syrup, along with fried Trail bologna, sausage patties, French toast, and Belgian waffles. Plus they will have craft displays, homemade candy, and quilts up for raffle."

Josie giggled. "Do you work for the Chamber of Commerce in addition to Mrs. Pratt?" She pulled a row of dish and hand towels from the line.

"No, one job is plenty, *danki*. But I think we'll have fun."

Josie's pretty face turned suspicious. "Who's this 'we'? What are you up to, Sarah Beachy?"

"Let's see…there will be me, Adam, my *bruder* Caleb, and James Weaver—producer of Ohio's best syrup." She grinned as though selling toothpaste on television.

Josie attacked a row of dresses, pulling until pins flew in every direction. "Oh no you don't. I like James well enough, but as a friend. Don't try fixing me up with him. If I give the tiniest amount of encouragement, his mother will plant half an acre of celery and finish our wedding quilt by month's end."

Sarah walked around men's trousers lofting in the March breeze. "No, not James," she said softly.

"Who then?" Josie yanked down socks and tossed them toward the basket.

"My brother. You once told me that you liked Cal. You thought he was kind, sweet, and very handsome."

Josie faced Sarah eye-to-eye, or to the best of her ability considering her stature. "I believe I was fifteen at the time. I'm twenty-one now, Sarah. People change. Your *bruder* sure did." She held Sarah's gaze without blinking.

"Maybe he's the same on the inside." Sarah tightened her cape against the wind.

"Maybe so, but my father would never let your brother court me. Everybody in the district has heard how he sneaked around to get a driver's license and then teamed up with a group of *Englisch* thugs. One of them hit a dog on Route 83 and didn't even stop to see if the dog could be helped." She shook her head.

"How could they be sure it was one of Caleb's friends? Anyway, you know very well my brother would never do such a thing, whether *Englisch* at the time or Amish."

"My *daed* said Cal threw keg parties where the sole purpose was getting drunk." Josie shivered.

Sarah paused to collect her thoughts. Once again she was defending Caleb's reputation—something that shouldn't be necessary. "I'm not condoning his behavior, but that's all in the past. He learned a hard lesson up in Cleveland. He's home and doesn't throw keg parties anymore. He intends never to touch beer again." She stomped her foot as her temper flared. "I didn't think you of all people would be so judgmental."

"Easy there, friend." Josie took her hand. "I'm not judging Cal, just saying my father wouldn't like me courting him."

"Don't you make your own choices?"

Josie grinned, slowly at first. "My, you have become persuasive under the influence of *Englischers*. Okay, I'll come to the pancake breakfast on Saturday with you and Adam, but I make no promises about falling in love with anyone." She reached for a pair of pants. "Just make sure *your mamm* doesn't start planting celery that's not intended for you."

On impulse, Sarah kissed Josie's cheek. "We'll pick you up at eight. Don't be late." She started down the hill. "Oh, I almost forgot. I brought two loaves of sweet bread to bribe you, but I didn't need them. Return the basket on Saturday." Sarah set the hamper in the tall grass and practically ran all the way home.

Mrs. Pratt's challenge had taken one giant step in the right direction.

3

Teach me some melodious sonnet,
Sung by flaming tongues above.

Caleb woke before his father on Saturday morning, dressed quickly, and hurried to the barn. Yesterday's cold wind had died down while the sky remained clear. When the sun finally rose above the eastern hills, the day promised to be quintessentially spring. By the time Eli arrived at the barn, the cows had been milked and Caleb was busily filling water troughs and feed buckets.

"You're up mighty early, son." Eli Beachy stood in the doorway with his battery lantern and an unreadable expression. "Develop a taste for night crawlers instead of your *mamm*'s bacon and eggs?"

The joke took Caleb a moment to comprehend. "No worms for me, *danki*. In fact, no bacon and eggs either. I've got plans for today. That's why I started chores early." He concentrated on filling the five-gallon bucket from the fifty-pound sack. They'd run out of last year's silage and had had to purchase local grain.

Eli set his thermos on the stall wall. "You already turn the sow and horses into the outdoor paddock?"

"*Jah*. I'll begin mucking out their stalls next."

"Mind if I ask what your plans are? I figured you were becoming another Amish hermit like your old pal, Albert Sidley."

Caleb peered up, unsure how to take his father. "Just waiting for the weather to clear before I make my social debut." He clamped the feed sack shut and carried it to the wheelbarrow.

"Debut? Rather fancy word for an ordinary Saturday morning." Pushing his felt hat to the back of his head, Eli leaned against a post.

Caleb realized his father wasn't leaving without an answer to his question. He waited, however, until he'd filled both cattle troughs with grain. "I'm going to the annual pancake breakfast in Shreve with James Weaver. He talked me into it, but I'll be back before afternoon chores. Sarah and Adam are coming too. Adam hired a van so we won't have to take our rigs." He wiped his hands down his pants.

The expression on Eli's face would be more appropriate after an alien spaceship landed in their recently plowed cornfield. "Your *mamm* and I went one year a while back. Big crowds. I couldn't see standing in line for a stack of flapjacks." He stroked his beard during the reminiscence.

"Hopefully, the crowds have died down since then." Picking up the shovel and pitchfork, Caleb headed toward the sow's pen. But his *daed* stepped into his path.

"I'll do that, since I won't have to wait an hour to eat." Eli pulled the tools from Caleb's grasp. "You jump in the shower so you don't keep Adam Troyer waiting."

"*Danki.*" A short word that Caleb found hard to utter on his way out the door.

Inside, his mother was in her usual position at the stove. "Coffee's ready."

"Exactly what I'm looking for." Caleb headed to the cupboard for a mug as his sister exited the bathroom, a thick towel wrapped around her long hair.

"All yours." Sarah smiled sweetly. "Adam will pick up James first and then come for us. We'll make one more stop and arrive in Shreve before you know it. I'm hungry already."

Caleb filled a mug with black coffee and tried to step around her, but Sarah blocked his path. "If you'll let me pass, I won't attend the event smelling like barn stalls."

Sarah glided toward the coffeepot, still grinning.

Caleb started to close the door behind him when a thought occurred. "What do you mean another stop? Who else did you invite along?"

She blew on the surface of her mug. "Only my best friend, Josie Yoder. You remember her, don't you? Tiny gal with dark hair, lives on Route 852?"

"Of course I remember Josie. I saw her last month at a preaching ser-vice." He shot Sarah a frosty glare before shutting the door.

How could any man with blood in his veins forget Josie Yoder?

The skinny little girl had bloomed into a beautiful young woman during Caleb's long absence. Josie had taken a shine to him when she was seventeen, but he had already been twenty. He decided to give her some growing-up time before asking her out. Then the whole world had shifted beneath his feet. His father took a contract to build a new hotel in Wilmot, working alongside *Englischers*. Caleb had met a skilled carpenter from Cleveland and they'd become friends. Pete encouraged him to apply at a major construction firm by Lake Erie when they fin-ished the hotel. Not that it was Pete's fault. That summer Caleb had lost his common sense and his way...spiritually and emotionally. And his journey back was far from over.

Adam Troyer picked them up at the appointed hour in a hired van. Always punctual. Adam might be wound a little tight, but he was a good man. And one thing was crystal clear: He loved Sarah and would be a dependable, devoted husband.

James, as bright-eyed and bushy-tailed as any squirrel, jumped out of the van as soon as it slowed to a stop. "Cal, let's sit in the backseat so the courting couple has a chance to be together." James imbued the term "courting couple" with a silly, juvenile inflection.

"*Guder mariye*, Adam," Caleb greeted, remembering to use only *Deutsch* with his future brother-in-law. "Hey, James, you scrub off all the dried sap just in time for today?"

"You bet I did. I can't wait to dig into those pancakes." James rubbed his hands together. Caleb bit the inside of his cheek trying not to laugh. He knew James's exuberance had nothing to do with food.

Sarah monopolized the conversation on the way to the Yoders, fill-ing Adam in with the latest news from home and the inn. Caleb con-tently watched the passing scenery. Everywhere were the green, fertile signs of spring and new life. When Josie Yoder skipped out her door and down the steps, Caleb forgot all about soggy farm fields. Dur-ing the five years he'd been gone, the pretty girl had morphed into a stunning beauty with creamy skin and sparkling green eyes. One lock of black hair trailed from her *kapp,* offering a hint of her luxurious mane beneath. Caleb's heart thudded against his chest wall. He glanced away before his blush revealed he was no more sophisticated than James, despite his years living with the *Englisch.*

"Hi Sarah, Adam. How are you doing, James?" Josie called the first two greetings en route, but waited for the third until she reached the van. "Good to see you, Caleb. This is my first chance to welcome you home." She locked eyes with him, much to his chagrin.

"Thanks, Josie. *Gut* to be back." Caleb studied the back of Adam's head. *Gut* to be back—as though he'd been vacationing in Florida?

"Josie, sit up here with me and the driver." Sarah instructed through the open window. "Adam can crawl into the back with the men."

As Josie Yoder climbed onto the front seat, Caleb said a silent prayer of thanks. Praying hadn't been a habit for a long while, but he thanked God Josie wasn't sitting next to him. Now he would have thirty minutes to pull his act together.

Once they arrived at the pancake breakfast, true to his father's prediction, the line snaked out the door of the elementary school. But customers chatted and laughed as though waiting hours to eat was normal. The party of five took their place in line in a crowd. Many of the people were *Englisch,* but there was a good smattering of Amish folks among them. Always the hostess, Sarah kept conversation lively, finding ways to include James, Josie, and Caleb.

Caleb had just begun to relax when the rowdy locals behind them caught his attention. From the corner of his eye, he assessed the group—three muscle-bound young men with their overly made-up girlfriends. The men talked as though they wanted the world to hear them while the women giggled shrilly. *Must Englischers be so loud?* Caleb tried his best to ignore them and concentrate on Adam's story about coaxing a bull back behind a fence. Then Caleb overheard the *Englischer's* taunt clear and true.

"Do you suppose there's only one Amish barber in town, or do all the barbers learn only one haircut?" Laughing, the three girlfriends stole not-very-subtle glances at them.

Caleb felt heat start in his chest and spread up his neck, but he focused on Adam. Adam either didn't hear the comment or was able to ignore it. Sarah pulled Josie closer to her side as though closing ranks.

"I know there's only one clothing store in town. They dress so much alike, I don't know how they tell each other apart." That particular remark came from the shortest of the men.

Caleb pivoted around to face them while his fingers bunched into fists. Five years of living in the city had taught him to be cynical, wary, and defensive—three traits frowned on in Amish society. He took a step toward his adversaries, but Josie Yoder grabbed his hand, halting his progress.

"If my stomach grumbles any louder, I won't be able to hear myself think," she said. "Could we skip pancakes for now and buy one of those giant funnel cakes? A booth is selling them near where the van dropped us off." Her dark lashes fluttered while she spoke.

"Great idea," said his sister. "I'm starving too. We can either check this breakfast line later or chow down solely on junk food. I vote for the latter." Sarah began dragging Adam in the direction of the vendors and craft tables. Adam continued his tale about the wily bull without interruption. Josie didn't release his hand as they fell in step behind them.

"Smart thinking to shake those troublemakers," James whispered to Caleb, joining his other side. "I saw plenty of Amish women at those food booths. Besides, I eat tons of pancakes with maple syrup at home." His spirits hadn't been daunted in the least by the *Englisch* thugs.

Caleb relaxed his shoulders and released his breath. "I could go for one of those greasy funnel cakes. I've been eating way too healthy since moving back."

"*Gut,* that means I won't have to share any of mine." Josie swung their arms like children on a playground.

Caleb smiled at the prettiest and most clever woman at the Shreve pancake festival. His temper had reared its ugly head, but Josie had diffused a bad situation. Even if the lovely Miss Yoder never spent another minute in his company, Caleb Beachy would remain forever grateful.

❧

Caleb turned over in bed early Monday morning. Sleep refused to come. Too much had taken place during the last forty-eight hours for his mind to stop spinning. He hadn't had so enjoyable a Saturday in a long time—five years to be exact. Who would have thought a tourist celebration in a small country town could change his outlook?

Like throwing sand on a fire, Josie had doused his anger at the rude *Englischers*. The last thing he needed was to pick a fight with plenty of Amish and *Englisch* witnesses. The Amish were known to be pacifists— to turn the other cheek as instructed in Scripture. So why had he been eager to wipe away that man's smirk with his fist?

After Josie had guided them to the funnel cake booth, they bought sweets and cups of hot chocolate. Adam groused they were spoiling their appetites while munching an enormous elephant ear. Next Sarah led them to the display of Amish quilts, birdhouses, and feeders, and just about everything that could be crocheted or knitted. Although not a big fan of handmade creations, Caleb savored the feel of Josie's small hand in his. When she finally let go, his fingers tingled for several minutes.

Caleb had forgotten how graceful, charming, and sensitive to the needs of others Josie was. She knew how to handle Adam's narrow viewpoint so she could enjoy the camaraderie of Sarah. Sensing James Weaver's shyness, Josie fanned his courage like a flame. James had wandered off looking for familiar faces and found former district members from across the county. These women hung onto every word of his sugar production explanation. When their newly expanded group returned to the school for breakfast, the crowds had died down. Pancakes, sausage, and orange juice had never tasted so good before. James relished five minutes of celebrity status as everyone raved about Weaver maple syrup, while Caleb enjoyed his first outing with Plain believers.

Josie had been so relaxed with him that for a brief moment, Caleb believed they might have a future together. Today he felt far less confident. Josie was an innocent girl whose *rumschpringe* probably consisted of buying lipstick or taking a trip to King's Island to ride the roller coaster. What would she think if she knew what evil he'd been part of? Would she court him? Invite him for Sunday dinner with her parents? Caleb thought not, despite her encouraging words on the way home: *I'm glad you've come home, Cal. If there's anything I can do to help you readapt, let me know.*

Readapt—a five-dollar word for giving up his driver's license and hitching up a Standardbred gelding whenever he wanted to go anywhere. *Readapt*—that meant throwing out his belts, Levis, and plaid flannel shirts. He'd looked for Josie at preaching yesterday, craning his neck left and right to no avail. Sarah heard from one of her siblings that Josie had come down with a cold. He'd endured a three-hour service, including two sonorous sermons, in hopes of seeing Miss Yoder.

He should have paid attention to the service to reconnect with his religious upbringing. But God and Caleb Beachy hadn't been on a first name basis for a long while. Once he left home and moved to Cleveland, he hadn't bothered joining an *Englisch* church. Late-night carousing and early Sunday services didn't usually mesh. And prayer? He'd prayed for a new job at the end of his first project, but God either hadn't heard him or decided one fallen-away Christian wasn't worth the trouble. Now he was between a rock and a hard place. You couldn't be agnostic and be Amish, yet religion without faith was pointless.

Caleb threw back the covers and climbed out of bed. He'd better not oversleep on his first day of working for his father. Downstairs, the Beachy family had sprung to action. Sarah and Rebekah filled travel mugs of coffee for their walk to Country Pleasures Inn. Katie was getting ready for school while his mother cooked a simple breakfast of oatmeal and toast.

His mother smiled at him over her shoulder. "I packed your lunch, Caleb. Two sandwiches with chips and bottled water. I put them in the small cooler."

"You didn't have to fuss, *Mamm.* I'm capable of making my lunch." Caleb gritted his teeth. Coming home had reduced a grown man to boy status.

"Oh, it's no trouble because I'm already fixing your *daed*'s."

Eli Beachy exited the bathroom dressed and ready to leave. "There you are. Jack's van will be here in ten minutes. Glad you've come down."

"I'll get my tools." Caleb carried his mug of coffee to the mudroom where he'd stashed his toolbox. At least they would be traveling back and forth to Millersburg in a vehicle.

Eli followed him to the doorway. "Jack and Bob are my *Englisch* carpenters. They'll run the power equipment if our hand tools aren't sufficient for a particular task. They've been on my crew for years and have adjusted to our *Ordnung*." He locked gazes with Caleb.

If he wasn't mistaken, his father's words were laced with challenge. "How many men on the crew?" Caleb dragged his case from under the stationary tub.

"Eight, counting you and me. You'll know some of them from building barns long ago. And today you'll meet two carpenters who live near Killbuck." Eli shrugged into his black wool coat.

Caleb pulled on his dark brown Carhartt jacket—the choice of outdoor American laborers everywhere.

"We'll have to replace that *Englisch* coat," Eli muttered as he marched back into the kitchen.

"The newest Beachy employee can't leave the house without breakfast." Elizabeth handed him a bowl of oatmeal and a spoon.

Caleb practically had to inhale the food when Jack picked them up right on schedule. Crawling into the van's third seat, he decided to remain low-profile on his first day. He had only a passing acquaintance with the Amish fellows. Surprisingly, they talked in *Deutsch* during the thirty-minute ride, even though Jack and Bob wouldn't understand a word they said. Once at the site, the crew wasted several hours standing around while Eli conferred with the building's owner. While they waited, the foreman closed the sidewalk in front and on one side with a yellow caution tape to protect passersby from danger. Caleb nailed up their work permits in a prominent position while two men moved the large dumpster into the best location for debris.

During lunch—a wholly undeserved break since no one had done a lick of work—Caleb acquainted himself with the rest of the crew. Finally, a city councilman and the safety director of the city of Millersburg allowed the project to proceed.

Eli divided the warehouse roof into sections so that the entire structure wouldn't be exposed to the elements at the same time. They worked in three teams of two men to pry up layers of tar and felt that covered leaky three-quarter inch plywood. The seventh man gathered the old materials with a pitch fork and shovel to heave into the dumpster. With the sun warming his back and a breeze cooling his skin, Caleb liked the work. If nothing else, it distracted him from wallowing in self-pity. Playing games of what-if or if-only never did anyone a bit of good.

After several hours, Caleb and his assigned partner hit a particularly rotted section of sheathing under the tarred felt. "Let me get something to cut out this whole corner," he said. "None of this is salvageable." Caleb climbed down the ladder to his toolbox in the van and returned within minutes. He had made only two cuts through the plywood before Eli appeared behind him on the roof.

"What have you got, son?"

Caleb glanced up. "It's a reciprocating Sawzall. I brought it with me from Cleveland. This can get into hard-to-reach places better than a circular saw." For demonstration he cut a second straight line through a section of underlayment.

Eli huffed. "I know what a Sawzall is, Caleb. I'm just wondering why *you* have one. You said you wanted to return to the Amish ways." Eli didn't try to hide his disappointment.

Caleb straightened, switched off the tool, and met his *daed*'s gaze. "The tool is battery powered. There is no cord. Nothing is connected to the grid."

"I understand how it works, but our district doesn't use them. The ministerial brethren have discussed power saws in the past."

"That's ridiculous." Caleb spoke without thinking. "If it's battery-operated, what's the difference between using a Sawzall or a flashlight or a nine volt wall clock? Jack or Bob could take my power pack home each night to charge it up."

Eli's face turned so red, Caleb feared he might suffer a heart attack. "Jack and Bob have their own power saws, including one exactly like yours. If you need to cut out some sheathing, Jack will do it. That's how it will be done on my crew on this project."

Caleb felt the presence of several men who'd apparently taken a break to listen to their discussion. His face flushed with embarrassment from the dressing-down. His father was treating him like a teenager instead of an experienced, twenty-four-year-old carpenter.

He set down the tool none too gently.

Jack materialized at his side. "Let me cut out that section, Cal. No big deal." The *Englischer* picked up the saw and put it to use, the noise effectively mitigating the tense situation.

Grabbing the pry bar, Caleb began lifting off boards from the roof rafters. One by one the other workers returned to their tasks. But his father remained in place for several minutes, as though expecting him to use the taboo tool the moment he turned his back. Caleb concentrated on the loosened sheathing, transferring his negative energy into the decayed wood. In a few minutes Eli climbed down the ladder and returned to his portable table of blueprints and specifications. But Caleb couldn't meet his eye for the remainder of the day.

He was too close to saying something he would undoubtedly regret.

※

Eli sat up front next to Bob while Jack drove the van back toward Fredericksburg. It had been a stressful day despite the fact that demolition hadn't even begun until after lunch. Problems with the city safety director, the utility company, and the owner's agent had upset his stomach during the morning hours. Not that construction projects ever began or ended without tension. It was the nature of the business—whether Amish or *Englisch*. But Eli really didn't need a confrontation with his son on the first day of the job. Perhaps he should have discussed what was and wasn't permitted on his crew, but Caleb had worked for him before he left to find his fame and fortune in Cleveland. He didn't think his son could have forgotten a lifetime of learned *Ordnung*.

Eli had been relieved when Jack picked up the saw and assumed responsibility. Nevertheless a heart-to-heart with Caleb was long overdue, but he would wait until they got home so as not to embarrass his son. At least Caleb talked to other Amish during the drive instead of forming instant bonds with the *Englisch* employees. Deep inside Eli feared a repeat of that heartbreaking summer years ago.

When Jack dropped them off, Caleb scrambled out to retrieve his toolbox from behind the seat. "I'm leaving my Sawzall and cordless circular saw," he said to Jack after walking around to the driver's side. "They're all yours, my friend." Caleb spoke with an ounce of emotion.

"Okay, but I'll return them if your district changes their policy someday. You never know what the future holds." Tipping his ball cap, Jack rolled up the window.

The man had learned much about the Amish after working for him these four years, thought Eli. "See you tomorrow," he called.

Eli followed his son through the back door into the mudroom. While they pulled off their boots, coats, and hats, Eli chose this opportunity to set some guidelines before more time elapsed. "I didn't appreciate you disagreeing with me on the roof, in front of the other men." He kept his tone nonconfrontational.

"I didn't argue about anything, *Daed*. I merely pointed out my tool ran without an electrical cord." Caleb hooked his coat and hat on a peg.

"You should have respected my authority as your boss and your father and set down the tool without backtalk."

"Discussing something in a calm manner isn't backtalk. It's how adults communicate in the world. I am a grown man, but I'm also more than willing for you to call the shots on the job. It's your company and I respect your position in it, in addition to you being my father." Caleb slicked a hand through his tangled hair. He hadn't raised his voice or used a defensive posture, yet Eli sensed resistance just the same.

"Most matters aren't up for discussion. We're Amish and therefore subject to my decisions as your bishop and our Old Order *Ordnung*, whether district members are young or old. You still manifest ego and pride—both traits learned in the *Englisch* society. Those won't serve you here." Eli hung up his hat and coat on the next peg.

"I doubt that *Englischers* are the only ones who develop pride. But I'll do my best to respect your authority while at work." Caleb leaned over the stationary tub to wash. His mother didn't need any tar residue tracked into the household bathroom. Turning on the taps, he tested the water and stuck his head under the stream as though cooling off his hot temper.

"That is true, but those in their permissive society learn no self-restraint or how to control their tongues."

Caleb straightened his spine, flinging droplets of water around the laundry and storage area.

"I gave Jack the tools that you won't allow. I don't know what else you want from me. I didn't argue. I only questioned what I didn't understand." While he talked, Caleb unbuttoned his navy blue shirt, dropped his suspenders to his waist, and pushed up the sleeves of his thermal undershirt. He was preparing to wash his neck and arms, but froze when Eli gasped. Every drop of blood drained from Caleb's face when he realized his mistake, his complexion turning the color of woodstove ash.

"What is that?" With a trembling finger, Eli pointed at a garish tattoo. The monstrosity stretched from his mid-forearm up to his elbow.

Caleb turned away, grabbing frantically for his shirt. "Nothing to concern yourself with."

"Let me see it," Eli demanded, holding Caleb's arm steady to get a better look. Twin snakes writhed and coiled around a fancy red heart. Inside the name *Kristen* had been inscribed in an old-fashioned script. Red outlined the bottom of the letters as though blood dripped from her name. "Vipers! That is an abomination." He didn't attempt to hide his disgust. "What kind of unholy alliances did you form in the city? Were you in some kind of cult?" He whispered the last word as though afraid of invoking evil.

Caleb pulled away from him and turned back to the stationary tub. He thrust his arms beneath the taps and scrubbed with the bar of Life-buoy soap. "I was in no cult. It only means I thought I was in love with a woman named Kristen."

"The body is a temple of the Lord. Yet you defiled yours with snakes and garish designs."

"Believe me, if there was any way I could rid myself of it I would. It was a mistake. I did a foolish thing when I wasn't myself."

"Were you drunk?" asked Eli.

"Yes, drunk and a fool. Two conditions I hope never to be again."

Eli rubbed his tired eyes with his fingertips. "You're certain a doctor can't remove this…this tattoo? Maybe scrape it off under anesthetic?"

"I'm sure. It goes too deep, through several layers of skin. But I will never roll up my sleeves on the job, no matter how hot I get." Caleb reached for the towel to dry his arms and pulled on the soiled shirt. No clean clothes were stored in the mudroom unless Elizabeth happened to leave her basket of laundry behind.

Eli clenched his eyes shut. "There must be something we can do. No Amish woman in her right mind will marry a man who is marked in such a fashion."

"Then I'll have to find one *not* in her right mind." Caleb pressed the towel to his face.

Grabbing the damp towel, Eli hurled it across the room. "Do you think this is a joke? I've never known an Amish man to disgrace himself like this."

"I don't think it's funny, but I can't change my past. If I could I would." Caleb's voice rose with anger as he glared with more venom than his inscribed snakes.

Shaking his head, Eli walked to where the towel lay and picked it up. "What about this woman—this Kristen? Were you betrothed to her? Is she waiting for your return to marry?"

"I thought she was my fiancée, but when I lost my job, she lost interest and started dating someone else." His voice cracked, betraying his emotion at last.

Eli stared at his arm where the tattoo lay hidden by the work shirt. "For now, tell no one about this abomination. But I will have to discuss this with the other elders during your membership classes. There's no way around it." His anger changed to pity for a man who'd fallen so far.

"I understand." Nodding, Caleb opened the mudroom door.

Inside the kitchen, they were greeted by an effusive Elizabeth. "*Ach*, my two hardworking men! How did it go on your first day on the job, son?"

Her face was so filled with hope and love that for a second Eli thought their son might cry. But instead he cleared his throat and spoke softly. "*Gut, Mamm.* Glad to be back to work. Excuse me while I change into a clean shirt."

Eli slumped into a chair, feeling close to ninety years old. And he wasn't even fifty.

4

Praise the mount! I'm fixed upon it,
Mount of Thy redeeming love.

*C*aleb walked onto the porch with a cold cup of coffee. He'd finished his share of morning chores while managing to stay out of his father's way the best he could. His mother had cleaned up the breakfast dishes and gone quilting with his youngest sister, Katie. Sarah and Rebekah were at Country Pleasures, leaving him alone in a large, silent house.

He'd endured his first full week of work without getting fired or pulled into another argument with his *daed*. He should celebrate, yet his day off stretched before him with few options. In the city he could go to the zoo or the lakefront park or ride the train downtown to watch the ships in and out of the harbor. Once he rode the elevator to the top of the Terminal Tower. What was there to do in March in Fredericksburg?

Of course, all he had to do was find his father. There was always something to do on a farm, even one as small as theirs. Tools needed sharpening, gardens could be tilled, and farm animals were always in need of some kind of care. But Caleb wasn't accustomed to only one day to himself—Sunday. He'd grown lazy while in Cleveland and old habits would be hard to break.

He sat down on the porch steps to pet his gray-muzzled sheepdog. It took little to make a dog happy. As long as someone regularly filled his bowl with kibble and occasionally scratched behind his ears, Shep wagged his tail, licked your hand, and would follow you anywhere.

And what would make Caleb happy? For the past week, all he could think about was Josie. They had gotten along well at the pancake breakfast. Unlike most women, Josie didn't chatter incessantly or pout for no reason. She knew the right thing to say in every situation.

Or maybe it just seemed that way because Caleb was smitten with her.

But each time he considered driving his buggy to her house after work or hiking the back path with a flashlight on some thinly disguised errand, he remembered his father's warning: *No Amish woman in her right mind would ever marry you.* What would Mr. Yoder think about his tattoo? More to the point, how would Josie feel about the name Kristen emblazoned on his arm until his dying day?

Caleb stared off in the distance. The sight of his father plowing the cornfield filled him with guilt. "Come on, old boy. Let's see if we can't make ourselves useful."

However, he didn't get a dozen yards from the house when the crunch of car wheels on gravel caught his attention. Shep started to bark. Lifting a hand to shield his eyes, Caleb watched a shiny gold convertible crawl up the lane. The top was up on the cool spring day.

"Cal Beachy, as I live and breathe." A familiar voice floated from the driver's window.

He waited at their turn-around for the fancy car to stop, unable to believe his eyes or his ears. Shep started to bark. "Quiet, boy," he ordered.

Pete Taylor opened the driver's door and jumped out. "You can run, but you sure can't hide. At least, not for long."

Caleb stepped forward to embrace his *Englisch* best friend in a clumsy man-hug. "How did you find me?"

Pete slapped him on the back. "It wasn't easy. Do you have any idea how many Beachys live in Wayne County?"

"Quite a few?" Laughing, he leaned on the car's fender.

"There are hundreds of them. And you left no forwarding address at that *luxury* apartment on Davenport Drive. Your former landlord couldn't believe you abandoned so much quality furniture." Pete rolled his eyes. He'd been appalled by Caleb's furnishing each time he visited.

"I am a firm believer in recycling," said Caleb, eager to forget his former residence. "Sorry I didn't send a letter or call. When I arrived home, I wasn't sure how long I would be staying." Regret over treating his only Cleveland friend shabbily brought a blush to his face.

"Don't worry about it. I know how touchy your homecoming might have been." Pete pivoted in the middle of the driveway. "Wow, your family has a really nice farm. This looks like one of those pictures on a calendar."

"Not one of your calendars." Caleb remembered seeing Pete's wall-hanging of women in very skimpy swimsuits. Leafing through the photos, he'd never felt so embarrassed in his life.

"Now that I'm about to become a married man, I threw that calendar in the trash. My new replacement has pictures of dogs, cats, and horses." He grinned and then hooked his thumb toward the car. "Do you remember my fiancée, Michelle?"

As though on cue, a long-legged, dark-haired girl got out of the passenger side. She wore a low-cut sweater, very tight jeans, and high-heeled leather boots. "Hi, Cal," she said, flashing a bright white smile.

He startled, not because of her appearance, but because he hadn't noticed anyone else in the car. Caleb had met her once and been thoroughly intimidated. He still wasn't accustomed to the *Englischers'* revealing clothes and heavy makeup. "Michelle, excuse me. I didn't realize you'd come along with Pete." Caleb strode to her side and accepted a loose hug.

"I decided to stay low-profile until you two had a chance to get reacquainted." Michelle stepped back, but her perfume continued to overwhelm his senses.

"Let's go up to the house. We could sit on the porch or maybe go inside." Caleb led the pair to the porch swing and a row of rocking chairs.

"Maybe inside would be better." Pete grinned. "We didn't dress for the weather. We've been relying on the car's heater to keep us from freezing to death."

"No problem." Caleb opened the door on his family's kitchen. Was this their first time in an Amish home? Of course it was. He wondered what they would think of the simple appointments. Most *Englisch-ers* adored gadgets, rooms filled with furniture, and endless decorative objects. But he didn't have long to wait for his answer.

"What a kitchen! It's so huge," said Michelle. "I love how unclut-tered it is." She pranced around the room like a spring filly. "And I'll bet you can fit twenty people around your oak table." She trailed her hand down the waxed surface with appreciation.

"Yeah, at times we've had more than that for dinner." Caleb pulled out two chairs at the table and then went for a hot drink.

"I understand why you decided to stay once you were home." Pete glanced around the room and then locked gazes with him. "So, how's life going?"

Caleb knew his friend didn't want some phony answer. They knew and respected each other better than that. "It's been fine with my mom and sisters, but tense with my dad. He keeps waiting for me to bolt for the door and not look back." He forced a wry smile.

"It takes time, I suppose. You were gone a long time. Once you stick around, he'll get used to seeing you." Pete chuckled, finally drawing a matching response from Caleb. "Did you find a job yet?"

"Just started work this past Monday. Roofing and general construc-tion for my father."

"Well, that might bring the pimple to a head sooner." Pete guffawed good-naturedly.

Caleb didn't quite understand the analogy but he nodded anyway, looking anywhere in the room but at the bubbly Michelle. The woman made him nervous. She was always watching him from the corner of her eye, like a bug under a microscope. "Tell me about your upcoming wedding—everything set for the big day?" he asked.

"Two months and counting. We've lined up eight bridesmaids and groomsmen, but I can make room for one more if you'd like to stand up as my best man." Pete lifted one eyebrow.

"Thanks, but I had better pass. I hope you understand."

"No problem. We've booked the Old Stone Church on Public Square with an evening reception in the ballroom of the Renaissance Hotel. Michelle's an only child so her parents have decided to pull out all the stops: open bar, heavy appetizers, and then a sit-down dinner of surf-and-turf."

"What's that—seawater and dirt?"

Pete smirked. "Even better—lobster tail and filet mignon. Nothing but the best for daddy's little girl."

"Good grief, for a wedding?" Caleb thought about Amish marriages. Although lavish in variety and quantity of food, they were just a step above a church potluck.

"Everybody is having extravagant weddings these days, so I said why not?" Michelle leaned forward to resume the narrative. "My parents have plenty of time to pay it off before retirement. We're flying in fresh flowers the night before from Hawaii, plus there'll be a molten chocolate volcano for the centerpiece of the dessert buffet." Her pretty face glowed with excitement.

Caleb was struck speechless. He didn't know whether to say "Congratulations on one-upping the competition," or "Sorry to hear your parents will be shackled to their jobs for years." However, his shock over their wedding arrangements paled in comparison to his father's.

Eli had entered through the mudroom and stood in the doorway, his mouth agape. "Caleb," he said, "who are these *Englischers*?" There wasn't a hint of hospitality in his tone.

Caleb sprang to his feet. "*Daed,* this is my best friend, Pete Taylor. Don't you remember him from the Wilmot project?"

Pete also scrambled up and stretched out his hand. "How do you do, sir? I'm very pleased to see you again."

Perhaps it was due to Taylor's formal and respectful tone and choice of words, but Eli's frown softened. "Thank you, young man. I trust you've been well." He shook Pete's hand briefly.

"Very well, thank you. May I present my fiancée, Michelle Moore. We're to be married in May, unless she comes to her senses." Pete laughed wholeheartedly, while Eli blinked like an owl.

Michelle jumped up and practically sprinted around the table.

Please, God, don't let her throw her arms around my father's neck. The prayer flitted through Caleb's mind in an instant. Even after five years, he still didn't understand *Englisch* forwardness or public demonstrations of affection. But thankfully, Michelle stopped short in front of Eli and kept her arms at her side. "I have wanted to visit Pete's Amish friends for months. You have such a super home. I want to live in a big house like this someday, but maybe one a little closer to civilization, and not set so far back from the road. Passersby can barely see it. And was that a pig I spotted next to your barn? Do you own a real pig? It's so huge compared to those potbellied mini ones." She grinned as though pleased with herself.

Eli was utterly flabbergasted. "Yes, the pig is real."

"Why don't we have some lunch?" Caleb broke his father's inertia. "I know *Mamm* left a plate of sandwiches. Why don't I get a jar of peaches from the pantry?"

"Lunch in a real Amish kitchen? Wait until I tell my friends at work. They'll be so jealous." Michelle returned to her seat next to her intended spouse.

Eli shook off his trance and began to wash at the sink. "Yes, lunch is a good idea. Then I'll need your help this afternoon in the fields, Caleb."

"I would love to pitch in too, Mr. Beachy," said Pete. "I'm fascinated with farming. What are you planting—wheat, hay, oats? Maybe soybeans? Alfalfa? Barley?"

When it became apparent that Pete's guessing would continue until he exhausted the name of every grain and vegetable, Caleb intervened. "We need to plant seed corn—both sweet and field."

"I should have known." Pete slapped his forehead with a palm. "Good cash crop, right?"

"The market fluctuates, but right now it's not too bad." Caleb fought back a grin. Pete hadn't known the difference between beets, turnips, or kohlrabi during their trip to an open-air market and had shown no interest in learning. "These sandwiches appear to be ham and Swiss cheese on rye with tomato—everybody okay with that?" He set the plate down on the table, along with jars of mustard and mayo.

"Knowing your *mamm*, there should be enough." Eli murmured, carrying over plates, napkins, and forks.

Pete placed a sandwich on both his and Michelle's plates. "We're fine with these, thanks."

"But they're ham!" Michelle gasped, pressing a palm to her chest. "I surely hope this isn't that pig's sister or brother."

Eli settled himself at the head of the table before answering his female guest. "Worry not; this particular hog was a total stranger to us." He fluffed his napkin over his lap.

"Oh, thank goodness." She bit into her sandwich with zeal. After Caleb spooned peaches into small bowls, Michelle's admiration rose to a new height. She forked one peach half and held it aloft. "Did your wife actually can these from your own peach trees, Mr. Beachy?"

"Of course she did." Eli began eating as though late for an appointment.

"Then she should put those little doily-hats over the jar lids and sell them at a roadside stand. I'll bet she could make tons of money." Michelle popped the entire peach half into her mouth.

"If we sold our peaches at a stand, Miss Moore, what would we possibly serve when *Englischers* drop in unannounced from Cleveland?"

That curtailed Michelle's enthusiasm a tad, along with the majority of the conversation for the rest of the meal.

❧

Sarah walked home from Country Pleasures with a spring in her step, mainly because she walked home alone. Mrs. Pratt had hired Rebekah for several hours of extra work. Apparently, she wanted to clean out closets and the attic—areas of her house unconnected with the inn. Rebekah had been the first to volunteer for overtime. Not that Sarah didn't need extra money with her marriage less than eight months away. But with *Mamm* and Katie at quilting all day, she vastly preferred an afternoon to herself. Maybe she would nap, or read stretched out on the sofa or under a quilt on the hammock. Maybe she could…

Her musings ceased when Sarah spotted an unfamiliar car in the driveway—an expensive sports car with shiny wheels and a license plate that read DADSGRL. Sarah ran up the steps and threw open the kitchen door. "Hello," she crowed, scanning the four people at the table. "I take it that car is yours?" Her focus landed on a pretty girl with a vast expanse of chest showing.

"It is," said the girl. "Are you Sarah?"

"I am." Shutting the door behind her, she heard her father release a deep sigh.

"I'm Michelle Moore. Pete told me so much about you—how you three walked the beach at Edgewater Park and ate lunch at the West-side Market. If I had known about your visit, I would have taken the day off. I'm a legal secretary, plus I'm taking classes at Tri-C to become a paralegal." She dabbed her lips with a napkin. "Your mom makes great peaches, by the way."

Sarah could barely take her eyes of the energetic woman. "Nice to meet you, Michelle. Hello, Pete. My brother said you were engaged. When's the wedding?"

Eli pushed his chair away from the table. "Fix yourself a sandwich, *dochder.* The ones your mother made are gone. Miss Moore has already described the lobster extravaganza her parents will be paying for into their dotage."

Sarah glanced between her brother and father on her way to the fridge. Caleb was glaring at his sandwich while her *daed* was frowning as though suffering heartburn. But the engaged couple didn't seem to notice.

"Thanks, Sarah," said Pete. "In less than two months we'll be honeymooning in Maui. That's one of the Hawaiian Islands."

Sarah winked over her shoulder as she fixed a sandwich. "Yes, I remember studying U.S. geography in school. Hawaii was our fiftieth state, right?"

Michelle squeezed Pete's hand. "That's right. Daddy rented us a condo for two weeks, right on the beach. Pete said you had a serious boyfriend too."

"Yes, Adam and I are getting married this fall."

"Where do you plan to honeymoon?"

Sarah carried her plate to the table. "Not as far away as Hawaii. We'll probably visit Adam's relatives in Indiana and Pennsylvania."

"Sounds nice. Why don't you plan a Saturday in Cleveland with us? We could go to lunch at the mall—I know a great home décor shop that sells every gadget shown on those TV cooking shows. If you stay overnight, we can visit the Cleveland Zoo and the art museum." Michelle's fervor knew no bounds. "I heard you missed those during your last trip. We could be like tourists."

Sarah glanced at her father. Her intuition was correct—*Daed's* face had turned so red she feared his head might explode.

"That is out of the question, young lady. My daughter is about to take classes to join the church, which means her *rumschpringe* is just about over. She has no use for art museums, or culinary gadgets, and even less for shopping malls. She's about to become an Amish wife and mother, very different from the life you're preparing for." Eli balled his napkin and tossed it down on his plate. "If you'll excuse me, Miss Moore, Caleb and I must get to work. You're welcome to join us in the fields, Pete, if you're not worried about ruining your clothes."

Caleb's face flushed almost as bright as Pete's red shirt. "I have a jacket and boots he can wear."

Pete carried his plate and glass to the sink. "I would love to, and these *are* my old clothes. I expected to get dirty in the country."

"You men run off," said Michelle sweetly. "The two brides-to-be will make short work of these dishes."

Sarah bit her tongue until Pete, Caleb, and her father had donned coats and left the house. Then she burst into giggles while Michelle stared with confusion. "I am so glad to meet you, Michelle," she said. "You and Pete will make a good match together. How about a slice of chocolate cream pie to celebrate your upcoming marriage?"

"That sounds wonderful. Say, you don't grow cocoa beans on this farm, do you? If so, I must text my mother—she won't believe how clever you Beachys are!"

Sarah and Michelle enjoyed their pie and cleaned up the kitchen in no time. Then Sarah took her on a grand tour of the house, chicken coop, and their recently tilled vegetable garden. Pete's fiancée had to be the friendliest person on earth. She asked dozens of questions—some ridiculous, some soul-searching, but never made a single disparaging remark. Despite working for a B&B that catered to *Englischers*, Sarah had never met anyone so curious about Amish life.

"My mom told me she used to dream about marrying an Amish man." Michelle pulled up a long, tasseled weed as they strolled back toward the house.

"Did your parents have Amish friends?" Sarah asked a fair share of questions too.

Michelle shook her head. "Mom didn't know a single one other than those we bought vegetables from. But she was fascinated with their large families and how they turned their backs on modern technology."

"Both are ways to stay close to God and His divine plan for our lives. The more children you have, the more you'll be centered on your family."

"I never thought about it like that. I hope Pete and I have at least six kids. My friends only want one or two, but not me. I can't wait until we marry and get started making babies."

Sarah blushed as they climbed the porch steps. She wasn't sure if anything would embarrass this young woman. "Let's have some iced tea on the porch. It's warmed up quite a bit, but I'll get a shawl to put around your shoulders." When she returned, Michelle was rocking in the porch swing.

"It is so peaceful here. I definitely want a swing for my back deck." Her head was back, her arms crossed, and her eyes closed.

"I brought a plate of oatmeal cookies to have with our tea." Sarah hated to interrupt.

Michelle opened one eye and then grabbed two cookies from the plate. "Did your mom bake these?"

"My twelve-year-old sister, Katie, did. She's getting quite good."

"Of course she is. Aren't all Amish women wonderful cooks and bakers?" She practically swallowed the first cookie whole.

"Of course not. Like every other group, some people are gifted in certain areas and some aren't. But we lock the bad cooks and bakers in the attic whenever tourists stop by to keep up our image."

Michelle's laughter could have been heard in the cornfield. "You have a great sense of humor. That's why we get along so well." She took another cookie from the plate. "Do you suppose I could see what your hair looks like under your bonnet?"

"This is called a prayer *kapp*." Sarah glanced around to make sure they were alone. Women's hair shouldn't be seen by men other than their husbands, but since they were both females she didn't see a problem. Sarah pulled off the covering and turned to show the back of her head. "It's just an old-fashioned bun held up with pins."

"My grandmother used to wear her hair like that." Michelle patted the knot of hair gently. "Do you take it down every night or only every other? How often do you wash it? Do you think I could see how long it is?"

Sarah pivoted around to assess the woman's face. Michelle's inquisitiveness appeared utterly earnest. "Yes, I take it down each night but sleep with a loose ponytail. Otherwise it would get too tangled. I usually wash it every third day unless my scalp sweats in the summer." She sipped her tea and nibbled a cookie.

"Makes perfect sense." Michelle couldn't take her eyes of Sarah's *kapp*. "Mind telling me how long your hair is? I've never been able to grow mine past my shoulders. Then it gets on my nerves and I chop it off." She fingered one of her own dark locks.

"Why don't I show you?" She pondered only a moment before pulling out the dozen pins that held her bun in place. *After all, the men would be in the cornfield for several hours.* When she shook her head, her waist-length hair cascaded down her back.

"My goodness, I've never seen such beautiful hair before." Michelle reached out tentatively to touch a strand. "It's so thick and shiny. You should do television commercials for hair care products."

"I don't think my parents would approve, especially since my father is the bishop." Sarah lifted the bulk off her neck, feeling the sins of vanity and pride take hold of her better judgment.

Michelle pawed around in her oversized purse, spilling half the contents on the porch floor. Finally she extracted a plastic brush. "Would you mind if I brushed it? I promise this brush is clean." When Sarah didn't respond, Michelle's face turned the color of ripe tomatoes. "You probably think I'm weird. Sorry. Pete says I always push things too far."

"I don't think you're weird in the least. When we were young, my sister and I loved brushing each other's hair. Now Rebekah would prefer pulling mine out by the roots." Sarah perched on the edge of the swing. "Go ahead."

Michelle dragged the brush through Sarah's long tresses, gently working out snarls instead of yanking them free. "Maybe I'll return to school for cosmetology. These paralegal classes get boring at times."

For five minutes Michelle brushed, Sarah rocked, and they both shared their plans for the future. Despite her fancy car, flashy clothes, and extravagant wedding plans, Michelle had a practical head on her shoulders. "When my children are old enough for school, I'm sending them to a Christian school where they'll get personal attention. Public school classrooms are too large." While she talked, she plaited Sarah's hair into two long braids.

"I haven't had pigtails since I was a little girl," said Sarah.

"And there's good reason for that—you're not a child anymore." The male voice from the other end of the porch nearly knocked both women off the swing.

Sarah turned to see Adam Troyer striding toward them with his coat buttoned up to his throat. "I didn't hear your buggy drive up. Where did you park?"

"I tied my horse in the front yard since a car blocked the driveway. I had no idea who would be visiting the Beachys on a Saturday afternoon." His stare rotated between Sarah's uncovered head and Michelle Moore like a pendulum. Judging by his expression, neither sight made him happy. "Where is your *kapp*, Sarah?"

"Right here." She held up the starched piece of white cotton. "Adam, this is Michelle Moore, the fiancée of Caleb's friend, Pete Taylor."

"From Cleveland?" he asked.

"Lakewood, to be exact. How do you do? I gather you're Sarah's beau. You are a lucky man, to be sure." Michelle extended her well-manicured fingers.

Adam's manners returned in the nick of time. He swept his felt hat from his head and shook her hand. "Pleased to meet you. And yes, God blessed me generously when I met Sarah." Embarrassment turned his cheeks a healthy shade of pink. His gaze shifted back to Sarah. "Why is your hair down?" he asked, settling into a rocker.

Sarah quickly coiled the two long braids around and secured them with pins. Nimbly she covered her head with the *kapp*. "Michelle was curious about Amish hair. Since we were alone on the porch, I saw no harm in showing her mine. I hope you don't think me vain." She folded her hands primly.

"No, I know you too well to think that, but Amish hair is no different than any other." Adam focused on the *Englisch* guest. "Did you drive to Fredericksburg by yourself?"

Michelle dropped the brush onto the pile next to her handbag. "Oh, no, Pete came to visit his old friend, Cal, just to make sure everything was all right."

"Why wouldn't things be all right? Caleb is back where he belongs with his people." Adam stared at the spilled contents of her purse. His frown returned for a second appearance. "You brought *a camera* to an Amish home?" He glared at Sarah. "Did you allow yourself to be photographed?"

Sarah inhaled through her nostrils as her temper flared. "You know me better than that. That camera hasn't left her purse. Please don't give Miss Moore the impression that Caleb's family is bad-mannered and inhospitable," she snapped.

Silence gripped the porch.

Michelle and Pete didn't stay long after that.

Adam tried to finagle an invitation to supper to no avail. If he could behave rudely, then so could Sarah. When she refused to budge, he finally returned to his buggy with his tail between his legs. By the time Elizabeth and Katie returned from their quilting bee, not one of the Beachys was smiling—not Eli, not Caleb, and certainly not Sarah.

෨෧

"Goodness, *ehemann*, are you sure you're not making a mountain out of a molehill?" Elizabeth peered over the top of her glasses, her sewing momentarily forgotten.

Eli shook his head. "You weren't there while Caleb was having lunch with those *Englischers*. He seemed to hang onto every word that woman said."

"Maybe Pete's fiancée was telling a fascinating story, and you walked in too late." His *fraa* returned to her needlework.

"She was describing her three-ring circus of a wedding. What Amish man would be interested in that?" Finally alone with his wife, Eli began to pace the kitchen floor. After Caleb left for an evening walk, he'd thought his girls would never go upstairs to their room.

"Sit down, Eli. I'm growing exhausted just watching you. Katie and I seemed to have stumbled into a hornets' nest instead of coming home to our family. All four of you glowering and pouting like *kinner*."

"I don't pout." Eli paused. "Four? What could Rebekah be riled up about? She wasn't even home during their visit."

Elizabeth winked at him. "That's just it—Rebekah is miffed because she missed the excitement. She believes Sarah planned for her to stay at the B&B."

"That's ridiculous. Sarah couldn't have known they would visit." Slumping into a chair, Eli released a sound similar to a growl. "First, Caleb getting excited about those *Englischers'* wedding, then Sarah disgracing herself with Miss Moore."

She dropped her sewing atop the basket. "Sarah said she simply showed the woman her hair and then Michelle decided to brush it. True, that shouldn't have happened outdoors, but Sarah believed they were alone. Why was Adam Troyer sneaking around the bushes like a prowling tomcat?"

"You're as bad as our daughter. Adam didn't sneak. He was calling on Sarah on his way home from work. Granted, he shouldn't have taken his reaction out on Caleb's guests, but he has a right to be concerned about Sarah's behavior. Aren't they announcing their engagement soon?" His tone dropped to the barest whisper.

"You know better than to ask me. We'll see this summer." Elizabeth reached for her cup of tea. "I'm glad you realized Pete and Michelle were Caleb's guests. According to our son, you treated them like house burglars caught red-handed in the strong box. Is that true?"

Eli pursed his lips. "I made no one turn out their pockets or empty their purse. But *jah*, I suppose I overreacted to their showing up unannounced."

"Were they supposed to *call* first?" She sipped her tea without taking her eyes off him.

"I don't know, *fraa,* but I'm afraid we'll lose Caleb back to their world of temptation."

"Then let's not drive him away with our lack of trust and faith in his judgment."

Weary beyond description, Eli nodded on his way up the steps. "I will try." He voiced the words, but in his heart he hadn't the slightest idea how.

5

Sorrowing I shall be in spirit,
Till released from flesh and sin

Caleb's second week on Eli's roofing crew started out very much like the first. By Wednesday, however, his *mamm* inadvertently provided the fly destined to embed itself in the family ointment. At their normal breakfast of toast and oatmeal, she entered the kitchen carrying a heavy, black wool coat.

"Look what I found for you secondhand—a still serviceable winter coat." She held out the garment for his inspection. "I lengthened the sleeves, mended a few moth holes, and cleaned it the best I could. What do you think?"

Caleb peered over his coffee cup at the fairly worn-out Amish jacket. "Looks fine. *Danki.* Where did you come across it?"

"Beatrice Black's husband passed away, so he had no further need of it. She was getting rid of most of Abraham's clothes at a rummage sale."

Caleb wished he hadn't asked. *A moth-eaten coat from a dead man at least half a foot shorter than me?* Knowing she meant well, he gritted his teeth and smiled at his mother. "It will come in handy for the rest of the season. By next fall I'll be able to buy a new coat."

"It won't be a perfect fit, but I couldn't see it going to waste. Abraham would be happy it was put to good use." Elizabeth bustled between the counter and the refrigerator as she packed their lunches.

His father listened to their exchange but said nothing. His silence ended when Caleb downed his remaining coffee and lifted his Carhartt from the hall peg. "Why are you taking that? Your *mamm* repaired a perfectly fine Plain coat."

"Which I intend to wear." Caleb spoke softly while shrugging on his mother's handiwork. Two inches of wrist dangled beneath the sleeves. "Since I don't need this one any longer I might as well give it away." He walked outside just as Jack pulled up the driveway.

"Sounds *gut*." Eli stomped down the porch steps, lugging his briefcase of papers, lunch cooler, and thermos.

Caleb followed him, carrying the *Englisch* coat and the last shreds of his dignity. He climbed into the back while his *daed* sat up front as usual. Caleb waited until they turned onto the state highway to address their driver. "I'm putting this Carhartt atop your toolbox, Jack, because I don't need it anymore and you're about the same size as me."

Jack repositioned the rearview mirror to meet his gaze. "Thanks, Cal. How much do you want for it?"

"Nothing. It's a gift. I bought it on *rumschpringe* while up in Cleveland." While he spoke Caleb noticed an overlooked moth hole in his sleeve.

"Your Carhartt looked brand new. Besides, you already gave me your Sawzall and Bob your cordless circular saw. I wouldn't mind paying a fair price for the jacket—that brand lasts forever."

Caleb didn't have a chance to argue, or decide upon a price for a used garment, or anything else. His father jumped into the discussion as though Caleb had been struck mute.

"No, just take it off our hands," said Eli. "It's a daily reminder of a place my son needs to forget. How about if Caleb foregoes his share of the gas money during the project in exchange for the tools?"

Jack glanced into the rearview mirror at him. "Sounds fair to me, if it's okay with Cal. But I'm still getting the better end of the deal."

Caleb stared out the window, not meeting Jack's eye. With two other Amish men in the van, he didn't wish to disagree with his father. "Deal sounds fair." Three words, barely audible, but it was the best he could do at the moment.

At the Millersburg job site Eli remained on the ground poring over blueprints and specifications, or on his cell phone ordering materials, or lining up their next project. Caleb and the rest of the crew worked unsupervised. All seven men were diligent and relatively proficient—the *Englischers* more so than the Amish, due to their experience. During their lunch break, Jack and Bob headed across the street to McDonald's while Eli met another contractor in a local diner. Caleb saw a chance to broach a subject that had been needling him with his fellow Amishmen. "I've noticed you continue to speak *Deutsch* even when Jack and Bob are with us. Don't you think we should speak English out of common courtesy?" He glanced around the group where everyone munched on sandwiches or pieces of cold fried chicken. All food consumption halted, sandwiches held aloft in midair.

Four sets of eyes focused on Josiah, Caleb's roofing partner. "I had a feeling that has been bothering you," he said. The Killbuck carpenter, a father of six with a seventh on the way, spoke in a calm manner. "We thought the same when we started working for your *daed*. So we spoke English in the van, at lunch, or anyplace else *Englischers* were present." Pausing, Josiah glanced around the group.

"Go on," prodded Caleb. He set his egg salad sandwich down on the waxed paper. "What changed? Did you get mad at Jack or Bob?"

"Of course not." Josiah looked bewildered. "Truth be told, Eli told us that on breaks and before or after work we should speak *Deutsch* and let Bob and Jack carry on their own conversations. Only when we're actually working with them should we converse in English."

Caleb waited for someone to burst into laughter to indicate Josiah was pulling his leg, but no one did. He received only nods of acknowledgement when he scanned the faces. "He instructed you to speak a language that Bob and Jack don't understand?"

Josiah took a bite of sandwich and chewed. "Eli has nothing but respect for them, but I have the feeling he doesn't want his Amish employees"—he paused as though searching for a word—"fraternizing with the *Englisch*."

"You've got to be kidding." Caleb's comment wasn't a question.

"No, I'm not, but Jack and Bob don't mind. Everybody is happy on this crew, Cal. Don't try to fix something that's not broken." Josiah locked eyes with him. "I'm offering brotherly advice from one Plain man to another."

Caleb found the notion ridiculous, but he had no choice but to agree. "All right. If you're sure we're not offending Bob and Jack, I won't rock the boat."

Josiah rose to his feet and shoved his trash into his lunch bag. "I'm positive. Things are different here than what you're familiar with, but you'll learn Eli's ways eventually." He patted Caleb's shoulder before heading toward the ladder to the roof.

You're not kidding they're different, Caleb thought. But what choice did he have? Eli was his boss as well as his father, and Caleb was in no mood to look for another job.

During the afternoon, roof removal moved at a speed slower than a three-legged turtle. Jack and Bob, crew partners, worked on a section half a story higher than the other crews. Each time an Amish team needed something cut with the Sawzall, Bob or Jack had to climb down the ladder. No one but Caleb found this arrangement of teams ridiculous. But considering his last clash with Eli in front of the men, Caleb worked without comment. At quitting time, however, his patience ran out. "Can you clean up the site without me?" he asked Josiah. "I'd like to speak to my father a moment."

Josiah shrugged. "Sure, go ahead. I'll see you in the van."

Caleb found his father stacking papers and rolling up warehouse blueprints. His glasses sat cockeye and a smudge of blue ink marred his nose. "Got a minute, *Daed*?" he asked.

"Of course." Eli pushed his glasses higher up his nose. "This job is coming along nicely. We'll be done within two weeks."

"Coming along, yes, but I don't know how nicely."

Eli frowned. "Did you run into trouble today—another section of deteriorated rafters?"

"No, nothing like that." Caleb sucked in a deep breath. Considering his years of commercial construction experience, perhaps his father would welcome his input. "But I have a suggestion. Today Josiah and I kept interrupting Jack and Bob. They had to climb down the ladder to make cuts for us. Instead of having three teams of two men, why don't we make two teams of three? Bob could work with one Amish crew and Jack with the other. Then our work can proceed smoothly and more efficiently." Caleb forced a smile, trying to reduce the confrontation factor as much as possible.

Eli shoved his papers into a leather case. "Is Josiah unhappy with the teams or did Jack speak to you about this?" His forehead furrowed into creases.

"No, neither. This is my idea, based on my years of experience." He crossed his arms. "I'm no novice. I know what I'm doing."

"You're a good carpenter, *jah*, but I prefer the teams to remain as they are." Eli reached for his empty lunch cooler. "Are you packed up, son? Did you load your tools?"

"Everything is stowed, but before we join the others, could you explain why you won't take my suggestion?"

Eli hesitated as though deciding whether or not to answer. Then he lifted his watery blue eyes to meet Caleb's. "Because several Amish fathers were concerned about their sons working for me. They knew that I also have *Englisch* employees. They didn't want their boys to jump the fence like you had done." Eli hoisted the strap to his shoulder. "If there's nothing else, let's head to the van. Men are eager to get home to their families."

Caleb followed his father to the parking lot, utterly speechless with his mouth agape. That had to be the last reason he would have expected.

᳗

There was something extraordinary about Saturdays in April. Maybe it was the intensity of the sun as it rose over the eastern hills. Maybe it was the breeze which no longer cut through one's clothes to the bone. Maybe the extra hours of daylight tipped the scales in April's favor. For whatever the reason, this particular Saturday was extra special for Sarah. First, she didn't have to work at Country Pleasures today; Rebekah would assist Mrs. Pratt by herself. Secondly, her best friend was getting a brand new barn. The entire community would show up to lend a hand, along with their *Englisch* friends and neighbors. Barn raisings were hard work for menfolk. But the women enjoyed plenty of free time between meals to catch up on news while they watched the transformation of a foundation and pile of materials into a finished structure.

Sarah washed her hands and face and dressed with care. Adam would be at the barn raising, so she wanted to look her best. They had not parted on the best of terms last week and she hadn't seen him since. Sunday had been an off-week for preaching.

Downstairs in the kitchen her *bruder* sat alone. "Where's *Mamm*?" she asked.

"In the henhouse." Caleb filled his thermos with black coffee.

"How about Rebekah?"

"Taking a shower. She plans to leave the inn early." He took three hard-boiled eggs from a bowl on the counter.

"Is James coming to the Yoders?" Sarah grabbed a couple of eggs for herself.

Caleb winked. "Why else would Rebekah want to arrive early to a barn raising?"

Sarah cracked an egg on the table edge. "May I ride with you and *Daed*? I want to get there early to help Josie and her family."

He lifted his straw hat off the hook. "*Daed* left while it was still dark. He went down the back path with the flashlight."

"Whatever for? You and the other carpenters helped him yesterday. Didn't you lay out the materials and pre-build some walls?"

"You know how he worries, Sarah. He's the master barn-builder, so this project rests on his shoulders." Caleb reached for a lightweight jacket and his tool belt. "I'm leaving now, *schwester,* so you'll have to ride with *Mamm*."

"Please, Cal? I'll be ready before you finish hitching the horse." Sarah flew up the stairs, not waiting for his answer. Ten minutes later, she ran to the buggy with her purse and two shopping bags of produce. A leafy bunch of celery peeked from the top of the tote.

Caleb offered his hand. "What's all that? I'm sure the Yoders have plenty of vegetables."

"My contribution to the buffet will be a giant tossed salad. I might as well fix it in Josie's kitchen while we chat." Sarah smiled sweetly as he released the brake. "How are things going at work?"

"Fine."

"Earning plenty of money for the future, maybe to build your own home some day?"

"*Jah.*" Caleb turned the buggy onto the township road.

"Are you excited that the barn raising will be at the Yoders?"

"I'm simply jumping for joy. Why don't you cut the small talk and get to the point? You didn't dash out with me at the last minute just to fix your salad in someone else's kitchen." He clucked to the horse to pick up the pace.

"No, I didn't, Mr. Man-of-few-Words." Sarah scowled. "I'm curious if you plan to pursue Josie, maybe see where you stand with her."

"That is not your business, little sis."

"I'll take that answer as a no." Sarah watched him bite the inside of his cheek. "Why not? True, it's not my business, but you're not getting any younger and neither is she. I saw sparks between you two at the pancake breakfast. Don't try to deny it."

"The sparks were caused by rude *Englischers,* not because of my infatuation."

"So you don't find Josie attractive? Or maybe she's not *nice* enough?"

Caleb stared at her. "You know that's not it, but you of all people should realize Josie wouldn't court someone like me."

She pivoted on the seat. "Me, of all people?"

"Have you forgotten?" He dropped the reins and rolled up his sleeve, revealing the bright red heart with snakes entwined around the name "Kristen."

Sarah gasped. "*Jah,* I had forgotten."

"Now that I've reminded you, could we talk about the weather, or problems at the inn, anything other than Josie?" He rolled down his sleeve and picked up the reins.

"That tattoo is ugly, to be sure, but Josie might be able to overlook it if you gave her the chance."

"Why would she do that?"

"Women are capable of almost anything if they're in love."

Caleb emitted a harsh, bitter sound. "Your friend is not in love with me, Sarah. Get that through your head."

"Not yet she isn't, because you haven't enthralled her yet with your stimulating, single-word conversations."

This time Caleb smiled and then laughed.

"Spend a little time with her, maybe at supper. The way I see it, you've got nothing to lose."

His reply was a grunt—one step lower than his usual monosyllable replies. But he didn't argue and for that Sarah was grateful.

Once they arrived at the Yoders two little boys took the reins from Caleb. They would park the rig and feed and water the horse so Caleb could head straight to the barn site. Sarah jumped from the buggy and joined a throng of women entering the kitchen.

Inside, Josie greeted her with boundless enthusiasm. "You're early—what a miracle! Work next to me since I see your salad's not done. Some things in life never change." Josie dumped vegetables from the bag and lined them up on the cutting board.

"Glad to see you too," she said. Sarah slipped on an apron and greeted the other ladies, settling into an enjoyable morning of female companionship.

It was almost time to carry lunch outdoors to the workers when she noticed Adam's sister staring at her. "Hi Amanda, how's married life?" she asked.

Amanda Stutzman set down her wooden spoon. "*Gut.* Would you mind taking this jug of lemonade out to the drink table? It's ready to go."

Sarah smiled over her shoulder. "Could you send someone else? I'm up to my elbows in flour. Josie decided we needed more pies." She lifted her powdery hands from the bowl.

Amanda set down the lemonade and strode across the kitchen. Halting next to Sarah, Amanda whispered into her ear. "You've not been out to the barn all morning to check the men's progress. Maybe you need a break."

"I've seen barns go up all my life, but I'll deliver the lemonade as soon as this batch goes into the oven."

"Adam has been heartsick since Saturday. Did you two have a spat? His neck is probably stiff from watching for you." Unfortunately, whispering wasn't one of Amanda's many talents. Her voice steadily increased in volume to become audible everywhere in the room.

"Maybe Sarah has no intention of marrying your *bruder,* Amanda. She might have her eye on someone she met at that fancy bed-and-breakfast." The speaker was Doris Schmidt—Rebekah's best friend.

"I assure you, Doris, that isn't the case." Sarah tried to remain pleasant to the girl, a duplicate thorn-in-the-foot to her sister.

"Adam is a catch, and yet you drag your feet. Won't you be happy married to a simple furniture craftsman?"

"What crawled under your *kapp*?" Margaret Yoder shook a spatula at Doris in warning. "Hush, if you can't say anything nice."

Sarah washed her hands at the sink and then lifted her skirt six inches higher. "See my feet, Doris? They don't drag; they don't shuffle. Amanda, I'll take the lemonade out if you'll finish this pie dough. I want to ask Adam what kind of furniture he plans to build for our new home." Sarah resisted the impulse to stick out her tongue at Rebekah's wily friend.

Outdoors, teenagers had set up a table of cool drinks next to where men could wash before their meal. Long tables had been moved into the shade where people could enjoy their lunch. Men would be served first and then the women would eat. Sarah scanned the dozens of men scurrying around the roof until she finally located Adam. Amanda had been correct—Adam had already spotted her and was frantically waving his arms. She waved and smiled until her face hurt. After pouring the lemonade into the drum, she busied herself wiping up spills and throwing away empty paper cups. But she didn't have to wait long for Adam to appear at her table.

"Can you spare a drink for me?" he asked. "I've been watching for you. Has Josie kept you busy?" Adam swept his hat from his head and smoothed his hair. His face looked sweaty but glowing.

"*Jah,* she has. I was making pie dough when Amanda suggested I bring this out." As she handed him a brimming cup, they locked gazes. "It gave me a chance to apologize for not inviting you to supper. I was out of sorts last Saturday and took it out on you. *Mir leid.*"

Adam drank half the glass. "I'm sorry for embarrassing you in front of Michelle. Land sakes, Cal's friends must think his family is a pack of wolves."

Sarah refilled his glass before stepping around the table. "Actually, Pete and Michelle said they had enjoyed their visit. And that the Beachys turned out to be *friendlier* than expected."

"No joke?" He spun his hat brim between his fingers.

"No joke, hard as that is to believe." Chuckling, she reached for his hand. "Can you spare another minute before heading back to work? I'd like to show you something on that tree." Sarah nodded her head toward a massive oak.

"Sure." Adam downed his drink, tossed the cup in the trash, and tightened his grip on her hand. They walked as slowly as humanly possible. Once they arrived at the far side of the tree, he studied the bark for an unusual carving or strange outgrowth. "What did you want to show me?"

"Only this." Sarah turned his face away from the tree and planted a kiss squarely on his lips.

"Well, doesn't that beat all?" Adam's face blushed brightly.

And in Sarah's mind, it truly did.

❧

Caleb, as an experienced carpenter, was in charge of a group of barn-builders. Eli had spread his employees out among the dozens of volunteers for leadership. After all, most men knew how to hammer a nail and it simply took the strength of twenty to stand up a wall that had been assembled on the ground. In the morning, Caleb's group worked on floor joists for the first floor. Then in the afternoon, Eli assigned them to roof rafters in the main section of the barn. Both rafters and joists were two-by-twelve solid oak boards in twenty-foot lengths—heavy pieces of lumber. Caleb had chosen only strong, brawny men for his team. He was the only underweight man around.

For lunch the various crews took shifts at the buffet. That way work never had to cease during precious daylight hours and men wouldn't waste time standing in a long queue for food. When it was their turn for a break, Caleb climbed down the ladder with growing anticipation.

He might get to see Josie Yoder.

He'd been able to think of little else since Sarah's heart-to-heart advice this morning. His sister was right—he needed to make an attempt. If Josie refused to take him seriously, or told him she favored someone else, then so be it. But he couldn't spend the rest of his life not knowing.

Caleb waited last in line to wash up at the stationary tub. Why hurry when the only females serving were older than his mother and long married? Finally, just as he scrubbed his arms and splashed cold water on his face, he heard a familiar voice behind him.

"You dawdled too long, Caleb Beachy!"

He jumped at the vehemence in Josie's tone, cracking his head on the faucet. Straightening, he shook back his wet hair. "Why? Is lunch all gone?" Caleb reached for a towel from the hook.

"No, if you're only interested in something to fill an empty belly. But my secret recipe four-bean salad is gone." Josie tilted the bowl to reveal a clean bottom.

"Four beans?" He moved away from the tub to make room for other workers. "My *mamm* only uses green, yellow, and kidney. What is the fourth?"

She grinned, deepening her dimples. "I won't say. You'll have to wait for the next potluck."

Caleb settled his hat on his head but kept his focus on Josie. How a woman could spend the morning in a hot kitchen and remain so cool, calm, and collected was beyond him. "Maybe some other lady brought a bowl of beans. I'll have to study the contents carefully." He walked toward the buffet, praying she wouldn't abandon him for chores inside the house.

She did not. Josie joined him at the end of the line. "Study those bowls all you want. The others have only *three* types of beans, no chopped celery, no black olives, and no sweet Vidalia onions."

"Those are your secret ingredients?" He gazed into her luminous green eyes for a brief moment.

"It's my secret seasoning that I refuse to divulge." Josie arched up on tiptoes to scan the table. "Looks like there's plenty of sandwich fixings and side dishes so you won't starve." She turned on her heel to leave.

He had mere seconds to react. "Wait, what about supper?"

She halted and glanced back. "What about it? You haven't even eaten lunch yet."

"I'll be working until almost dark to build your family a new barn, while you tease me with recipes you didn't prepare enough of? I'm surprised at you, Miss Yoder."

Josie marched back to him, shaking her finger en route. "I've got chickens to fry this afternoon. You expect me to make another bowl of beans when there are two others on the buffet?"

They had attracted a bit of attention. Several men waited to hear his answer. "Yes, please," he said.

She smiled. "I will try, but you had better like them." Josie stalked off as though angry.

But he knew differently. For the rest of the day, he couldn't get her off his mind. And it had nothing to do with side dishes or secret recipes. Josie had been flirting with him. Plain women usually didn't flirt. Flirting wasn't a game like it was for the *Englisch* women he'd met in bars. An Amish gal wouldn't purposely encourage someone she wasn't interested in.

Hope began to grow deep inside Caleb's chest—hope he hadn't felt in a long time. Could a person as pure and sweet as Josie find something worthy in him?

When the sun dropped behind the western woods, men climbed down the ladders to the ground. The barn was up, roofed, and enclosed. Although much work remained on the interior, the Yoder family now had a three-story, usable structure. Caleb kept working, helping other teams until everyone was finished. He was in no hurry to leave.

"Ready for supper?" Eli called to Caleb just as he started down the ladder.

"You go ahead, *Daed*. I'll go tend our animals and come back for supper."

Eli looked weary and older than his years. The responsibility of the project had taken its toll. "*Danki,* I intend to eat and go home. I'm ready for bed, if truth be told." His father limped in the direction of the tables.

Caleb didn't hurry tending the livestock, and he changed clothes before returning to the Yoders. Although most of the workers had eaten and left, plenty of food still remained. He spotted his sister eating with Adam Troyer, his mother and Katie with a group of women in the shade, and lots of strangers milling around, perhaps too tired to go home.

But no dark-haired beauty waited in the dark with her empty bowl magically refilled. Caleb grabbed a plate and walked to the buffet. Platters of ham and roast beef had been picked over. The roasters of fried chicken contained wings and thighs—the drumsticks and breasts all gone. But a hungry man wasn't picky. He speared two slices of ham and three chicken wings, scooped up some sweet potatoes and coleslaw, and headed to an empty table. After his long day of constantly answering questions, he chose to dine by himself. However, Caleb didn't remain alone for long.

"You'd better have saved room for this." Stepping from the shadows, Josie sat down on the opposite picnic bench. She placed a plastic wrapped bowl in the center and peeled back the covering.

Caleb refrained from jumping up and down with glee. "Are you kidding? I've been unable to think about anything other than your secret recipe." He pushed the coleslaw into the potatoes to make room.

"Your father said you went home for chores. Considering all the hearty appetites, I got worried that we would run out again. So I scooped a small bowl and took it back inside. Good thing, the rest of the batch is gone."

"You deprived people a taste of your special salad?"

"I did." Not an ounce of guilt shaded her words.

Caleb scraped a hearty amount onto his plate. "Ah, garbanzos are the fourth bean." He ate a forkful, chewing slowly to savor. "As promised, lots of celery and sweet onion, plus the eggs are a nice touch. I suspect the seasonings are Old Bay, celery seed, and cayenne pepper." It was purely a guess.

She broke into an ear to ear grin. "*Jah*, those three along with Hungarian paprika. Does it meet your approval, Mr. Beachy?"

He ate another forkful. "It does. I've never had better. My only question is why would you grace me with your side dish while you deny other men equally worthy?" He knew he walked on thin ice, yet Caleb wanted to know where he stood. He was no teenager and refused to get his hopes up.

"I'm not sure." His directness caught her off guard. "I like you, Cal. At least, I did before you moved away."

"You're not afraid to associate with me?"

"No, I'm not, but I would like to know your plans."

"I don't intend to move back to Cleveland if that's what you're asking."

"In part, yes, but are you planning to return to an Amish social life?" Josie imbued the last words with an amusing inflection.

"That's a contradiction in terms, no?" Caleb picked up his chicken wing and ate. "I go to preaching every other Sunday, and I'm here today."

"What about singings? Are you willing to come back?"

He dropped the wing bones and cut his ham into small pieces. "Sixteen-year-olds go to those. I'm twenty-four, Josie."

"And I'm twenty-one, but I still attend. They're for single people of any age."

Caleb knew that wasn't the case, but he shouldn't argue with the woman who'd occupied his every waking thought. "If you tell me the time and place." He concentrated on the meal so as not to betray his nervousness.

"This coming Friday night at the Robert Miller farm." She lifted one dark eyebrow.

"In that case, I will be there with my usual singing voice."

Josie smirked and recovered the four-bean salad with plastic wrap. "Do you intend to join the Amish church?"

"Wow, you don't beat around the bush, do you?" He set down his fork.

"As you aptly pointed out, we're not sixteen anymore."

"I do plan to join with the next membership class."

She pushed the bowl across the table, her left dimple returning. "In that case, the rest is yours. Sarah can return the container. Enjoy your dinner. Eat hearty, but I must help *Mamm* in the house." She pinned him with an uncompromising stare. "And I trust you'll keep my ingredients secret." Then she vanished into the shadows.

6

Yet from what I do inherit,
Here Thy praises I'll begin

The fourth week of work on the Millersburg warehouse began with a downpour. For two hours Caleb and the other men sat in Jack's van waiting for the rain to stop. But it never did. That was the difficulty of roofing projects—heavy rain rendered work impossible. His father had left long ago after calling another contractor on his cell phone. The builder, also stymied by the weather, agreed to drive to Millersburg to discuss potential future work. Huddled under his umbrella, Eli hadn't thought twice about abandoning his employees in the van in favor of a warm and dry coffee shop.

For a while the men listened to the radio. Then they took turns reading aloud from the sports section of the newspaper. Several alternated between rolling down windows for fresh air, and then rolling them back up when shirts and upholstery started to get soggy. After Josiah fell asleep and began to snore, Caleb had had enough. "This rain isn't letting up," he announced loud enough to awaken his partner.

Jack cleared a patch of windshield condensation with his sleeve and peered at the low, grey clouds. "Gotta agree with you, Cal." He switched on the ignition to run the defroster. "Judging by the clouds, this slop might last all day."

A few men grunted in agreement. Josiah merely closed his eyes and shifted to get comfortable.

"This is supposed to be our last week on this project," said Caleb. "I can't see how we could possibly finish on time." He waited for a response, but heard only wiper blades flapping against the glass. "It's taken us three weeks just to remove the old roof and replace rotted joists and underlayment. Three weeks." He repeated in case someone hadn't been keeping track. "That only gives us this week to nail down new insulation boards, cut the rubber roofing to fit, and then glue it down on the three different buildings. There's no way we'll be done by Friday night."

"We can't do much about the weather," said Josiah. "Only pray for sunshine and blue skies tomorrow." The man had replied with his eyes shut. He'd only been pretending to nap.

"Maybe Walmart sells block-sized umbrellas," said Daniel. The suggestion came from a young, easygoing Amish newlywed, also from Killbuck.

"Just in case they're sold out," said Caleb, "we'll need to speed things up this week. I proposed changing to two teams of three men, so Jack and Bob can be nearby if power saws are needed."

Jack swiveled around on the front seat. "What did Eli say?"

"I think he'll go along with the idea if it originates with someone other than me. I have the least amount of seniority among his employees." Caleb tried not to reveal his father's total lack of respect for his opinion.

"It would be fine with me if Eli agrees," said Bob. "I thought that a while ago, but I never said anything." Bob fiddled with the radio knobs for the tenth time. He didn't seem to like any of the music being played.

"No point changing teams now." Josiah straightened his spine, abandoning his attempt to nap. "We don't need power tools to roll out rubber and slice it off with utility knives. As long as you've got a sharp blade, you're in business. Glue is spread with a long-handled paint roller—no power cord necessary." He scratched his jawline.

"I know how to install a flat roof. But I'm talking mainly about future work, so we don't get this far behind."

Josiah smiled at him with the patience of Job. "Let's take life one day at a time. We'll probably pray for this kind of downpour in June to make the corn grow, *jah*?" He focused his attention on a mother and child crossing the street without paying much attention. A pickup truck splashed the pair with a wall of water.

Caleb leaned his head back and shut his eyes. He needed to find a way to change the inefficiency without alienating the other men or angering his father. Then maybe his *daed*'s opinion of him would improve. On Saturday at the barn raising, Eli had organized two hundred men to assemble a complete barn in less than twelve hours. No one had gotten injured; no one had gone home mad because they'd been slighted for some task. So why couldn't Eli run his commercial crew with the same effectiveness? True, no power tools had been used on the Yoder barn, not even by the *Englischers*. But that was because the vast majority of lumber had been cut to correct lengths at the mill. You can't expect that on a small warehouse project. For several minutes, he debated how to proceed while listening to rain beat steadily on the vehicle's hood. Finally irritation and claustrophobia got the better of Caleb Beachy. "This is ridiculous," he announced.

"What do you suggest?" asked Josiah.

"We're wasting the day parked here doing nothing. Let's head to that café across the street to buy a slice of pie and cup of coffee. Then we'll go home. Every man here has better things to do in his house or barn or garage than sit listening to the rain."

Two or three seconds passed before Bob spoke. "Sounds like a good idea to me. I need to change a leaky faucet valve before we run the well dry."

"I could be sharpening the plow and checking my seed corn," Dan added in a soft voice.

"Do you think they will have cherry pie?" asked Josiah.

Caleb laughed. "If they don't, I'll treat you to a slice of your second choice."

Simultaneously, four van doors swung open and seven men lumbered out, stiff from sitting too long. They sprinted across the street to where neon soft drink signs drew them like beacons in a fog. Caleb headed to a large table in the center of the diner. During the short walk from the van, rain had soaked him to the skin. He slapped his hat against his leg and shook like a dog, sending water droplets flying. Being inside and dry in a sweet-smelling restaurant lifted everyone's mood.

"Look at this dessert rack," exclaimed Daniel. "They have every type of pie known to man." He stared at the display like a kid in a candy store. "Plus giant cream puffs, raspberry crumb cakes, and little pecan pies."

The crew settled on red vinyl chairs just as a pretty redheaded waitress ambled over. "What'll it be, boys? Coffee?" She offered a toothy smile.

"Seven coffees, six slices of pie, and one of everything for our friend over there." Jack hooked a thumb at Daniel, who was still gaping at the assortment of pastries.

"And we are not *boys*, young lady," Bob added an inflection of indignation.

"Then what are you—ducks? You're sure wet enough." The waitress giggled behind her order tablet, but never took her eyes off Bob.

As the only other single member of the crew, Bob had a penchant for attracting females wherever he went. But Caleb didn't mind. After the attention Josie Yoder paid him last Saturday, he would be walking on air for quite some time.

"Not ducks," said Bob. "We are big strong men, roofers to be exact." He rolled up his sleeve and flexed a bicep in an exaggerated fashion, mimicking a cartoon muscleman.

The waitress's giggles escalated into laughter, drawing the attention of nearby diners. "You don't say. Well, you sure picked a lousy day to put on a new roof." She shifted her weight from one hip to the other, all thoughts of coffee forgotten.

"You said a mouthful, darlin'." Bob leaned back in his chair.

"Caitlyn," she said. "My name is Caitlyn. With a C, not a K."

"Your parents chose a special spelling for a special girl."

"Could we order and have that coffee now, Miss Caitlyn?" Jack took a fatherly command of the situation.

"Sure, what kind of pie?"

As requests for apple, blueberry, and peach rang out and Caitlyn scribbled furiously on her pad, Caleb glanced around the diner. A bent, dark-haired man struggled to his feet at a booth—a very familiar man.

Eli Beachy and his *Englisch* business associate approached the front cash register. Eli's eyes rounded as he recognized his crew as those creating a fuss in the restaurant. "What are you all doing in here?" He halted at their table while a middle-aged woman leaned between men to fill coffee cups.

"Getting out of the rain and enjoying a cup of java." Caleb lifted his brimming mug.

"Plus dessert," added Daniel. "I ordered chocolate mousse pie with a scoop of vanilla ice cream."

"It's barely ten o'clock." Eli's tone expressed disapproval with morning sweets.

Daniel clamped his lips together as though duly reprimanded.

Caleb blew out his breath. "You left us in that van, twiddling our thumbs for hours, while you came inside where it's comfortable."

Eli glared at him. "I came to talk to Mr. Emerson about future construction work." He half-turned to the *Englischer*. "Ralph, this is my son. Caleb, this is Ralph Emerson."

Darkening with embarrassment, Caleb extended his hand. "How do you do, sir."

"Fine, Caleb. The fact Marge has the best pie in Millersburg probably influenced your decision, eh?" He smiled at the woman filling their mugs.

"Ralph Emerson—like the poet?" asked Bob. He also extended a hand.

"That's right, but I have no 'Waldo.'" Ralph shook hands vigorously.

"Who's Waldo?" Daniel inquired of no one in particular.

Eli fumed like a hen shut out of the coop during cleaning. "These are my carpenters, good workers—every one of them, whom I intend to pay half a day for their down-time." His glare landed squarely on Caleb.

At that point, the lovely Caitlyn-with-a-C delivered a tray of delicious-looking pies. "I see you have your coffee. Now here's the best part."

Before she had a chance to distribute the plates, Josiah stood abruptly. "We'll take to-go boxes along with our checks. Sorry to trouble you today." He tipped his hat as the rest of the crew clambered to their feet.

"But it's still raining. What's the rush?" she asked.

"One check and I'll take it," murmured Eli. "I will meet you at the register, miss."

One by one the men finished their coffees and filed out the door with Styrofoam boxes in hand. And once again, Caleb felt he'd been reduced to teenager status.

❦

Eli paid the bill for his coffee with Ralph, along with the pointless expense of seven slices of pie. *Who eats dessert before they eat lunch?* After parting with the contractor, he walked to Jack's van without bothering to raise his umbrella. Maybe the cool spring shower would wash away his irritation with his son.

All the way to Killbuck and then to Fredericksburg, he had to listen to men eat pie while planning how to approach the inevitable showdown. Caleb wasn't the boss; he wasn't even his foremen. Yet today he took charge and made decisions for the crew.

In the van Caleb said nothing. Each time Eli stole a backward glance his son was staring out the window as though he'd never seen farm fields buffeted by heavy rain. Better to let the sleeping dog lie until they were home. When he finally walked into his warm kitchen his wife greeted him with surprise.

"Home so soon? It's barely eleven. *Ach*, the weather. Not fit for man or beast." Elizabeth turned the burner on under the cold coffeepot. "I imagine you'll want a hot lunch."

"No, don't fuss, *fraa*. We'll eat the sandwiches you packed this morning and look forward to a hot supper." Eli buzzed her cheek with a kiss.

By the time he hung up his coat, he realized Caleb hadn't followed him into the house. Through the window he spotted his son entering the barn carrying their lunch cooler. For the rest of the day, Caleb avoided him as though he carried an infectious disease. When Eli arrived in the main barn, Caleb decided to restack hay bales in the loft. When hunger sent Eli searching for his portion of the sandwiches, he found the tote at the foot of the ladder with half the contents gone. Caleb was nowhere around. How had he gotten down from the loft? When Eli finished chores and headed indoors to wash, his exasperation had reached a boiling point.

Caleb sat nursing a cup of coffee at the kitchen table as Elizabeth fried pork chops at the stove. Rebekah, peeling potatoes, and Sarah, fixing a salad, argued over some mishap at the bed-and-breakfast. Rebekah felt she should make up rooms instead of being on constant kitchen duty for a change, while Sarah felt Mrs. Pratt assigned tasks based on proficiency and overall pleasantness of the employee. Hence, Rebekah should *always* toil alone in the kitchen.

Sighing wearily, Eli sat down at the head of the table. "And how was school today, *dochder*?"

His youngest, Katie, grinned warmly. "*Gut.* The teacher called on me three times and each time I knew the answer. She was shocked!"

"Shocked, but pleased, I'm sure." Eli patted Katie's hand. Unfortunately, Rebekah and Sarah's discussion lifted a notch in volume. "Enough!" he thundered. "Kindly confine your work problems to the walk to and from the inn. You don't need to spoil supper with your quarreling."

"*Mir leid*," they muttered in unison.

Silence reigned in the room for several minutes, since apparently neither girl had anything agreeable to say. After Elizabeth carried over the chops and they said silent prayers, Eli chose the opportunity to speak to Caleb. "I'd wanted to talk to you in the barn but I couldn't find you. How did you get down from the hayloft?"

His son fixed him with a stare over a pork chop. "I swung down on the rope."

"You're too old for that. I'm trying to break Katie of the dangerous habit." Eli shook his head.

"Apparently, I'm not old enough to decide when it's time to come in out of the rain." Caleb spooned parsley potatoes onto his plate next to the chop.

"Nobody was getting wet inside the van."

"No, but it wasn't exactly homey either. Not as comfortable as inside the restaurant."

Eli felt his gut tighten. "I had a meeting to discuss specifics for our next job. As the head of the company, business meetings are part of *my* job."

His son took a long swallow of milk. "I understand, but there was no harm in waiting indoors to see if the rain would let up."

"I don't pay men to sit around and eat pie. Like I told you, I planned to pay my crew for half a day today."

Caleb shrugged. "So what difference does it make where we waste the morning?"

Eli realized four sets of female eyes rotated between him and Caleb like a volleyball over the net. "Let's finish our *work* discussion after supper. I'll take the same advice I doled out to Sarah and Rebekah." Thus, peace returned to the Beachy dinner table for the remainder of the meal.

When everyone finished eating and his daughters began stacking plates, Eli cleared his throat. "*Dochdern,* please bring the pot of coffee to the table and leave the dishes to soak. You can wash them before bed."

Dutifully the girls did as he asked and left the room, while Elizabeth waited in the doorway. "Do you need me to stay and referee?"

"No, *danki.*" Eli didn't laugh at her jest. Once his wife went upstairs, he picked up where they'd left off. "The difference is that none of you knew where I had gone with Ralph Emerson. I might have completed the meeting earlier than your snack and not been able to find anyone."

Caleb reflected on this for a moment. "I suppose you have a point, but it had become downright suffocating with seven men in that van."

Eli refilled their mugs. "Did the other men wish to leave the vehicle?"

His son's fingers tightened around the cup. "*Jah.* I didn't force them against their will. Plus, it was a little cumbersome with five of us speaking in *Deutsch* and Jack and Bob trying to carry on an English conversation. Cumbersome, and a little silly."

Eli peered into his coffee, allowing Caleb to fully vent his spleen.

"In the diner everybody spoke English. Once we had our pie, I'd planned to discuss how we might complete the roof on schedule."

Eli could stay quiet no longer. "What do you mean?"

"We are so far behind I can't imagine being done by quitting time on Friday. Your insistence of having two Amish crews and one *Englisch* has hobbled the warehouse project."

"Hobbled?" Eli slapped the tabletop with a palm. "According to you, son? This is your first project since you came back to work for me. I have installed plenty of new roofs while you were twiddling your thumbs in the Cleveland union hall." In frustration, he repeated Caleb's pet term.

Caleb lifted his chin. "You still believe we can finish by Friday afternoon?"

"I do, barring any more days like today. We can't predict or change the weather, nor will we be held accountable."

Caleb arched an eyebrow. "The owner won't hold you to the schedule if it continues to rain cats and dogs?"

"He won't, within reason, of course. But a week won't cause either of us sleepless nights."

"You won't be fined for each day you run over deadline?"

"I will not." Eli took a swallow of coffee.

"That's quite different from the commercial projects I've worked on. Fines are always levied for non-completion. Nobody gives allowances for rain delays."

"Perhaps I deal with more reasonable owners in Wayne County than those up in Cuyahoga."

Caleb nodded, yet didn't appear convinced. "Will you at least consider my suggestion of two crews instead of three for future projects?"

Eli chose his words carefully. "If the situation warrants, or if we're hindering another trade by not finishing early, then *jah*. But I already explained my reasons for three crews last week. The feelings of the other district fathers have not changed."

"Fair enough." Caleb drained the contents of his mug and rose to his feet.

"Sit. I'm not finished. Give me another minute of your time."

His son frowned but slouched back into the chair.

"You have expressed a desire to return to Amish ways and restore yourself to your family and this district." Eli paused as they both listened to the ticking of the wall clock. "If that remains the case, you must reacquaint yourself with humility and restraint. You are not in charge of this crew, nor should you want to be. Although we work *in* this world, the Amish do not concern themselves with matters *of* this world. Do your job, praying daily for patience and strength of spirit. Don't place yourself above your fellow workers because of your past experiences. Let me worry about schedules, contracts, and efficiency. Be thankful that those concerns aren't yours."

"In other words, you're the boss and I am not." Caleb's tone turned harsh.

"If you insist on the simplest of terms…then *jah*. You're not an *Englischer* anymore and my crew isn't a democracy."

For the second time, Caleb jumped to his feet. "At long last, I think I've got it, *Daed*. Now if you'll excuse me I'll make sure the livestock have enough fresh water for the night." He grabbed his hat and coat and strode from the room.

Eli stared at the closed door long after he had gone. Although his son had voiced the words, something told him that Caleb was as close to "getting it" as a plow horse learning to read.

⁂

Sarah crept from her bed before dawn on Friday morning, careful not to disturb her sister. Rebekah had been in a foul mood all week. After their father's scolding on Monday, at least she hadn't argued with her openly, not at home or at the B&B. But Rebekah's sullenness could be almost as tiresome as bickering. She never missed a chance to pout, roll her eyes, or sigh like a long-suffering saint on the way to a martyr's death.

Rebekah could be overly dramatic at best. And so Sarah decided to cook breakfast on her own. Downstairs in the kitchen she found Caleb sipping coffee, deep in thought. "Why aren't you outside helping with morning chores?" she asked.

His head snapped up. "*Guder mariye.*" He used a *Deutsch* greeting, unusual for him if their parents weren't within earshot. "*Daed* asked me to pack our lunches while he fed livestock. *Mamm's* down with a cold, so she's staying in bed this morning."

Sarah spotted the loaf of bread, block of Swiss cheese, and tub of sliced ham still untouched. "You haven't gotten very far. Let me help." She pulled waxed paper and plastic bags from the drawer and mustard and a tomato from the refrigerator.

"*Danki.* I've been distracted by something else." Caleb filled their thermoses with hot coffee.

"How's the Millersburg warehouse project coming?" She deftly cut the tomato into uniform slices.

"Fine. We'll be done today by four o'clock, amazingly so. I didn't think it would be possible, but the weather cleared. *Daed* might have been on target all along." He murmured the words as though they were distasteful to say.

Sarah glanced at both doorways. "Don't you just hate it when parents are right?" They shared a good-natured sibling laugh.

"I should lower my defenses and learn from him. He certainly knows what he's doing." Caleb retrieved the cold pack from the freezer, two bottles of water, and their soft-sided lunch cooler. "I'll work up my courage and tell him."

"Is work the only thing on your mind, big *bruder*?" Sarah angled a droll expression. "I find that hard to believe."

"Whatever do you mean?" he said, feigning confusion.

"Don't play innocent with me. I saw you and Josie at the picnic table last Saturday. You were eating supper long after everyone had finished. Then Josie just *happened* to bring more of her bean salad, straight from the house?" She winked. "Come to think of it, what happened to that bowl of salad in the fridge? It wasn't there when I looked for it." She wrapped the four sandwiches, slipped them into bags, and dropped them in the cooler.

"I washed her bowl and left it in the mudroom. Don't worry, I'll return it."

"You ate all those beans yourself? You weren't much of a fan before." Sarah twirled a *kapp* ribbon.

"Tastes change as we grow older, little *schwester*. Besides, this was Josie's secret recipe—a bit different from yours or *Mamm's*. No offense."

"None taken." Sarah chuckled. "She saved the salad especially for you?"

"*Jah*, I guess so. Thanks for packing our lunch. Maybe I'll wait for Jack on the porch. Looks like fine weather today."

"Oh, no, you don't." She grabbed his arm with a viselike grip. "Sounds to me like you took my advice—to be nice to Josie and see what happens."

"I'm nice to everyone." Caleb glared at her hand like a spider was crawling up his arm.

"Sure, and Josie saved a separate bowl for every man who returned after farm chores were done. How did you two leave matters on Saturday? Have you seen her since?"

"For your latter question, no—too much to do after work this time of year. For the former, I defer to a charming *Englisch* acronym: N-O-Y-B."

"What's an acronym?" Sarah perched her hands on her hips.

"Letters that represent words." Caleb tugged his arm free.

"Wait!" She re-fastened her hold while her brain figured out the meaning. "None of my business? After I've been your successful social advisor?"

"What's none of Sarah's business?" Rebekah appeared in the doorway. "Or should I say what *hasn't* she made part of her control?"

Caleb smirked, shaking his head. "Oh, no, you don't. I refuse to be drawn into the ongoing Beachy sister war of words." He freed himself again from Sarah's restraint.

"Are you going tomorrow night?" whispered Sarah, close behind him.

"To the singing?" demanded Rebekah. She moved to effectively block his exit at the kitchen door. "Or did you think I hadn't heard about the singing like I didn't hear about the Shreve pancake breakfast?" Crossing her arms, Rebekah stomped a booted foot.

"Simmer down. Let's not start the day—" Caleb attempted to placate the sixteen-year-old.

"I won't simmer down. That was downright mean of you, Cal. I would have expected it from Sarah, but not you."

Sarah intervened on his behalf. "We weren't trying to be mean, but Mrs. Pratt can't spare us both on a Saturday morning. She always has a full house Friday nights." Sarah patted her sister's shoulder hesitantly like an unfamiliar stray dog that wandered into the yard. "But I promise I'll work instead of you for the next Saturday event."

Rebekah's gaze remained cool as she refocused on Caleb. "Is there some other reason neither of you told me? Such as James Weaver saying something negative about me?" Her voice sounded plaintive.

"Absolutely not. It was as Sarah explained. But take heart, neither of you have to work at Country Pleasures tomorrow night, so both can attend the singing."

With eyes filling with tears, Rebekah didn't move from the doorway.

"Why are you crying?" asked Caleb. "I heard straight from the horse's mouth that James plans to be there. Now may I get past you? I hear Jack's van in the driveway."

Rebekah blinked several times. "The horse's mouth?"

Caleb grasped Rebekah's upper arms, lifted her into the air, and set her down two feet to the left. "It's an expression. It means you'll see James tomorrow night, so wear your prettiest dress and be on your best behavior." He ran from the house before either could utter another word.

"Does that make you feel a little better, because we also need to leave for work?" Sarah asked, feeling a surge of pity for the girl.

She nodded, swiping at her tears with a hanky. "I suppose so, but neither of you understand. You've got Adam Troyer wrapped around your little finger while Caleb seems to have caught Josie Yoder's eye. I'm all by myself in the world."

Inappropriately, Sarah laughed. "Forgive me, *schwester*, but you're only sixteen. You've got plenty of time for courting. I'm twenty, nearly twenty-one, and Cal's already twenty-four."

"*Mamm* was only sixteen when she married *Daed*." Rebekah marched to the sink to fill her water bottle.

"True, but nobody Amish marries that young anymore." Sarah's assessment of their culture met with no reply as they both pulled on sweaters.

"Are my girls ready for work?" asked Elizabeth. She entered the kitchen wearing her heavy flannel bathrobe.

"*Jah*, but where's Katie?" Sarah realized she hadn't seen the youngest Beachy sister yet.

"Down with a cold, same as me. I'm keeping her home so she doesn't spread germs throughout the school." Elizabeth set the kettle on a burner. "I believe I'll have ginger tea today instead of coffee."

"Hope you feel better, *Mamm*." Rebekah offered a lopsided smile and hurried out the door.

"Stay bundled and drink lots of fluids," added Sarah. She chanced catching the virus by kissing *Mamm's* cheek.

On the way to Mrs. Pratt's B&B, Sarah would have been content to simply enjoy a perfect spring day. The sun was shining, the breeze felt warm, and daffodils and grape hyacinths bloomed along the fence. Young calves frisked in the pasture, bravely venturing from their mother's underbellies. But Rebekah's insecurity would not let the pancake breakfast matter drop.

"Since you walked with Adam, and Caleb with Josie Yoder in Shreve, who did James walk with?" Rebekah kept her eyes trained on the gravel.

"He seemed to amble competently along by himself." Sarah chose not to mention the gaggle of women from another district who hung on to every word of his maple sugar saga. "He didn't fall face-down in the dirt once."

Rebekah turned on her, scowling. "Must you always be such a smarty pants? Always clever—that's Sarah. But you're sarcastic, not clever. The young minister said sarcasm is just another form of self-absorption. You're in for a rude awakening when you start membership classes." After another frown, Rebekah lifted her skirt and ran the rest of the way to work.

Sarah sighed, regretting she'd annoyed Rebekah with their entire shift ahead of them. During her solitary stroll to the Pratt back gate, she mulled over her sister's prediction. She probably *was* in for a rude awakening at the classes. And it had nothing to do with her wry sense of humor.

7

Here I raise my Ebenezer;
Here by Thy great help I've come

Caleb paced from one end of the porch to the other. No matter where he sat—porch swing, rocking chair in the front room, kitchen chair, or hay bale in the barn—he couldn't remain stationary. Would their Sunday afternoon guests never go home? Not only had his grandparents dropped by, but the entire Troyer clan was visiting. Adam had three sisters and three brothers, all but one married, with thirteen children among them. When Sarah and Adam tied the knot, she would gain an enormous extended family. Sometimes Adam's sisters and sisters-in-law overwhelmed Sarah, but she adored their *kinner*. So she would do fine as a Troyer…as long as she kept plenty of food in the house at all times. Every single one of them possessed a hearty appetite.

The younger females planted themselves in the kitchen with Sarah, Rebekah, and Katie. His mother entertained the middle-aged and older ladies in the front room, where they alternated between sewing, gossiping, and sipping coffee. His father and John Troyer were holding court in the main barn, surrounded by the Troyer sons, sons-in-law, and grandsons. Caleb couldn't concentrate on their chatter about seed corn varieties, new equipment purchases, and endless boasting about spring lambs, newborn calves, and recent foals. He was happy as a part-time farmer, but with his first singing in five years later this evening, he yearned for some solitude to sort out his thoughts.

"Say, why don't you bring Sarah and Rebekah tonight to the Millers? I'll see that they get safely home." Adam's question nearly jolted

Caleb out of his shoes. He'd been leaning on a tree, contemplating his next place to hide from the Troyer youngsters.

Caleb peered down at his future brother-in-law, a man at least five inches shorter than him. "Sure, no problem."

Adam removed his glasses and cleaned them with his hanky. His striking blue eyes were definitely his best feature. "Since every Troyer is here, we'll need the buggies to take my family home. But once I drop off *Mamm* and *Daed,* I'll have the rig for the rest of the night." Anticipation turned his blue eyes very bright.

"Thanks for taking Rebekah too." Caleb wanted to verify Adam's intentions for his other sister. If God was merciful tonight, he might have some time alone with Josie.

"No problem." Adam replaced his glasses and rubbed the bridge of his nose. "Your first singing in a long time, no?"

"*Jah,* I'm not sure why I'm going. I feel downright elderly next to Rebekah's friends."

"Nonsense. I'll be there and I'm almost your age. Besides, it's still the best place to meet an eligible Amish girl. Good luck, Cal." Adam slapped him on the back before heading toward the kitchen, no doubt to see what Sarah was doing.

Hopefully, some will be women and not girls, Caleb thought grimly. What if Josie didn't show up? She barely said two sentences to him after preaching this morning. Josie treated him no differently from the man who delivered propane or the milk hauler from Walnut Creek. Of course, her mother and sisters had been present the entire time of socialization after the service.

Caleb waited another ten minutes before walking into the house. Blessedly, people were packing up pie carriers and salad bowls, gathering children and sewing baskets in preparation to depart. After twenty minutes of goodbyes as though it would be ages until the families saw each other again, the Troyers finally left. Caleb headed straight into the bathroom for another shower, a shave, and fresh clothes. All that exciting talk about Nathaniel's new thresher had made him sweat. Turning the shower taps to full blast, Caleb couldn't wait for the water to wash away his anxiety. In the steamy mirror, he saw bags beneath his eyes, indicative of too much worry about his future…or the lack of one.

Suddenly, the sight of the name "Kristen" stopped him short. Caleb stared with horror at the colorful reminder of lost love and a drunken stupor. Funny how dressing and undressing in the dark, along with wearing long sleeves, had allowed him to forget his shame. Two ghastly serpents with long fangs writhed around a blood-red heart. His anticipation ran headlong into a brick wall. Some Christians considered vipers aligned with the devil. But he had played with garter snakes as a child and even kept one as a pet for a while. Snakes helped to keep the rat and mouse populations under control, so they were no more evil than rabbits or squirrels. But the Amish abhorred garish tattoos adorning a person's body. Not to mention how Josie might feel about seeing another woman's name on his arm. Would she be curious about his past or only repulsed by his actions? Stepping into the shower, Caleb let the water cascade over him until his sisters knocked on the door. Unfortunately, the twenty-minute shower did little to wash his sins away.

On the way to the Miller farm Sarah and Rebekah kept up a lively discussion about who might be there and who might ride home with whom. For Sarah, the conversation was merely to pass time because she would marry Adam in the fall. But Rebekah grew more boy-crazy each day and more obsessed with James in particular. At least their chatter distracted Caleb from his worries. Tonight, he would be fully Amish— no *Englischers* attended singings. They would speak and sing solely in *Deutsch*. This would be a major transition for him—one he would survive as long as *she* was there.

Josie Yoder strolled into the Miller barn ten minutes late. The songbooks had already been passed out. Young men and younger women sat on opposite sides of long tables in an almost spotless outbuilding. The deacon's son had been appointed song leader and was already calling the next page number when an ethereal angel glided into the room as though on air. Josie wore a dress of deep mauve with a crisp apron and starched *kapp*. She had tied her ribbons behind her neck as though toiling in the garden. Her fresh face looked burnished from the sun while her emerald eyes sparkled and danced in the kerosene lantern light.

"Josie, we'll make room for you down here," a girl called from the far end.

"Josie, I've got room for you next to me." April Lapp half-stood and waved her hand.

But the object of Caleb's affection seemed not to hear them. Josie's eyes scanned the room until they landed on his sister, directly across from him and Adam Troyer. Unlike either of the women who'd summoned Josie, Sarah was wedged between people. But that didn't stop his *schwester*.

"Scoot over a smidge," said Sarah to those on both sides. Using her hip, she banged her way into compliance.

Josie's decision had already been made. "*Guder nachmittag*, Sarah, Caleb," she greeted. Hastily, she slipped onto the bench as the leader began the next song.

Throughout two hours of singing, Caleb alternated between periods of contentment and anxiety during the age-old courting tradition. His *Deutsch* readily came back to him as the hymns oddly soothed his nerves. Singing about a God of infinite power and mercy made his earthly worries seem miniscule. As Scripture attested, nothing was beyond the healing power of God. Then Josie would turn her beautiful eyes his way, and he felt as helpless and out of place as a worm at a robin reunion.

How could someone as pretty as Josie be interested in him?

Sarah kicked him under the table each time he stopped singing. He could be in his buggy and on his way home before anybody recognized the streak of lightning as a human being. But cowardice had never done a man a bit of good, whether *Englisch* or Plain. At long last the leader closed his songbook and invited them to eat the snacks set up outdoors.

As though on a mission of mercy, the angel across the table looked him straight in the eye and announced, "I'm starving. Let's run for the desserts." As tiny as she was, Josie had no trouble extricating herself from the tight fit on the girls' side.

Caleb, however, had to squash poor Adam Troyer to get out before their bench unloaded in an orderly fashion. He followed the scent of peaches and cream out of the Miller grain barn and into the cool night air.

Josie hadn't been joking about running. She sprinted across the lawn to the tables with trays of brownies, cookies, and pies that had been arranged under a hanging lantern. She picked up a paper plate as he reached the table. "Since I'm first, I can take one of everything."

Caleb glanced at her slim figure. "You can, but I doubt you can eat that much."

"You'd be surprised by my appetite." Josie selected a Rice Krispie treat, a brownie, and two peanut butter cookies.

Because he was incapable of making logical decisions at the moment, Caleb duplicated her choices for himself. "Would you like a cup of lemonade or iced tea?" he asked as they stepped away from the food.

"Iced tea, please. You fetch our drinks while I find seats away from the crowd." She disappeared into the shadows as though still in a hurry.

Caleb discovered his muscular legs would barely bend at the knee. Josie wanted to be alone with him? The paralysis soon spread upward into his chest, turning his breaths into short, desperate gasps. Hopefully by the time he returned with the drinks, his vocal cords wouldn't be locked in place. With shaky hands, Caleb carried two cups of iced tea to the dense canopy of a maple tree. Little illumination from the barn's solar floodlight reached into the gloom. "Who are you hiding from, Miss Yoder? I hope it's not me." He set the cups down before they spilled.

Josie ate half her brownie before replying. "Your sister and my three sisters." With a wink, she popped the other half into her mouth.

"Why would you hide from Sarah? She's your best friend." Caleb picked up a Rice Krispie bar for something to do with his hand.

"Because she's constantly pointing out your attributes. *Doesn't Cal look handsome in a navy shirt? Don't you think that horrid Englisch haircut has grown out nicely? Did I mention that my brother saved enough to buy his own buggy and Standardbred horse?* Sarah has appointed herself your PR director." She sipped her drink.

"Hopefully she won't send a bill for her services at month's end." Caleb chewed some of the square nervously. The marshmallow practically glued his dry mouth shut. "Don't you agree with Sarah's generous assessment of me?" He focused on the dark pasture instead of her.

"Sarah isn't known for telling lies, but I prefer to draw my own conclusions." Josie began to nibble a cookie.

"Fair enough," he said, downing his tea. "What about your *schwestern*? I would guess your reasons for avoidance aren't the same."

Josie didn't bat a single long eyelash. "Quite the contrary. *Why are you hanging out with wild Caleb Beachy? Anyone separated from the fold that long will never commit. Why waste your time on a man who'll run back to Cleveland the moment he builds up his bank account?*"

Caleb dropped the rest of his dessert onto the plate. He couldn't have eaten another bite if someone put a gun to his temple. "I had no idea the other Yoders held me in such low esteem."

"Rest assured each of my sisters spoke to me in private—not in front of my parents. They aren't ganging up on you."

"I suppose I should be grateful for small blessings."

Josie laughed as though she hadn't a care in the world. "*Jah*, we all should."

"What about you? Do you hold the same opinion as Laura and Jessie?"

"If I did, would I be sitting with you now?" She consumed her Rice Krispie treat in three bites and then licked her fingertips. The stickiness apparently wasn't a problem for her vocal cords. "I told them the same thing I said to Sarah: Please let me make up my own mind."

Caleb released his death-grip on the plastic cup before he destroyed it. "Another blessing—this one not so small."

"You're not saving money to head back to the city, are you?"

Loud laughter and chatter carried on the breeze from the young people clustered around the barn, but Caleb heard her clear as a bell. "I certainly am not."

"Are you planning to commit to the Amish faith?"

"I intend to take membership classes the next time they're offered."

Josie finished the last dessert on her plate. "*Gut.* Then why don't you stop beating around the bush and ask me out on a real date?"

Caleb coughed as saliva slipped down his windpipe. "What would you like to do, Miss Yoder? Your wish is my command."

"Funny that you should quote one of those storybook Prince Charmings. Since we're both still on *rumschpringe* for a couple more months, I want to go to the movies in Wooster to see one of those animated fairy tales on the big screen. Plus I want a tub of buttered popcorn. Then let's stop for a deluxe pizza in Shreve on the way home."

"I won't even ask if you can eat all that." Caleb grinned at her empty plate, relaxing for the first time that evening.

Josie scrambled up. "Let's get more sweets for the ride home."

"Would you let *me* drive you home tonight?" He rose to his full height.

"Hmmm," she murmured. "I guess so, as long as nobody better asks between here and the parking area." She grasped his arm on their walk back to the snacks.

"I'll hold them off with a rake if need be." At the table, Caleb loaded his plate with six Rice Krispie squares.

"Looks like you were hungry after all."

He reached for a piece of foil. "These are for Sarah; they're her favorites. My PR director is about to get her Christmas bonus early this year."

Josie stood at the front window watching for Caleb's buggy. She wanted to know the moment he pulled into their driveway to avoid any unpleasant scenes with her family. Her parents weren't happy about her dating Caleb, while her sisters were downright hostile. But since the Bible was full of stories about people getting second chances, they couldn't easily forbid them from seeing each other.

Caleb deserved a second chance. Since he'd returned from Cleveland he resembled an old hound, scolded once too often for jumping on the furniture. It couldn't be easy having Eli for both his employer and father. The bishop struck her as unyielding at best. Not a good match for someone as spirited as Caleb. At least, he used to be spirited. Now he just seemed sad. What was it like to not fit in anywhere?

Her oldest sister asked if she was courting Caleb out of pity. Josie had been stuck for a quick reply but had since thought carefully. Even though his situation seemed pitiful at times, she was dating him because of the way he treated her. If some men wore their hearts on a sleeve, Caleb used every stitch of clothing he owned. There was nothing quite as irresistible as somebody's adoration. No one had ever looked at her the way Caleb did.

"A watched pot never boils." Her *mamm* spoke from over her shoulder.

"I want to leave the moment he arrives. It's a long ride to Wooster. If it had been anyone else, *Daed* would have permitted a hired van." Josie didn't turn to face her mother.

"But it's not anybody else; it's Caleb Beachy."

Did those three little words sum up the entire district's opinion? "There he is," she said, hurrying toward the door. "See you later."

"Enjoy your movie, *dochder*."

Josie heard *Mamm's* final comment while halfway down the steps. She jumped into Caleb's buggy before he could brake to a stop.

"You seem eager for some hot buttered popcorn." His smile lit up his whole face.

"I'm anxious to get there before the matinee starts. If my father had allowed a hired car, we wouldn't have to leave so early."

"I'm glad he didn't. I get to spend that much more time with you." With a flick of the wrist, Caleb guided the horse in a circular arc. "Besides, I've had the week off since we finished the Millersburg warehouse. What a lovely way to spend my day."

"Will we find enough to talk about for the next two and a half hours?" Josie braced her feet against the wooden buggy slats.

"Are you joking? The last time we really talked you were barely sixteen. I want to hear everything that happened since then." Caleb slicked a hand through his hair before replacing his straw hat.

"Okay, I'll touch on the high points—all six or seven of them. Then you can tell me where you found this gorgeous horse and buggy. Your father must pay well."

Caleb laughed in a companionable way. "He does, but this rig took most of my pay from the last four weeks. Good thing this movie will have an early-bird special price."

"In that case let me pay for the popcorn." When he started to object, Josie held up her hand. "Stop. This is the twenty-first century, even in our community. You can save your money for the pizza tonight. I have a taste for every topping plus extra cheese."

"You've got a deal, Miss Yoder. But I warn you, I've been known to steal pepperoni when folks aren't looking."

"Good thing I have eyes in the side of my head, according to my sister Anna. You don't stand a chance getting mine."

One would think people would run out of things to say during that long a drive to Wooster. But not her and Caleb. When one mouth grew tired, the other picked up the thread of conversation. At no point was she bored or uncomfortable. Caleb was attentive, entertaining, and utterly charming. Yet during the entire drive, he didn't mention God or his faith once. And for an Amish man on the verge of baptism and joining the church, that was rare.

Few mountains can be scaled during a single afternoon, so Josie sat back to enjoy his company, the animated movie, and the largest tub of popcorn she'd seen in her life. Caleb never tried to hold her hand or drape his arm around her shoulders like many men would have done. Just the same, when their fingers touched in the barrel of popcorn, she felt a jolt of electricity that had nothing to do with pity.

"How did you like the movie?" he asked on their way out of the theater.

"It was wonderful! I can't believe they created such perfect expressions and mannerisms for the animals."

"Are you acquainted with lions and wooly mastodons?" His smirk deepened the lines around his eyes.

"No, but I own both a dog and a cat and can imagine what they would say if they could."

"I noticed some of Shep's body language on the big screen as well." Caleb took her arm as they crossed the stony, unused portion of the parking lot. They had left the buggy off the pavement so the horse wouldn't create a mess.

Josie peered at the sun. "We've still got plenty of daylight, which is *gut*. Shreve isn't exactly around the corner." Pulling away from him, she ran the rest of the way.

"Starting a date early has its advantages." Caleb helped her up and loaded the water bucket into the back.

Josie thought about the pizza shop in Shreve. She couldn't eat another bite if her life depended on it. The popcorn, followed by a sixteen ounce soda, had expanded her belly to capacity. If she were a horse, she would founder. But if she said, "Let's skip the pizza," their evening would be cut short. And this was one date she wanted to last until noon tomorrow.

Caleb entertained her during the drive as he had earlier. He described a beach close to his Cleveland apartment so beautifully, she longed to see Lake Erie for the first time in her life. Hundreds of seagulls diving for fish, sailboats bobbing on blue waves, and children soaring kites in the air currents—Caleb had a gift with words as well as with wood. Yet most of his time spent as an *Englischer* remained a mystery. And for now, that was how Josie preferred it to stay.

The buggy rolled in to Shreve. When they entered the town's sole pizza parlor, barely a head turned in their direction. Amish people were so common that the proprietor installed a hitching post out back with a water trough refilled from his garden hose.

"What'll it be, Miss Yoder?" Caleb perused the menu as the waitress set down two glasses of water. "An extra-large deluxe pie with double cheese?"

With a groan she pressed both palms against her belly. "How 'bout a medium with mushroom and onions?"

"Mushrooms sound fine, but why don't we skip the onions? I don't want breath like that dragon if you get the urge to kiss me goodnight." He fastened his dark brown eyes on her.

"If I get the urge?" Josie nearly choked on an ice cube. "You are absolutely horrible, Caleb Beachy." She felt her face and earlobes grow warm.

He leaned back in the red vinyl booth. "Do you mean horrible in a good way?"

After glancing around the shop, Josie relaxed in their private enclosure. "In absolutely the best way."

They talked for hours in the restaurant until finally able to eat a slice of pizza. With the remainder boxed up for their siblings, Caleb clamped the battery lights on his buggy for the drive back to Fredericksburg. It was two o'clock in the morning when they arrived home. As expected, her house was dark and silent when Caleb walked her to the door. As *unexpected*, his presumption proved correct. Without waiting for him to utter the standard post-date niceties, Josie stretched up on tiptoes and kissed him fully on the mouth.

"Thank goodness we didn't get the onions," she whispered, and fled through the kitchen door.

※

On Saturday morning, Adam walked onto the porch with his second cup of coffee. His day off from the furniture factory stretched before him like a gift. He had a perfect spring day and all he could think about was seeing Sarah that evening. But after she put in her shift at the *Englisch* bed-and-breakfast, she would be too tired to take a walk or play a game of volleyball with his family. She would be too tired for much of anything other than a buggy ride to the old grist mill. And the last time they went there, Sarah had fallen asleep during the drive back. So much for romantic conversation or making plans for their future.

Adam gazed across the hayfield, where the first crop was already up and doing well. With three brothers, his *daed* didn't need his help to plant corn and soybeans on their farm. He could busy himself in the barn since there would always be another horse stall in need of cleaning.

"Son?" his *mamm* called through the open kitchen window. "Would you mind splitting another half-cord of firewood?"

"This time of year?" he asked. Everyone teased his mother about being the freeze-baby of the Troyers.

"The nights have still been chilly." She offered a sweet smile.

"I would be happy to. It'll save me from mucking stalls until later." Adam left his coffee mug on the porch rail and headed to the woodpile. Chopping firewood gave him an excellent way to burn away his impatience and frustration. He was now twenty-three years old and still single—the last unmarried Troyer except for his sixteen-year-old sister. At this rate, even she might beat him to marriage vows. He had been baptized and joined the church several years ago, hoping his beloved Sarah would soon follow in his footsteps. They couldn't get married until she joined their church. Then her decision last fall to track Caleb down in Cleveland delayed their plans by a full year.

What would he do if Sarah changed her mind? Not about accepting the Plain way of life. She'd never given him any reason not to believe she loved being Amish. With her father serving as bishop, that part of her future seemed assured. But what if she had changed her mind about him? Tall, willowy, and blond, Sarah was lovely to look at. He, on the other hand was short, stout, and as appealing as a goat. How many tall women married shorter men? He'd once torn an advertisement from a magazine for elevator wedges for his boots, making himself the laughing stock among his *bruders* for a week.

I 'spose you're about as tall as God reckons you should be. His father's sage conclusion put an end to their teasing and any plans he had for plastic inserts. At least Sarah had sought him out at the Yoder barn raising. How he longed to make her his bride, to build a cabin near the road with a small barn for their horse and a fenced garden for her. With his job as a furniture craftsman, he didn't need to buy a farm. He only needed her... and a way to spend the next eight hours without obsessing about her.

"Working with wood is the last place I thought I would find you today."

Adam glanced around to find his sister Amanda several feet away. With her heavy bonnet and wool shawl clutched tightly, she looked as cold as a January afternoon. "What are my favorite newlyweds doing here?" Adam split a section of log into two equal halves.

"Nathan wished to talk to *Daed* about buying his new Belgian foal, and I wanted to speak to you." Amanda reached to touch his arm.

"Could you take a break for a few minutes? Looks like you've split quite a bit already."

"*Mamm* wants another half-cord to last into May. You know how she loves to keep the stove going until it's in the seventies outdoors." Adam buried the ax head in the chopping block so his nieces and nephews wouldn't get hurt. "What did you want to talk about?"

Amanda pushed off her outer bonnet, letting it hang down her back by the ribbon ties. "I wanted to make sure you're not pressuring Sarah before she's ready. I'm offering some free advice from one stubborn mule to another."

He stared at her. Despite the fact that Amanda had married and moved several miles away, she still knew what went on in his mind… and in his heart. "Me, impatient? You must be confusing me with someone else."

His attempt at humor didn't alter the uneasy expression on her face. "I saw you and Sarah at the Yoder barn raising. You seemed to be getting along well."

"And why wouldn't we be?" Adam felt his defenses lift a notch.

"Because the next baptism and wedding season isn't until fall. It's still only April."

Adam crossed his arms. "We should be married by now instead of her working every day at that fancy inn."

Amanda's eyes grew very round. "Tell me you haven't ordered Sarah to quit her job."

"I didn't, but I would like to."

She shook her head. "Don't bully her. Let things fall into place according to God's plan. She will quit work when the time is right."

"I don't think it's God's plan for an Amish woman to cook and clean up after *Englischers*," he muttered half under his breath.

"Is that what this is about? You don't like the fact that Country Pleasures caters to *Englisch* tourists here on vacation?" Amanda didn't wait for his answer. "Because who do you imagine buys those handcrafted dining room tables, writing desks, and extravagant shelving units? I assure you no Plain folk can afford the kind of oak or walnut furniture you make, Adam Troyer."

For a few minutes, he was speechless. "I suppose you've got a point. I never thought about it like that. But I want to be the breadwinner; Sarah doesn't need to work anywhere."

"The two of you can work that out once you're wed. Just don't lay down ultimatums you'll live to regret." Amanda glanced back at the house. "*Mamm*'s waving from the doorway so I need to go inside." She pointed an index finger at him. "But don't forget where I live. You can always stop by for pep talks, like we did in the old days."

"Don't worry, sis. I've got my bossy inclinations under control. But thanks."

Funny, he thought, as Amanda walked toward the house. The idea of laying down an ultimatum had just crossed his mind.

8

And I hope, by Thy good pleasure,
Safely to arrive at home.

Caleb watched the approach of his father from the grassy bank of the pond. The pressure of running a business eight months out of the year while serving as district bishop was starting to take its toll. He'd grown frailer in the last five years, with a definite curve to his spine. It was a good thing he did little more than study blueprints these days on the construction site.

"Your *mamm* thought I might find you here." Eli stopped close to the water's edge. A sheen of sweat covered his face from the May sunshine.

"Nice day to throw in a fishing line." Caleb pulled up a dandelion by the roots.

"It's still the Sabbath—no labor should be performed."

"Believe me, no work has been. Nary a fish biting." He shielded his eyes to peer up at his father.

"Your *grossmammi* wanted to know why you didn't come by today." Eli slowly lowered himself to the sloped hillside. "She baked a peach pie especially for you. Isn't that your favorite?"

Caleb felt a pang of guilt. His grandmother was the sweetest woman on earth. But he couldn't tag after his parents every non-preaching Sunday on their endless rounds of social calls. There were only so many cups of coffee, glasses of lemonade, and homemade cookies that a person could consume. Now if they had been visiting the Yoder family, it would have been a different story. "I'll stop by to see her during the week," he said. "With any luck, *Grossmammi* might still have a slice of pie left."

"You'll have to go after hours because I've lined up work for the crew." Eli skipped a flat stone across the water.

Caleb straightened from his inclined position. "That's great to hear. Lately, I've been carrying around my wallet for no reason whatsoever. That Standardbred and new buggy wiped out everything I had saved so far. I haven't been able to give *Mamm* money toward groceries these past two weeks."

"No son or daughter of mine has to worry about paying room and board—that's an *Englisch* custom." Eli's second stone sunk to the bottom on the first skip.

"*Danki,* but I would feel funny not contributing. I'm a grown man, not a teenager. What kind of job will this be?"

"An expansion of a restaurant and tavern in Ashland with a large banquet room for weddings and reunions. They want the rustic, historical look of the original building to carry over into the new addition. The owners hired *Englisch* plumbers, electricians, and tile setters, but we got the contract for the rough and finished carpentry. He's already found oak siding from a dismantled barn that he wants to use on the interior walls."

"Old barn siding?" asked Caleb. "That ought to supply the rustic ambience he's looking for."

Eli screwed up his face. He hated it when people used words like *ambience*, despite knowing clearly what it meant. "Yes, well, let's hope none of the wood is wormy or decayed. Hopefully, there'll be enough without piecing together short lengths. Are you ready to start tomorrow?" He threw one final stone into the pond with a resounding *plunk*.

"Nothing else on my Monday social calendar."

His father rose slowly to his feet. "*Gut.* Jack will pick us up at six thirty. Don't oversleep." Eli started for the house on the same weedy, overgrown trail.

Oversleep? Hardly. Caleb hadn't much to do after chores other than doze in the porch rocking chair. When he wasn't pining over Josie, of course. Their date to the theater and pizza shop had been his most enjoyable day in too many to count. And when she'd kissed him good night on the porch steps, he practically started shouting. But that wouldn't have been wise at two o'clock in the morning.

He'd seen little of her lately. Without five dollars to his name, he couldn't very well take her out for a cup of coffee or an ice cream cone in town. And when he walked the back path to the Yoder house during the late afternoon, her sisters stalked them to the tree swing, the front porch, or the apple orchard—wherever they went. Her family didn't allow Josie out of their sight, as though he would spirit her off to the city if they turned their backs. The two of them had chatted last week after preaching and then shared a drink in the cool shade. She had laughed at his jokes and listened to his stories of Sarah and Rebekah's ongoing rivalry at work. But all too soon, her *daed* rounded up the family to visit some relation several miles away.

Caleb could think of little else beyond her. Yet nothing had overtly signaled she was his girl. One little kiss did not a future make. At least if work started tomorrow, he would have something other than watching hay grow occupying his time. And some money in his pocket to properly court Josie. Amish people didn't go out often or buy costly gifts like courting *Englischers*. But he couldn't tolerate empty pockets for long. It smacked of no future—the last impression he wanted to give the woman of his dreams.

The next morning he awoke at four o'clock to shower and shave before his sisters got up. By the time Jack picked them up, he'd fed the horses, milked their two cows, gathered eggs for his *mamm,* and eaten more breakfast than he had in a long while. He would enjoy the camaraderie of the other men again, even if two languages were spoken during the drive to Ashland.

At the site they unloaded their tools into a chaotic construction site. Deliveries of restaurant food and supplies competed with the cleanup of the adjacent building's demolition. Eli's employees set to work building new interior walls to the architect's specifications. By the third day, they finished roughing-in two bathrooms in preparation for plumbing and electrical works to be installed. When those tradesmen arrived, their crew focused on meticulously matching oak boards in the main banquet hall to ensure the best possible appearance. The final step would be to remove the temporary wall separating the old establishment from the new. The partition allowed business to continue in the bar and restaurant during renovation.

"Say, aren't you Cal Beachy?"

A voice broke Caleb's concentration with his hand sander. He glanced up at a vaguely familiar face. The contents of his tool belt indicated the man was an electrician. "I am." Caleb offered a faint smile.

"It's me—Dave Whitaker. We worked together at that big hotel complex in Wilmot a few years ago. Have I changed that much? We went out for beers after our shift a few times, remember?" The bearded, crew-cut man grinned and stuck out his hand. "Good seeing you again!"

Caleb wiped his hand on his pant leg and shook heartily. "Good seeing you too. Small world, no?" He gestured around the banquet hall with his tool.

"Unbelievable, considering the number of construction projects happening all at once. Say, are you still in contact with Pete Taylor? He was one heck of a finish craftsman."

He nodded affirmatively. "I saw him a few weeks ago. He's getting married one of these days."

Dave Whitaker gazed over Caleb's clothes as though noticing their crew for the first time. "I had heard that the carpenters would be Amish, but I thought you had moved north after the hotel project and left the Amish faith." There was nothing critical or snide in his comment, merely an honest observation.

"I did move to Cleveland for a few years. Turned out I wasn't cut out for the big-city life." He forced a laugh. "I'm back now with my family." Caleb stopped short of adding, "And with my faith." Despite going through the motions in church, he usually felt like a poser—one big hypocrite.

"Well, that would explain the hand sander. Actually, you'll get a smoother surface with one of those. I'm glad you're back with your family. Hey, we're gonna eat lunch out back in about twenty minutes. Why don't you join us so we can get caught up?"

Before Caleb could respond, his partner on the Millersburg roof stepped in between him and Dave and started talking in *Deutsch*. Josiah had been on the other side of the room hanging freshly sanded boards just a minute ago. Caleb focused on Josiah, his mind quickly adjusting to the German dialect. "All right," he said to Josiah. Then to Dave he said, "My friend needs advice on something and he had hoped to talk on break." Caleb felt like an inadequate version of a United Nations interpreter.

"Sure, no problem. Good running into you, Caleb." Dave tipped his hard hat and resumed stringing wire through bored holes in the framing studs.

Caleb turned back to Josiah, but his roofing partner was already halfway across the room, leaving him scratching his head. When the Amish crew members opened their lunch coolers an hour later, Josiah seemed to have forgotten his urgent conundrum. "What did you want to talk to me about?" Caleb asked after swallowing a mouthful of bologna and sliced tomatoes.

Josiah blinked several times. "My oldest son will soon need his own buggy and horse. I'd heard that you landed a great pair. Mind pointing me in the right direction? I don't want to overpay."

Caleb glanced over at his father, who seemed engrossed in a set of blueprints. Then he described the buggy maker and the Mount Hope horse auction that occurred the first Wednesday of the month. Anybody Amish in the three-county area would know exactly where the few buggy makers lived and the best places to buy a Standardbred or draft horse. Josiah hadn't wanted him getting friendly with his former *Englisch* friends. And as much as he liked and respected the man, his interference grated on Caleb for the rest of the afternoon.

At the end of the workday, he wandered over to where the electricians were locking up their expensive tools. "Maybe we'll get a chance to have lunch some other time," he said quietly to Dave.

"Sounds good. I'll bet you've got great stories from when you were living up in Cleveland." Dave slung his coiled extension cord over one shoulder and his tool belt over the other.

"Yeah, I had some interesting experiences in the city, most of which just about curled this country-boy's straight hair." Caleb pulled on his suspenders.

"A few of us are going across the street for a couple beers before heading home. Why don't you join us…just like old times?"

Caleb gazed into Dave's honest, forthright face while several emotions fought for control. Part of him would like a small taste of the "old days," but a bigger part remembered the shameful things he'd done while under the influence of "a few beers." One moment, then two spun out while he waged war with his inner demons. "Nah, I'm not going back to my old habits. I need to walk the straight-and-narrow, but thanks for the offer."

"Sure thing, Cal. See ya tomorrow." Dave slapped him on the back and offered a genuine smile.

When Caleb turned around to head toward the van, he met his father's eye. The man wasn't smiling at all—genuinely or otherwise.

�❧

Eli tried to recall any of the numerous passages in the Bible that referred to anger. Bits and pieces came to mind, yet his irritation continued to build on the drive home from Ashland. Finally his mind fastened on Ecclesiastes 7:9—*Be not hasty in thy spirit to be angry: for anger resteth in the bosom of fools.* But how could he put aside his need to exert authority over his son? Besides the fact he was Caleb's father, he was also the district's bishop. He had drawn the lot, bestowing on him the lifelong responsibility for the spiritual well-being of his flock. He had failed before to keep Caleb in the Amish fold. Would he fail again? Couldn't the boy turn his back on worldly temptations?

Why don't you join us for a few beers across the street before heading home? If Caleb had his own transportation, would he have gone with his old *Englisch* friends? Eli shifted on the van's front seat as his back spasmed with muscle tension. The defroster blew warm air into his face, along with the pollen from budding trees and blooming flowers.

"Can't you shut off that fan, Jack?" he snapped. "There's no more condensation on the windshield."

"Sure thing, Eli. Guess my mind had wandered." Jack switched off the blower without taking his focus off the road ahead.

Silence filled the vehicle without even the radio blasting its nonsense. His Amish crew members had been unusually quiet since leaving Ashland. Jack and Bob had been chatting about the Cleveland Indians ball team until he interrupted them. Now they too fell mute. "Sorry, Jack," he murmured. "I didn't mean to bark at you."

"Don't worry about it. My daughter plays around with the vents every time she's in the car. I'll readjust how they're pointed when I get home tonight." Blessedly, Jack turned on the radio to a country station to relieve the uncomfortable silence. Eli lapsed back into his quandary over Caleb. He couldn't let his son venture down the same road as before. He had an obligation as a parent and as a bishop.

In Killbuck, Daniel and Josiah climbed out with the barest, "*Guder nachmittag.*" Josiah probably felt responsible for the trouble brewing. But if he hadn't intervened between Caleb and the electrician, Eli wouldn't have known that bad influences from the past had returned to his crew. Why had the Lord placed temptations in his son's path so soon? Caleb hadn't been back long enough to strengthen his resolve against worldly sins.

At long last, Jack drove up their rutted lane. "Looks like your driveway could use a grading and a load of gravel."

"It can at that," agreed Eli. "I'll have the neighbor scrape the surface with his tractor blade after the next heavy rain. Then all we'll need is another load of stone. Thanks for the ride."

"See you tomorrow, Eli, Cal," said Jack with a wave.

But his son was halfway to the house before the van turned around. Eli hurried after him as though haste were of particular importance. Inside the kitchen Caleb stood at the sink, pouring a glass of cold water. "Is that how things will be this summer?" he asked.

Caleb peered up with exasperatingly coolness. "Is that how *what* things will be?"

"Don't play games with me, son. You know I refer to you socializing with those *Englisch* electricians." Eli struggled to keep his voice down. For the time being they were alone in the room, and he preferred to keep it that way.

"Dave Whitaker recognized me from the Wilmot hotel project and walked over to say hello. What would you have preferred? That I pretended not to know him? Or perhaps demand he keep a six-foot perimeter at all times to keep from spreading his Englischness?" Caleb drank the full glass without breaking eye contact.

"Don't talk back to me. What did Dave want? I'm sure it was more than just to say hello."

"He asked if I wanted to eat lunch with the electricians. Workers often do that on construction sites. It fosters good communication among the various trades. But Josiah apparently has as much trust in me as you do. He interrupted Dave with a phony request for my advice. Then during lunch, Josiah asked about where to buy a horse and buggy. Honestly, *Daed*, he should have thought up something better than that."

"Josiah was only looking out for you." Eli eased himself into a chair.

Caleb's eyes darkened into black pools. "I understand that. He's a good man, but I don't need someone watching me like a babysitter. If I wanted to stay *Englisch*, I would have remained in Cleveland. But you don't seriously expect me to never talk to an *Englischer*, do you? That's a little ridiculous since we work with them."

Eli flexed his fingers to unlock his balled fists. "There's more to this than talking to Dave Whitaker or even eating your sandwich with electricians. I heard him invite you to go drinking after work. What would you have said if you had your own way home?"

Caleb pondered the question for a long time—an action that should have been wholly unnecessary. "I would have said no thanks. The same as I did. I have no desire to drink alcohol. It didn't do me any good five summers ago and did even less good up in the city." He refilled his glass to the brim. "But I don't need you or Josiah making decisions for me. Showing a little trust would go a long way."

Eli slapped the tabletop. "Trust must be earned."

Caleb's head reared back as though he'd been struck. "Since coming home, what have I done to deserve your lack of faith?" He wiped his damp hands on a towel and tossed it across the countertop. "I'm to be held accountable because someone asked to have a beer with me? I said no and would have declined even if you and Josiah hadn't been there to intervene. I don't plan to repeat the mistakes of my *rumschpringe*."

"The problem isn't what you have done, Caleb, but what you have not." Eli sucked in a deep breath to steady his nerves. Why did the kitchen seem so overbearingly stuffy? No cook pots were simmering on the stove.

"You'll need to be a bit more specific." Crossing his arms, Caleb glared down his nose.

"You haven't talked to me about joining the church or getting baptized in the Christian faith. You go through the motions during preaching without absorbing a single word that's being said."

"God gave you the ability to read people's minds?" he asked.

"Stop that sass!" Eli struggled to his feet.

"Perhaps you should postpone this conversation until your tempers have cooled down." Elizabeth had entered the kitchen unnoticed. "What on earth are you arguing about?"

Caleb turned his focus to his *mamm*, his face softening. "He expects me to join the church when they haven't even started classes yet. The next baptism and communion isn't until fall. I would happily adjust to his rules if it were humanly possible."

Elizabeth stared at him as though he were the unreasonable one. "Eli?"

"You plan to join the membership class?" he asked.

"I intended to all along."

"All right then." Eli cleared his throat. "I might have overreacted today. I will do a better job of displaying my trust in you."

"You must have some before you can display it." Caleb stalked out the door and down the steps, heading toward the barn.

Elizabeth waved her hands at him. "Please don't go after him. Let Caleb have the last word for a change. You've both been speaking out of anger and spite. Simmer down before you say another word."

Eli bristled like a startled stray cat, unaccustomed to his wife lecturing him. But in all fairness, Elizabeth made a good point. "My anger is born of fear," he whispered, deflating like a punctured balloon.

"What are you afraid of, *ehemann*?"

"Of losing him again to *Englisch* temptations. Old friends invited Caleb to go drinking with them."

"They came to your construction site for that specific purpose?" She sat down at the opposite end, her lashes fluttering in confusion.

"No, they're electricians working on the same project. I'm fearful our son will fall back into old habits."

"You cannot control him. You couldn't years ago, and you'll have even less success now. Caleb must come to the Christian faith and our Amish lifestyle of his own free will. It is the only way this will work."

"Caleb is right about one thing—I haven't trusted him." Eli covered his face with his hands. "And my lack of trust has driven him further away. I'm probably the reason why he left the first time."

"Let's not worry about the past. And regarding the present, it sounds like you've lost faith in the One who can work miracles. God has performed harder tasks than bringing one Plain man back to His flock."

Eli peered up and stroked his beard. "My faith in God never falters."

"Then give this matter over to Him and let go. Show faith in our son and in the Lord."

"What would I do without you, *fraa*?" He closed the distance between them in a few strides and encircled her with his arms.

"*Ach,* you'd probably flounder like a cow struck in the mud. Be thankful that I found you many years ago." She patted his hand.

"I do, each and every day of my life."

֍

When Sarah walked outdoors after preaching on Sunday, the breeze felt wonderful on her overheated skin. The Miller house was too small to host services, in her humble opinion, and should be skipped during the rotation. Neither their grain barn nor their livestock barn would clean up sufficiently to host the district. Thus fifty-some people had jammed into their living room and overflowed down the hallways. A few teenagers sat on the stairs to the second floor. Even with every window open in the house and several fans, the room had become oppressively hot before they reached midway in the three-hour service.

On the lawn Mrs. Miller set up a table with pitchers of cool drinks. Aware of the stifling temperatures of his home, Mr. Miller carried benches into the shade of several ancient maples. Without waiting for her *mamm* or sisters Sarah headed straight for the drinks. She drank most of her first glass of lemonade before looking for her beloved. But instead of Adam, she spotted his mother hurrying toward her at a brisk pace.

"My, it's awfully warm for May, no?" Anna Troyer reached Sarah's side huffing and puffing. She cooled herself with a plastic fan from the dollar store. "If it's in the eighties already, what does that bode for July and August?"

"That would leave the nineties and hundreds." Sarah poured her future mother-in-law a large glass of iced tea and stirred in a round tablespoon of sugar as she preferred.

"*Danki,* my girl." Anna accepted the glass, braced one palm on the table, and finished it in several long swallows. "That hits the spot, but I need to be quick. John is loading our buggies while Adam hitches the teams. I've come to invite you to dinner this afternoon. Since it's the Lord's Day, it'll just be cold fried chicken and salads. But we'll eat outdoors on the porch and in the yard. Adam says you love picnics." A lock of gray hair peeked from under Anna's *kapp* while her apron pulled tightly across her midsection—a testimony to the excellent cooks in Adam's family.

Sarah had been looking forward to a quiet Sunday afternoon rather than the entire Troyer clan. But there was no way could she refuse. Several of his sisters already thought she was dragging her feet with Adam. "*Danki,* I would love to come. I'll have my *daed* drop me off as we pass your farm."

"*Ach,* you're so skinny, I'm sure we can squeeze you in one of the buggies." Anna eyed her figure like a challenge to be dealt with.

The idea of squeezing in with Adam's siblings held little appeal. Their chatter would wear her out on a day as hot as this. "No, my *mamm* wishes me to speak to Rebekah on the drive back, so I'll see you later this afternoon." Smiling, she finished the rest of her lemonade.

"As you wish." Anna tossed her empty cup into the trash can and hurried toward the parking area. The woman never seemed to stroll, meander, or dawdle.

Sarah didn't fib about needing to talk to her sister on the way home. Her mother had requested that she *speak nicely* to Rebekah for practice. And that proved to be a tougher challenge than Anna Troyer adding meat on her bones.

The moment she relayed her plans for the afternoon to her parents, her sister jumped on the opportunity to nettle. "I bet I know why Anna and not Adam asked you to dinner today."

Sarah pivoted on the seat to gaze out the window. "That's nice," she said to Rebekah, sweet as honey. "Goodness, look at that huge flock of geese. I wonder if they'll stay in the U.S. or keep going to Canada for the summer."

Katie stuck her head out the other side. "It doesn't look like they're carrying passports, so they'll probably settle down in Wooster."

Rebekah had no interest in migrating birds. "His *mamm* wants to figure you out, Sarah, to make sure you're not leading her poor son on."

"In that case, Anna is in for a pleasant surprise." Sarah looked past Rebekah in favor of her friendlier sister. "Look, Katie. See how they changed positions in the formation? That will give the leader a chance to catch his goose-breath."

Katie giggled, bobbing her head. "Maybe he honked his way to the head of the line, just like cars on the freeway."

"The Troyers will probably grill you—"

Mamm cut off whatever nugget of possibility Rebekah had surmised, pivoting around on the front bench. "I want you to figure out how to be kinder to your *schwester*! This is the Sabbath and yet you poke and prod Sarah like a cow in the milk stanchions. If you cannot find anything nice to say, then I suggest you watch the scenery with your lips buttoned shut."

Seldom did their mother speak so sternly. Seldom did she need to, and never on the Sabbath.

The drive home from the Millers' was ten miles, but the Troyers' driveway arrived early in their journey. Before her father brought the buggy to a stop, Rebekah turned to her with teary eyes.

"*Mir leid*," she apologized. "I've been feeling sorry for myself about my miserable life. So I took it out on you. Forgive me." Rebekah sniffled, because as usual, she'd forgotten her hanky.

Sarah handed her a tissue and kissed her forehead. "Everybody's life seems horrible when they're your age. Be patient. Your turn will come."

"Will Adam bring you home tonight?" Eli asked as she climbed out of the buggy.

"You can count on it," she called. Then Sarah ran all the way to the Troyer backyard where tables had been set up on the lawn. Amanda and Adam's sisters were already carrying bowls from the house.

"Aunt Sarah," cried Lydia Troyer, one of Adam's many nieces. "I couldn't wait for you to get here." Lydia threw her arms around Sarah's waist and peered up through long, dark eyelashes. "Will you sit next to me at supper?"

"I can't think of a better companion." Sarah patted the top of the child's *kapp*.

"How about me?" Adam came up behind her, carrying fresh picked flowers in his hand.

Sarah grinned and grabbed the massive bouquet. "Does your *mamm* know you raided her garden?"

"*Jah,* she gave me the thumbs-up." Adam leaned over Lydia's head for a quick kiss on Sarah's cheek.

"Would you please put these in a coffee can of cold water?" Sarah asked Lydia. "And make sure I don't forget to take them home." As soon as the child sprinted away, Sarah wrapped an arm around Adam's waist. "I'm glad your *mamm* invited me. You saved me from a dull afternoon in the porch swing."

"We don't spend anywhere near enough time together, not with your job and mine."

"The days are starting to get longer. We should have plenty of chances to count stars and chase fireflies this summer."

"Sarah, I've been meaning to—"

"Time to eat, Uncle Adam," hollered Joshua. "Or we'll throw it to the hogs." Adam's favorite nephew giggled all the way to the tables.

As Sarah took her seat on the women's side next to Lydia, Adam sat down directly across from her. Unfortunately, his busybody sister joined her left side. "Would you like some potato salad?" asked Amanda after their silent prayer.

"*Jah, gut.*" Sarah accepted the bowl while Lydia scooped baked beans onto her plate.

"How about some chicken?" Mrs. Troyer appeared at her shoulder with the platter. Before Sarah could request a drumstick, her hostess plopped a breast and two wings onto the plate.

"Would you like some bean salad?" asked Lillian. Adam's sole shy sister-in-law appeared the moment Anna moved away.

"No, *danki*," she said. "I have plenty to eat already."

Lillian's smile faltered. "But I made this from Josie Yoder's recipe. Isn't she your best friend?" The bowl hovered before Sarah's nose.

"She is, indeed. I suppose I can fit a spoonful next to the baked beans."

Lillian dished a mound that threatened to shift into her lap. "Let me know if it's as good as Josie's."

As Sarah began eating, she noticed Adam biting the inside of his mouth more often than the chicken. She tried kicking him under the table but connected with the post instead. During supper, the topics of conversation moved from optimum lettuce varieties for hot weather to the likelihood of rain this evening to whether or not snakes had been aboard Noah's ark.

"Of course they were," said Adam. "But not the poisonous ones, just the good kind that keep the mice in line." Sarah expected one of the youngsters to ask how rattlers survived the flood, but no one did.

Instead Joshua, well-known for telling jokes, popped up with his latest. "Uncle Adam, why did the celery think the tomato was mad about something?"

"I haven't a clue." Adam wiggled his thick eyebrows.

"Because he was stewing in his own juices." Joshua broke into uproarious laughter.

"Let's wait until after supper for any more jokes, son," said the boy's father. "Folks need a full belly to appreciate your brand of humor."

When everyone finished eating, Sarah scrambled up to carry left-overs to the kitchen. With thirty people, there would be plenty of dishes to wash. But Anna Troyer stopped her at the back stairs. "No guest of mine helps with cleanup." She pulled the bowl of coleslaw from Sarah's hands. "You run along. My son wants to take a walk with you."

Sure enough, Adam waited near the barn, spinning his hat between his fingers. She knew she should have insisted on helping, but yearned for some time alone. When she reached his side, she took his hand. "Let's hurry before Joshua or Lydia or *someone* tries to follow us." Sarah picked up her skirt and they loped down the path.

When finally out of view of the house, they slowed their pace. "I apologize for my family. They can be pushy at times." His warm breath tickled her ear as he wrapped an arm around her.

"Your *mamm* and sisters sure want me to eat more. They mean well, or at least I hope they do. They're not fattening me up for fall butchering, are they?"

"Absolutely not. I have other plans for you." His voice was barely audible.

An uneasy sensation ran up her spine. She didn't want him spoiling an otherwise perfect afternoon. Couldn't he enjoy her company without exerting pressure? For the next ten minutes they strolled arm in arm to the river. Cold water rushed over moss-covered rocks in a ravine where sunlight rarely penetrated. Just as she lowered herself to a boulder, Adam broke the serenity with his usual question.

"Is this how it will be forever, Sarah? We court until I'm an old man and you're an old woman?" His lips drew into a poignant smile.

Sarah's breath caught in her throat. This wasn't what she'd expected. It occurred to her that Adam probably *would* wait forever, despite whatever consequences ensued. "Nobody should give up on this old woman yet." Grabbing his arm, she pulled him down to her rock. "Classes are starting in a few weeks and I will be there. You can count on it."

9

Jesus sought me when a stranger,
Wandering from the fold of God

osie glanced over at the men's benches as though Caleb would
suddenly appear in the Miller's sweltering living room. But no
matter how many times she scanned the familiar faces, she didn't see
the one she yearned for. Why hadn't he come to the preaching service?
It had been two weeks since their trip to the movies in Wooster, and
she'd seen very little of him since. Of course, anytime he came by the
house, one of her sisters managed to turn up without something better to do than eavesdrop on their conversation.

Josie didn't know what to make of him. Was he really interested in
her, or merely passing time until he figured out how to spend the rest
of his life? Her parents hadn't been pleased when they'd stayed out so
late. And they weren't happy that she was courting Caleb...if that was
indeed what she was doing.

"Stop daydreaming," Margaret Yoder whispered in her ear, along
with a companionable nudge to the ribs.

She smiled at her mother and then gave full attention to the bishop's sermon. Sarah's father spoke of turning one's back on sin without
passing judgment. *So hard to do*, she thought. Didn't people always
want to condemn those who acted in ways they felt were wrong? How
difficult a walk Bishop Beachy must have had during those years his
son had been gone.

When the service concluded, Josie was trapped behind her formi-
dable *mamm* and *grossmammi* for another ten minutes until their row
emptied out. Why her family couldn't chat outdoors where it would

be cooler, she didn't know. Next Josie needed to assist her grandmother over to the chairs since she was staying for lunch with the Millers and other district members. Then *Mamm* sent her on errands back to the buggy to get their hamper. By the time she put the food in the house and searched for Sarah, her friend had already left. Sarah had said nothing about Caleb before the service and Josie hadn't thought to ask. Now she had plenty more questions than just why hadn't he come to church.

When her family arrived home that afternoon, Josie's anxiety began to ebb. After all, Caleb lived within walking distance—a long walk to be sure, but he was accessible. And the fact that his sister was her best friend provided an excuse to pay a social call. After packing a basket of cold pork chops, homemade applesauce, and chocolate chip cookies, Josie set out on the back path to the Beachy's. A gentle breeze lifted her *kapp* ribbons, along with her spirits. Caleb could be sick in bed with a rare, fatal disease while she was getting annoyed about lack of attention.

As she passed the old gristmill she heard the soothing sound of rushing water. She couldn't imagine grinding your own wheat, corn, barley, or oats each time you wanted hot cereal or to bake a loaf of bread. Life had become so much easier with the invention of the bulk foods store. Everything you possibly needed, plus the treats you loved, could be purchased in quantities from a cupful to a hundred pounds. When she reached Sarah's backyard, Josie swung her basket while humming a tune learned from a Mennonite friend.

Elizabeth sat rocking on the porch with Katie. The bishop appeared to be asleep in his chair while Sarah and Caleb were nowhere in sight. "Hello, Josie," called Elizabeth. "Come to see Sarah, I imagine?"

"*Jah*, I missed her after preaching. We didn't get much chance to talk." Josie lifted one foot to the bottom step.

"You're out of luck. She went to the Troyers for supper. 'Spose it'll be dark by the time Adam brings her home, but I'll mention that you stopped by." Elizabeth smiled fondly while continuing to rock. "Care for something to drink?"

"No, *danki*." Josie considered her options. "Say, is Caleb around? Could I have a word with him?"

"Don't see why not. He's down at the pond with a fishing line thrown in. Not that there are any fish left. I think they died off this winter when we had month-long subzero temperatures. Want me to send Katie to fetch him?"

The youngest Beachy turned up her face expectantly.

"No, no, stay where you are, Katie. I prefer to go myself to get more exercise." Josie hurried away before somebody questioned her logic—she'd just walked two miles and must walk another two to get home.

Josie spotted Caleb as soon as she crested the hill. He sat underneath a swamp willow on a campstool with his nose buried in a book. She'd almost reached his side before he heard someone approach.

"Goodness, Josie! Are you trying to give a man a heart attack?" Caleb jumped to his feet, losing his hat and dropping the book in the process.

Josie marched to the shade and set her hamper in the grass. "You're too young for a heart attack, but I did fear something horrible had happened, or at the very least, you were gravely ill." She pulled a tattered patchwork lap robe from the basket. After spreading it out, she plopped down in the middle.

He plucked his hat from the weeds and slapped it against his leg. "Why did you think I was sick?" His warm brown eyes locked on hers.

"Because you weren't at preaching, silly. I can't imagine why your *daed* didn't drag you by your ear. After all, he's the bishop." She laughed despite the fact she wasn't joking. "I'm sure that's what my father would do." Josie dug a jar of lemonade from the basket along with two plastic cups.

Caleb ignored his folding stool and crouched down beside her small quilt. "I'm rather surprised *Daed* said nothing when I decided not to go this morning. Those services are so long and the minister drones on about situations that don't apply. Those people have been dead a long time and faced trials and tribulations different from ours."

She handed him a drink. "Maybe you need to look deeper into his message, keeping in mind our individual wills hold little importance. We are to surrender ourselves and walk the path Christ taught us to the best of our abilities."

"Oh, *is that all?*" Caleb stretched out his legs.

"*Mamm* says it gets easier with practice and that yielding is hardest when you're young like us."

Caleb sipped his drink and picked up his leather bound book. "I derive more good from reading by the pond than I do jammed in somebody's hot living room or outbuilding." He splayed his fingers across the well-worn cover.

Josie noticed it was an English version of the *Holy Bible*. "The Good Book won't let you down. It has helped Christians for two thousand years. What have you learned today?"

"I like reading the Psalms—all things seem possible in that book. And I've read through the Gospels four times. Now I'm finishing the rest of the New Testament, and then I'll start at the beginning with Genesis."

"I applaud your efforts. I listen to my father read *Deutsch* Scripture in the evenings. But most of the time I just pay attention during the sermons." She lifted out the jar of applesauce, three wrapped pork chops, and some foam plates. "*Daed* says our goal is to live in submission to God, to the ministers and bishop, and to him and *Mamm* until I marry. So I don't need to study much by myself." After spooning apples onto their plates, Josie began to nibble her pork chop.

"Each to their own, Miss Yoder." Caleb settled back on one elbow to eat. "Thanks for bringing me lunch. It saved me a trip to the house until I'm ready. But I suspect you had a better reason to walk here than making sure I wasn't lying on my deathbed."

She glanced nervously over her shoulder. "You talk so much like an *Englischer,* but you're right. I've been thinking since we went to Wooster together. In two weeks the membership classes start—the first preaching Sunday of June. I plan to go and so does Sarah. You still intend to take the classes, don't you? Because if you don't, it would be pointless for us to spend any more time together. I'll be ending *rumschpringe* before my baptism." Desperate for a distraction, Josie picked up her plate and devoured the applesauce.

"Wow—that sounded like an ultimatum." Caleb grabbed his throat with both hands as though being strangled. "But since you're the prettiest girl in Fredericksburg, besides the best cook, I would be a fool not to join the class." He chomped into his second pork chop.

"Just to set the record straight, my sister fried the pork yesterday, *Mamm* made the applesauce, and I only fixed the lemonade from a powdered drink mix."

"I was referring to your roast chicken and four-bean salad." Caleb winked playfully. "But I would like you to fill me in on exactly what happens at these classes." He finished his chop in another two bites.

"You're pulling my leg, right?"

"I assure you, I am not."

"Your father is the bishop, Cal. How could you not know what goes on?"

Staring off at the water, Caleb set his empty plate in the grass. Low clouds were forming above the horizon, promising a shower before dark. "I seem to have trouble talking to him lately. We've been butting heads since I came back to work. So I can't find the right time to discuss his hopes for my salvation."

Josie reflected a moment. "You're not getting along on the job? But Eli is the boss."

"Don't worry your pretty head. Things are improving in that regard after a period of readjustment."

"*Gut* to hear." She exhaled slowly. "Okay, from now on during preaching Sundays those who wish to join the church will meet in the kitchen of wherever the service takes place. For forty-five minutes, one of the ministers will teach us the eighteen articles of the Anabaptist faith. Plus your father will instruct us on our *Ordnung* to make sure folks understand the district rules. After our class, we go to preaching."

"I've noticed that during years gone by. What else?" Caleb pulled up a weed, not meeting her gaze.

"Those who remain throughout the classes and wish to join the church will have one final session with their parents. It will be the day before baptism. Your *daed* and the other ministers will ask questions to make sure we're ready. Plus the men will be asked if they would be willing to be ministers if chosen by lots. That's it. You've watched people take their vows and get baptized at fall communion services."

He nodded. "*Jah*, I understand that part."

"Anytime during the classes if a person decides they're not ready, they just stop coming. No hard feelings. They can wait until next year."

"Well, my dear girl, I've got every incentive in the world to be ready." He rose to his full height, grabbed the handles of their hamper, and pulled her to her feet. "Now I'd better see to evening chores. Even on the Sabbath, horses still need to eat."

And Josie strolled back with more confidence than she'd known for quite some time.

❦

It was a Monday morning in June when Eli stood on his front porch sipping his second cup of black coffee. He'd already completed his morning prayers and eaten all the breakfast his unsettled stomach could handle. For some reason the usual orange juice and fried eggs churned his gut like the spicy burrito he'd once had at a livestock auction. Thank goodness he'd been born Amish instead of Spanish or he would be a very skinny man.

He had no idea what had tied him in knots. Their last project at the Ashland restaurant had finished on schedule without further incidents. When Caleb ran into some former *Englisch* friends, Eli had feared the worst. But his son hadn't spent lunchtime with the electricians. And more importantly, he hadn't started drinking with them after work. Mostly Caleb had avoided Dave Whitaker on the job except for the requisite greeting or farewell.

What could he have done if it had gone the other way? Absolutely nothing. Caleb had to make his own choices in life; he especially must make up his mind about remaining Amish. Eli's only option would be to ask Caleb to move out. And that would be a last resort since it would break Elizabeth's heart...along with his own. His best course of action was to pray, and hope God was merciful to one Amish farmer who'd stumbled on the Christian path too many times to count.

"Why are you waiting for Jack out here?" Caleb's voice broke Eli's concentration.

He turned to find his son dressed for work with coffee mug in hand. "I love the view from this porch—so much better than the side or back." Eli stepped back into the house, letting the screen door slam.

"If you say so, but it all looks like corn to me." Caleb followed him down the hallway into the kitchen.

Elizabeth smiled as she industriously packed their lunches. "I've made you each two sandwiches, because you never know how long your first day will be. And I have chips and a walnut brownie for both my boys." She planted a kiss on Caleb's cheek, initiating a blush.

"You act like this is our first day of school instead of just another construction project," said Caleb. "We'd better watch for Jack outside before you send us upstairs to comb our hair once more." He hugged his *mamm* before picking up the bulging cooler.

Despite occasional rough patches between the two of them, Caleb always treated Elizabeth with love and respect. And for that, Eli was grateful.

"What's our new project?" asked Caleb when Eli joined him on the porch. "All I know is we're heading to Ashland again."

Eli sipped from his travel mug. "We landed a good contract this time—finished carpentry and cabinetmaking in a new building close to the interstate. A large law firm wants fancy offices for their corporate attorneys. The rough carpentry work has already been done. We should have three weeks of bookcases and shelving for electronics, conference room wainscoting, installing hardwood floors, and building cubicles for administrative assistants. The kind of work you love."

"In Ashland, Ohio?" Caleb smirked with disbelief.

"*Jah*, the college has brought new development to the area. Wealthy *Englischers* will always need wealthier lawyers." Eli chuckled as Jack's van pulled up the driveway.

"Will we have quality materials to use, not like that knotty old barn siding in the banquet room?" Caleb set his empty mug by the door for one of his sisters to find.

"Nothing but oak, walnut, and cherry. Every board will be rated grade A."

"Sounds like a walk in the meadow on a summer day," said Caleb.

"With a pretty girl by your side," Eli added to the analogy.

"With fresh apple pie and hand-churned ice cream when you get home," Caleb concluded on their walk to the van.

"What are you two talking about?" asked Bob as Eli opened the door.

"About the stacks of perfect wood waiting at the next job site." Caleb stowed his tool belt in the back and climbed in.

"Remember the nest of termite eggs I found in that stack of old siding?" Bob shook like a dog in the rain. "I still have nightmares about those disgusting bugs."

"Those days are behind us." Eli rolled down the window and leaned his head back.

However, the Ashland construction project turned out to be anything but a walk in the meadow.

"Uh-oh," moaned Jack. He pulled the van to the berm while still two hundred yards away, but they could already see and hear loud commotion. "There was something about this on the radio this morning, but I didn't catch the whole story."

"What's going on?" asked Caleb from the backseat. He leaned forward to see out the windshield.

"A strike," said Eli. "The building's owner feared this might happen."

"Which union?" Caleb demanded.

"It looks like the plumbers." Jack crept forward another fifty yards. "The radio said something about the local union being upset because nonunion contractors were being used on a major commercial project. It doesn't help that contract negotiations have stalled over wages and benefits. They've reached some sort of impasse." Jack clucked his tongue against the roof on his mouth.

"This matter doesn't concern us," said Eli. "Drive into the fenced parking area, but be careful. With so many men milling about, we don't want to run anybody over." His stomach took another nasty turn. It was as though his body had sensed trouble as soon as he woke up this morning.

"What do you mean this doesn't concern us?" Caleb asked his question in a soft voice. "I'm still in the Carpenters' Union, Local

Brotherhood Number 21. I remember sitting in the union hall plenty, waiting for jobs to come in. If too many owners use nonunion contractors, families of the men down at the hall are forced to do without."

"Work is work. Let's not worry about a disagreement between plumbers and contract negotiators. This strike has nothing to do with carpenters, whether union or not." Eli ate three Tums from his pocket container.

Caleb leaned over the seat between him and Jack. "But we should show support for the strikers by not crossing their line. Otherwise they'll lose ground at the bargaining table. If the other trades don't respect their picket line, it hurts all trades in the end."

Eli swallowed a mouthful of stomach acid and pivoted to face his son. "Need I remind you that I'm a nonunion builder? Since I signed a contract for my crew to work this project, I can be sued for nonperformance. Besides, you left the union when you moved from Cleveland. So this is not your business."

"Aren't I still a man of integrity who respects his fellow workers?"

Turning back to peer out the windshield, Eli thought carefully before answering. The strikers marched back and forth, waving signs and shouting at passing cars. "You're a Plain man now. We report to a higher authority than business owners or labor negotiators."

For a minute or two, a person could hear a pin drop inside the vehicle. Then Jack cleared his throat. "Looks like the strikers are blocking the entrance to the site, not letting anybody cross. They usually do that on the first day. But the police will come to make them abide by the letter of the law."

"What do you suggest, Jack?" Eli asked as calmly as he could manage.

"Why don't I drop the men off at a restaurant in town? They could have coffee and listen to the local news. No doubt it will be the top story on TV and radio. Then you and I can come back and park down the street. We'll walk around, look for the owner, and get a feel for the situation. Nobody will bother us if we're on foot. By tomorrow the police will have established rules for those on the picket line."

"Those are good ideas. Everyone in agreement?" asked Eli, not turning around.

"Sounds fine to me," said Caleb. He was the only man to speak.

৯৯

Caleb thought Monday would never end. He couldn't remember a more onerous day—not down at the union hall waiting for assignments, not during a horrible hangover from drinking, not even walking home on Christmas Eve in a blizzard. By the time Jack and Eli picked them up after stale pie and weak coffee, the picket line was exactly as it had been earlier. Trucks and vans were afraid to cross. Strikers taunted and jeered any tradesman who tried to enter the construction site. Caleb thought his stubborn father would insist that Jack inch the van forward into the parking lot. Not that he was afraid for his physical safety. Although the strikers threw out plenty of trash talk, these plumbers were decent men who went home to families each night and might even attend church on Sundays. No, Caleb feared he would be forced into a showdown with his father—one he wasn't ready for. Although he still carried a union card tucked in his wallet, he'd quit the carpenters' union when he left the city, regardless of his paid-up dues. If he was Amish, then he shouldn't be a member of a labor organization.

He would never vote, sit on a jury, or serve in the armed forces, except in humanitarian capacities. He would pay his taxes, obey the law, and never turn his back on a man in need, whether Amish or *Englisch*, because all that was mandated in Scripture. But he could never place the rules of society above the Lord. Caleb understood all this, but he still didn't want to cross the picket line. Why couldn't they simply wait until the strike was settled? Then they could finish the three weeks of cabinetry without interruption. Most likely the completion date would be pushed back considering that circumstances were beyond their control.

Luckily his father decided not to jump into the fray. Eli had instructed Jack to drive them home. Few crew members talked during the ride. Even Josiah and Daniel seemed uneasy about what they'd seen and heard. After Jack dropped them off, Caleb occupied himself for hours in the barn, allowing his father to explain the situation to his mother. Caleb didn't wish to discuss this with her or his sisters, especially since he hadn't sorted out his plans for tomorrow. What would he do? Jack would surely pick them up at the appointed hour. And if the police had the picketers under control, Eli would take his crew into the building, business as usual.

During supper, Katie entertained the family with stories about the end-of-the-year picnic at school. Then Rebekah described in detail the odd goings-on of two couples at Mrs. Pratt's B&B. Sarah interjected her observations until *Mamm* put a stop to their fascination with *Englisch* tourists. At least none of the Beachy females had heard about the strike in Ashland. Why would they? Just like his *daed* had said—it was of no concern to anyone Amish.

When Caleb finished supper, he left the house for a long walk through the woods. The substantially cooler temperatures under the trees refreshed his spirit. With the morning's events running through his mind, he weighed the various possible outcomes. In the end he did what he should have done in the first place. He sat down on a mossy log and prayed—a habit neglected for a long time. *Please, Lord, show me what to do. How can I honor my father while respecting my fellow man, even if he's an Englischer? Give me patience, give me strength, and most of all give me peace. Let me rest knowing You will take care of this.*

Caleb walked back to the house where his father sat reading in his chair and his mother darned socks in the front room. Briefly he considered joining them, perhaps to pick up the New Testament where he'd left off. But instead he went to bed and slept like a baby that night, deep and dreamless. The next morning, he threw back the covers full of energy. He knew exactly what to do and found his father at the kitchen table with his first cup of coffee.

"Where's *mamm*? Should I get out a box of cereal for us?" he asked.

Eli peered up with red-rimmed eyes. "Let her sleep for another hour. I told Jack to pick everyone up an hour later. We'll give the construction site time to sort things out."

Caleb doubted an hour would make much difference, but he didn't say so. Eager for something to do, he sliced ham off the bone to fry instead of their usual bacon. Taking his lead, Eli cracked eggs into a bowl, added milk, and scrambled them with a fork. After he poured the mixture into a skillet, his father said, "Looks like we can survive one morning without womenfolk taking care of us."

"Who says men are helpless in the kitchen?"

However, by the time Elizabeth arrived downstairs, Caleb had over-cooked the ham and burned the toast while Eli had created a mess in her favorite skillet. Both men were pleased with their efforts. When Rebekah and Sarah left for Country Pleasures and Elizabeth headed to the henhouse for more eggs, Caleb and Eli sat down to eat. It was bliss-fully quiet in the kitchen for a full two minutes.

"Have you given much thought about today, son?" asked Eli. "Will you cross the picket line with us?"

Caleb chewed and swallowed his rubbery ham, and then balanced his fork on the plate. "I couldn't think of much else last night. After I turned the matter over to God, I slept well, surprisingly enough."

"Not surprising to me."

"*Jah*, but you've got more experience with praying than me." Caleb wiped his mouth on a paper towel. "I agree with what you said in the van. If I'm Amish—and that's what I want to be—then a labor strike has nothing to do with me. Part of me hates crossing their line, but I know it's what I must do. You're my boss besides my father. I cannot live in two worlds."

Eli concentrated on his breakfast. "I'm glad prayer helped you make the right decision. Our lives aren't easy. According to Scripture, they're not meant to be. Paradise awaits those who live by Christ's example. But each time you deny your willfulness, the next day becomes a little easier."

Caleb pictured sheep mindlessly following each other into the slaughterhouse, but shook off the image. "I hear Jack's van in the yard. I'll get my tool belt."

❧

When Eli's carpenters arrived in Ashland, they found matters hadn't simmered down at the site. Local police and the sheriff's department were engaged in verbal disputes with several angry strikers. As soon as law enforcement cleared the driveway for a cement hauler, strikers surged from the other side to fill the gap. Two trucks laden with building materials blocked the road with no place to go. Not until the sheriff dragged several men away in handcuffs did the protestors move their picket line onto the sidewalk.

Jack's van crept through the opening in the fence behind a paneled van of nonunion plumbers. However, they did not cross the line unnoticed.

"Respect your fellow workers!" yelled a striker.

"How can you sleep at night?" hollered another.

"Go home, you scabs!"

A few hurled foul language while Caleb and the crew stared straight ahead. Josiah and Daniel turned pale as skim milk. Inside the fence, an armed security guard eyed them carefully as they entered the office carrying tool belts, lunch coolers, and coiled extension cords for Jack and Bob.

The situation outside didn't make for an enjoyable workday, no matter how grade A the quality of wood. No one left to go out for lunch. Jack checked twice on his truck, parked only a hundred feet from the angry strikers. While the men sawed, hammered, and stained, they talked little and joked not at all. Everyone wanted this project finished as soon as possible. Even Bob, who'd been known to take fifteen-minute coffee breaks, never left his sawhorse. Instead he measured and cut, measured and cut, board after board, like a machine. By quitting time, the office for the senior law partners was starting to look magnificent. But no one stood around slapping each other's back or snapping photos with cell phone cameras.

When Eli's crew walked outside with other nonunion tradesmen, Caleb noticed the private security detail had increased by threefold. Local police and the sheriff's department were still positioned at the gate to the complex. The number of strikers hadn't dwindled during the day, despite arrests. In fact, some women had joined their ranks carrying placards. One sign read, "Honk to support the families of Ashland's union plumbers."

Several passing cars honked as Jack's van crawled through the gap in the fence, heading to the county highway. The pickets stepped back to allow them through. No nasty profanity or name-calling rang out as the carpenters remained motionless as statues inside the van. Caleb thought the worst was behind them, that they had survived the ordeal with little personal affront. But as he turned his focus toward the window, a twenty-something man in jeans and a dark T-shirt spit on the glass, inches from Caleb's face. Shame filled every inch of his body. For a brief moment, his throat swelled shut with emotion. Caleb closed his eyes and remained oblivious to his surroundings until out of Ashland. When Jack braked to a stop in his driveway, he staggered from the van like an old man.

"We should finish the contract within two weeks instead of three at the rate we're going," said his father, halfway up the walk. "Then everyone will have a month off to cut hay, plant soybeans or a late corn crop, or help their wives in the garden."

"Time off for the men is a good idea. And I'll stick with the project out of respect for you, but when it's done I quit," said Caleb. "I need to find another job—something far removed from the *Englisch* world, if me becoming fully Amish is ever going to work."

10

How His kindness yet pursues me
Mortal tongue can never tell

For four days, Caleb endured crossing the picket line to work on the new law offices of Ashland. He put up with the strikers' heckling, the hateful glares, the sign waving, and the occasional foul language to prove something to his father...and to himself.

To Eli, he wanted to prove he knew how to take orders like every other working man in America. And to himself he wanted to show he could tamp down his need for individuality and personal expression. An Amish man submitted to his district, to his ministers, and to their *Ordnung*. Caleb might demonstrate these traits, but he hadn't necessarily proved anything. But just like any other learned behavior, progress often begins with baby steps.

At least he had honored his father. And God thought that was important enough to make one of His commandments.

Inside the law offices, work proceeded at a rapid pace. Conference rooms, libraries, executive offices, and break rooms took shape with the best wood, brass, beveled glass, and imported area rugs that money could buy. The construction crew of Eli Beachy would have an accomplishment they could be proud of, if such things mattered to six Amishmen. Even Bob and Jack said little and labored industriously to distance themselves from the dispute as quickly as possible. Most nonunion tradesmen took no pleasure in crossing a picket line.

Today everyone held their breath when the van left the office building for the last time before the weekend. Another five days, maybe six, and they would be done. Relief washed over Caleb like a shower when the van turned onto a rural back road. The sight of farmers in their fields, either on tractors and driving teams of draft horses, salved his soul. This past week he wished he'd become a full-time farmer or a furniture craftsman like Adam Troyer—anything but a carpenter.

Caleb showered as soon as he arrived home. The scent of sage, onion, and celery meant his *mamm* was cooking chicken soup, one of his favorites. After supper, he planned to call on Josie. It had been five days since he'd last seen her pretty face, and he'd become a lonely man. When Caleb exited the bathroom in clean clothes and freshly washed hair, his *daed* was waiting at the table.

"Have a minute, son?" asked Eli.

Crossing his arms, Caleb leaned against the kitchen counter. "Sure. What's on your mind?"

"We've made good progress this week, so you don't have to return to Ashland on Monday."

This was the last thing Caleb expected. "I told you I would finish the project. Are you *firing* me?" He didn't hide his astonishment.

"No, nothing like that. Josiah has a nephew who needs a job. The young man is getting married this fall and wants something more dependable than occasional side work. Josiah says he's good with hand tools." Eli drummed his fingertips on the table. "This past week has been tough, besides a constant reminder of your former life as an *Englischer.* I thought we could end your misery a week early." Eli met Caleb's gaze. Considering the deep lines around his eyes, the week hadn't been easy for his father either.

Caleb's initial thought was the loss of one week's wages. He'd been trying to rebuild his savings since buying the horse and buggy. But Plain men weren't supposed to be overly concerned with money.

Secondly, without a job he would be stuck at home with little to do. Most of the spring planting was already finished.

But giving the position to Josiah's nephew made sense for both of them. Caleb would never be comfortable working for his father, no matter how Amish he became. "*Jah*, it's for the best, I suppose."

Eli stroked his long dark beard. "I'm not good at phrasing things in a diplomatic way. You might have noticed that over the years." He arched an eyebrow and smiled.

It took Caleb several seconds to realize that his father was joking. "Diplomacy isn't a subject taught in school and few are born with a natural ability." He uncrossed his arms, willing himself to relax.

"I wasn't gifted with that particular talent, so I hope you'll take what I'm about to say as advice instead of criticism." Eli allowed a few moments to pass. "Since you came home, you've been concerned solely with yourself: how to readjust to our *Ordnung*, earn a living, buy a rig, and ridding yourself of *Englisch* clothes, tools, habits, and mind-sets. It's time to think about somebody else for a change."

Caleb felt the back of his neck start to sweat. "I've tried to help you and *Mamm* around the farm with chores. I worked for James Weaver without pay in his sugar shack. And I've mediated between Sarah and Rebekah on more than one occasion." He forced a small but sincere smile.

Eli chuckled. "I have noticed, and we're in your debt. But I want you to look beyond our family and neighbors."

"I take it you have someone in mind?"

"I do. Your old friend Albert."

"Albert Sidley?" he asked, despite knowing only one Albert.

Following an affirmative nod, Caleb tried to remember his old pal. Albert had refused to write back after Caleb moved to the city. He had made no effort to get in touch since Caleb returned. Now that their district had split into two, the Sidleys attended preaching services elsewhere. According to Sarah, Albert's family lived in the most woebegone farm in the county after Mrs. Sidley died many years ago. No matter how many frolics the district scheduled to paint, repair, or restock the pantry, conditions returned to normal within a year or two. "What made you think of Albert?" he asked.

"*Ach*, that family is always in need of assistance. Recently I heard that the health of John Sidley has deteriorated, so I doubt things have improved for the boys." Eli pushed up from the table and limped to the sink for a glass of water. Sitting for any length of time stiffened his knees and hips. "If we're looking for people to help, the Sidleys were the first that came to mind. Once you focus on someone else's problems, yours won't seem so burdensome." His voice dropped to a soft caress.

"I might be ready to take advice along those lines, but how do I begin? I haven't talked to Albert in years. Sarah said that when she stopped there to get my Cleveland address, Albert was downright hostile. He's angry that I moved away and never responded to the letters I wrote."

Eli shuffled back to his chair with his water. "Those Sidleys were never easy to reason with or eager to accept the district's help. But maybe Albert will listen to you, Caleb."

"You think one stubborn man might listen to another stubborn man?"

"Something like that." A smile spread across Eli's face—an infrequent expression lately.

Caleb's mind wandered back to his schoolyard and teenage years. He'd gotten along well with Albert. They shared similar interests such as riding, fishing, and exploring the forested hills. One year they'd built a treehouse in the woods about midway between their two farms. Neither of them knew who'd owned the land and to this day, Caleb still didn't know. Carrying canteens, old quilts, and bags of snacks, they met at the treehouse to sleep under the stars on summer nights. While munching cookies, they would invent stories about early pioneers while they waited for deer to come browse the nearby berry bushes. Neither of them hunted deer after watching those gentle does and fawns. Even the bucks seemed trusting and timid—not exactly worthy opponents for high-powered rifles with night vision scopes.

Albert only went squirrel or rabbit hunting after that summer, and only when they needed meat for the stewpot. The Sidleys were always in financial straits. Either their small farm was too worn out to produce or his *daed* was too untalented or lazy to coax much from the soil. Caleb suspected John Sidley drank in secret, but Albert refused to talk about it. When Mrs. Sidley died giving birth to her fourth son, life on that hardscrabble homestead went from bad to worse.

Feeling a sorrowful pang of nostalgia, Caleb met his father's eye. "I'll go Monday after morning chores to see if there's anything I can do to help."

"You'll find plenty if you're looking for holes to patch in the roof or fences to mend. That house should probably be torn down and a new one built. I'm hoping you'll look beyond the surface. Maybe you can give Albert something that will change the rest of his life."

Caleb scratched a mosquito bite. "You mean teach him carpentry?"

"If he's willing to learn, but I wouldn't suggest that right after 'hello.' Start with getting the Sidleys straightened around, but make sure Albert works with you. They have too much done for them and that could be part of the problem. Too many kind folks cleaning up the mess and sticking a bandage on their problems. Albert might slam the door on your good intentions, but it's worth a try."

"I agree. He might be willing to learn after all these years. Sitting around feeling sorry for yourself gets boring after a while. I know it did for me up in Cleveland." Caleb hadn't meant to divulge that detail, but it slipped out unintentionally.

Eli let the comment slide. "I plan to pay your wages for next week while you're at Albert's."

His chin snapped up. "That's not necessary. If I'm no longer working for you, I shouldn't get paid."

"You had planned to work another week before quitting. Besides, whatever help you give them relieves the district of its burden for a while. Believe me, you might discover the task more challenging than the Ashland office building, even in the middle of a labor disagreement."

"A week, no more. I won't take charity if an Amish man is supposed to give without expecting anything in return."

"One week," agreed Eli. "Now I need to find out why my gourmet supper hasn't been started yet."

"Maybe because *Mamm* is no gourmet," Caleb joked, experiencing a level of compassion that had been as long absent as his father's smile.

❧

On Sunday morning Josie repinned her hair for the third time, attempting to contain all stragglers neatly inside the bun.

"I don't understand why you're fussing so much," said Laura. Her *schwester* had entered the bedroom they shared very quietly. "It'll be hidden under your *kapp* anyway."

"I want to look nice at my first membership class."

Laura flounced down on her twin bed. "But why bother? Unless a *special person* will be at the class." She dragged out her words for emphasis.

Josie put on her head covering and studied her reflection in their small hand mirror. Her face was already tanned. She'd better switch to her wide-brimmed bonnet whenever working in the garden. "You're right about someone special. My best friend in the whole world will be there. If I get there early, I plan to save her a seat." After a final perusal, Josie added a slicker of ChapStick, loving how it tasted like lemonade.

"Sarah isn't the Beachy I had in mind. Didn't you wear your favorite dress for Caleb?" She tugged the hem of Josie's apron.

Deciding that Laura wouldn't be easily put off, Josie sat down and took hold of her younger sibling's hand. "I'm not sure if Cal will show up or not. But if he does, I want to look my prettiest."

Laura's eyebrows shot to her hairline. "Rumors are true—you are sweet on him."

"I am."

"*Mamm* hoped he was just a passing fancy," Laura whispered into her ear. "A phase that you were going through."

"She said that?" Josie was shocked that her mother would talk about such a personal matter.

Laura nodded. "*Jah*, but she didn't know I was listening."

"You shouldn't eavesdrop. One day you might overhear something you wish you hadn't."

"Aren't you afraid Caleb will get bored and move back to the city? Then you will have wasted precious courting time on a dead end. You're twenty-one, almost twenty-two." She lowered her voice as though Josie's age were a big secret.

"I was at first, so I asked him. He assured me he wasn't leaving and that he planned to join our church. I'm willing to take his word and give him a chance. For all I know Cal might chew with his mouth open or burp loudly in public. Then it won't make any difference if he gets baptized." Josie walked to their bedroom door and grabbed her purse off the hook.

"Sounds like you haven't heard the news."

Josie stopped in her tracks. "What news?"

"David told me James told him that Cal quit his job." Laura joined her in the hallway.

"How could he quit? His boss is his father."

"I don't know. Maybe it's just a rumor that isn't true. Let's go before everyone leaves without us. I just heard the buggy stop by the steps. We don't want *Mamm* to start yelling."

"Indeed, we don't." Josie followed her down the steps in a mood that was rapidly deteriorating. Caleb quit his job? As bad signs went—that one had to be the worst.

The buggy ride to the hosting farm was long and hot. Her brother kept bumping her shoulder while her sisters wouldn't quit chattering about nonsense.

Finally her father spoke in an unarguable tone of voice. "Silence. Let's prepare ourselves for worship by stilling our tongues and opening our hearts." Josie had a few quiet moments to pray that she wasn't skipping merrily down a dead-end street like Laura suggested.

After *Daed* dropped them near the house, he parked the buggy in the recently mown hayfield. The Zook family held services outdoors in a spacious outbuilding. Since the benches had been delivered during the week, people clustered near the open door waiting to be summoned inside. Two lines—one male and one female—would soon form to fill the benches in an orderly fashion. Josie headed inside the house for her first of eight membership classes. She'd already chewed off her flavored lip balm, her dress was sticking to her back, and her face felt like she'd coated it with olive oil. But when she entered the kitchen, her heart skipped a beat. Scanning the rows of folding chairs that filled the room, she spotted Sarah and Caleb in the back row. Sarah lifted her hand in a wave, while Caleb pointed at the empty seat between them.

Bishop Beachy cleared his throat. "If you would sit down, Miss Yoder, we're ready to start."

Josie hadn't noticed him standing with his Bible clutched to his *mustfa* vest. "*Guder mariye,* Bishop." She hurried to the chair before another late arrival grabbed it.

"What took you so long?" asked Sarah near her ear.

"It's about time," said Caleb. "I was ready to let the swarm of single women fight over that chair." The two siblings whispered simultaneously.

Josie grinned at both of them until her face cramped. Any attempt to form words in her current state of mind would only result in an embarrassing squeak.

"*Welcum*, young people," the bishop greeted after clearing his throat. "You have come because you wish to learn the meaning of *Gelassenheit*. Our *Deutsch* word means many things, including resignation, composure, long-suffering, collectedness, calmness of mind, inner surrender, victory over selfishness, and detachment. My favorite definition is 'quietly residing in Christ.' If it is your wish to be baptized and join the church, then rise to your feet and repeat after me."

Every person in the Zook kitchen stood and repeated after the bishop. "I am a seeker desiring to be part of this church of God."

Eli gestured for them to sit. "We will begin each class with that statement of intention. If at any time you choose not to continue, you can come back next year. There is no shame in waiting. This is the most important decision of your life, and shouldn't be entered into without considerable contemplation." When no one got up to leave, the bishop began his first lesson.

Josie had known Sarah's father her entire life. But today he wasn't pushing them on the tire swing or comforting Sarah after she scraped a knee or got stung by a bee. The bishop was all business. He didn't crack a smile until they solemnly filed out to join their parents in church.

"Try to be on time next week, Josie," said Eli. "I would hate for you to miss a single minute of my instruction."

"I will, Bishop," she said as she walked by.

Sarah was waiting for her on the path, but Caleb had already entered the barn with the other men. "What did my *daed* say?"

"Be on time in two weeks." Josie shivered as they walked toward the open doors.

"Don't worry. He always liked you."

Josie had no chance to ask Sarah if Laura's rumor about Caleb was true. With the service underway, they slipped in silently without dilly-dallying. When preaching concluded several hours later, they both had to help the women set out lunch. After she placed her cornbread with the other desserts, Josie stood behind the table as men moved through the buffet.

Caleb appeared second in line, preceded by his pal, James Weaver.

"Cal, James, how about a slice of cold roast beef?" Rebekah Beachy materialized out of nowhere with a long-handled fork.

"*Jah,* please." They both held out their plates.

Rebekah slapped a slice on her *bruder*'s plate without hesitation, but searched for the most succulent piece in the roaster for James. "This one should cut with your fork," she purred, adding a ladleful of brown gravy.

"Say, Josie," said Caleb. "I see potato, macaroni, and cucumber salads, but my heart was set on four-bean." He brought the forward movement of hungry men to a dead stop.

"Not today, Cal. Please select from the bounty the Lord has provided." Josie flourished her hand over the assortment of side dishes. "I will make some for our next gathering." Smirking, she spooned marinated beets next to his beef and focused on the next man.

When it was the women's turn to eat, she got in line as quickly as possible without knocking down elderly *grossmammis* with their canes. Paying little attention to her food selections, Josie searched the crowd with a keen eye for a certain tall man.

Caleb leaned against a tree to eat, without the benefit of a flat surface.

She crossed the lawn at an amazing speed. "Why didn't you sit at a picnic table? That beef isn't as fork-tender as your sister implied." When he trained his dark eyes on her, her knees went weak.

"I wanted to take no chances on missing you," he said. "I don't care if the meat is tougher than boot leather."

Josie glanced around before lowering herself to the grass. Crossing her legs Indian style, she pulled her dress down discreetly. "I wanted to talk to you about something too."

"That's *gut* to hear. Why don't you go first?" He plopped down on the lawn beside her.

"My sister Laura heard a rumor that you quit your job. Is it true?"

The corners of his mouth dropped. "It's no rumor. I left on Friday. I would have stayed another week, but my father has already replaced me. A new carpenter from Killbuck is ready to start." Caleb hacked at the beef with his pocketknife.

Josie shooed away a gnat that refused to leave her coleslaw alone. "May I ask why you quit? Jobs aren't easy to come by in Wayne County." She blanched, knowing she sounded exactly like her mother.

"Several reasons, but mainly because my father usually works with *Englisch* contractors. At least for now, I prefer not to be reminded of my old life on a daily basis." Caleb chewed his meat with deliberate slowness, not taking his eyes off her.

"Is your *daed* mad about you leaving his company?"

"Not in the least. He gave me an idea for work that I'll look into on Monday." He swallowed and frowned. "What's this about, Josie? Are you afraid my quitting means I intend to leave town?" He set his plate in the grass.

"I suppose I was a little worried." She ate every one of her baby beets without breaking stride.

"Ye of little faith." He lifted her chin with a finger. "Lots of Amish men quit their jobs. I told you I'm here to stay. Even if you decide I'm the last man you wish to court, I'm not packing my bags. I'll cry my eyes out right here in Fredericksburg, surrounded by my family."

"You would cry your eyes out over me?" Josie set her plate atop his.

"Most likely for a few months. Then I would probably suffer in silence." He took a celery stick from her plate to nibble.

Relief washed over her. "Crying, at least for now, is premature and unnecessary." She grinned as he popped a cherry tomato in his mouth. "I was really happy to see you in class. *Danki* for saving me a seat."

"I told you my intentions. Where I find a job or how I earn a living has nothing to do with joining the church." He reached for the last tomato, but she grabbed his hand with a firm grip.

"You should know that there are ants crawling all over those plates."

Caleb peered at their lunch with a scowl. "And you couldn't have mentioned that first?"

"I was saving the best for last."

&c.

Sarah peeked around the craggy willow tree again. Each time she spied on her brother and her best friend, her exhilaration ratcheted up a notch. Josie and Caleb. If they continued to gaze at each other like that, *Mumm* and *Daed* might as well plan a double wedding in December. Nothing could make her happier than having Josie for a sister-in-law. They would become family, as well as the closest pals in the world.

She'd had her doubts Caleb would show up at class until he followed her into the Zook kitchen. Whenever he and their father argued about work, Caleb withdrew deeper inside his shell. Working with *Daed* wouldn't be easy because they were too much alike. Two people exactly the same usually rubbed each other wrong. Maybe that's why she and Rebekah seldom agreed on anything. They were both stubborn and opinionated. If there was a person in the world who could keep Caleb on the correct path, it was Josie Yoder. Who could resist those emerald green eyes? Caleb was a goner, and Sarah was pleased as punch.

"Who are you spying on?"

Sarah jumped a foot at the sound of a male voice, spilling her iced tea down her dress. "Adam, look what you've done! Now I'm all wet."

"I'm sorry. I didn't mean to scare you," he said. Joining her side, he peeped around the willow tree. "Caleb and Josie—that's what has you fascinated? You already knew they were courting."

"True, but Caleb quit his job last Friday and I wanted to make sure that didn't make a difference to Josie." Sarah stole another glance around the massive trunk and then brushed bark from her palms. "Looks like it didn't. Let's get something to eat. There's no more line at the buffet." She took a step toward the tables.

Adam tugged on her sleeve. "Why did Caleb quit his job? I thought he loved carpentry and construction. There aren't that many Amish contractors in Wayne County and none can line up as much work as Eli."

"He left because of the temptation to slide back into old bad habits." With her mind at ease regarding her future sister-in-law, Sarah was famished. She shook off his restraint.

Her comment silenced Adam long enough for them to load their plates with sliced roast beef and cold salads. "Your family doesn't own enough land to do any serious farming." Adam balanced a glass of lemonade on his plate.

Sarah decided to wait for more tea since she was wearing her first glass. "He's going to visit Albert Sidley tomorrow to help him fix up their farm. That's all I know." She headed toward a table of other courting couples in the shade, many of whom had been in her membership class.

Adam latched onto her sleeve a second time. "Let's sit somewhere where we can talk privately."

After scanning the Zook backyard, they walked to a pair of webbed chairs near the garden. A bower of grapevines offered some cool, midday relief from the scorching sun. "You must admit the Sidleys certainly can use help. I was a tad frightened when I called on them last summer. Their driveway had so many potholes, I feared my mare would twist an ankle and end up lame." She wrapped two slices of bread around her beef to eat as a sandwich. Slathered with mayonnaise, the beef wouldn't taste so dry.

"You had no business going alone," said Adam. "If you hadn't chosen to be secretive, I could have taken you after my shift or on Saturday." When he bit into his tomato, seeds and juice sprayed his pressed white shirt.

"*Gut,* now we're both a mess." Chuckling, she stretched out her long legs. "Do you think Albert Sidley will ever join the church? He might if Caleb renews their friendship. This could be the best thing for both of them."

Adam dabbed at his soiled shirt to no avail. The orange blotch darkened against the fabric. Tossing the paper napkin to the ground, he swiveled to face her. "I don't know him well enough to form an opinion. But could we talk about a subject other than Caleb and Josie or Albert perhaps?"

Sarah cocked her head on one side. "I suppose. What topic did you have in mind?"

"Us—you and me." A bright pink flush rose up Adam's neck. "Do you know how relieved I was to see you in the membership class this morning?"

Frowning, she lowered her sandwich and wiped her mouth. "You knew I would be there."

"*Jah*, but now that you've stated your intentions we can plan our future. As soon as you're baptized we can announce our engagement. We could be married by Christmas." When he attempted to cut his beef, the plastic knife snapped in half.

"It occurred to me that Josie and Caleb might want a double wedding this fall. After all, many of our guests will be the same." She pressed a hand to her mouth. "Oh, dear, I just brought up the forbidden subject."

Adam shook his head, fighting back a grin. "You're impossible, but I'm hopelessly smitten with you, like a bug trapped in a spiderweb. Just don't get too far ahead of yourself with Cal."

Sarah leaned over to pat his cheek. "You're the cutest bug in our district. What else is there to discuss? It's too soon for me to buy fabric and make my dress." She finished off her sandwich in three bites.

"It's not too soon to talk about where you'd like to live. Since my *bruders* help *Daed* with the farm, the eldest will live in the big house when my parents move into the *dawdi haus*. Right now James lives with my grandparents to help with chores. The other two have already built homes on Troyer land. I thought we could buy a small parcel midway between my job at the factory and your parents so you wouldn't be too far from your family. Maybe three or four acres, just enough to pasture our buggy horse, along with a nice garden plot."

"Buggy *horses*," she corrected. "I need my own rig. How would I get to quilting or to *Mamm's*? Don't even think of locking me in the house, cut off from the world." She angled a suspicious expression.

"Of course not. I meant to say *horses*—plural." He jammed the beef inside his biscuit and took a bite. After a full minute of chewing, Adam was able to swallow and speak. "Would you prefer a newer ranch house, a farmhouse to fix up, or open land on which to build? If it's the latter, I need to look for available acres now so I can build in the fall. We can start with one bath and two bedrooms and then add more rooms as needs arise." His face blushed to a shade that rivaled the ripest Beefsteak tomato.

Sarah fluttered her eyelashes. "What do you mean, Mr. Troyer? Why on earth would we need more than our bedroom and one guest room?"

A bead of sweat formed above his lip as he pushed to his feet. "No one can hold a serious discussion with you. I'm going to dump the trash and pick out our desserts. If you haven't composed yourself by the time I return, I'll wave over your father. Then you can repeat what you said to him." Adam buzzed her brow with a kiss before marching across the yard.

"I'll concentrate on sad thoughts while you're gone," she hollered, "so hurry back."

How she loved to tease him. How she loved that man.

11

How His kindness yet pursues me
Mortal tongue can never tell

Caleb jumped out of bed at the regular hour even though as of today, he'd joined the ranks of the unemployed. In Cleveland he would have signed up for government compensation during periods of layoff. The weekly check, although not close to his normal salary, still kept a roof over his head and the lights on.

Now the house where he lived didn't have electric lights anyway.

Although the Amish never collected unemployment, workers' compensation, or Social Security, few worried about where their next meal would come from or where they would live. Caleb had never heard of homeless Plain folks. Families or district members stepped in and shared whatever they had. If he developed the same mind-set, his future would no longer seem so frightening.

Downstairs, he found his father doing paperwork at the kitchen table. "Getting ready for the new man to start?" Caleb poured a cup of coffee.

Eli peered over his reading glasses. "I am, always another form to fill out. I've been thinking...would you like me to send Bob along for a few days at the Sidleys'? You might need his help, at least in the beginning. And Bob wouldn't mind getting away from the Ashland plumber strike."

Caleb didn't need much time to consider. "No, Albert never cared for *Englischers*. He always thought they were staring at him, even when they weren't."

"Will you be okay by yourself?" His *daed* took a muffin from the plate.

"Of course. Why wouldn't I? Albert and I used to be friends. Even if he doesn't want my help, he's not going to shoot me with his squirrel rifle."

Eli buttered the cornbread without breaking eye contact. "No, John Sidley would use his shotgun filled with pellets."

"I will be fine," Caleb said, his bravado slipping a notch.

"In that case your *mamm* packed plenty of sandwiches to take." Eli pointed at a hamper near the door. "She's sending jars of vegetables, pickled meat, and fruit preserves too. Who knows how well those five men eat with no *fraa* in the *haus*?"

When a car horn drew their attention, Caleb followed Eli onto the porch. "Hi, Jack, Bob," he called as the van pulled to a stop.

Bob rolled down his window while Jack popped open the back for Eli's briefcase and blueprints. "Where's your tool belt, Cal?"

With as few words as possible, Caleb explained why he'd quit his job, along with his plans for the immediate future. Then he wished for a speedy resolution to the strike. No one man seemed surprised by his decision. Before the van could reach the county road, Caleb had hitched his horse and loaded the hamper, his thermos, and tools into the buggy. For a brief instant, he considered borrowing a battery powered Sawzall and cordless drill from the neighbor, but he reconsidered. *Ordnung* was *Ordnung*—whether the bishop was there as witness or not. Besides, Roy Pratt probably wouldn't have charged them anyway.

During the hour-long drive to the Sidleys', Caleb viewed the countryside. Each year the number of farms shrank while the number of houses increased. At this rate there would be no land left in the county to grow food. Even among the Amish, farms were frequently split up between sons into smaller and smaller plots.

Caleb sighed as he turned onto Albert's road. Sarah hadn't exaggerated the condition of the roadbed. Some ruts were deep enough to break an axle. After half a mile, Caleb passed a sign announcing: WARNING—TOWNSHIP ROAD CLOSED. TRAVEL AT YOUR OWN RISK. The Sidley mailbox leaned crookedly against the sign. Even the postman refused to endanger his vehicle by delivering an occasional tax bill or supermarket flyer.

"A little late for the warning, no?" Caleb asked his gelding.

Although the horse had no reply, when he reached the next cavernous pothole he shook his silky mane and refused to step around it. Caleb climbed down to walk the remaining distance, keeping a tight grip on the bridle. *Not a good omen*, he thought. And nothing changed his mind the closer they came to the one-hundred-fifty-year-old homestead.

Poison ivy vines entwined every upright post. Strands of barbed wire, which substituted for missing fence slats, had rusted to the point of uselessness. Caleb soon understood why the Sidleys had little motivation for fence repair. Five Holsteins with saggy udders and sad faces chewed their cud with no interest in escaping. They barely turned their heads as Caleb's buggy passed just yards away. An ancient windmill stood sentinel on the far hill, its blade long corroded into immovability.

However, the landscape appeared practically Eden-like compared to the ramshackle house. Paint had chipped and peeled down to bare wood on the side exposed to prevailing winds. The front porch canted at an angle due to a collapsed corner of the stone foundation. A smoke stack now poked through a hole where a chimney had toppled long ago. Blue plastic patched the opening while strategically placed wires held the metal pipe upright. Only half the home's windows contained panes of glass. The rest either had cardboard tacked in place or were open to the wind, rain, and flying insects.

Caleb muttered a vulgar word—residue of his years on an *Englisch* construction crew—and shook his head in frustration. After tying the reins to a scrawny sapling he ambled toward the back door. He didn't know if he should chance the rotted porch boards or simply yell to the inhabitants to come outside. Opting for polite behavior, Caleb sprang up the steps and knocked. He waited for a full minute and then knocked again, harder.

"You can pound on that door all day long. *Daed* ain't gittin' outta that chair to answer."

Caleb spun around on his boot heel to gaze into the hooded, gray eyes of Albert Sidley. Five years had done the man no favors. He had always been tall and rangy, but now his clothes hung from him like a scarecrow's rags. At twenty-five, Sidley could easily be mistaken for forty. A shameful lump rose up Caleb's throat as though he were personally responsible for his friend's deterioration. "Albert, it's me, Caleb Beachy." He tipped his hat and smiled.

"I know who you are. I ain't addlebrained." Albert shifted his weight between hips just as a yellow dog wandered up to sniff the intruder's leg.

Caleb stood very still, not trusting the dog's intentions. "I've come home, been back since December. I was wondering how you were."

Albert's hooded lids drooped. "Took ya six months to come 'round? Sounds like I wasn't the top of your list of priorities."

Albert so badly mispronounced the final word Caleb needed a moment to decipher it. "I helped James Weaver make maple sugar until the sap stopped running, and then I went to work for my *daed*."

"How'd that work out?" Albert reached down to ruffle the dog's fur. The mutt's leg began scratching his hind flank in reflex.

"Not so well." Caleb laughed, relaxing somewhat. "This morning he replaced me with a carpenter from a town south of Millersburg."

Nodding, Albert glanced over his shoulder as a younger sibling approached.

"Is that your little *bruder*, Elijah?" Caleb stared at the boy. Although not as thin or wasted appearing as Albert, Elijah was muddy from head to toe.

"Who else?" Albert mumbled. "He's been mucking out the hog pen and apparently he forgot to use a shovel."

Elijah stopped ten feet from Caleb. "We got us a pregnant hog this *Englischer* didn't want no more. Now we got eleven piglets. We'll have us some good ham and bacon to smoke come fall." His smile revealed white teeth in stark contrast to his dirty face.

"You go on now and shower off," Albert spoke softly. "And put on some clean duds too. Leave those on the porch. I want to visit my old pal without you for an audience." Unlike Elijah's, Albert's clothes were clean. Plus someone had sewn a cloth patch over the right knee.

Elijah sauntered off with the dog at his heels. Once he reached the porch, the boy stripped bare as the day he was born. The dog ran off as soon as Elijah entered the house.

Caleb watched, speechless with shock. No Amish person would ever disrobe in front of strangers, especially not outdoors. Of course, normal Amish homes were neat and tidy beyond reproach. Throughout his entire life, Caleb had never seen a farm in such a miserable state of disrepair. "Where are your other *bruders*?" asked Caleb, eager for conversation to dispel his growing uneasiness. Although barely nine o'clock, sweat ran down and dripped off his chin.

"If we're gonna chat, let's sit in the shade." Albert pointed at two lime green chairs under a tree. Along the way, he offered a full explanation for the unusual color. "Somebody threw a can of paint out their car window. I found it in the ditch, and there was enough to paint these chairs. First I sanded them to bare metal so the rust wouldn't come back so fast."

"They look good. And they still rock somewhat too." As Caleb leaned back to demonstrate his focus landed on a doghouse, perhaps home to the yellow mongrel. Like the two chairs, the doghouse sported a fresh coat of paint along with a red shingled roof. Fresh straw poked from the opening and covered the ground all around the doghouse. Compared to the Sidley residence, the dog's accommodations were downright luxurious. "Tell me about your family." Caleb turned his attention back to his friend.

"My *bruder* Joe went to Indiana to look for work. The second youngest is hiding out in the woods somewhere. Tobias will be back for supper. An empty belly brings him home every night."

"How's your father?" Caleb interlaced his fingers across his belly.

Albert's sociable expression faded to one of pure contempt. "How do ya think he is? Barely gets off the couch these days. Sometimes I gotta bring him supper on a tray like this was some kinda hotel. *Daed* chows it down without even bothering to sit up." Albert shook his head, sending his lank hair into his eyes. "But at least he quit drinking."

At long last, the truth about his suspicion. "There's a blessing," Caleb said.

Albert snorted. "Too late to make any difference. Only reason *Daed* stopped is because he's too weak to walk up into the hills. He made corn whiskey for years at a still he built. One night Joe and I followed him when he thought we were doin' our chores."

"Nobody ever found out about the still?"

"Nope. *Daed* never told anyone and never sold any whiskey. When Joe and I caught him red-handed, he said it was for medicinal purposes." Albert spat on the ground. "How stupid did he think we were? *Medicine?* Liquor is the reason his liver and lungs are shot." Releasing the weariest of sighs, Albert leaned back and closed his eyes as though taking a nap.

Caleb was uncertain what to do. Should he keep up the banter of conversation? Creep away silently and come back tomorrow? Or close his eyes and try to catch forty winks? "Sorry to hear about your father's health," he said after a pause.

"You were curious 'bout my family…well, now you've got your answers." Albert spoke without opening his eyelids. "As for me? I'm fine and dandy, but this place might blow away in the next strong wind."

"How come the district hasn't helped with a frolic?" Caleb asked hesitantly, unsure about his friend's pride.

Albert took no offense. "They tried plenty of frolics over the years you were gone. At first *Daed* let them come and just stayed out of their way. Afterward he complained about those nosy do-gooders, and why can't folks just mind their own business. But he sure dug into the food they left behind." Albert shook his head. "And he never refused new quilts or blankets with the cold winters we've been havin'. For the last couple years, he stopped letting folks inside the house." Albert pinned Caleb with haunted eyes. "I think he's afraid people will notice how sick he is and take him to a hospital. Or maybe a nursing home. Every day he says he wants to die right here where he was born."

"I don't think outsiders can force him to leave."

Albert spat again next to his chair. "We'll see 'bout that if *Englischers* get involved. When the district came for the last frolic, *Daed* ran them off with scatter shot. If you shoot at people, they usually don't come back." Albert moistened his lips with his tongue.

"You got a point there." Caleb turned his focus toward the back door.

"Don't worry. *Daed's* probably passed out. Or maybe he recognized you when you walked up the drive. I think he used to like you, so he probably won't shoot." Albert's voice contained a hint of his former self.

"Hopefully he still likes me, because I aim to be a one-man work frolic." Caleb pushed up from the lime green chair.

"You're joking, right?"

"*Nein*. I have no job, but I've got tools and I'm strong like a bull." Caleb flexed a bicep as some of his old personality returned. "With your help we can fix up this place. Not to tour-of-homes caliber, but maybe how it was when your *mamm* was alive."

Albert reflected for a moment. "I've kept the roof patched. If you let rain get in, you'll end up with crumbling walls and buckling floors."

"In that case, our job won't even be very hard." Caleb grinned wryly.

"*Ach*, materials cost money. I ain't got any and you just lost a job with a paycheck."

"Let me worry about materials. My *daed* works commercial construction. You've got no idea how much stuff is thrown in the dumpster at the end of each project. *Daed* has plenty stored in our old barn as long as you're not that particular."

Albert scratched the thick beard on his chin—something a single Amish man wasn't permitted to grow. "Look around—do we look picky? But why are you doin' this? What's in it for you?"

Caleb knew better than to reply carelessly. "I ran into trouble in Cleveland. Now I have things to live down that I don't want to talk about. I'm not an *Englischer*, but I don't feel very Amish either. If we work together this summer, maybe I can forget the past and start over."

Albert gazed over a weedy pasture where his yellow dog chased an unseen critter. Overhead, buzzards circled ominously while the oppressive sun slipped behind a cloud. "Stuck in between worlds, eh? That's pretty much how I feel. We might as well give it a try. I ain't got nothing better to do." Without another word, Albert rose and started walking toward the barn.

Caleb jumped to his feet to follow. After all, they would have time for more small talk in the weeks to come.

On Saturday evening, Josie waited for Caleb with far too much
anticipation regarding their second date. She hadn't been able to keep
her mind on chores all week. Josie and her sisters picked strawberries
until their spines were as bent as ninety-year-olds and juice permanently stained their fingers. Then she and *Mamm* canned twenty-five
pints of strawberry preserves, enough to last through winter. Since
Caleb had a long buggy ride home after work, he no longer had time
to sit on her porch in the evening. But she would see him tonight, and
unless she stopped grinning, her family would know how head over
heels in love she'd fallen with Sarah's prodigal brother.

Caleb's horse trotted up their drive at exactly the appointed hour.
Josie flew down the steps to greet him before his buggy rolled to a stop.
"*Guder nachmittag!* How are you, Cal?"

"Fine and dandy, Miss Yoder." He jumped down and leaned against
the wheel. "You look particularly fetching in that purple dress."

"*Danki*, but this shade is called mauve, not purple." Josie clasped
her hands behind her back.

"Going to be one of those afternoons, *jah*?" Caleb winked.

"Yep. After spending five days with Yoder females, I'm in rare form."

"In that case, where would you like to go? We could get pizza in
Shreve, or try that tourist buffet, or maybe go for ice cream? We probably shouldn't attempt the movies unless we want to end up on your
daed's bad side." Laughing, he ducked his head with embarrassment.

"No, we don't need to spend money to have fun."

Caleb's head snapped up. "I'm not broke, Josie. I've got last week's
paycheck, plus extra put aside from the previous week."

"Don't get your dander up. I only meant I prefer a picnic down by
the gristmill. It's cool by the river, and without horses around we won't
be bothered by flies." She scratched the gelding's muzzle.

"In that case, I'll turn this old swayback into the paddock and wash
up at the pump. Your plan sounds better than mine."

"I'll get our lunch and meet you behind the barn." Josie ran to the
house and quickly loaded the food into a hamper. When she spotted her

father cutting the strawberry pie she'd baked for Caleb, she refrained from pulling the plate from his hand. Going dessert-less would be better than not going at all...or with one of her sisters along to chaperone.

Caleb stood waiting on the path, hat in hand. "I was afraid you'd changed your mind."

"It's only been ten minutes. You need to slow your expectations to Amish time." As soon as she spoke, she regretted her thoughtlessness. Caleb didn't need to be reminded of his former estrangement.

But Caleb didn't seem to mind. "You're not kidding. I'm learning how long repairs take without an *Englischer* with power tools nearby and with only unskilled helpers."

Josie fell into an easy stride at his side. "Are you referring to work at the Sidleys'? How's that going?"

"It's going better than I figured. According to Albert, the foundation and walls of the house are sound, but I've yet to step inside."

"He doesn't want you to see how they live." Josie shuddered involuntarily. Having been to a frolic there a long time ago, she preferred never to return.

"Maybe, but eventually he'll have to let me in. We've already repaired the fence around the entire farm with posts I found out back and an extra roll of barbed wire from *Daed*. The pasture will need to be disked and reseeded in the fall, but grass will have to wait. First we'll install a new roof on the barn with rubber leftover from the Millersburg warehouse. Like my father, Bob has saved all kinds of stuff in his pole barn. He dropped off roofing materials yesterday, and said he will bring more as needed."

"Very generous of him. Does Albert help, or are you doing all the labor yourself?"

Caleb shrugged. "Albert works very hard and he has some good ideas. Lately, his brother Elijah has also started pitching in."

"That surprises me. None of the Sidleys worked at the frolic I attended. They stood on the porch steps, scowling." Josie shivered a second time, remembering the scruffy condition of the youngest boy.

"It's different with only me there." Caleb reached for her hand once they were beyond view of the house. "I've noticed a change in all of them within five days."

"How so?" She loved the strong feel of his callused hand around hers.

"Elijah took a bath and put on clean clothes."

Josie burst out laughing.

"It's not funny. That family needs our prayers, not our ridicule." Caleb's admonishment was soft as a baby's breath.

"*Mir leid*, forgive my reaction. I will pray for the Sidleys tonight. And request a dose of sensitivity for me."

"You're already a sensitive woman." Caleb kissed the back of her fingers. "But it's hard dealing with folks so long away from the Amish flock."

"Why do you suppose they live like hermits? Does John still grieve for his late wife?"

As the historic gristmill loomed into view, Caleb paused on the path to admire. "I think there's more to his separation than grief. John has had a drinking problem for years. Now alcohol has damaged his health." Caleb's hand tightened around hers. "That information isn't to be repeated. I don't want my friend's family subject to cruel gossip."

Josie squeezed his fingers in return. "You have my word, Caleb. I'm glad you called Albert your friend—sounds like he sure could use one."

"You've got no idea." Caleb snaked his arm around her waist, pulling her close. "He told me about his father firing pellets at district members. John doesn't want people to see how bad things are."

Josie thought for a moment and then spoke frankly. "You can't help people without their cooperation. And where on earth did John Sidley buy alcohol? He would have to take his buggy to Wooster or to Millersburg. I can't imagine him traveling so far very often. People would find out."

Caleb also reflected before replying. "He had a still up in the woods."

"The wild, wild West, right here in Fredericksburg?"

"This isn't funny."

"I'm not poking fun, but you must admit this is an unbelievable situation that apparently went on behind the bishop's back."

"True enough. I doubt my *daed* knows. He thinks Sidley is still depressed about losing his *fraa* in childbirth. And if John found a new wife, all would be well."

"Not for the new wife in that kitchen," Josie muttered, and then held up her palms. "I'm sorry. I promised not to poke fun, but that house scares me. During the frolic I used their outhouse because it was the lesser of two evils."

"That's what I aim to fix." Caleb steadied her arm as they picked their way down to the gristmill. Tall grass and tumbled stones had turned the trail treacherous. "Tell me this place doesn't inspire awe, even without a roof." Caleb cleverly changed the subject from the Sidleys.

"It's my favorite spot in three counties." Josie ducked her head to enter the low doorway. "This piece of history warms my heart on even the coldest winter day."

He led her to a low wall where she spread her small quilt. "Mine too. It's a good spot to clear your head of cobwebs." Caleb sat and dangled his legs over the edge.

"Are you certain John Sidley is ill?" Josie pulled a thermos of tea from the hamper.

Caleb nodded. "According to Albert, he's very sick. He sleeps most of the day and can barely sit up to eat his meals."

Dropping her chin, Josie uttered a prayer for the man she had so recently mocked. *Please, Lord, I pray for John's recovered health or his painless passing to the life yet to come.* When she opened her eyes, she saw Caleb was also in prayer. "Will you talk to your father about how the district could help him?"

"No, I will not." Caleb locked eyes with her. "John Sidley fears being taken from his house. It might not meet our standards, but it is his home."

"He probably needs to see a doctor and be put on medication. Without proper care, he might die." Josie handed him a drink.

Caleb kicked a clump of debris on the plank floor. "*Jah,* he probably will."

Josie reached for his hand. "When your dog was sick, you took Shep to the vet. Would you do any less for a human being?"

Every ounce of color drained from Caleb's face, while a vein bulged from the side of his neck.

"Forgive me. I've said too much and overstepped the boundaries of friendship."

"*Nein*, you have every right to voice your opinion…even if you weren't my girl." His lips curled into a smile. "And since you are my girl, feel free to overstep the boundaries left and right." He drained the contents of his glass as she spread the containers of food across the quilt.

"Did you speak to him?" Josie spread the containers of food across the quilt.

"No, we've had plenty to keep us busy outdoors, but soon I will speak to John. Albert thinks if a doctor or someone from the county comes, they will cart his father away in an ambulance. Who knows what laws *Englischers* have invented regarding old people? John would surely die of sorrow in a hospital. Albert doesn't want this on his conscience and neither do I."

She nodded. "I trust you will do the right thing."

"As long as God shows me what that is. If given the chance, I'll try to convince John to seek medical help. You can rest assured of that."

Josie wrapped her arms around his neck and hugged him in an improper fashion for two people who hadn't announced their engagement. "You're a good man, Cal Beachy."

"So are you, Josie Yoder. Although I recently noticed you're not a man at all." His laughter lifted the somber mood in the ancient mill.

"I'll not talk about this to anyone and I will keep the Sidleys in my prayers. In the meantime, let's eat. This is a picnic, no?"

"It is." Caleb took a chicken breast and picked off the breading piece by piece. "This tastes *gut*. Who made this, your *mamm*?"

"No, not my *mamm*."

"One of your sisters then?"

"It was me! Put it back if you think I've poisoned you." Jumping up, Josie attempted an indignant pose.

"Afraid for my life? Nope. I wanted to make sure the correct Yoder received the highest compliment I can pay someone." Caleb wiggled his eyebrows. "This chicken is even better than my *mamm*'s."

Gasping, Josie pressed her palm against her chest. "Even better than Elizabeth Beachy's?"

"I tell no lies." He took a huge bite.

"In that case I have decided to kiss you, so put down that chicken." Josie scooted along the stone wall.

"Can't this wait until after lunch?" Caleb licked the tips of his fingers.

Josie grabbed the piece of chicken, dropped it back into the container, and planted a kiss firmly on his mouth. It was short, sweet, and rather chicken-y. "How was that?" she asked, but didn't need a verbal answer. Caleb's expression said it all.

"Now I know you do *two* things better than anyone else in Wayne County," said Caleb with a grin. "Should we forget about the picnic and just kiss until it's time to walk home?"

Josie returned to her original spot on the wall. "Absolutely not. My parents trust me to behave properly, so we're going to eat." Reaching into the tub, she grabbed a wing and handed him the half-eaten breast.

For the rest of the afternoon they strolled under leafy willows along the river. They talked and laughed with no more kissing, but Josie had never enjoyed herself so much. Caleb asked questions and actually listened to her answers instead of thinking about what to say next. He was so unlike other men she'd met. Now that he'd found work he truly enjoyed, the relationship was starting to look better and better.

It might be the one she'd been waiting for all her life.

12

Clothed in flesh, till death shall loose me
I cannot proclaim it well.

Caleb pulled into the Sidleys' driveway at nine o'clock as he had for the previous three weeks. The July sun already warmed his neck and soaked his hatband with sweat. But Caleb didn't mind the heat. With no foreman or boss lurking nearby, the three of them could take coffee or water breaks whenever they chose. Yesterday Albert decided it was time for a swim midway through the afternoon, so into the creek they went. After all, who was he to argue? As he parked his buggy under the barn's overhang, Elijah appeared out of nowhere.

"I'll rub him down and turn him into the pasture," said Elijah in *Deutsch*. He seldom uttered a word of English.

"*Danki*, I'll get a bucket of water." Caleb smiled at the boy's improved appearance. Elijah wore coveralls that were frayed at the knees and bleached to the color of a robin's egg, but he and his clothes were clean. Apparently, Elijah had found a suitable shovel for the hog pen.

"Gonna be another hot one." Albert walked around the corner with two cups of coffee. Sipping one, he handed the other to Caleb.

"Just thinking the same thing." Caleb swabbed his forehead and neck with a handkerchief.

"What's on your task list for us today?" Swallowing a deep gulp of coffee, Albert rubbed his smooth jaw with the back of his hand.

Caleb noticed Albert had started shaving each morning, as required of single men by their *Ordnung*. "We have repaired the fences, replaced your barn roof, and built an outdoor paddock for Elijah's brood sow to sun herself. We jacked up the corner of the porch and put in a new flat rock foundation. Bob told me his neighbor owns a SkidSteer. The neighbor agreed to grade your driveway after the next rain in exchange for some sweet corn next month."

"Much obliged. Now our buggy won't throw a wheel in one of those potholes." Albert drained the contents of his chipped mug, his expression souring. "Does that mean you're almost finished here? Because if you are, I'm grateful for your help."

Caleb met Albert's pale grey gaze. "I'm not done by a long shot. It's time to sweep out the barn and swab the loft with bleach water. The Troyers have cut and dried more hay than they can store. They only need so much covered with plastic out in the fields. Adam doesn't want leftover hay turning moldy after the next rain. Once he finishes baling, he plans to bring over a wagonload."

"Is this the Adam that will wed your *schwester*?"

"It is. He's a *gut* man. The hay might be enough to see your livestock through winter. Let's go get your loft ready."

"Much obliged to him too. I suppose then you'll look for a better paying job?" Albert grinned.

"*Nein*, I'm having too much fun here. When the loft is clean, it's time for me to see inside your *haus*."

Albert's smile vanished. "Don't know if my father would like that much."

"Surely he's noticed me around the farm."

"Of course he has. He asks every time I come in what you've been up to."

"After lunch I want to get reacquainted, face-to-face." Caleb took hold of his friend's shoulder. "I won't talk about anything I see inside with anyone. You can trust me."

Albert didn't shrug him away. "I know that, but I would hate for you to pick buckshot from your backside all night." As usual, he started walking toward the barn without a word of preamble.

Caleb caught up within three strides. "It's a chance I'm willing to take for the Sidley home to be restored to its former glory."

"To look how it did when my great-great grandfather built it?"

Caleb didn't think that would be possible without a federal grant from Washington, but there was no point in admitting that to Albert. "Too bad we don't have an old photo of the place."

After Elijah finished caring for Caleb's horse, he joined them in the loft. With three men, the barn was ready for the hay delivery by noon. They moved to the porch steps to eat sandwiches and drink honey-sweetened iced tea. Caleb kept watching the kitchen door anxiously. "Ready to head inside?" he asked, wrapping up his trash.

A frayed scrap of cloth in the window fell back into place as the Sidley brothers scrambled to their feet. Even a person with a vivid imagination couldn't call it a curtain. "As much as we ever will be," said Albert. "Let's pray *Daed*'s in a friendly mood."

It was Albert's first reference to anything spiritual or religious in three weeks, but it did little to raise Caleb's optimism. When he pushed open the warped door, he breathed a sigh of relief. There were no stacks of boxes up to the ceiling or trash bags filled with roadside discards—typical of most hoarders. No gaping holes in the floor waited to devour the unobservant or provide easy access for snakes and mice from the cellar. And Caleb spotted no dangerous black mold on the walls or ceiling, common in neglected houses with moisture problems. Caleb walked to the center of the room to assess the structure with a carpenter's trained eye.

"I told you I patched the roof holes," said Albert, sounding defensive.

"That was a *gut* idea. The load-bearing walls and floors appear sound, at least in this room."

What he didn't mention was the appearance of dire poverty and prolonged neglect. Nothing looked clean, although from the pattern of dust, someone had recently swept the floor. Cupboard doors were either absent or crooked due to broken hinges. Dishes and cups comprised a hodgepodge that any charitable collection center would reject, while a greenish scale clung to water spouts and faucets.

Albert peered around the room as though suddenly unfamiliar. "'Spose I could have done more in here, but at least I make everyone wash their dishes. I can't abide by picking a plate from the sink and loading it with food."

To that Caleb had no comment. Blessedly he saw no crawly critters in the sink or on the countertop. "I want to speak to your *daed*
now," he said.

"He's in here." Waving his hand, Elijah led the way as their self-
appointed tour guide. While Albert hung back, Caleb followed Elijah
into the living room, which reflected the same sad state as the kitchen.
"I found that sofa in somebody's yard down by the road." Elijah pointed
to the piece proudly. "*Englischers* throw out all kinds of decent stuff."

Caleb murmured agreement to the boy before turning his attention to the patriarch of the family. John Sidley sat in a red vinyl chair.
He wore work boots indoors as though ready for the fields. His suspenders were down, food particles spotted his shirt, and his trousers
were several sizes too large for him. Although the other rooms simply
smelled old, a foul odor emanated from Mr. Sidley. Decay seemed to
seep from his pores like perspiration. At first, Caleb thought the man
was dozing until he opened one red-rimmed eye.

"Caleb Beachy, come to see the old man at last?"

"How do, John? I thought you and I should have a chat."

"I've known every time you've been here." Oddly, Sidley spoke in
English, not *Deutsch*, even though his sons talked solely in the Amish
dialect.

"I had no intention of working behind your back."

"You some kind of a do-gooder because your pa's the bishop?" His
voice sounded raspy, making his words difficult to understand.

"No, I'm here to help Albert fix up this place."

"You ain't touching nothing in my house. It's fine how it is." John
Sidley spat into a coffee can on the floor. "Don't care much what y'all
do in that old barn or in those rocky, worn-out fields. Never got a good
corn or hay crop, not even thirty years ago."

"No," said Caleb. "It's not fine. You might choose to live like this,
but you don't have the right to force it on your sons. If you remain in
your chair or on that couch I won't bother you, but we will repair this
house." Caleb strolled to the corner of the room where a pump action
shotgun leaned against the wall. A box of shells sat on a nearby three-
legged table. Grabbing the gun and the shells, he turned back to the

broken man. "I'll keep these in a safe place until my work here is done. Then I will return them to you."

"You ain't got no right!" John half-stood from the chair and shouted to the best of his ability.

Caleb planted his feet wide, although the smell was becoming too much to bear. "Probably not, but you don't have the right to treat Emma's sons this way. So I figure we're even." It had been the first time Caleb had used the name of Albert's *mamm*, but his tactic worked.

John slouched back into the stained chair. "*Ach*, go off with you then."

Elijah entered the room carrying a dented can of tomato soup on a tray, along with a spoon. Apparently, Mr. Sidley preferred his soup cold. "Here's your lunch, *Daed*." When Elijah lowered the tray to his chest, John sent his lunch flying across the room. Tomato soup splashed and pooled across the floorboards.

Pulling on his earlobe, Caleb nodded to his work partners. "I think we'll repair this room last."

"*Gut* idea," Elijah agreed, while Albert merely grunted. Then the men walked outdoors into the remarkably fresher air.

"I gotta check on my hog and piglets to see if they have enough water." Elijah skipped off, unfazed by the soup incident.

"So the house will keep you here another month or so?" Albert's face remained unreadable.

Caleb stared at the distant pastures where the yellow dog chased a squirrel at least half an acre away. "That's something else I wanted to talk to you about. What do you say we form a partnership after the repairs here are caught up, splitting the profits down the middle? We can establish our own handyman and construction business for the Amish, on a small scale, of course. We won't take side jobs for *Englischers* unless we can't find enough work. I need to distance myself from my old ways."

"*Ach*, you saw how little I know about construction during the last three weeks."

"*Jah*, but I also saw how fast you learn—much faster than most men."

Albert scraped his boot heel across the porch floor. "I don't know,

Cal. Sounds like something I might like, but how can I leave the farm from sunup to sundown, especially since Joe's off in Indiana?" He, too, focused on the yellow dog that had given up on the squirrel and was off on another adventure.

"If you want my two cents, it's about time Tobias hangs around the house more. He needs to step up to his responsibilities if you take a job for money."

Suddenly, a wasp stung Caleb's upper arm through his thin cotton shirt. "Yeoow!" he howled. Jumping off the porch, Caleb rolled up his sleeve to access the sting. Unfortunately, his hasty reaction revealed the snake-infested tattoo. His arm advertised "Kristen" while his heart belonged to Josie Yoder of Fredericksburg. He dabbed a drop of saliva on the bite mark before rolling down the sleeve.

Albert hadn't missed the display. "One of those mistakes you're trying to live down from Cleveland?" His eyes bulged from his face like an owl's, while revulsion radiated in waves.

"It is." After a few uncomfortable moments, Caleb said, "Give the business proposition some thought. No need to make up your mind now. I'll get the ladder to finish dismantling the chimney from your roof." For the first time, he walked away from his friend...as fast as his legs could carry him.

๛

"Josie, come downstairs, please."

Mamm's voice carried up to her bedroom as Josie put the final touches on her Sunday evening *toilette*. She read that word in a historical novel at the library and had been shocked. When the librarian explained the archaic definition, Josie had chuckled for the rest of the day. Not that she had much of a *toilette* to perform. She wouldn't wear makeup, and her thick hair would be bound under a *kapp*. Flossing her teeth and applying lemonade ChapStick would have to suffice.

In the kitchen her mother set out a plate of cold ham sandwiches and a pitcher of tea for supper. "Are you going to the singing tonight?" she asked.

Josie joined Laura in setting the table. "I am. Caleb lives on the same road as the hosts, so I'll walk to his house. Afterward he can drive me home."

"You will walk to the Beachys with your two *schwestern*. Then he'll drive all three of you back." Margaret never raised her voice, yet still managed to convey nonnegotiable decisions with perfect clarity.

Josie glanced at Laura, who lifted and dropped her shoulders. "All right. May I take some brownies for the dessert table?"

"You may, but that's enough discussion about tonight's singing." John Yoder spoke from the doorway. "Let's sit and bow our heads in prayer."

❧

An hour later the three Yoder women met Caleb in the turn-around. If he was disappointed, he hid it well. "Ladies, your carriage awaits." Caleb flourished his hand toward the horse and buggy.

"Looks like your same old rig to me," Laura teased. "In storybooks, the carriage is solid gold and the horse pure white." Laura climbed into the backseat, pulling Jessie in next to her.

Caleb helped Josie climb up beside him. "I'll keep that in mind when I turn this horse out to pasture. For now, we must use our imaginations."

"*Danki* for letting my sisters come with us," said Josie very softly.

"What man wouldn't appreciate being surrounded by such beauty?"

Sounds emanating from the backseat were less than ladylike as Josie settled back for the drive. Caleb entertained them with stories of progress at the Sidleys'. He discussed none of the brothers, but she got the distinct impression the situation had improved for them as well.

"All I can say, Caleb, is you're a braver man than most." Laura summed up Josie's opinion as well.

Once they'd reached their host's farm and joined the singing, Josie felt Caleb's gaze. But if the truth be told, Josie couldn't stop thinking about him either. She hoped God would forgive how often her mind drifted from hymns of praise to a tall man with chocolate brown eyes.

When the singing concluded, Josie headed toward the dessert table with her sisters. Laura grabbed Josie's arm before they reached the line. "I have *gut* news for you." Laura spoke from behind a raised palm. "I found a ride for Jessie and me."

"With whom?" Josie didn't bother hiding behind her hand.

"My friend Kathleen agreed to take us home, even though it's a tad out of the way." Laura grinned affectionately.

"*Danki,* dear one." Josie kissed Laura's forehead, knowing her girlfriend lived in the opposite direction. Piling brownies and Apple Betty bars onto a plate, Josie hurried to where Caleb had found a place to sit. "You won't believe this." She lifted her legs over the picnic bench.

"Your *schwestern* rounded up a ride home tonight?" Caleb leaned so close she could smell the scent of Ivory soap.

Josie punched his arm. "How did you guess?"

"I saw Laura talking to folks on her way out of the barn and then you in the dessert line." Caleb lifted a brownie from the plate. "It didn't take a genius to figure out."

"Are you pleased, or should I tell her to forget it?" Clucking her tongue, Josie crossed her arms over her apron.

Caleb's dimples deepened. "My heart soars into the stratosphere with just the possibility."

"That's better." Josie nibbled the crusty edges of an Apple Betty bar. "Where on earth did you learn to say such things?"

"From an *Englischer*, who else? I heard my friend Pete say that to his fiancée, Michelle."

"In jest?" She sucked out the apple filling.

"I don't know. Michelle was miffed with him at the time, and it did seem to soften her up." A cloud seemed to cross Caleb's face that, unlike Pete's, was dark and ominous.

"What's wrong?" she asked. "Aren't my brownies sitting well on your stomach?"

"The brownies are great, but I realized Pete and Michelle are probably married by now. I didn't attend their wedding, or buy a gift, or even send a card. Pete even invited me to be his best man." Caleb sighed.

"You're feeling sad for not going to an *Englisch* wedding?" Josie licked sticky glaze from her fingers.

"*Jah*, he was my friend, my only friend in Cleveland. Pete helped me through several tough situations." Caleb cracked his knuckles one by one, his mood deteriorating with each.

"Didn't he have any *bruders* or other friends to be his best man? Considering the situation, I'm sure it should have been another *Englischer*."

"That's not the point, Josie. Pete only asked *one* favor of me the entire time we knew one another. And I not only didn't stand up for him, I've made no effort to recognize his marriage to Michelle. Even Plain folks give wedding presents." Caleb sprang to his feet as though too agitated to remain seated.

For some odd reason, Josie felt uncomfortable with Caleb's loyalty. "I'm sure Pete understood that your decision to come home meant returning to Amish ways. And that means cutting your ties to the past. It's what's expected and necessary to focus on a godly life."

Caleb produced a crooked grin. "If you weren't so pretty, I'd think I was listening to one of *Daed*'s Sunday sermons."

"*Mir leid.*" She apologized and forced herself to meet his gaze. "I didn't intend to lecture you, only to say Pete probably wasn't disappointed."

Caleb rubbed the back of his neck. "But *I'm* disappointed. He and Michelle were important to me. A man doesn't—or shouldn't—forget his friends so easily."

Josie searched her mind for the right thing to say but came up empty. Few life experiences had prepared her for this debate. "It's not too late to send a gift. Don't we have a year according to *Englisch* rules? Maybe I can make a quilt for the newlyweds with my *mamm*'s and sisters' help. Sarah and Rebekah could help as long as they sit at opposite ends of the table. We might even finish the quilt by midsummer."

Caleb studied her closely. "You would do that for me?"

"Well, *jah*. We're a courting couple, aren't we? Or at least that's what I was led to believe. I know we haven't announced our engagement and won't until the fall, but I thought we were serious about each other." The longer she rambled, the more like an idiot she felt.

Pushing away from the tree, Caleb returned to where she sat. He splayed his hands on the table. "How could I spend my life with a woman so shy and uncommunicative? I would never know what you're thinking or what you expected from me."

Josie huffed out her breath. "Right now, I expect you to eat so we can leave. Then I expect you to choose a roundabout route so we can enjoy a perfect summer night. We have clear skies, plenty of stars, and even a moon to light our way." She tilted her head back to look up.

Caleb reached for another brownie. "Sounds like a plan. Let's take these desserts for the ride. What if we became hopelessly lost? Without a GPS we could be stranded for days."

Josie covered the plate with a napkin and brushed crumbs from her skirt. "I don't know anyone Plain who owns a GPS. Standardbreds usually know the country roads better than any gizmo mounted to the windshield."

As they walked to his buggy, she reached for his rough, callused hand. But during the long, circuitous route home, something other than an occasional mosquito bothered Josie. Each time she inquired about his plans for the future—his plans for *their* future—Caleb sounded vague and confused. His favorite topic of conversation was Pete Taylor, the *Englisch* carpenter. Caleb filled the drive with an endless stream of tales about his life in the city.

Yes, living near Lake Erie with seagulls, sailboats, and flying kites from the bluffs sounded lovely. And yes, she was certain the diversity of food from the area markets and restaurants would be delicious. But frankly, Josie didn't understand what any of this had to do with *them*. Perhaps Caleb needed a chance to vent because he'd missed his friend's wedding.

She just hoped he would lose his fascination with the past before autumn leaves changed to the first lacy flakes of snow.

ॐ

Eli climbed his porch steps a weary man. Monday, and it already felt like the end of the week. His recent hire, Josiah's nephew, didn't possess the same skills as his son, even though the man tried his best. Caleb had a good eye for rough cuts, seldom wasting more than the barest minimum of lumber. Their new construction project, although free of labor disputes, offered a fresh set of headaches, including an owner who watched over his shoulder and questioned every decision. At least Eli had no obligations this evening. After supper he planned to relax in his recliner with the Good Book and a cup of honey tea.

"Hello, *fraa*." Seeing his wife stirring a pot on the stove never failed to lift his spirits. Several gray wisps escaped her bun while her face glowed with the sheen of perspiration.

"*Ach*, I'm glad you're home. You had better see to the milking. Caleb's not home from the Sidleys' yet."

"Where are my *dochdern*?" He bit back a surge of irritation.

"Rebekah is cleaning the henhouse and gathering eggs, but she must have fallen asleep out there. I haven't seen her in hours. Sarah had to work late for Mrs. Pratt. Now she's in the garden picking lettuce, carrots, and tomatoes for supper. I'll send Katie out to help you." Elizabeth winked one brown eye.

"She'll have to do." Eli resettled his hat on his head and turned all the way to the barn. Even though they owned only three cows, he'd hoped one of his *kinner* would have assumed milking chores. Everyone was always so busy, and Katie helped little because she was afraid of cows. After Katie tried to pet a nursing calf, the annoyed mother had chased her across the pasture. Now she admired new babies from behind the fence.

When Eli returned to the kitchen an hour later supper wasn't ready, despite four Beachy women present and accounted for.

"You're adding too much milk to the mashed potatoes." Rebekah peered into Sarah's saucepot with a frown. "Turning them into soup won't take the lumps out."

Sarah lifted up the masher. "Would you like to take over while I fix the salad?" Her sugar-sweet tone fooled no one.

Rebekah pursed her lips. "I had better, or we'll be eating oatmeal that tastes oddly like potatoes."

Wordlessly, Sarah dropped the utensil into the pot and walked to the sink.

Eli slumped into his chair with a glass of milk to coat his stomach.

"Brown gravy for the meat loaf, *ehemann*? Or will catsup be okay?"

Intent on watching his middle *dochder* attack the spuds with her masher, he didn't answer.

"Eli, do you want brown gravy?" Elizabeth placed her hand on his shoulder.

"Catsup will suffice so we don't *dine* at midnight."

Elizabeth tugged on his earlobe. "Things only look like chaos. We'll be eating before you know it."

Katie carried plates and bowls to the table while Sarah placed a bowl of salad in the center, a mound of chopped vegetables covering the lettuce and spinach. Within minutes his *fraa* delivered sliced meat loaf, a bowl of buttered yellow beans, and the resuscitated mashed potatoes.

"At last," Eli muttered.

But not a half-minute after their prayer, Rebekah delivered her second complaint. "Must you drown the entire salad with Ranch dressing, Sarah? Why can't you let folks add a choice of dressings to their bowls?" Rebekah's nostrils flared like an angry bull's.

"So thoughtless of me," murmured Sarah. "I forgot that everyone loves Ranch dressing, except for you."

"Why can't you speak to your *schwester* in a nice way?" Eli glared at Rebekah.

Her complexion flushed brightly. "I guess because of what happened at the singing. Sarah could have saved me a seat next to her, but she called over Laura Yoder." Rebekah dabbed her salad with a paper napkin before adding Italian dressing.

Eli speared two slices of meat loaf. "Considering you work with Sarah all day, you should welcome time spent with your friends. Especially in light of how you two get along."

Sarah speared a radish before replying. "James sat down next to Adam on the bench. That's why Rebekah wanted to stick to me like gum on my shoe."

"If you're trying to fix Laura Yoder up with James, I will pull your hair."

Eli dropped his knife with a clatter, but Elizabeth was first to respond. "You will do no such thing, young lady. What has come over you lately?"

Large tears rolled down Rebekah's cheeks. "You only see my retaliation and not when Sarah is unkind to me. She's sly like a fox around the chicken coop."

Caleb returned from work, washed up in the mudroom, and had entered the kitchen silently. "James has no particular interest in Laura," he said. "I can assure you, little *schwester.*"

"Sit down, son," said Elizabeth. "Start eating before the food gets cold."

Rebekah glared over her shoulder at Caleb. "Are you trying to make up after the stunt you and Josie pulled last night?"

Eli drowned his meat with catsup, attempting to tune out his offspring. "This meat loaf is loaded with onions—just how I like it." He smiled at his wife as though they were alone in the room.

"What stunt would that be?" Caleb slid into his chair and reached for the salad.

"After Sarah left in Adam's buggy I searched for you, Caleb. But you and Josie had already left." A hiccup punctuated Rebekah's mournful grievance. "I had to walk home by myself."

Eli stopped ignoring his *kinner.* "*What?* You walked all that way in the dark?" He glared at his son and daughter in succession. "It's not safe. You could have been hit by a car that doesn't see you in time. And who knows what kind of people prowl country roads these days?"

Caleb leaned back in this chair, his food untouched thus far. "I thought Adam would bring you home, or I would've sent you with Josie's *schwestern.* Or asked James to take you," he added after a pause.

"You're only saying that after the fact, when it's too late for me to spend time with James." Tears streamed down Rebekah's face.

Eli waved his fork in the air. "Forget about James for a moment, *dochder.* You're too young to think about courting anyway. Let's focus on the fact your siblings abandoned you." He swiveled in his chair toward Sarah. "What say you?"

Sarah had paled to a sickly pallor. "I'm truly sorry, Rebekah. I'd believed you were riding with Caleb." She turned to face him. "I'm sorry, *Daed*."

"*Ach*, a matter of miscommunication." Elizabeth speared several yellow beans. "One that I hope won't be repeated soon."

"It won't, *Mamm*." Caleb sounded appropriately contrite.

"This isn't satisfactory in my estimation." Eli thumped his palm on the table. "According to Rebekah, plenty happens behind our backs. I won't have this sparring between my girls. Any disagreements that occur at work should remain at the bed-and-breakfast. Talk things out on the walk home and don't bring your problems into this house."

"*Jah, Daed*," his daughters replied in unison.

"When did you three become so uncaring, putting your own selves before one another? Even if I weren't the bishop of this district, I would be discouraged by your behavior. And because I am the bishop, our family should set an example...in a positive way."

Everyone sat very still—even Katie, who'd not been to the singing.

Caleb cleared his throat. "I apologize, Rebekah. As long as I live here you have my word, *Daed*, I'll take better care of my sisters."

Eli nodded. "Let's finish this meal and make time to read Scripture. I would say we could use extra prayer time this evening too."

While his daughters cleared the table and Caleb headed out the door toward the barn, Eli carried his coffee to the porch. Heat lightning in the distance foretold of rain later that night, much needed by the crops. Hopefully, the rain would relieve the humidity that had shortened tempers.

Elizabeth soon joined him with a glass of tea. "I gave Katie the night off. I don't intend to lift a finger in the kitchen either. A bit of penance will do Rebekah and Sarah some good."

"Where did we go wrong, *fraa*?" Eli gazed at the night sky as though it might hold clues to his family's problems.

"Isn't that the question asked by parents everywhere in the world?" She laughed merrily.

Grunting, he leaned his tired body against the post. "This isn't how we raised them. Maybe I've been too lenient."

"I don't think so. They are *gut kinner*, but are going through adjustments with each other. Give them a few years and all will be well."

"My hair will turn white as snow by then."

"It probably would anyway." Elizabeth slipped her arm around his waist, a rare gesture that he cherished.

"They are in God's hands." Eli pulled her close.

"They are indeed. Let's take a walk, *ehemann*. I don't want to set foot in that house until there's not a chore left to be done."

13

O to grace how great a debtor
Daily I'm constrained to be!

On Sunday Caleb couldn't wait to get to the preaching service. Not particularly because of the forty-five minute membership class, but because he would be taking Josie home in his open buggy. They needed to spend as much time as possible with each other, especially in such lovely weather. Sooner or later they would be expected to give up *rumschpringe* in preparation to join the church and follow the *Ordnung.* He'd finally found the first Amish woman he wished to court and he had only ten or twelve weeks left to do so. Then the singings, volleyball parties, hayrides, cookouts, and drives on starlit nights would become pleasant memories. By the time people reached his age, they were ready to give up running around to get married and raise families. But was he? Without a doubt he loved Josie, but he wished they had more time to get know one another.

So much time wasted in Cleveland.

So much money wasted in Cleveland.

And so many mistakes to live down. Between now and baptism, he and Josie must cross some troubled waters—something he'd hoped to avoid for the rest of his life.

When the preaching service concluded, he found Josie helping her *grossmammi* to a lawn chair in the shade. He waited patiently until she delivered a glass of lemonade and then approached with hat in hand. "Care to take a walk with me, Josie? Or maybe a Sunday drive in the country?"

"We live in the country, Cal, and have done so our entire lives.

Where else would we go?" Perching one hand on her hip, she looked adorable when piqued…and adorable when things were right-as-rain.

"Oh, I don't know. Maybe to the bike trail to watch the riders whizzing past at great speeds, as though the trail actually went somewhere other than sleepy little Millersburg."

Josie massaged her grandmother's shoulders. "They'll probably be in just as big a hurry on their way back. But what about lunch? I prepared a huge bowl of four-bean salad especially for you. And you want to rush off like those *Englischers*?"

"Don't be a stick in the mud," said *Grossmammi*. "Take a few sandwiches for the ride with a thermos of drinks. Maybe there'll still be beans when you return." She reached up to pat Josie's hand.

"Fat chance any will be left," Caleb said in English since the expression had no meaning in *Deutsch*. "Josie's salad is the best."

The elder Yoder nodded in agreement.

"All right, I'll make sandwiches while you hitch the horse. We'll meet at your buggy in fifteen minutes." Josie brushed a kiss across her grandmother's forehead and skipped off without a backward glance.

So like Josie—not a woman to ponder or vacillate or discuss plans endlessly. Just set a course of action, whether for the afternoon or the rest of your life, and go for it.

In exactly a quarter of an hour, Caleb helped her into his open buggy. "What type of sandwiches do we have?" He flicked the reins lightly on the horse's back.

"Ham and Swiss on rye with mustard. They're my favorite. Will that be okay?" Josie turned her dazzling green eyes in his direction but didn't wait for an answer. "Your *schwester* Rebekah followed me around the buffet table, very curious about what we're doing. I thought she might ask to tag along. What's going on with her?"

He shrugged. "Rebekah is having difficulty being sixteen years old. She wants to grow up but can't quite figure out how. I need to be more patient with her."

Josie issued a sound similar to a snort. "Good luck. Rebekah will create a ball of trouble if none's waiting when she arrives. Where are we headed?"

"To the booming metropolis of Fredericksburg. We'll watch the river flowing under the bridge if the cyclists don't interest you."

"Fine with me. Maybe I'll cool my heels if there's a place to sit on the bank."

"So, Josie, why don't you fill me in on what I missed during the last five years?"

"You mean in our district?"

"*Nein*, in your life."

Josie's expression turned skeptical. "You're teasing, right? What do you suppose I did? You're the one who left for a grand adventure. I stayed in town and planted five gardens, pulled millions of weeds, picked thousands of vegetables, and canned corn, cucumbers, lima beans, beets, green beans, peas, potatoes, okra, and spinach." She ticked off her impressive list on her fingers. "And those are what come readily to mind. I'll save the fascinating stories about laundry and cleaning for another day."

"Didn't you get a job at some point?" Caleb prodded the horse into a fast trot.

Josie pivoted toward him on the seat. "I did take care of an *Englischer's boppli* when she went back to work. But after six months, the woman decided it wasn't worth it, not once she added up the cost of fancy clothes, gas for her car, and paying me. So Mrs. Wilson quit and stayed home. Now she's expecting another." Josie smiled. "I still get to babysit a few times a year."

"You didn't work anywhere else? How about a restaurant, or gift shop, or maybe a B&B like my sisters?"

She shook her head. "What's this about? Are you worried I'm lazy or useless? Good grief. I'll ask *Mamm* to fill out a list of how much work I do at home. Maybe *Grossmammi* will testify on my behalf regarding the *dawdi haus*."

They locked gazes for a moment and then burst into laughter.

"I'll accept your word that you didn't spend those years in a hammock, reading romance novels." Caleb wiggled his eyebrows.

"You forget the part about eating bonbons."

"Not in my mental picture, I didn't." They laughed again, sending birds flying from overhead branches. "Sorry," he said, sobering. "I don't think you're lazy, but I'm curious how you spent your running-around years. Were there places you wanted to visit or things you wanted to do before baptism? Where have you gone?"

"Let me think." Josie looked toward the clouds. "I went to the Akron Zoo and out to dinner at a Mexican restaurant. They had the best tortilla chips. And I went canoeing in Loudonville."

"Did you camp in a tent?" he asked.

"No, a bus brought us home. But it was after midnight when they dropped me off in my driveway. Is that worth extra points on your tally board?"

"At least an additional ten. What about an overnight trip to see the ocean or the mountains? Didn't you want to go to Disney World?"

Josie shrugged. "The travel bug never bit me like you and Sarah. Don't worry about me, Caleb. Even if I never see a larger body of water than Charles Mill Reservoir, I can still die a happy woman."

"So at least you've been there."

She punched him in the arm. "Yes, and I brought home a nasty case of poison ivy as a souvenir."

Caleb snaked his arm around the back of the seat as the buggy rolled downhill into Fredericksburg—a town so quiet people didn't bother locking their doors at night. Josie waved at locals who were strolling the main thoroughfare, eating ice-cream cones.

"Let's park near those picnic tables." She pointed at a gravel parking area close to the bike path.

Caleb dutifully applied the brake and tugged on the reins. His gelding tossed his head but slowed down to a walk. "What about courting?" Caleb waited to ask until he'd tied the reins to a post. "Didn't you date while I lived in Cleveland?"

Josie pulled the picnic basket from the back, her mouth scrunching into a frown. "I've courted a few men before you. You're not my first beau, if that's what you're worried about." She sat, but didn't swing her legs under the table.

"Who were they?" he asked. "Or are their identities a deep, dark secret?"

Handing him a sandwich, Josie looked rather bewildered. "I'm not sure why this is important, but I courted Benjamin Fisher and Joel Bent." She filled their cups with lemonade until they nearly overflowed.

Caleb repeated the names, trying to put faces to the names. But he couldn't remember meeting either man at preaching and didn't recall them from school either. "Were they from a different district—or Mennonite perhaps?"

Josie's complexion darkened a shade. "They are Old Order, same as us. Joel moved out west with his parents, and I seldom saw Ben after our last redistricting. I believe he's courting a Miller girl, if you're worried he still pines for me."

Caleb knew he should change the subject. It was none of his business. Yet he couldn't seem to stop himself. The thought of Ben or Joel holding her hand or kissing her soft lips sent him into a jealous rage. "I was curious why I didn't know them."

"And I don't know why you're so inquisitive. You don't hear me demanding to know who you dated while you were gone. That's in your past—over and done with." She took a small bite of ham and cheese.

"Kristen," he said.

Josie was about to take a second bite before she realized he had spoken. "What?"

"The name of the woman I'd been involved with was Kristen. There were several others, but I honestly can't remember their names." His collar grew tight and suffocating under the shady canopy of the town park.

"Fine, your former girlfriend's name was Kristen. For some reason, it was important you told me, and now you have. Can we get on with lunch? You haven't touched your sandwich and I plan to go wading before we head back." Her face returned to its carefree composure.

"There's plenty more to the story." His voice turned raspy, his mouth dry, as he rolled up his right sleeve.

Josie blinked several times. "That is awful, positively dreadful." She pressed both hands to her throat.

"I agree. It's something I'm ashamed of and deeply regret. If I could remove it I would, but I can't. So I'm asking you to forgive me."

She peered at the tattoo and then glanced down at her lap. "There's nothing to forgive. You did a stupid thing that has nothing to do with me, but the past is the past. I'm more interested in our future."

Josie had said the right thing—the perfect words that should have eased his mind. Yet for some reason, tension still surrounded their picnic table like a fog. Caleb believed that for the first time, the woman he loved had just lied to him.

᧞

"*Mamm,* do you think I'm lazy?"

With her concentration focused on sorting clothes, Margaret Yoder took a moment to glance up. "What?"

"Am I lazy? Or do I give people the impression I don't do my fair share of work?" Josie stuffed dark trousers and shirts into the washing machine.

"You've never heard me complain once about you. What's this about, *dochder*?"

"Yesterday when I went for a ride with Caleb, he asked me plenty of peculiar questions." Josie reached for another shirt in an effort to evade her mother's eye.

"What do you mean, *peculiar*? If you want my opinion, you'll have to be more specific."

"He asked me if I ever worked at a real job. Maybe he's afraid of getting saddled with a lazy wife. The only job I ever held was for Mrs. Wilson, watching her *boppli* when she went back to work. Caleb sounded surprised I never clerked in a store or waited on people at the buffet restaurant."

"Most Old Order gals stay home if their families don't need extra income. There's plenty for women to do around a farm. Your job is to learn to cook and clean and can garden produce, not refill glasses of iced tea in some tourist trap." Margaret punctuated her opinion of girls working the tourist industry with a click of her tongue. "However, you don't seem to have mastered laundry. That basket of wet clothes sits while you stare into space."

Picking up the basket, Josie followed her *mamm* out to the clothesline. "In the city, he probably knew women who managed their households and held down full-time careers."

"*Englisch* women don't usually cook and bake from scratch. Plus their canned food comes from the grocery store. Is that what Caleb asked—how busy you stay during the day?" Frowning, Margaret crossed her arms over her ample chest.

"*Jah,* and he asked what I've done during *rumschpringe* thus far. I had little to tell him." Josie picked up one of her father's shirts and pinned it to the line.

Mamm hung a row of dark socks in quick succession. "He probably wanted to make sure you saw and did what you needed to before becoming a wife and mother. You're reading too much into his questions, *dochder.*" Margaret pinned the rest of the shirts to the line and started across the lawn with the empty basket balanced on one hip.

Josie hurried after her. "He also asked who I courted while he was living in Cleveland."

That stopped her *mamm* in her tracks. "He's got no cause to be questioning you. You're not the one who ran off with a wild group of *Englischers.*"

"I don't think his carpenter friends were exactly wild."

"Nevertheless." She dragged out the word for emphasis. "Caleb had better not cast any accusations on a Yoder girl. Or I'll march over to the Beachys with my porch broom."

Josie dropped their topic of conversation, but couldn't stop thoughts of Caleb quite so easily. As soon as they finished with laundry, she slipped on her sneakers and headed down the path for a heart-to-heart with her best friend.

Sarah usually arrived home from Country Pleasures around lunchtime, except for spring or fall cleaning days. With perfect timing, Josie spotted Sarah and Rebekah on the lane from the inn to their house. They were smiling while they chatted—a good sign Rebekah wasn't in her normal crusty mood.

Josie hid behind a tree until the sisters walked by and then she jumped out to startle them. "Hi, girls!" she said.

Once her feet landed on gravel, Sarah turned on her. "Will you still pull that old childhood prank when we're gray-haired old grannies?"

"Most likely, if I can still get behind a tree with my cane."

"Josie, you have a wicked sense of humor." Rebekah shook her index finger and ran the rest of the way home. The two friends were left in her dust.

"Worked like a charm, once again." Sarah flashed a toothy smile.

"I had something to discuss that required privacy and your undivided attention."

"Ah, sounds like you seek knowledge from someone older and wiser than you." Sarah swung her tote bag like a schoolgirl.

"You're only four months older and even the wiser part is debatable. But I do need your advice in the romance department. You have been courting Adam for ages now. That should make you an expert." As they rounded a curve the Beachy house loomed into view.

"You're starting to sound like him," Sarah cautioned, "but I'll do my best. Go wait by the tire swing in the orchard. I want to wash off the dust and grab us a couple Cokes."

Josie's optimism rose a notch. If anybody knew Caleb it would be his sister. Hadn't Sarah tracked him down in Cleveland with nothing more than an old mailing address? She sought reasons for his leaving the Amish church and their family when he was nineteen. Sarah must have found answers, because she not only returned promptly, but Caleb came home soon after.

With her feet dangling in the air, Josie waited in the sunshine and cool breeze. "I thought you'd forgotten me," she called the moment she spotted Sarah.

"Relax." Sarah handed her a cool drink. "What's got you stymied on a Monday? Some horrible laundry stain refuses to budge from your favorite dress?" With a push of the tire, Sarah sent her soaring.

Josie dragged her feet through the dirt. "It's your *bruder*. He's been asking odd questions and doesn't seem excited about planning our future."

Sarah rolled her eyes. "Oh, dear, man-type questions. Purple juice stains on white linen would be much easier to tackle. But I'll try my best."

"Cal has been asking about my past beaus. That has me worried."

"You have so few past beaus, why should it concern you?" Sarah shoved the tire a second time.

Josie jumped off the swing and faced Sarah eye to eye…or as close as possible when one person stood five-ten and the other was barely five feet. "I suspect he has plenty of history he wants to share, but doesn't know how to broach the subject."

"I believe your suspicion is correct." Sarah held the frosty soda bottle to her cheek.

Josie waited for additional comments to no avail. "Caleb showed me the ugly tattoo he can't get rid of."

Sarah's brown eyes turned round as saucers. "He rolled up his sleeve?"

"*Jah*, it seemed important I discover his stupid mistake now, in case it made a difference regarding our future."

"And does it?" Her eyes narrowed into slits.

"It does not. I love your brother. People make mistakes—nobody is perfect."

Whistling through her teeth, Sarah plopped into the empty swing. "I'm glad to hear that. I had my heart set on you for a sister-in-law."

"Me too, but Caleb thinks I should know about every *Englischer* he dated. Whatever happened in the city made him so suspicious about *my* running-around years."

Sarah shook her head from side to side. "That's something you should ask him. I don't want to get in the middle of problems or cause any new ones."

"You don't understand. I'm not interested in who he dated or what he did on *rumschpringe*. We're taking classes to prepare for baptism. Soon our sins will be washed away; our lives will begin anew. We start with a clean slate after we're baptized."

Sarah abandoned the swing and wrapped an arm around Josie's waist. "That's what you should tell him—you want to leave the past exactly where it's buried."

"If I say that will Caleb relax and stop fretting so much?"

"*Jah*, I'm sure everything will be fine."

Josie saw the truth instantly in Sarah's eyes, even though her words said something altogether different.

❧

Sarah loved to let herself in the back door of the inn while the guests slept and Mrs. Pratt was still in the shower. The house was peaceful yet somehow filled with the anticipation. People on vacation or getaway weekends were universally in good moods. That was why she enjoyed cooking and serving breakfast here. Not only was the work easy in a beautiful house, but everyone was so nice. Besides, Mrs. Pratt gave her plenty of delicious recipes she never would have learned from *Mamm*. Not that her future husband would expect fancy casseroles or layered fruit and cream parfaits each morning. Adam was a simple man in their Plain culture. A bowl of oatmeal and a glass of milk, a sandwich with a shiny apple, and meat loaf with green beans and boiled potatoes could satisfy his daily requirements for the rest of his life.

Sarah washed, slipped on a white apron, and started the huge coffee-maker. Early risers would soon venture from their rooms seeking a cup of coffee before their showers. Mrs. Pratt had left a brief to-do list on the counter before going to bed, but she entered the kitchen before Sarah had a chance to read it.

"Good morning, Sarah! You're exceptionally bright-eyed and bushy-tailed today." The innkeeper wore a smile that could melt the iciest heart. She pulled on a full-length Country Pleasures apron and took a basket of brown eggs from the refrigerator. "Is Rebekah still dawdling on the lane?"

"She couldn't wait to give Bo and Princess treats she brought from home." As Sarah spoke, Rebekah walked through the door.

"Am I late, Mrs. Pratt? Sorry." Rebekah headed straight to the sink.

"Not at all, we're just getting started. Today let's have fresh fruit cups, cheddar biscuits, and a sausage, egg, and cheese casserole. Rebekah, please start browning the sausage and a little chopped onion. Sarah, you wash and slice the berries and other fruit. Everything is where you expect it to be. I'll mix and roll my biscuit dough." Lee Ann Pratt flew around the kitchen issuing orders like a drill sergeant, even though their routine seldom varied. Sarah's parfaits were artistic creations while Mrs. Pratt loved to bake. That left bacon or sausage frying to the person with the least seniority—Rebekah. Lee Ann turned the radio to soft music and they went to work.

Within the hour, delicious aromas filled the inn. The guests milled around the great room, chatting amiably and sipping coffee while they waited to be called to eat.

"Sarah, the casserole needs about ten or fifteen minutes," said Mrs. Pratt. "I want to show my Michigan guests the front garden. Don't let that top layer of cheese get too brown." She hurried from the kitchen as the door swung closed behind her.

"What am I supposed to do?" asked Rebekah, peevish.

"Make sure the table has been set correctly and fill the goblets with ice water. This isn't your first day on the job, sister." Sarah concentrated on adding a whipped cream curl to the top of each parfait. Just as she finished, she heard a timid knock behind her.

A well-dressed *Englischer* and her son appeared in the doorway. The boy was around fifteen with thick glasses and shaggy hair. "May we interrupt you a moment, miss?" The woman talked with an unusual voice. "My son, Jason, wants to ask you something."

Sarah wiped her palms down her apron and turned to greet them. "No interruption whatsoever. What can I help you with?"

The woman nudged her son, who turned a bright shade of pink under double female perusal.

Clearing his throat, the boy dug his hands into his jean pockets. "We live in a condo in Lakewood so I've never seen a horse up close. I heard Mrs. Pratt mention she owns a pair of Haflingers. Could you take me to see them?" He sounded indifferent but his soulful eyes revealed something else.

"Of course I can, right after breakfast." She smiled, hoping to put the shy boy at ease.

Jason rolled his eyes toward the ceiling. "My dad wants to leave as soon as we eat. He's in a big hurry to get back. I'm afraid it's now or never."

The dire finality in his last words broke her heart. "In that case, now it is." Sarah grabbed several apples from the bowl on the counter just as her sister entered the kitchen. "Watch the casserole, Rebekah. Don't let the cheese get too crisp."

"Where are you going? It's almost time to serve." Rebekah set down her pitcher of ice water, her peevishness reaching a new high.

"Jason and I are going to the barn. We'll be right back." Sarah yanked her apron over her head. "Follow me," she said to the boy with a wave of her hand. Without another word they ran out the door as the *Englisch* woman wandered back to the great room.

Sarah slowed her pace once they reached the flagstone path. "Can you see Lake Erie from your condo?"

The question took Jason by surprise. "Sure, we can almost see Canada from our balcony. We live on the top floor."

"That's amazing. When I visited my brother last year, we walked the beach at Edgewater Park. There must have been five hundred seagulls that day."

"There's that many every day. But it's the countryside that's amazing—open land, rolling fields, beautiful farms. This is where I plan to live someday."

Sarah cocked her head to one side. "Everyone takes the beauty in our own backyards for granted, or in your case, the view from your balcony."

"I suppose you're right. The grass is always greener." Jason offered a shy smile.

Inside the barn, the teenager's mouth dropped open. "They are so much bigger in real life than on TV. Are these as big as the Budweiser draft horses?"

"Haflingers aren't even close to a Clydesdale." Sarah nudged him forward the same way his mother had. "Don't worry. Bo and Princess are gentle as lambs. Just hold the apple flat in your palm." She demonstrated with one piece of fruit.

Jason took an apple and stepped to the stall wall. Princess slurped it from his palm with her long pink tongue.

"Wow!" he murmured with reverential awe.

"What about Bo? We must feed both and not play favorites. Horses can be as jealous as little kids."

Jason extended his hand to the second Haflinger. Bo took the apple with a friendly toss of his mane. When all four apples were gone, he backed away from the stall. "Thanks, Sarah. This has been the best part of Amish country."

"You're welcome. The next time you and your parents stay here my brother will take you for a ride through our pasture."

"He could teach me to ride?" Astonished, Jason arched up on tiptoes.

"If you give Caleb thirty minutes, he'll have you trotting and galloping like a cowboy."

"I can't wait." He hooked his thumbs into his pockets as though getting into mode.

"Me too, but right now I must serve breakfast.", Sarah turned on her heel and sprinted back to the house. Jason stayed behind her until they slipped through the back door.

In the kitchen Mrs. Pratt frowned while scraping off a layer of blackened cheese. "Sarah, I asked you not to let our breakfast burn. Now we'll have to melt more cheddar and hope the burnt taste hasn't permeated the entire casserole." Her gaze flickered over Jason as he slinked through the room to rejoin his family and then landed squarely on Sarah. "Please serve the biscuits and fruit compotes. Can you do that for me?"

"Yes, ma'am. I'm so sorry." Sarah washed her hands and carried the tray to the dining room. Her fingers shook as she placed a parfait at each place setting. On her way back to the kitchen, she passed Rebekah with a fresh carafe of coffee. "I asked you to watch the casserole," Sarah hissed through gritted teeth.

"I did, for a while. Who knew you and that *Englisch* man would be gone so long?" Rebekah wrinkled her nose like a rabbit. "Looks like you're not the perfect employee after all."

"*Man?*"

But Sarah had no time to argue. They had to serve breakfast and deliver whatever the guests needed. Blessedly, no one complained about the retouched casserole which Lee Ann served a few minutes later. Jason's family left immediately after breakfast. The other guests soon packed up and headed to the furniture stores, farmer's markets, and cheese houses of Mount Hope or Kidron. Once the inn emptied of tourists, the sisters stripped beds and cleaned rooms without exchanging a single word of dialogue. Not until all chores were finished, a little after noon, did Sarah explain to Mrs. Pratt about Jason's lifelong passion for horses.

The innkeeper peered up from her ledger. "I appreciate that you took an interest in our guest, particularly one with such…overbearing parents. But I can't fathom why you didn't pull out the casserole and leave it on a trivet to cool."

Sarah kneaded her hands behind her back. "I don't know why that never occurred to me. I'm sorry."

"I'll see you tomorrow, dear," she said in frosty tone and returned to her ledger.

On the way home, Sarah attempted to discuss her grievances with Rebekah in a calm manner, as *Daed* had suggested.

Her sister refused to concede her point. "Mrs. Pratt put you in charge of the casserole. You should have taken it out before you left, or given me explicit instructions such as 'remove it from the oven in eight minutes.' But you didn't, so don't blame me because you messed up. Besides, you had no business running off with that boy when we had work to do, especially since you're pledged to Adam Troyer." Rebekah picked up her skirt and ran the rest of the way home.

Sarah chose not to chase after her or broach the subject again later. Sometimes she was just on a different page—or an entirely different chapter—from her sibling.

14

Let Thy goodness, like a fetter,
Bind my wandering heart to Thee.

Saturday was a day off from the Sidleys, but Caleb still had plenty to do. Chores around the farm needed attention, so he rose early to muck stalls, cut the grass, and fix his mother's broken clothesline. *Daed*'s head would be buried in Scripture for hours to prepare for tomorrow's preaching service. With weekends busy at the inn until December, his sisters would be gone until one o'clock. When they walked through the kitchen door, they would join *Mamm*'s canning frenzy.

No rest for the wicked during the month of August.

Lately, Caleb hadn't felt quite so wicked as he usually did. They were making good progress on Albert's home. His brother Tobias had joined their small crew two weeks ago. Now Tobias talked eagerly about which room they would tackle next. The roof proved to be a major undertaking. First, they removed the rotted shingles and colorful patches, along with every bit of the old masonry chimney. Due to the unsafe nature of the project, they ripped off the entire roof at once instead of section by section. Yet God provided five consecutive rainless nights. A full moon and bright stars shone into the attic where Elijah temporarily made his bed.

Dad assigned his full crew to the Sidleys because they were in between projects. He'd planned to pay them full wages but once the men arrived, they insisted on donating their time. Bob brought over plywood from his barn to replace the underlayment, while Eli purchased felt and shingles out of profits from the Ashland law offices. Albert never realized *no one* would have enough leftovers to reshingle an entire house, and John Sidley didn't care where the materials came from. Usually the eldest Sidley, sprawled on the couch or in his recliner, kept his eyes closed to the transformation taking place around him. Caleb had come to terms with the man. He stayed as far away as possible, but paid him appropriate respect whenever their paths crossed.

After the roof was done, a heating contractor installed new flue stacks for the wood-burning stoves in the kitchen and front room. Vents cut in the floors would allow heat to rise to the second story bedrooms, keeping them sufficiently warm in winter. The *Englisch* contractor, who knew Eli from previous projects, provided a friends-and-family discounted price. His father paid the bill without letting Caleb see it. Eli had yet to confront John Sidley, but he inquired every day as to what supplies were needed or how his crew could help. District involvement would come later, after order had been restored to the farm. And memories of buckshot flying through the air faded away.

Once Caleb finished his farm chores, he hitched up his buggy for a trip to Shreve. It was a nice day to go to town. All around him, fields were filled with corn, wheat, and soybeans ready for harvest. Roadside stands along every road offered sweet corn and every variety of vegetables. Although he loved carpentry, nothing gave a man satisfaction like producing food for his fellow man. Wherever he and Josie lived, they must have a huge garden plot.

Josie. Could even a single idea come to mind without him fixating on that raven-haired girl? He hated to think about her being courted by someone else. Lately, he was losing the battle against jealousy, envy, and covetousness.

In Shreve, Caleb parked close to the hardware store and walked the distance, nodding at passersby on the sidewalk. The Sidleys needed inexpensive but sturdy plumbing fixtures. Caleb planned a new bathroom for the house with a fiberglass shower enclosure, standup pedestal sink, and a water-saving commode. They had already hauled everything from the old bathroom to the landfill. Albert and his brothers would use the outhouse and a garden hose rigged over a tree limb to take showers. At least it was August and not January…and the Sidleys had no neighbors for miles.

Caleb selected bathroom fixtures and plumbing supplies from in-stock inventory and a full color catalog. His father insisted that he charge the Beachy account because even Bob didn't have free-standing sinks in his cornucopia of supplies. After loading all he could carry into his buggy, Caleb arranged delivery of the heavier pieces to Albert's farm. With the anticipated shipment date in his pocket, Caleb climbed into his buggy with a feeling of accomplishment. Albert and his brothers were just weeks away from their first hot shower. Then an odd sight across the street caught his attention—Josie's small Morgan and her open buggy.

Caleb stared, momentarily befuddled. Had Josie mentioned a trip to town the last time they had talked? He was certain she hadn't—other-wise they could have ridden to Shreve together. After all, he tried to squeeze in every opportunity to be with her, since long days at Albert's left little time for visiting. While Caleb stared, unsure what to do, a fancy Dodge truck pulled into the parking stop nearest the hitching post, and a young, blond-haired man climbed out. The *Englischer* didn't gaze left or right but headed straight for the Yoder rig.

Caleb reset the brake and leaned forward for a better view. When the man reached the buggy's door, he swept off his ball cap and offered a phony smile. He was apparently talking to someone in a buggy Caleb thought had been empty. Then to Caleb's utter amazement, Josie stepped down and paused on the lowest step to chat eye to eye. Or in her case, laugh and flutter her eyelashes.

Caleb's blood pressure ratcheted up a dozen points while his shirt collar contracted around his throat. Beads of sweat formed on his upper lip and forehead, which had nothing to do with August humid-ity. For several minutes, the love of his life *flirted* on the sidewalk of the Shreve coffee shop.

How had Josie met this man? She didn't work outside the farm and thus seldom dealt with *Englischers*. Could he be one of the men she had courted in the past—an old flame who jumped the fence? Grind-ing down on his back teeth, Caleb opened his buggy door. But before he could get out, the blond *Englischer* and Josie strolled into the diner. *Just like business as usual.* Caleb's mouth gaped wide enough to catch flies. Were they on a date—a prearranged meeting in public where anyone could see them? Caleb swabbed his face with his hanky and closed his eyes. He needed a course of action before he did something stupid.

Should he storm the restaurant and drag Josie out by the arm or maybe her *kapp* ribbons?

Should he demand to know what this *Englischer* was doing with *his* girl?

Or perhaps he could opt for the subtle approach—wander in, peruse a menu, then casually spot the pair. *Say, Josie, I don't believe I've had the pleasure of meeting your secret admirer...*

Without a clear plan in mind, Caleb simply waited in his buggy. He wanted to see how long the rendezvous would last, and if it would conclude with a warm embrace or passionate kiss.

Caleb sat for thirty-eight minutes while his personal green-eyed monster reared its ugly head. When Josie and the man finally exited the shop, they paused at her buggy to chat and smile some more. Then they shook hands as though priming a well.

Caleb swallowed the bitter taste in his mouth. At least Josie didn't cry when the young man climbed into his four-wheel drive pickup. She glanced at traffic in both directions and slowly backed her buggy away from the post. Caleb debated his next move. No one had noticed him across the street, three storefronts down. Should he follow the truck and demand satisfaction at dawn with dueling pistols? But he wouldn't be able to follow the vehicle with his horse and buggy. So when Josie left town in the opposite direction as the Dodge, Caleb trailed her instead.

Staying well behind her rig, Caleb searched his brain for a logical way to broach the subject. How could he determine the nature of their relationship without sounding jealous and insecure—exactly what he was? He was so busy weighing various scenarios he missed the turn for his road. But at least now he could make sure Josie arrived home safely.

However, Miss Yoder had a few more surprises up her sleeve. As Caleb rounded the curve, Josie stepped into the middle of the pavement, letting her mare nibble grass along the driveway. Her arms were crossed, her chin was lifted, and Josie was not smiling. Caleb realized his surveillance hadn't been anywhere near as clandestine as he thought.

❧

"Why on earth are you dogging me? I waited for you to pull alongside me since leaving Shreve, but you never did. You kept slowing your horse to stay far behind."

Caleb reined his gelding to a stop. "You knew I was back there?"

"Of course I did. I try to stay aware of my surroundings whenever I'm out by myself. It's unsafe to be oblivious on the road."

"But you weren't alone, were you?" He took off his hat to slick a hand through his hair.

She blinked with confusion. "Nobody rode with me today, not my *mamm* or my *schwestern*."

"I saw you go into that coffee shop with a man."

Reality finally dawned on Josie. Up until that moment, it had been a lovely summer afternoon. She and Caleb could have floated on the pond in her *bruder*'s rowboat or waded in the river with their shoes off. They could have strolled through the apple orchard, picking a snack when they got hungry, or lain back on a quilt, finding animal faces in the cloud formations.

But they wouldn't do any of those things. In an instant, Josie knew it was time for a long overdue chat. "You're blocking traffic. Pull your buggy into our driveway." She marched from the roadway with hands balled into fists.

Once his wheels were safely off the county highway, Caleb stuck his head out the window. "Should I drive to your paddock? I could rub down both your horse and mine."

"No, you won't be staying that long." She tried not to grit her teeth as she tethered her horse to a tree branch. "We'll sit in the shade for a few minutes." Waiting for him to join her, Josie settled her skirt primly around her ankles.

Caleb lowered himself to his haunches as though ready to pounce at a moment's notice.

"What's this about?" she asked. "Why did you follow me home?"

"I didn't know the *Englischer* you met in Shreve, so I wasn't sure if he could be trusted." Caleb rested his wrists atop his knees.

"Is that why you tried to stay out of view, because you didn't trust *him*?"

"He could have been up to no good. I also thought you might get mad if you found out," Caleb added after a slight hesitation.

"You're the one up to no good," she snapped. "And I am mad that you were checking up on me."

Caleb shook his head. "I accidentally spotted your rig when I came to Shreve to buy plumbing supplies for the Sidleys. If you had an errand, we could have ridden to town together." His tone of voice was soft as though he possessed the upper hand. "You can be so independent at times."

"I didn't know about my trip until Steve Strickland sent word he would be in Shreve on business."

Thus began a series of questions and answers which went nowhere.

"Who's Steve Strickland?" asked Caleb.

"Mrs. Angela Wilson's younger brother," she said.

"Who's Angela Wilson?"

"The *Englisch* woman I used to babysit for. I told you about her." Josie bit her lip, her patience waning.

"How come you never mentioned Steve Strickland before?"

"Because I never met him before today." She rubbed her neck, which had stiffened during the ride.

Caleb emitted a long, protracted sigh. "Could you explain why you snuck out to meet a total stranger at a coffee shop?"

Josie matched his sigh with orchestrated mimicry. "I didn't sneak out. My *mamm* knew about my errands and that I was meeting a beekeeper."

Her beau stared at her mutely.

"Steve and his family are moving to South Carolina due to a job transfer. He's not moving his honey production business, so he's willing to sell the queen bee, along with his equipment, for a very reasonable price." Josie tugged up a handful of crabgrass.

"Steve Strickland is a beekeeper and you wish to become one?" Caleb sounded both shocked and skeptical.

"Correct. I thought you would be proud of me." Josie tossed the clump of grass at him, hitting his chest squarely.

"Proud of what, exactly?" He brushed away the grass without breaking eye contact.

"That I had devised a way to make money. You seemed concerned that my income-producing ability was zilch. Real clover honey fetches a good price in the tourist shops. Plus I could sell it in the natural food market in Berlin."

Caleb squeezed the bridge of his nose. "If this Steve Strickland wanted to sell his beekeeping supplies, why would you meet him at a restaurant for forty minutes?"

"You were *timing* me?" Josie hopped to her feet and pointed a finger at him. "You sound jealous. I have no idea why you would be... or should be. Steve is a married man. Besides, I've already made my feelings for you clear."

"Mr. Strickland could have delivered everything in his truck, taken a check from you, and then been on his way to South Carolina."

Josie lowered her finger and explained with as much control as possible. "Beekeeping isn't the same as hanging a birdfeeder in the kitchen window. It's complicated; plenty of things can go wrong. If you suffer total hive collapse, the profits and maybe even your whole business might be out the window." Pulling a spiral notebook from her bag, she fanned pages of neatly printed notes beneath his nose. "I wanted to know exactly what I was getting into before deciding yea or nay."

"I see why it took forty minutes." His voice lost most of its vehemence.

"After Steve explained the work involved, I picked his brain for helpful hints and what I should watch out for. He's had years of experience. After his family moves to South Carolina, it'll be hard to ask questions. It's not like I can stay in contact by email."

Caleb rose to his feet stiffly. "Beekeeping—that's the last thing I would have guessed." One of his dimples deepened as though this were merely a misunderstanding.

"What would be the first—that I was meeting an *Englischer* for a romantic date?"

He blushed, but didn't deny her preposterous suggestion.

"Oh, Caleb, is that what you thought? How could you possibly have so little faith?"

His flush deepened. "I suppose my past history would be the easy answer." He gazed down on her with a face filled with sadness.

"We don't have time for the long, hard answer. I need to help *Mamm* with supper." Josie pushed up from the grass.

"I asked you earlier about the men you courted, but you provided few details. Maybe I had distracted our conversation with this." Caleb clamped a hand over his arm where the horrid tattoo lay hidden.

"I courted boys, not men. Because I was a girl, not a grown woman. You shouldn't ask such questions, but since this apparently bothers you, I will answer." Josie meted out her words succinctly. "My relationships with previous suitors never got beyond hand-holding or perhaps a goodnight kiss. Those boys had been my friends. We wanted to see if we could spark something more, but we couldn't. End of story." She inhaled a deep breath before continuing. "I thought I was ready for a grown-up relationship with someone I had fallen in love with, but now I'm not so sure."

"You must admit it looked a tad suspicious. Steve Strickland is a handsome man." Caleb used his honey-sweet, teasing voice.

It had no effect on her. "Honestly, I hadn't noticed if that *married Englischer* was handsome, or if his face contained more warts than a horned toad." Josie tapped her toe in the tall grass.

Caleb stared at his boots, as though finally realizing his blunder. "I apologize, Josie. I misjudged you and insulted you. Then I threw salt in your wounds by pressuring you for details that weren't my business. *Mir leid.*"

Josie unclenched her fists and released her pent-up breath. "All right, I forgive you."

A dark cloud lifted from his face as Caleb put his hat back on. "Why don't I rub down our horses and give them a bucket of oats? They could probably use a drink of water too."

Josie stared at him, stunned. *One apology and that's it?* "I thought you needed to deliver plumbing supplies to the Sidleys."

"While I was busy following you, I missed their road by a country mile. Now it's too late. I'll just take everything with me Monday morning." Closing the distance between them, Caleb took her hand. "Maybe I could wrestle an invite to supper."

Josie yanked her hand away. "You may certainly *not* stay for supper. I might have forgiven you because it's my Christian duty, but I need more time before things are peachy between us."

"All right, should I come back later to sit on your porch for a spell? It's Saturday night and we get few chances to be together." He lifted one eyebrow.

"If rocking on a porch with a woman who's not talking to you sounds *gut*, then by all means."

Caleb's head reared back as though slapped. "*Gut nacht*, Josie. I'll look for you after preaching tomorrow." He politely tipped his straw hat and strode toward his buggy without another word.

Josie remained on the lawn for several minutes, feeling worse than the time she'd eaten potato salad left in the sun too long.

❧

Eli had been on his way to the house when he spotted his son's buggy rolling up the drive. He waited to talk, because lately, progress at the Sidleys' had captured his imagination. Who would have guessed Albert and his *bruders* would be such hard workers or so eager to learn a trade? Every previous encounter had led him to believe the sons would end up exactly like their *daed*—cut off from their community and from God. Caleb had reached not only Albert, but also Elijah and Tobias.

"You're late, son." Eli called. "But your *mamm* left a plate for you on the stove."

"*Gut* to hear. I'm starving." Caleb climbed down slowly, instead of jumping like usual.

Eli couldn't help notice the long CPVC pipes sticking from the back of his buggy. "You've started their new bathroom?"

He nodded. "We gutted the old one and hauled everything to the dump in their hay wagon. Thank goodness they only had one bathroom in the house." Caleb moved stiffly as he unhitched the horse.

"Did you run into any trouble with the interior walls? Any black mold or dry rot of the timbers?"

"*Nein*, the worst problem was a huge yellow jacket nest living in the wall. John Sidley had punched his fist through the plaster years ago, leaving a big hole. Albert said his *mamm* had burned the biscuits on the bottom and John flew off in a rage."

Father and son exchanged a sorrowful glance. "John had a mean temper," said Eli. "What about this insect nest? Are you saying none of them knew it was there?" He picked up the harness and followed Caleb into the barn.

After cross-tying the horse, Caleb picked up a brush. "Oh, they all knew its location. Hornets were flying in and out through an open window in Elijah's bedroom."

"Did that boy sleep in the same room as an active hive?" Eli walked around the stall wall to make sure his son wasn't pulling his leg.

"Every single night for the last year. His window contained not a bit of glass. Elijah said he left the bugs alone and they left him alone. I asked if he got bit by mosquitos all night, and he said that he didn't think so. Apparently, mosquitos no longer raised welts." Caleb paused in his grooming. "Once a bat flew into Elijah's room and spent an entire day hanging upside down from the ceiling. The critter flew out the next morning, never to return."

"The bat probably didn't want to share space with a bunch of yellow jackets." Eli hung the harness on a hook.

Laughing, Caleb drew a metal comb through the gelding's mane. "If you repeat this story, which I hope you won't, no one will believe you."

"You're right about that. Insects aside, how is the reconstruction going? Has John stood in your way?"

Caleb grinned. "It's coming along better than my fondest hopes. My prayers have been answered."

"You prayed for the Sidleys?" Eli didn't hide his surprise.

"*Jah*, I pray for them. God has been with us every step. So many bad things could have happened while dismantling the roof and masonry chimney, but so far nothing has. Plus, Mr. Sidley hasn't shot at me or done anything worse than holler foul names."

Eager to help, Eli filled the grain bucket and hay stanchion. "I'm curious, how did you get rid of the hornets—a giant can of Raid?"

"That had been my suggestion, but Elijah wouldn't let me. He insisted he knew a better way." Caleb made eye contact before continuing. "He rigged up a pot of smoldering grass and herbs, then placed it under the hole in the wall. The white smoke put the hornets into a deep sleep, allowing us to dismantle the wall around them. Then Elijah carried the nest out on a stick. He insisted they had as much right to live as we do."

"Did he sleep in the same room with a smudge pot?"

"He had planned to, but I insisted he bunk in with Tobias." Caleb rolled his eyes. "Albert made Elijah carry the nest far from the house. When the last stragglers flew out the window, I boarded up the opening until I can get new replacement glass. And the yellow jackets now reside in a pine tree in the north woods."

"Amazing," said Eli. Although the word was inadequate for what was happening on that dead-end road.

"That's not all. Elijah had a black snake living under his bed, sort of like his pet. It would eat any mice that lived upstairs. He or she—hard to tell with snakes—came and went through a hole in the wall to a tree outside the bedroom."

Eli held up his hands. "Enough. Perhaps I don't need to hear every detail of the Sidleys' former existence. I trust you also found a new home for the snake?"

"Now he lives in a rotted log near the river." Caleb released the horse from the ties and returned him to the stall. "The snake seemed happy when he slithered off, but Elijah was sad to see him go."

A shiver ran up Eli's spine. "When the house is done, maybe he can adopt a dog from the shelter. I'll donate a fifty-pound bag of chow. In the meantime, let's go inside so you can eat. You've had quite a week. Did it get too late to drop off the plumbing supplies? I noticed them still in your buggy."

Caleb closed the barn door behind him. "No, I left in plenty of time, but I saw Josie in Shreve and decided to go to the Yoders."

"All the way by road? Why didn't you just talk in town?"

"Because she was having coffee with an *Englisch* beekeeper." Caleb climbed the back steps and toed off his boots.

"A *beekeeper*? You've lost me." Eli scratched his head. "Are you sure this isn't part of the Sidley story?"

Caleb opened the kitchen door for him. "I couldn't figure out what she was doing with him so I followed her home. She got a notion to raise bees and sell their honey. She thinks I want her to earn an income." He walked straight to the fridge for a Coke.

"And you don't?" Eli set the kettle on for a cup of tea.

"Not at all, but how can I discourage the idea?" His son drank half the can in several swallows.

"Bees will be good for their peach and apple trees. I read in *The Budget* that it's difficult to get one hundred percent pollination of blooms." Eli selected a chamomile teabag from the metal canister.

"What if she invests her money but doesn't like tending the colony?"

"She could sell the hive to someone else." Eli stood at the stove as though watching a kettle made water boil faster. "What did you think of the former beekeeper? Was he covered in suspicious-looking red welts?" He tried his best to suppress a chuckle.

Caleb didn't appreciate his humor. "I didn't go inside the diner. I sat in my buggy, watching the door until Josie left to go home."

"Why on earth didn't you speak to this *Englischer*? Then you could have judged for yourself how difficult or dangerous her new undertaking was. Josie might be biting off more than she can chew." The moment the whistling began, Eli removed the kettle from the heat. His *fraa* and *dochdern* could be asleep upstairs by now.

Caleb carried his supper plate to the table and peeled off the cover. Under the foil were two pork chops, a mound of green beans, mashed yams, and an ear of corn. He picked up a piece of meat. "*Mamm* won't be happy until she fattens me up."

Eli waited several minutes until Caleb devoured his first chop and put a dent in the side dishes. Then he repeated his question. "Why *didn't* you join them for coffee, son?"

"Because I didn't realize it was a business meeting. I thought my girl was on a date with another man." Caleb tipped back his head to finish his soft drink.

"But you said he was an *Englischer*."

"*Jah*. What does that have to do with it?"

"Plenty. I've known Josie Yoder from the day she came into the world. She would never court someone *Englisch*."

"Then I guess you know her better than me." Caleb bit into the second pork chop.

"You're almost midway through the membership classes, preparing to join the Amish church and pledge your lives to Christ. Yet you assumed she was sneaking around behind your back? I thought you two would soon speak to me about intentions to marry this fall after your baptism."

Caleb dropped the bone onto the plate. "I know that, but I didn't like seeing her walk into Cup-of-Joe with another man."

Eli continued to dunk his teabag in the cup far longer than necessary. "So you followed her home in your buggy. Once at the Yoder's, Josie explained her idea to sell honey?"

"*Jah.*" Caleb didn't lift his focus from the meal. "She explained why she went to Shreve. Then she sent me home, all but slamming the door in my face."

"Women, or men for that matter, don't like to find out they're not trusted. You can't blame Josie for being angry."

"I don't, but if this situation were to happen again, I wouldn't do anything different." Caleb balled up his paper napkin and tossed it into the trash.

Eli's years of studying Scripture, along with leading the district as their bishop, momentarily failed him. He didn't know the right words to say to a troubled young man. "Even when your distrust had been misguided?" he said. "Josie had only been buying a beehive, of all things, which you would have discovered had you not stewed in jealousy out in your buggy."

"I understand, but I couldn't tolerate that *Englischer* laughing and talking with my girl. The man even shook her hand!"

"If you keep up this kind of behavior, she might not be your girl much longer." Eli had spoken more to himself, but his son heard him nevertheless.

"A man wants to protect those he loves and keep them safe. Josie is an innocent babe in the woods. She has no idea what kind of men are out in the world. I do know. I saw plenty in those Cleveland bars." Caleb carried his empty plate to the sink.

"Maybe you shouldn't have been in those bars in the first place. You too could have remained oblivious of things Amish folks don't need to know."

"Maybe not, but I can't do anything about it now."

"You need to study the *Gelassenheit* tonight and focus on implementing those principles in your life. Once you've learned resignation, detachment, and calmness of mind, then jealousy won't be an issue nearly so often."

Caleb met his gaze and nodded. "All right," he said. *"Gut nacht."*

But as he headed upstairs, Eli felt he might as well be trying to teach geometry to a goldfish.

15

Prone to wander, Lord, I feel it,
Prone to leave the God I love

Caleb slouched at the breakfast table, not in the best of moods. The thumb he'd hit with the hammer twice yesterday was swollen and throbbing. The steady rain thrumming on their steel roof meant little work would get done on the Sidleys' back porch that day. They had already burned the rotted, warped boards from the previous porch in a bonfire, the sparks and flames shooting twenty-five feet into the air. The shower enclosure he'd ordered had yet to be delivered, stalling progress in the bathroom. But at least Albert and his brothers had a new flush toilet and pedestal sink, even if cold water was their sole option. Two days ago *Daed's* foreman stopped after work with his plumber friend. Within a few hours, Bob and the plumber had installed both fixtures, to Elijah's utter amazement. The boy watched over their shoulders the entire time. Caleb had been amazed by the number of questions Elijah asked.

But it wasn't the rain delay that had Caleb down in the dumps. A full week had passed since his spat with Josie and they were no closer to mending fences. He'd seen her the next day, but she offered no more than a half-hearted smile…one more of pity than affection. After preaching, Josie insisted she needed to sit with her grandmother during lunch. *Grossmammi* Yoder had trouble eating with her new dentures. Then she and her family drove off while he'd been occupied with a debate over soybeans versus more corn next year.

Three times Caleb had walked the back path to the Yoders' after supper to make amends. The first evening he took wildflowers, which her *mamm* didn't appreciate: "Truly, Caleb, these should remain where God planted them." But at least Margaret promised to deliver them. Josie had gone to town for ice cream with her sisters. During his second ill-fated visit, he tried to entice her outdoors to view the first harvest moon of the season. The yellow aura surrounding the moon had always intrigued him, but it failed to draw Josie away from her needlework. His third unsuccessful trip ended with a closed kitchen door in his face. Jessie, her younger sister, informed him that Josie had gone to bed early with a headache.

Was *he* the headache in her life—the thorn that had buried its tip just beneath the surface, refusing to be removed with needle or tweezers? How he missed her sweet smile and pretty face. Thus, when Sarah bounded down the stairs, Caleb wasn't ready for unmitigated cheeriness.

"Why are you still home?" she asked.

"Look outside. It's raining."

"Ahh, you'd planned outdoor work at Albert's. Would you like me to fry ham and eggs while you wait for the skies to clear?" Sarah poured coffee to the rim of her mug.

"No, *danki*, cornflakes will be fine." Caleb didn't glance up from his perusal of a dried blob of jelly on the oilcloth.

"Suit yourself. I'll eat with Mrs. Pratt after we serve last night's guests." Sarah rummaged around in her purse. "Where are my keys to Country Pleasures? Lee Ann sometimes runs to the market for more fruit while her guests sleep, as long as Roy is awake." She dumped her purse contents onto the table. "There they are." Sarah grabbed the ring from the clutter.

As fate would have it, a slip of paper landed faceup amid the sprawl. Like a hummingbird drawn to the next succulent flower, Caleb focused on Josie's name.

"What's this?" he asked, reading aloud. "1230 Mercy Drive NW, Canton."

"It's the address of Timken Mercy Medical Center in Canton." Sarah swept contents back into the purse and slung it over her shoulder.

"I know where that hospital is. What does this have to do with Josie?" An uncomfortable tension tightened his belly.

"I don't know why exactly. I'll get the full story from her tonight after work." Sarah busily filled an aluminum water bottle at the sink.

"Tell me what Josie said to you, Sarah. Stop being evasive. Is she sick or injured?"

"Goodness, *bruder*. Why would you jump to such dire conclusions? I'm sure she's fine. She probably wants to visit someone in the hospital."

"Who?" In a few sort strides, Caleb blocked his sister's exit. There would be no mad dash out the door until he had answers.

"I have no idea. Josie left a message on the Country Pleasures' answering machine. She said she needed the address to give her hired driver. I was to leave the address on her *daed*'s machine out in his barn, which I did. All I know is she's going today."

"Hired cars know where the Canton hospital is." Caleb felt the vein in his neck start to throb.

"True, but driver's love the exact address to punch into those locator machines. Then they'll know about traffic jams ahead of time." Sarah pursed her lips. "Right now I need to get to work. Rebekah is staying home because she doesn't feel well." She pushed past him in the doorway, leaving the scrap of paper where it lay. "Why don't you find out the whole story tonight and then tell me."

For no apparent reason, Caleb tucked the slip into his pocket. It would be a long, worrisome drive to Albert's house, because once again Josie decided to be secretive and sly.

Despite the rain, indoor work at the Sidleys' continued. All morning they filled holes and cracks in the plaster walls with spackling. Once the compound was dry, they sanded in preparation to paint the upstairs bedrooms. Even Josiah pitched in, although he never caught on that a light touch worked best when patching cracks. The walls in his room would forevermore undulate like ocean waves, but they would be clean and free of critter access. After all, the Amish didn't open their homes to decorator magazines anyway.

Caleb's spirits lifted when the paneled van for Dave's Plumbing rolled up the driveway. Dave Wilhelm, Jack's best friend, climbed out with his usual cheeriness.

"How's it going, Albert, Cal? Guess what I've got in the back of my truck?" Dave resettled his ball cap backwards.

"A pepperoni pizza?" Elijah asked with wide-eyed eagerness.

Albert nudged his brother with an elbow. "We're fine, but we don't know what's in your van." Albert never could relax with *Englischer's* mannerisms and redundant questions.

"Your new fiberglass shower enclosure. I went to Shreve to pick up my order for a job in Mount Hope, but mine hadn't arrived yet. Some kind of computer glitch—typical, no?"

Shrugging, Albert looked to Caleb for the appropriate response.

"That happened once on the Ashland office building too," Caleb answered on behalf of the Sidleys. "Will this glitch impact your completion date?"

"Not enough to worry about. Anyway, although my order wasn't in, *yours* had just been delivered. It was still sitting on the loading dock. I told them I would bring it out if they would deliver mine for free when it came in."

Caleb was first to speak. "We're much obliged, Dave. The four of us can unload so we'll be ready for the next time you have a day off."

Albert and Elijah nodded enthusiastically.

"Oh, I can do better than that. Without my order I've got nothing to do. We can set the fiberglass stall in place and I can start hooking it up. I'll run both hot and cold water lines, so once you have a propane and a hot water tank delivered, I'll come back to hook the tank up to the plumbing."

"We surely intend to buy one before winter," said Albert, rocking on his heels.

"You sure there's no natural gas in this area? It's cheaper in the long run." Dave peered toward the road even though gas lines ran underground.

Caleb and Albert exchanged glances. "I've already discussed different fuels with a neighbor," said Albert. "And he recommended this propane type of fuel."

"The gas company won't extend lines for only one house," Caleb added. He smiled inwardly on two counts: Albert had made propane sound like a newfangled invention, and he had chatted socially with one of his neighbors.

"Propane it is. Now let's get that baby unloaded." Dave hooked his thumb over his shoulder.

While they worked Caleb continued to smile for no reason. He enjoyed seeing the Sidley house turn into a habitable, if not comfortable, home. Helping Albert and his family had given him a rare sense of accomplishment. Was this what it meant to be a Christian—to put someone else before your own personal problems? Each time he lost himself in construction, he forgot his courtship woes, at least for a while. And Albert's carpenter skills were improving each day. With a valuable new connection with Dave Wilhelm, Caleb felt more optimistic about their business partnership.

It had taken four men to unload and carry the shower stall to its new location. But that many pairs of hands were unnecessary for the hookup. Dave needed only one helper and Albert readily volunteered. Elijah soon wandered off to the river to fish while Caleb devised a spur-of-the moment plan. "Say, would you mind if I borrowed your truck for an hour or two?" Caleb asked. "I'll replace any gas that I use."

Dave peered up from opening a plastic sack of copper fittings, his expression quizzical. Albert's jaw dropped to his collarbone.

"You have a drivers' license?" they both asked simultaneously.

"I do, and it's still valid. I passed the test when I lived in Cleveland. I owned a car for a while too."

Dave replied after a brief hesitation. "Sure. I left the keys in the ignition since I figured this wasn't a high crime area." He laughed alone at the under-appreciated joke.

Albert wasn't nearly as amenable as Dave. "What are you up to, Caleb? You said you were taking membership classes to join the church. That means ending your running-around, which has gone on far too long anyway. You're supposed to give up your *Englisch* ways." Albert looked as though Caleb's suggestion was a personal affront.

"Simmer down. I do intend to join, but I'm on *rumschpringe* until

I do. This will be my last chance to drive and I'd like to go to the Canton hospital to visit a sick friend." The lie slipped out of his mouth effortlessly.

"You know somebody who's sick in Canton?" asked Albert.

"I do." The second lie issued forth even easier than the first. He bore false witness as easily as putting on his hat.

"All right. I'll help Dave while you're gone." Albert stared at a tube of plumber's putty on the floor.

"Be back as soon as I can." Caleb marched from the house before he lost his nerve. It had been over two years since he'd been behind a wheel. Yet once he spotted the van was automatic, he breathed a sigh of relief. Shifting standard transmissions had never been one of his talents, but just like riding a bicycle, his ability to control a three-thousand pound vehicle returned. Caleb punched the address from the slip of paper into the dashboard GPS—another skill learned from Pete Taylor—and then pulled onto the rutted dirt road. He inched along, reaching the county highway, and then escalated to the posted speed limit. Relaxing against the headrest, Caleb listened to a country music station—another pleasure he'd surrendered after moving home.

But instead of humming along to the tunes, he should have considered what he would do in Canton.

He should have been planning what to say if he bumped into Josie. What logical explanation could he have for following her twice in one week? But Caleb put thoughts of the future foolishly out of mind until he parked near the main entrance. Then he stood in the lobby, clueless as to his next move. He approached several volunteers at the front desk who were ready to direct visitors to a patient's room.

Excuse me. Did you happen to notice a tiny, green-eyed Amish girl today? If so, could you tell me where she went? Even in his petty, jealous mind, that sounded ridiculous. *Or maybe you ladies could look at the roster to see if Joel Bent or Benjamin Fisher is a patient here? I'm anxious to know if my girlfriend is visiting a former beau.*

Standing in the middle of the Timken Mercy Medical Center, Caleb scraped his hands down his face. He should find Dave's van in the parking lot and go back to Albert's house before more people realized he was a hopeless fool. But his luck had run out. The elevator door suddenly opened and Josie stepped out with a thirtyish *Englischer*. The man carried a little girl of around four in his arms. Both spotted him immediately. An Amish man in work clothes with suspenders and a straw hat would be hard to miss.

"Caleb, what on earth are you doing here?" Josie's face changed from shock to confusion to rage in quick progression. She marched toward him as fast as her legs could carry her. The *Englischer* and his child also approached, but at a much slower pace.

"Sarah told me you were headed to the hospital, but she didn't know who was sick. I decided to come in case you needed me for moral support. We are supposed to be a couple, aren't we?"

Her forehead creased with deep wrinkles. "How did you get here?"

"I drove." Caleb angled the man a disdainful perusal. The *Englischer*'s expression of benign confusion didn't falter.

"You drove *a car*?" Josie hefted her purse higher up her shoulder.

"The plumber's van, to be exact. Once again I find you secretly meeting *Englischers* and telling no one of your plans." Caleb crossed his arms as his temper began to build.

Josie closed her eyes and appeared to be counting. When she lifted her gaze, her face was composed. "Caleb, I would like you to meet Justin Wilson and his daughter. Isabella is the child I babysat when her mom went back to work." She grinned at the little girl who squirmed in her father's arms. The moment Mr. Wilson set the child down, she immediately ran to Josie.

"Mr. Wilson, this is Caleb Beachy, the man I might marry in the fall." Her lips compressed into a thin line.

Her former employer held out his hand. "How do you do, Caleb? It's nice to meet you. My wife and I are very fond of Josie and her family."

Caleb shook hands as his anger waned. Once again he felt like the world's biggest fool. "I'm fine, sir. Josie mentioned she enjoyed working for your wife. How are you?"

"We're better now that the obstetrician had good news for us."

Josie hefted Isabella to her hip. "Yesterday I heard that Mrs. Wilson had gone into premature labor. But by the time I got to her house, the rescue squad had rushed her by ambulance here." Josie blushed with the delicacy of the topic. "Things weren't proceeding as expected. The baby's placenta had torn from Mrs. Wilson's insides." Her flush deepened and spread to her hairline.

Mr. Wilson picked up the narrative. "The tear caused massive hemorrhaging. My wife could have died if she had called me at work instead of 911, or if the EMTs hadn't responded so quickly. Surgeons performed an emergency cesarean to first deliver the baby and then repair the damage."

Unlike his fiancée, Caleb felt every drop of blood drain from his head. All this fuss he created while this man had almost lost his wife. "How is Mrs. Wilson now?" he asked, fearful of the answer.

"She will be fine. Praise the Lord! And so is our son." Mr. Wilson couldn't have looked prouder or more relieved.

"Yes, praise Him for His mercy." Josie murmured while pinning Caleb with a frosty glare.

Caleb felt too ashamed to add his own words of praise. "Congratulations on your new son," he added after an uncomfortable hesitation.

Justin Wilson took his daughter back from Josie. "God has blessed us with both a daughter and a son. Our family is complete."

As Josie nodded with grave solemnity, Caleb finally realized that Mrs. Wilson couldn't bear any more children. "I'm sorry for the ordeal you had to endure."

"I have my wife and my family; we'll be fine." Justin glanced at his watch. "Angela will sleep for a few hours, so I volunteered to drive Miss Yoder home. There's no reason for her to call a driver. She's also graciously agreed to watch Isabella so I can return to the hospital. Isabella is long overdue for a nap."

"Your daughter is no trouble whatsoever…unlike *some people* I know." Josie squinted at Caleb under her long eyelashes.

Blushing to the roots of his scalp, Caleb cleared his throat. "I would be happy to drive Josie and your daughter home to save you the trip. I have a valid license and I'm a very safe driver." He lifted his gaze to meet the man's eye.

Mr. Wilson opened his mouth to reply, but Josie cut him off. "Could you excuse us for a moment, please? I need a private word with my *boyfriend*." Her inflection on the normally endearing moniker couldn't have sounded more caustic. Josie marched to a cluster of potted plants while he trailed at her heels. Then she turned on him like a mother bear separated from her cubs. "Nothing doing. I'm on to you, Caleb. You're here because you didn't trust me. Once again you assumed I was meeting someone in secret." She practically hissed her admonishment.

When Caleb noticed Mr. Wilson watching them, his humiliation grew by leaps and bounds. "Even if it was part of the reason I came, why cause Mr. Wilson to make an extra trip? I could take you home on my way back to Albert's in the plumber's van. Mr. Wilson is probably eager to get back to his wife."

"If it's any of your business, Mr. Wilson has been here for over twenty-four hours. He's *eager* to take a shower, grab a bite to eat, and catch an hour of shut-eye now that Angela is out of danger." Josie leaned close to his face. "And furthermore, I'm so angry with you I might be tempted to pull you by your hair all the way back to Fredericksburg. What kind of an example would that set for Isabella? So you, Mr. Beachy, can climb back into Dave-the-plumber's van and go home. Alone. Perhaps you can use the time to ponder why an Amish man about to join the church is driving in the first place." She lifted her chin. "Your father wouldn't like hearing what you've done. Or don't you plan to tell him? Seems to me you're the one sneaking around and keeping secrets. I was simply visiting a friend…who almost died."

"Josie, calm down and let's—"

"I'll calm down after I say my piece." Josie's tone turned annoyingly smug. "I'd planned to stop by tonight to tell you and Sarah all about what's been going on." She backed up a step. "But right now, I'm leaving with Mr. Wilson."

Caleb yearned to reach for her, to beg for forgiveness for the second time in a week, but he didn't dare. Josie looked mad enough to pull his hair inside the hospital lobby. "Will you still come over tonight?" he asked. "Or maybe I could stop by your house? I'll tell Sarah what happened to your friend."

Josie huffed out a breath. "I'll walk to your place after supper, because we definitely need to talk." Then she turned on her heel and marched back to the Wilsons. The threesome left through the revolving doors while Caleb remained where she'd found him—a Plain man without a rudder to guide him in this relationship...or anywhere else in life.

֍

Josie trudged the back path toward the Beachy home as soon as the supper dishes were put away. This conversation with Caleb was long overdue. She would not sleep until she got a few more things off her chest. Forgiveness and turning the other cheek were all well and good, but she couldn't marry a man who wouldn't let her out of his sight. Marriage in the Amish community was forever. Trust and respect were as important as physical attraction and love...more, if you came right down to it.

Caleb was sitting on his porch, deep in thought, when she arrived. "Mind if I sit a spell?" Josie pointed at a rocking chair.

His head snapped up. "Of course not. I've been waiting for you."

Josie sat next to him, anticipating another sorrowful apology along with a promise of improved behavior for the future. But what she received was entirely different.

"I had no reason to follow you to Canton today," he said. "I gave in to my out-of-control jealousy. Because I'm a deceitful man, I assume everyone else is also untrustworthy." Caleb rubbed a spot on his forehead where tension often collected. "But my excuses are more hollow words that no one wants to hear or believes sincere."

Josie chilled at his ominous tone of voice. "An apology is usually a good starting point."

Caleb peered up with red-rimmed eyes. "I'm sorry, Josie. I've done nothing but anger you and hurt your feelings. As beaux go, I'm the dregs of the barrel." He held up his hand when she began to protest.

"There's no need to disagree. You were correct at the hospital. I'm the one keeping secrets, but I refuse to keep them any longer."

Her blood froze in her veins. "I told you that I'm not interested in your past."

"But my past has me trapped and I won't let you marry someone you don't know. So whether you want to hear this or not, you're going to listen." Inhaling a breath, Caleb stared straight ahead. "For several years in Cleveland, I drank six days out of seven. I only stopped when I had no money left to buy beer. I squandered my paycheck buying drinks for complete strangers. Sometimes I didn't leave the bar until my last cent was gone."

She clamped her lips together to stem a gasp. "At least you've lost your taste for the stuff. Especially after witnessing what it did to John Sidley."

"That's not all. I picked up women in those bars and took them home or back to their places. I had relations with women who meant nothing to me." His dark eyes deepened to almost black.

Josie pressed her hands to her churning belly. "Do you mean that girl named Kristen?" She gestured toward his right arm.

He shook his head. "Many more than her. Kristen was the only one I got to know. I fancied myself in love with Kristen, but she dropped me when I lost my job." A muscle tightened in his neck as he stared at the floorboards. "You are pure, but I'm tainted with more sins than I can count. I lied on my unemployment forms just to keep the checks rolling in. I often sneaked away from work early if the boss had left the job site. That's stealing time from my employer. I didn't keep the Sabbath for five straight years. And honoring God? I never prayed or went to church the entire time I was gone. Wait—make that exactly once after Sarah came to visit." Caleb finally met her gaze. "A Catholic priest helped me decide to return."

"A step in the right direction." Josie knew how weak that sounded, but she had nothing better.

"Coming home was only a mirage in the desert. I've broken almost every commandment God gave Moses. My future will be no different than those who cast the golden calf the moment Moses turned his back."

"You don't know that for sure. God offers grace to those who repent."

"Not to those who've fallen as far as I have. And I won't saddle you with a lifetime with a man doomed to damnation."

"You can change, Cal. It's not too late. That's what these classes are for. Baptism will wash us clean." Josie scooted forward on the rocker, growing more anxious by the second.

He snorted with disgust. "Do you really believe half a cup of water will wash away my sins? Weren't you listening to me?" Caleb was practically shouting.

Her own ire ratcheted up a notch. "Sounds like we don't have a future because you're not willing to change." Josie stood ready to bolt down the path.

"I've already given up my bad behavior but nothing feels different in here." Caleb thumped his chest with a fist. "Not anything my *daed* said in class or anything I've read has made a bit of difference. I'm still as far apart from God as I was on that barstool in Cleveland."

"Then we have no future." The breeze picked up her *kapp* strings and sent them fluttering, but Josie ignored them. Her entire world perched on a narrow precipice.

"No, Josie, we don't." Caleb sounded miserable as he buried his face in his hands. "And you have no idea how sorry that makes me."

For a short while, Josie remained frozen in time and space until she heard the unmistakable sound of a man crying. It was so foreign a sound she didn't know what to do. On shaky legs she started for home...and did some crying of her own along the way.

᠙

Sarah tucked the ribbons behind her ears and began to rock. Yet even the porch offered no reprieve from the heat. Summer was her favorite season of the year, but if this oppressive humidity didn't break soon, she would go stark raving mad.

"You've been awfully quiet today." Elizabeth Beachy stepped onto the porch with two tall glasses of iced tea. She handed Sarah one before dropping down into an adjacent chair.

"*Danki, Mamm*. It's too hot to talk or even think, for that matter." Sarah gripped both arms of the chair.

Leaning back, her mother stretched out her legs. "Don't you feel that breeze from the north? I'll bet it's raining in Wooster. We could sure use some down here. Wooster always gets more rain than us. Maybe those tall buildings at the college catch hold of the clouds." Sipping her drink, Elizabeth clinked the ice cubes against her teeth.

Sarah released her breath in exasperation. "That makes no sense. There isn't a building on campus or downtown taller than eight stories. I would hardly say that's up in the clouds." She rocked harder, fanning herself with a pamphlet about fruit trees.

Elizabeth paused for a few moments of uncomfortable silence. "I was joking, *dochder,* apparently not very effectively. What's the matter with you?"

"*Mir leid, Mamm,*" Sarah apologized. "My sense of humor is gone until the fall, but I have no right to snap at you." She patted her mother's hand, feeling the dry, paper-thin skin.

"Autumn? I'm not sure your family or your fiancé can stand you that long." *Mamm* picked up another pamphlet to help circulate the air.

"I'll try my best."

"Is everything all right—other than the weather? I saw you fall asleep during preaching this morning. I thought you enjoyed your father's sermons."

"Did I hurt *Daed*'s feelings? His message about grace and not good works was *gut,* but I didn't sleep well last night. Rebekah was snoring, plus not a bit of breeze entered our window." Sarah dabbed her upper lip with a tissue.

"It would take more than droopy eyelids to offend your father." Elizabeth took a sip of tea. "I noticed you barely touched your lunch. Chicken salad with walnuts and grapes has always been one of your favorites."

"In my opinion, Ruth Ann added too much mayo. There's no need to drown the chicken. The poor bird is already dead." Sarah wiped her damp forehead.

"Perhaps you could open a cooking school in your new house for other brides. However, I would recommend a more subtle approach than accusing Ruth Ann of attempted chicken-murder."

Sarah scowled at her *mamm*'s second attempt at humor. "Ruth Ann is too stubborn to take culinary advice from me."

Elizabeth stopped rocking and pushed herself to her feet. "I see Adam coming up our driveway. It's nice of him to stop by after taking his *grossmammi* to visit her friends."

Sarah grunted in agreement.

"I wish him the best of luck with *you* today." Elizabeth picked up her glass and headed inside the house. Sarah chuckled at her parting comment—her third attempt had finally been successful.

With only five minutes to shake off her bad mood while Adam turned his horse into the paddock, she concentrated on pleasant thoughts of winter. Since they were mere weeks away from announcing their engagement, it wouldn't do if she offended her third loved one in an afternoon.

She popped a breath mint in her mouth and plastered a warm smile on her face. "Adam Troyer, the handsomest man in Wayne County, is paying me a social call," she said.

Her flattery always produced the same reaction. Adam flushed a deep shade of red. "Hullo, Sarah. Perhaps you need to have your vision checked the next time we're in Wooster. You might need glasses." He settled into the chair recently vacated by *Mamm*.

"My eyesight is twenty-twenty." She squeezed his hand affectionately. "Mrs. Pratt always asks me to read the fine print on medicine bottles or in catalogs. I don't know what she does on my days off."

"She'll purchase a pair of magnifiers at the Dollar Store because your days off are about to increase dramatically." Adam set his straw hat on the porch rail and slouched down in the rocker.

"What do you mean?" Sarah's hackles rose like goosebumps on chilled skin.

"I mean you'll soon be hanging up your chief cook and bottle-washer apron forever. Mrs. Pratt should start advertising for your replacement. Surely she can't manage with just Rebekah." Adam dropped his voice to a whisper. "That girl is no Sarah Beachy." He gave one of her *kapp* ribbons a tug.

"Down the road, *jah*, but not yet." She stared at a row of crows on a dead tree branch. With dozens of branches to pick from, why did they huddle close on the same limb?

"It will be September next week. At this point in your membership classes you're to give up *rumschpringe* and start following the *Ordnung* to the letter. I had expected you to give your notice at Country Pleasures weeks ago."

He didn't raise his voice or whine, but Sarah knew Adam wasn't happy. "I intend to, but this will be Labor Day weekend. Lee Ann not only has a full house for a family reunion, but she's allowing the children to sleep in tents in her back garden. The reunion people will stay for three days."

"You're not working on the Sabbath." Adam stated a fact, not asked a question.

Perspiration ran down Sarah's face in rivulets. "No, I'm not. Lee Ann arranged temporary help from an agency to replace Rebekah and me that day. But I'll bet we'll serve thirty breakfasts over those two days."

"All right. First thing Tuesday morning you should give your two-week notice. The inn will be back to normal by then." Adam sat up straighter. "Say, do you think there's any tea left in the fridge? My mouth could use something wet."

"Of course, I'll be right back." Sarah sprang from her chair into the house. The errand provided an opportunity to compose her thoughts. She'd planned to quit her job, just not yet. A few minutes later she handed him a glass brimming with ice. "For my thirsty traveler."

"Much obliged." Adam swallowed several gulps.

"Now that you're refreshed, I hope you can see my predicament clearly." She blotted her face with her hanky.

His expression of relief vanished. "Haven't you been listening to your father or the other ministerial brethren in class?"

"I've listened, but I believe each person's situation is different. Labor Day starts the busiest season for Country Pleasures. Tourists flock in from Cleveland and Columbus to view autumn foliage and buy pumpkins from the produce stands."

Adam grimaced. "Leaves change colors throughout October. You had planned to stay until November?"

Sarah closed her eyes as a wave of dizziness washed over her. "Well, *jah*. This isn't a good time for Lee Ann to hire and train somebody new."

"That will be only a couple weeks before our wedding. When would you prepare our first home? The house should be finished by then, at least the starter version."

She swallowed hard, her throat dry and scratchy. "I promise to make time."

"Maybe she's waiting for her *Englisch* boyfriend to come back for his riding lesson." Rebekah appeared in the doorway, unseen until she'd spoken.

Sarah's head snapped around, the sudden motion triggering a second dizzy spell. "Jason is a *child* who stayed at the inn once, not my boyfriend. How dare you eavesdrop on our conversation?" She struggled to stand but found her legs too weak.

"I was bringing Adam some cookies that I baked and couldn't help but overhear." Rebekah set a plate of sugar cookies on the railing. "I'd wondered whether you'd told Adam about Jason."

Adam looked from one sister to the other, bewildered.

"No, because there was no reason." Sarah finally struggled to her feet. "If you'll both excuse me, I need to lie down." She clung to every piece of furniture between her chair and the door.

"What's wrong? Are you sick?" Adam jumped up to support her elbow.

"The heat has gotten to me today. I'm sure I'll feel better tomorrow." Her words sounded oddly muffled in her ears. Ignoring Rebekah, Sarah forced a smile for Adam. Then she staggered inside and practically crawled up the steps to her room.

16

Here's my heart, O take and seal it,
Seal it for Thy courts above.

Despite a ferocious thunderstorm surrounding the Yoder house, supper conversation carried on like usual. Kerosene lamps might have been lit earlier than usual, but no one else seemed concerned that the skies had opened with a deluge. But Josie had noticed. She jolted in her chair with each bolt of lightning and subsequent rumble of thunder.

"Something wrong with you, *dochder*?" asked Margaret, ever observant of her *kinner*.

Josie shoved her lima beans to the opposite side of the plate. "No, I'm fine."

"You've been moping around for days, jumping at every strange noise." Her mother set down her fork to devote her undivided attention.

"I don't like thunderstorms." Josie spoke just as another brilliant blaze illuminated the room.

"Since when?" Laura peered at her. "When we were little, you would press your face to the bedroom window so as not to miss a single flash, while Jessie and I cowered under the bed."

Josie aimed a meaningful glare at her sister—something she'd been doing often lately. "I used to stomp through mud puddles as a kid too. You don't see me doing that anymore, do you?"

"Who knows what you do when our backs are turned?" Laura winked with mischief.

Josie smiled at the memory of playing in the rain. Why did every pleasant reminiscence underscore how miserable she was now? She stabbed a row of beans in succession, forcing herself to eat to deflect further scrutiny. However, she wasn't to remain under *Mamm's* radar for long. While washing dishes, a serving bowl slipped from her sudsy fingers and shattered on the floor. It was a common occurrence in most households, yet coupled with the tempest raging outside, the crash pushed Josie's frayed nerves to the breaking point. She burst into tears like a six-year-old.

Margaret responded like a mother hen with one of her chicks in peril. Shutting off the water taps, she snaked her arm around Josie's waist. "Jessie, go tell Laura to come help with kitchen cleanup. We're switching Laura's night off. I need some private time with your *schwester.*"

Jessie bolted down the hallway as Josie bent to pick up the pieces. "I'm sorry about the bowl. I'll be more careful. Laura doesn't need to do my work." Josie quickly dabbed her eyes with her apron.

"*Jah,* she does. Because it's not a discount store bowl I'm worried about. Why don't we stroll to the barn where we can talk, woman to woman?" Margaret pulled her apron over her head.

Despite her sour mood, Josie snickered. "Am I the only one to notice it's raining outside?"

"Your *daed* and I are thrilled about the rain. It's perfect timing for the final crop of hay. And you won't melt from a little water. I have this clever contraption we can use." Margaret lifted the plain black umbrella from its hook by the door.

"Why do you want to go to the barn? Our chores are done." Josie cleared a patch of condensation from the windowpane.

"That's not why we're taking a walk." *Mamm* dragged her along as though she were a naughty child.

Josie grabbed her outer bonnet and stopped resisting her mother's unflappable will.

When Margaret stepped onto the porch she breathed deeply. "Do you smell that? Lightning must have struck nearby. I don't know what it's called, but I love that smell."

"It's called ozone. And you're the only one who appreciates it." Josie huddled close for their march across the lawn. The soles of her house slippers were instantly soaked through. "If I'd known we're going on an adventure, I would have put on leather boots." They ducked inside the barn where the interior smelled sweetly of stored hay in the loft, along with a sour tang from horse stalls in need of fresh bedding.

"Worry not about your feet for one moment." Margaret lowered her umbrella to her side. "I want you to unburden your heart. Why have you been brooding for a week as though your favorite pet just died?"

Josie glanced around for an escape route, but *Mamm* was blocking the doorway. She released a sigh with feelings of impending doom. "I have no reason not to tell you, other than I'd hoped it wasn't true. There will be no engagement to announce this fall." Her tears returned with fresh intensity.

Margaret's demeanor instantly sobered. "Dear me, I feared that was the case. What happened? Did Cal change his mind about taking the kneeling vow? Is he not ready to commit to our ways?" She broke eye contact. "Of course, if you don't wish to discuss the matter, I understand."

Josie perched on a stack of grain sacks. "I don't mind talking, and no, Cal hasn't changed his mind about joining the church. He's just not ready to commit to me."

"What's wrong with you? Has he heard some false gossip about one of my girls?" *Mamm's* hen-feathers ruffled with alarm.

"I don't think so. Apparently, whatever happened up in Cleveland has shamed him, and he can't seem to forget. I told him I don't care what he did, but it does no good. He said nothing he's heard during membership class has made any difference. He doesn't feel any closer to God being Amish than he did being *Englisch*. He said he prays, but God ignores him."

That generated a *harrumph* from her *mamm*. "God never ignores a contrite heart. Maybe he's not all that sorry about his mistakes." Margaret shook water droplets from her umbrella onto the recently swept floor.

"I believe he regrets his past, but can't forget long enough to plan a future." Josie paused to choose her words carefully. "I hope this doesn't sound prideful, but he acts like he's not worthy of me."

"*Ach*, maybe that's because he's not worthy of you."

Josie blanched. "*Mamm,* it's not like you to be so uncharitable. Don't you like Cal?" Suddenly, she felt like that little girl stomping through mud puddles in their lane instead of a grown woman.

"My opinion of him is of no consequence. I used to like the old Caleb Beachy before he left on *rumschpringe*, but he was gone a long time. Five years in the city isn't the same as a month of camping out West. Plain folks who are gone that long usually don't return to the fold."

"He shouldn't even try? We should wash our hands of a tainted man? Who among us is without sin?" Josie's voice rose in increments with each word until she was practically shouting.

Margaret arched one eyebrow. "Control your temper, young lady. I didn't say that and your courting woes aren't my doing."

Josie abandoned the feed sacks to encircle her mother's waist with both arms. "*Mir leid.* I'm so miserable that I'm lashing out at everyone. Maybe I should move into the hayloft for a few weeks. You could set my meals beside the bowl of cat food." Josie laid her head against her mother's shoulder.

"Nothing doing. Tomorrow is your night for dishes. We're not letting you off the hook." Margaret rubbed Josie's back in a circular pattern.

"Even though we've broken up, I still love Caleb. How can I help him? Surely he can't be a lost cause. Look at Mary Magdalene's past history."

Elizabeth held her at arms' length. "Of course he's not a lost cause. God often allows His children to fall far before drawing them back. But understand me: *You* can't do anything. The only person who can help Caleb is himself. He must want this. And I don't mean just marriage, but to be restored to God's grace. Going through the motions of membership won't suffice. I respect him for not falsely taking vows just to marry you. Now you're free to court someone else once your heart heals."

Josie stepped back from her *mamm's* embrace. "I don't want to court somebody else. Aren't you listening to me?" Tears streamed down her face as though in competition with the downpour outside. "I love him."

"I have listened to you." Margaret spoke with the patience of a veteran parent. "But I repeat: You can't change Caleb's future. You can make a life with someone else or remain single, wallowing in grief until you die. Caleb must choose his own path…with or without you. With or without God, for that matter."

She slid back the door and opened her umbrella. "Looks like it's not letting up. Are you ready to make a run for it?"

Josie shook her head. "No, I'll stay here a little longer. I've got some thinking to do."

Margaret's mouth drooped. "Suit yourself, but I'm ready for coffee and apple pie." She turned and vanished into the growing gloom.

With her mother gone, Josie was alone to pace the aisles, climb the steps to the loft, and peer out the window on a soggy world. But no clever plan or new attitude arrived no matter how hard she mulled the conundrum. In the end she knew *Mamm* was right. There was nothing left for her to do but go to bed. And forget about ever sharing a life with Caleb.

❦

On the Saturday after Labor Day, Adam Troyer limped back to the barn while gnats buzzed about his head. As days went, he'd had better. Although his brothers usually managed the farm under *Daed's* direction, harvesting demanded everyone's help—even those with full-time jobs elsewhere. He had little time to work on his new cottage for his bride to be.

It also left little opportunity to even see Sarah.

This week the inn would be recovering from the onslaught of the family reunion. Serving and cleaning up after thirty men, women, and children with only Rebekah and Mrs. Pratt must have been exhausting. The sooner Sarah quit her job the happier he would be. Yes, tourists arrived eager to see fall colors, but didn't leaves change on city streets and in suburban subdivisions? Lee Ann would have to hire someone else. Plenty of women were looking for jobs in this economy. If she would simply hire *Englisch* employees, she wouldn't be left in a pinch when Amish girls decided to marry.

Bending over to search *Daed*'s toolbox, Adam clunked his head on the vise handle. "Ow!" he muttered. While cutting hay, his brother declared the blade needed adjustment, so Adam volunteered to hike back for the tools…and twisted his ankle in a gopher hole along the way. Now he would have a goose egg on his forehead to go along with the swollen ankle.

"Are you all right?" a voice sounded from behind.

Adam turned to see his future brother-in-law's apprehensive face. "*Jah*, I'm fine. What's another lump on this old melon?" He forced a smile despite the start of a headache. "I don't know which of my *bruders* can't remember to turn the vise handle toward the wall." After retrieving the screwdriver, Adam slowly straightened his spine.

"That lump is starting to swell." Caleb stepped closer to inspect. "You might need some ice."

Adam waved off the suggestion. "It's nothing to worry about. Why have you come this fine September morning? Did the Beachys run out of chores so you decided to lend the Troyers a hand?" He stuck the tool into his back pocket. "Everybody's out in the fields, cutting, raking, baling, or moving hay to the loft. We had a good crop this year. We'll have enough left over to share."

Caleb shifted his weight between feet. "We don't own close to the size of your spread, but I still have plenty of chores. Especially since I'm gone all week at the Sidleys'. But the reason—"

"The Sidleys are who came to mind about sharing our hay. How is the house reconstruction going? My father said he'll send over a few heifers in the spring in case John wants to increase his herd. Even some bulls that he could raise for beef."

"Albert will be much obliged, but John takes no interest in farming these days. The reason I came—"

Adam interrupted Caleb a second time. "Sarah told me what you've done for Albert and his *bruders*. You're a *gut* man, Cal. Few would take an interest in people who slammed the door in their face too many times to count."

Caleb crossed his arms. "Sarah is why I'm here."

Adam sighed. "Did you hear about our spat last week? I sure wish

Rebekah would find something better to do than eavesdrop on conversations. You needn't worry about us. Sarah will quit her job when the time is right. I just wish it would be sooner, rather than later. Say, would you like to see how our new house is coming?"

Caleb lifted both palms into the air. "What I would like is to get a word in edgewise. I've never heard you run on so, Adam."

"Sorry. I'm excited about finishing our home." His expression turned to that of a chastised dog. "You wanted to talk about your sister?"

Caleb blew out his breath. "Sarah is sick. She's been feeling poorly for a while. *Mamm* thought the heat had brought her low. Out of everyone, Sarah tolerates humidity the worst. And *Daed* thought she was simply exhausted from working too hard at Country Pleasures."

"She seemed okay at preaching last Sunday," Adam interjected softly.

"That was an act she put on for your benefit and my parents'. Sarah doesn't want folks worrying about her…or forcing her to leave the inn short of help during the busy season. Sarah gave Mrs. Pratt her notice. As soon as her replacement is hired and trained, she'll quit."

Adam waved off his reassurance. "I know that. Get on with what you came to say."

"After I brought her home after church, she fell asleep in the hammock and spent the entire day under the tree. She didn't eat lunch and would have missed supper if *Mamm* hadn't dragged her into the house. *Mamm* insisted Sarah eat a bowl of cold cereal and drink some milk." Caleb stepped closer as though he were whispering a confidence. "I heard her throwing up later in the bathroom. 'Spose I'm no better than Rebekah spying on my *schwester*'s business."

Adam shook his head as blood drained from his face. "It's not the same thing at all. I'm grateful that you're concerned about Sarah. Tell me what I can do."

"I'd like you to come home with me to see her. Then you decide for yourself what needs to be done."

Adam felt his knees and legs weaken. "What do you mean 'what should be done'? Should I call the doctor from our neighbor's and ask him to meet us at your place?"

Caleb dropped his arms to his side. "I think she should be in a hospital. But when I suggested it, my father accused me of making his decisions. He's of the opinion I haven't given up my willfulness."

"If you believe Sarah should be in a hospital, why are we standing here chewing the fat?" Adam pulled the screwdriver from his pocket. "I'll deliver this to James in the hayfield to fix the cutting blade. Then I'll meet you at your buggy." He started toward the door.

"I hired a car to bring me—no time to travel by horse and buggy."

Adam's heart contracted in his chest from the implication. "I'll be right there." Forcing his legs to move, he bolted into the hayfield, ran back to the house for his wallet, and delivered a one-sentence explanation to his mother. He ignored his throbbing ankle and the knot on his forehead as he jumped inside the hired car. He prayed silently as icy fingers crawled up his spine.

Please, Lord. Don't let anything bad happen to my Sarah.

At fifty miles per hour, the car cut the distance between the Troyer's and Beachy's into a fraction. While Caleb paid the driver, Adam ran to the porch and took the steps two at a time. Not waiting for an answer to his knock, he threw open the kitchen door. "*Guder mariye,* Mrs. Beachy. May I see Sarah?"

Elizabeth looked like she'd seen a ghost. "*Jah,* she's still abed, but Rebekah will take you upstairs."

"*Danki.* Cal said she's feeling poorly."

The troublesome younger sister rose from the table where she'd been coring apples. "If Sarah would stop refusing to eat, she might start to feel better." Rebekah delivered her unsought advice on their way up the steps.

"I didn't realize you'd gone to medical school, Rebekah. Perhaps you could look at my sprained ankle after I finish visiting Sarah." Scorn rolled off his tongue. Adam wasn't a man of sarcasm, but Rebekah tended to bring out the worst in people.

Since he and Sarah were merely engaged, an unchaperoned bedroom visit wasn't permitted. But at least Rebekah sat quietly. It took him little time to arrive at the same conclusion as Caleb. "Sarah. How are you feeling, *liewi?*" Adam asked from the doorway.

His *Deutsch* endearment brought a grin to Sarah's wan face. "I've been better." She tried to rise up on one elbow. "But I'll be fit as a fiddle by November for our wedding. How is the house coming along?" During the question, a fit of shivers wracked her thin frame, followed by a convulsive cough.

Terrified, Adam rushed to her side and covered her hand with his. A fistful of ice cubes would feel no warmer. Dark smudges underscored Sarah's eyes and her cheeks had sunken beneath her skin. How was it possible that two weeks could so adversely affect a twenty-one-year-old woman? "The house is coming along nicely," he said. "Almost ready for a woman's touch when you're feeling better."

As Sarah labored to breathe, her haunted eyes tore a hole through his gut. He turned to Rebekah, sitting on the other twin bed. "Pack an overnight bag of your *schwester*'s toiletries and sleep clothing. She's going to the hospital in Canton." To Sarah, he replied in a calm voice. "I'm sure you'll improve faster with medicine other than aspirin, honey lemon tea, and chicken soup."

"*Mamm*'s cure-alls haven't worked so well this time. *Danki*, Adam." Sarah spoke with great difficulty.

The fact that Sarah didn't argue about a trip to the ER scared him more than anything thus far. "I'll be right back." He squeezed her fingers but felt no return response. After a pointed glare, Rebekah sprang to action while he hurried downstairs.

In the kitchen Caleb, Eli, and Elizabeth sat at the table, waiting. They neither ate, nor drank, nor talked—a rare occurrence for Plain folks. "I'm calling an ambulance," Adam declared. "Is your cell phone charged up?" he asked Caleb.

"No, I don't use it anymore." Caleb's healthy complexion faded to match Sarah's pallor.

"Mine is charged. I'll get it from my briefcase." Eli pushed himself to his feet and hurried to the mudroom faster than he'd moved in years.

"The hospital?" asked Elizabeth, covering her face with her hands. "We should have called you sooner, when I realized she wasn't getting better. I let Sarah talk me out of calling the doctor. She said she didn't want to waste the money. This is my fault."

Adam had no time to comfort the woman. He had to get EMTs

to the Beachy's before another minute passed. He had a bad feeling about Sarah's future. And it had nothing to do with bed and break-fasts, or new cottages in the woods, or a trip down the aisle in a brand new wedding dress.

❦

Sarah awoke for the first time without a throbbing pain in her head. It had seemed that whenever she opened her eyes, every part of her body ached. Not that she'd been awake much. Despite sleeping end-lessly, she could only keep her eyes open for short periods of time. Thus, one day seemed no different from any other. Had she seen Adam ear-lier this morning or had that been last week? What about her parents? *Mamm* had brought some oatmeal cookies which had all disappeared, but she couldn't remember eating a single one.

"Ah, I see you're back with us!" A dark-haired nurse, wearing a bright smile, wheeled a cart with dozens of drawers into her room.

"I am." Sarah tried to push herself into an upright position.

"Easy does it, Miss Beachy. You're still very weak." The nurse with a name badge that read "Peggy" pressed down a button on a remote control. The top half of the bed rotated forward, giving Sarah a better view of her surroundings.

"*Dank*—" she began and then switched to English. "Thank you, I mean."

"Do you know where you are, Miss Beachy?" Nurse Peggy jammed a second pillow behind Sarah's shoulders and pushed a tray with a pitcher and plastic cup in front of her.

"I'm in a hospital. And please call me Sarah." With extreme effort she reached for the water. Her arm felt weighed down by twenty-five pound feed sacks.

"Correct. You're in Timken Mercy Medical Center in Canton to be exact." Peggy supported her elbow while she drank the glass of water.

When Sarah finished the cup, she burped rudely. "I beg your pardon."

Nurse Peggy laughed. "Burp all you like. It's good for you."

"Do you suspect I have amnesia? Should I recite details about my home and family?" Sarah tried to refill the cup but spilled most of it onto the tray. Her hand wouldn't cooperate with her brain.

The nurse wiped up the spill while replenishing the water, adept at doing two things simultaneously. "Not unless you want to. Memory loss isn't usually a symptom of West Nile Virus. I was checking to make sure your fog had cleared. Your high fever had put you out of commission for a while."

"Nile, like the river in Egypt—that's what I had?" Sarah blinked, her hand gripping the tray. "But I've never left Ohio."

"I understand, but birds and insects often travel great distances. You were bitten by a mosquito that had bitten an infected bird."

"How could a mosquito make me so sick?" Sarah rubbed her forehead.

"You would be surprised how much disease insects spread. But your doctor will be in soon if you have more questions. I'm here to dispense your meds. Don't worry; you can't spread the virus to other people." Nurse Peggy placed a paper cup on the tray.

Sarah peered in at eight pills in various colors and sizes. "All these? What are they for?"

"Yep, every last one of them. Some are fever reducers, pain relievers, antinausea, antispasmodics, anti-inflammatories, and antibiotics. Now, down the hatch." Peggy handed her the water.

Sarah swallowed a huge capsule and clutched the thin white blanket. "Will I be okay? I'm supposed to get married in a month or two."

"You're expected to make a complete recovery." Peggy swept a lock of hair from Sarah's forehead. "But you'll be weak for some time to come. So the longer you can postpone putting on the white dress and strolling down the aisle, the better."

"Blue," she said, after swallowing two more pills.

"Excuse me?" The nurse glanced up from marking a chart with red pen.

"The wedding dress I'm sewing is blue."

"Is that right?" The nurse studied Sarah over her half-moon glasses.

"I'm Amish. We don't wear white gowns."

"A person learns something new every day. I figured you were Amish or Mennonite, judging by the clothes worn by your visitors."

"Have I had many?" Sarah finished the last of the pills. "Everything is sort of a blur."

"That's normal after a prolonged fever. And yes, you've had tons of visitors—young and old, male and female. My guess is one of them was your groom-to-be." Peggy winked and rolled her cart out the door, onto her next patient. "I'll be back later."

"Wait!" Sarah called. "One more question."

Peggy's expression of irritation lasted only half a second. Then it was replaced by another toothy grin. "One more for our bride to be."

"How long have I been...out of it?"

"A week, Sarah. You've been here seven days. My guess is your doctor will release you in a day or two to finish recuperating at home. Your mother said she could care for you better there."

"Thank you, Peggy."

Sarah settled back against the pillows as the nurse slipped away, leaving her alone in a room designed for two. No one slept in the other bed. Sheets were tucked tightly beneath the mattress. Maybe patients didn't want to share space with someone with an Egyptian ailment. Gazing around the room, she saw a bathroom, two green vinyl lounge chairs, and a wooden dresser. A potted plant and a vase of flowers, balloons, and a stuffed teddy bear covered the entire surface. Sarah also noticed her navy cardigan sweater hanging in the closet. With her inventory complete, Sarah closed her eyes to piece together events in her mind. She remembered getting a horrible headache along with chills and body aches. Then her stomach churned with nausea with even the thinnest chicken broth. Sarah recalled vomiting into a pail next to the bed. Her arms and legs had turned numb and then, nothing else. Seven days of her life gone. It seemed like yesterday she'd come home from preaching and collapsed in the hammock.

Just as she drifted to sleep, the hospital intercom announced visiting hours had begun. Within minutes, her mother bustled into the room with Rebekah behind her. One was carrying a foil covered plate, the other a soft-sided cooler.

Elizabeth stopped short, causing Rebekah to collide into her backside. "Praise the Lord. You're awake!"

"I've been awake before, haven't I?" asked Sarah.

"*Jah,* for a few minutes at a time, but you didn't answer a single question I asked. When you talked, you didn't make a lick of sense. I figured you were still dreaming, but I prayed each night that you weren't permanently addle-brained." *Mamm* pulled a green chair to her bedside and plopped down.

Sarah choked back laughter, which still caused her pain. "Am I making sense now?" she asked.

"So far, so good." Elizabeth wiggled her brows.

"Hello, *schwester.*" Rebekah approached the bed cautiously. "How are you feeling?"

"By all reports, much better than I had been." Sarah lifted one hand from beneath the blanket to reach for her sister. "I'm very glad to see *you.*"

Bursting into tears, Rebekah threw herself prostrate across the bed. "I'm so sorry I made trouble for you and Adam. I'm ashamed of how mean I've acted. If you get well, I promise to be kind and sweet until the day I die." Sobs wracked Rebekah's thin frame while the covers under her face grew damp.

Sarah stroked her sister's head, knocking her *kapp* askew. "You're only sixteen. That's a long time to stay sweet. I would settle for most of the time. After all, I haven't set a very good example for you." She hugged with every bit of strength she could muster.

After another minute, Rebekah lifted her wet, streaky face. "Don't make excuses for me. I've been a horrible person, but I aim to change." She planted a sticky kiss on Sarah's cheek.

"All right, sit down, *dochder,*" said *Mamm.* "We have only a limited time before the next group comes up. Let's not spend it crying."

"What have you brought me?" Sarah pointed at her *mamm's* lap. "I'm a tad hungry."

"The cookies are for the nurses. I've been bribing them so they take extra good care of you." Elizabeth unzipped the cooler and set two containers on the rolling table. "But I brought blueberry yogurt and sliced peaches for you, two of your favorites." She clucked her tongue. "The fruit served on hospital trays looks like colored mush."

"*Danki, Mamm.* You're the best."

Elizabeth rose to her feet and planted a kiss in the same spot that Rebekah had. "Get well. We miss you so much at home. Our prayers have been answered." Then *Mamm* grabbed Rebekah's arm and dragged her out the door.

Sarah had ten minutes to sample sliced peaches from the Beachy orchard before Caleb and Eli crept into her room. Both displayed matching expressions of shock.

Eli stared at her for a long minute. "Your *mamm* said you were back to normal, but we had to see for ourselves."

"Sit, both of you," she said. For the next ten minutes Sarah answered questions that would be repeated many times before the ordeal concluded. Her father kept twirling his hat between his fingers while her brother patted her shoulder as though she were Shep, his pet dog.

Before their allotment of visitation ended, her father stood and cleared his throat. "Sarah, you probably owe your life to your *bruder* and Adam. I thought you just had a case of the flu. Lots of sleep, your mother's chicken soup, plenty of honey tea, and you would soon be back to normal. But I was wrong." *Daed* met her gaze with eyes ringed with dark shadows. "You could have suffered permanent paralysis or gone into a coma. You might even have died. The doctor said you were the worst cast of West Nile he'd seen in years. I'm sorry for not listening to Caleb sooner." Eli turned to his son. "I'm sorry for not giving your opinion the respect it deserved."

Caleb put his hand on his shoulder. "It's all right. No one could have foreseen this."

"God took pity on us all." Her father cupped her chin, his fingers cool to the touch.

"I'm okay, so please don't punish yourselves. Instead let's eat some of *Mamm*'s cookies. My nurses have already had plenty if I've been here a week."

Caleb peeled back the foil. "You go ahead and eat every last one. You're skinnier than a walking stick. We need to leave so Adam can have the remainder of visiting hours. That man has worn out the lobby carpeting."

Sarah scrunched her face with the comparison to a green, beady-eyed bug. After both men kissed her forehead and left, she began to eat. However, the plate of cookies was far from empty when Adam sprang into her room.

"I thought your family would never stop jaw-boning!" Adam said on the way to her bedside.

"Sounds like you missed me. I've never received so much attention before in my life." Sarah brushed crumbs from her faded gown.

"I missed you more than I thought possible." Adam glanced over his shoulder before kissing her firmly on the lips.

"Wow, you taste like peppermints."

"You taste like heaven."

Blushing, she chose not to ask how he would know. "My nurse said my doctor will soon release me. I can't believe they let me stay this long without insurance."

Adam settled on the edge of her bed. "Don't worry about the bills. Neighbors and district members have been stopping by your house to donate money. Your *daed* probably collected enough to build the Sarah Beachy Troyer hospital wing."

"That sounds prideful, so we'll let the new wing remain unnamed." She gripped his hand tightly. "Hope you didn't think I was faking illness to postpone our wedding. I would marry you right now, if I had already been baptized."

"That never crossed my mind." Adam caressed her cheek with one finger. "Since we have a little house and you've got an in with the preacher, we'll be ready whenever you're strong enough."

"You're a patient man, Adam Troyer." Sarah's breath hitched in her chest.

"It's been a long time coming."

17

O that day when freed from sinning,
I shall see Thy lovely face

A decidedly cooler breeze hit Caleb's face as he left the Troyer outbuilding. According to the calendar, it was autumn, and he was glad to see the end of a long, humid summer. He glanced around the yard where people clustered after preaching. He needed a place to hide until lunch was set out. Then he would grab a sandwich and something to drink and go home. Caleb wasn't fond of socializing these days. The less time he spent with district members the better off they all were.

"Do you plan to block the doorway all afternoon, Cal Beachy?"

Feeling a sharp pain between his shoulder blades, he pivoted to greet his former fiancée face-to-face. "Excuse me, Josie." Caleb stepped to the side to open the passageway.

Surprisingly, she followed him, looking as tender and beautiful as ever. "How is your *schwester*?" Josie asked.

"*Gut,* I'll tell her you asked. Sarah gets stronger every day. She intends to come to the next service. *Daed* holds private classes so she can join the church with the rest of us in November." Caleb clamped his teeth together. *A one or two word response would have been sufficient.*

"Maybe I'll drop by later this afternoon. It depends on how things go."

"I'll tell her." Caleb touched his hat brim and stepped to the left.

"What did you think of the sermons this morning?" Josie rejoined his side.

Caleb thought for a moment. "The Book of Peter provides good reasons why we should behave as Jesus instructed. It's not just rules for the sake of rules."

"Ah, you were paying attention to your father."

His head snapped around. "Of course I was paying attention. My desire to be Christian hasn't changed." *Just because we're no longer together.* Caleb met her luminous green eyes, feeling a pain sharper than her poke to his back.

Josie smiled. "I saw you came to the membership class too. Front row—that must have lifted a few eyebrows."

"It was the only seat left when I arrived."

"So you plan to take the kneeling vow and get baptized, *jah?*" She was studying him carefully.

"I'm willing to go through all of it. I'm trying to make this work."

"Trying?" Josie repeated his word with a raised eyebrow.

"Yes. I'm trying to change. Where is this conversation headed?"

She ignored his question. "Either you're Amish or you're not. The same is true of being a Christian. We don't try, we just are. Sometimes we fall short, but it doesn't mean we look for a new religion."

"I'm willing to see if a cupful of water makes me feel any different. I want this baptism to work." The muscles in his gut tightened, giving him indigestion without eating a bite.

"What do *you* think the water is supposed to do?"

He stared at his boots for half a minute, composing his answer. "The water is supposed to wash sins away. Then I can begin anew." The admission somehow embarrassed him, as though he was revealing every doubt and skepticism he had inside.

"Do you think a cupful will be adequate? It might be like trying to rid your dog of skunk spray with a single cup of tomato juice. Believe me, when our spaniel tangled with a skunk last summer, we went through three or four big cans." Josie smiled as though her analogy would somehow amuse him. Or that everything between them was back to normal.

"Do *you* think it will be enough, knowing my history?" Caleb didn't mask his irritation.

"Nope, not for you, not by a long shot." She meant it to be funny, but at the look of chagrin on Caleb's face her grin faded, replaced by the look of pity.

"Are you trying to hurt me because we broke up? Somehow make me suffer for wasting a valuable summer of your life? I assure you, I'm sorrier about us than anything else in life."

His heartfelt admission had little effect on her. "Nope, I'm just trying to figure you out. I might have a solution."

He stared, confused. "I've done all I can."

"No, you haven't. On the inside you're still an *Englischer*." Josie thumped her chest with a fist. "You might have given up your driver's license and stopped using fancy power tools, but you haven't surrendered to God."

For several moments, they just stared at each other. Caleb hoped her tirade was done so he could sprint to his buggy.

But his green-eyed tormentor had more to say. "Since you still think like an *Englischer*, why not get baptized like one? Wash yourself clean of your past their way. Angela Wilson invited me to her baptism a couple years ago. It was a very nice service. Afterward the congregation threw a potluck picnic for everyone who got dunked in the lake by the preacher."

"Dunked in a lake?" Caleb rolled his eyes skyward where two red-tailed hawks circled on warm air currents. "That might have worked for the Wilsons, but it's not our way. I'm serious about becoming fully Amish."

"You could do this *first* and then take the kneeling vow with us during fall communion. You can start with a fresh slate." Josie's face glowed with enthusiasm.

Her earnestness was hard to bear. She still cared about him, even though he'd treated her poorly. "I appreciate what you're trying to do, but your suggestion amounts to getting baptized twice. Once should be sufficient."

Josie nodded. "Of course it is. But Mrs. Wilson said lots of *Englisch* Christians get baptized twice, when they start to take their faith seriously."

"Again, you're talking about *Englischers*. We're Amish."

Her eyes turned very shiny. "I know what we are, but you have special circumstances."

Caleb realized she was on the verge of tears. "Do you think my father or the other ministerial brethren would consider me a special case?"

The sag of her shoulders betrayed her answer. "Maybe not, but this is what you need. Maybe the elders wouldn't have to know."

Tentatively he reached for her. "Your idea sounds *gut*, and I'm grateful for it. But I must tell my *daed*. I don't want to keep any more secrets."

Josie grasped his hand and moved only inches apart. "Would you be willing to try this for my sake? Because I know that once you forget the past, welcoming God into your heart will be as easy as eating apple pie on the porch."

Caleb drew her head to his chest and lowered his chin to her *kapp*. He could neither speak nor meet her eye. Tears were streaming down his face, unbidden and unmanly, but they felt human. Maybe he'd just taken another step toward becoming a Christian.

"I love you, Cal Beachy," she said, her words muffled against his chest.

"And I love you, Josie Yoder."

"Are you willing to get dunked in a lake?"

"I am, as soon as it can be arranged." Caleb answered without the slightest hesitation.

"You will need an *Englisch* preacher. Should I talk to Angela Wilson tomorrow?" Josie peered up at him.

"Not quite yet. Let me talk to my old pal, Pete Taylor. I owe him a phone call anyway. If my memory serves, this might be something he can help with."

"Then I'll leave the next step in your hands."

"I'm sure I'll have plenty of questions before all is said and done." Caleb patted her back and then released her before he squeezed the air from her lungs.

"If you think of a question take the path around the barn, through the woods, and along the river past the old mill. Then cut in between hayfields and keep walking until you see a white house with porches on three sides. That's where I'll be living maybe until Christmas. After that, I've got big plans for the rest of my life." Josie winked and scampered off to find her family.

Caleb remained where he stood, until he could stop the flood of emotion too long held in check.

❧

With his new project only a mile away, Caleb beat his father home from work that day. By the time Jack dropped *Daed* off in their yard Caleb had milked the cows, cleaned the horse stalls, and swept out the barn. Eli stepped from the van laden down with long rolls of blueprints, a bulging briefcase, and his thermos. Caleb sprang to meet him on the walkway. "Here, let me carry some of that." He greeted his former workmates as Eli handed him the blueprints.

"*Danki.* Every project the drawings get thicker and more complicated." Eli shuffled wearily up the flagstone path. "How goes it at the Sidleys'?" No matter how tired he was from his own responsibilities, Eli never failed to inquire about Albert's family.

"*Gut,*" Caleb said. "For now, the house is done, and it looks great. Once we earn enough profits from our current project, Albert will buy a hot water tank. Then Bob can return to hook it up to the propane line."

"I'll check if any scratch-and-dents are available at the builders' outlet store." Eli labored up the steps, breathing hard.

Cal knew his father would do more than check. Without a doubt a serviceable, under-warranty water heater would materialize on the Sidley porch after his next trip to Wooster. "In the meantime," said Caleb, "Joshua Miller hired us to add on to his *dawdi haus.* One of his sons wants to marry but doesn't intend to farm. Joshua said his parents can use help around the clock from the new wife while his son works at the lumberyard."

"What kind of addition does Joshua need?" Eli hung his wool coat on a peg.

"Another two bedrooms, plus a downstairs bathroom equipped to handle a wheelchair. *Grossmammi* can no longer climb steps." Caleb emptied out his father's lunchbox into the sink.

"That should keep you and Albert busy all winter."

"That's what I figured too, but I need to ask you something unrelated to work." Caleb waited until he had *Daed's* attention. "Can I use your cell phone? It's important."

Eli stopped rummaging around in the refrigerator. "Of course. Let me get it from my briefcase."

"Don't you want to know what the call is about?"

"*Nein.* If you say it's important, that's good enough for me." Eli dragged his leather bag to the table and searched until he found it. "It's time you start charging up your phone, if you haven't already thrown it in the trash."

"I still have it." Caleb didn't quite know how to respond. His father had loathed what he'd brought home from Cleveland.

"Now that you have your own construction business, you'll need a phone. It's permissible to use for business. Not to call your customers, because most of them will be Amish, but to order materials, arrange deliveries, and schedule other subcontractors to the jobsite. Besides, construction work can be dangerous. I'd like you to be able to call 911 without running a mile to a neighbor."

Caleb accepted the phone from his outstretched hand. "*Danki.* I'll give your idea some thought."

Eli poured a glass of tea and headed to the front room. "You can charge yours in the barn with the generator. The outlet has room for another plug."

Caleb walked outside and punched in a number he still remembered a year later. *Maybe Pete has a new phone or a new number.* But just as the thought occurred, Pete Taylor answered on the fourth ring.

"Hello?"

The familiar voice filled Caleb with guilt. "Pete? It's me, Cal Beachy."

"Wow, you must be able to read minds. Michelle was asking about you today, whether or not I'd heard from you." Pete laughed in his easy, relaxed manner. "I told her not a word, so you'd better have plenty of news that I can relay."

Just like that…all those months with no communication fell away. Pete sounded as though only a week or two had passed since they'd last talked.

"I'm working for myself these days, so I'll keep my cell phone turned on. But first I want to hear about you and Michelle. Tell me about your wedding, and the honeymoon vacation, and your new home. How is construction going in Cleveland? Have you been to the beach at Edgewater Park lately?"

Laughing, Pete launched into a male abbreviated version of major life transitions—those that a woman could talk for hours about. All in all, Pete was a happy man. And that mitigated some of Caleb's shame in being such a poor friend.

"I'm glad you're both well and that your wedding was…exactly how Michelle dreamed it would be. I wish you both all the best." For a moment Caleb had been at a loss how to describe the expensive, over-the-top extravaganza. "I'm embarrassed I didn't send a card or gift or acknowledge your marriage in some way."

"According to Michelle's bridal magazines, you've got a full year. And she takes those magazines very seriously."

They both laughed, alleviating the last of Caleb's discomfort. "Josie—she's my fiancée—told me about the time limit. She's working on a quilt for your wedding gift. We'll send it to you when she finishes it."

"A real, live Amish quilt?" Pete asked. "Do you know how much those things cost in a gift shop?"

"No, I don't, and please don't tell me."

With more laughter and each passing minute, their friendship and familiarity with each other returned. Pete described his tribulations as a new project manager for a large construction firm.

"You had to turn in your union card?" said Caleb.

"I did. I'm considered management, for better or for worse."

Caleb relayed the course of events during the Ashland strike, followed by the renovation of the Sidley homestead and finally, his recent partnership with Albert.

"You're the owner of your company? That's quite a step up from a plain old carpenter, my friend."

Caleb hooted. Pete's excitement was infectious. "We're a pair of Amish handymen, trying to scratch out a living with household repairs and small additions. A businessman I am not, at least, not yet."

"It's good to start small and learn as you go."

"That's true. We're learning plumbing and heating systems so we can do more than work with wood or install a new roof."

"Did I hear you correctly—you have a fiancée? Good for you, Cal. Since I broke the ice, you're the second of my friends to get engaged."

"I'm not officially engaged yet. In fact, we've been going through a rough patch." He waited a moment to see if Pete would comment, but he remained silent. "I can't seem to live down the mistakes I made in the city. I've told Josie more than she ever wanted to know."

"And she's throwing it back in your face?" Pete asked.

"Not at all. I'm the one who can't seem to forget and move on."

Again Pete didn't comment, perhaps bewildered by the change of topics. Men could discuss work endlessly, but relationships? Those conversations usually lasted a scant sixty seconds.

"I know I have no right to ask for more favors, but you might be best suited to help."

"Sure, what can I do?" Pete replied without another thought.

"Josie watched her *Englisch* friend get baptized in a pond a couple years ago. She thinks that kind of baptism could…get rid of my guilt. Isn't that what you did after you met Michelle and joined her church?"

"Whew." Pete whistled through his teeth. "For a moment I thought you wanted me to be some kind of counselor. I can't even remember to take out the trash without constant reminders."

"Would your preacher be willing to baptize someone about to join an Amish church?" Caleb held his breath, waiting for the answer.

"I don't know why not. I'll call the church office when we hang up. Our minister would want to meet you to make sure you understand what this entails. And he'll ask you plenty of questions."

"I'll do whatever is necessary. I had planned to do this for Josie's sake, but the more I think about it, I'm doing this for me."

"I'll be in touch after I set up the preliminaries," said Pete. "Do you still have the same cell number you did before?"

"Yes. Today I used my father's because mine wasn't charged. But I'll plug it in as soon as we get off the phone. Call me any time, night or day."

"Sounds like you're taking some big steps—starting a business, joining a church, getting hitched."

"In case you haven't noticed, we're not getting any younger. Thanks, Pete."

"You're welcome. It's a small favor in exchange for a handmade Amish quilt."

"Thanks, Pete." After clicking the phone shut, Caleb gave thanks for his friend. Once again Pete had come through for him. Another flicker of light appeared at the end of a long, dark tunnel. And he thanked God for lighting the match.

❧

Eli awoke with a start and glanced around. He'd fallen asleep in his chair while studying the Book of Peter to prepare his next sermon. Now his notes and papers were scattered across the floor, his tea was ice cold, and he'd developed a crick in his neck. His *fraa* had dozed off in the rocker, her needlework abandoned in her lap. On the other side of the room sat his son, neither reading nor napping. Caleb seemed to be studying them.

"Have you taken up the exciting pastime of watching your parents sleep?" Eli kneaded the tight cords at the back of his neck. "I'd better wake your *mamm* and help her upstairs. Sleeping upright isn't good for our old bones." He slowly rose from the chair to loosen his tight vertebrae.

"*Daed*, I've been waiting to talk to you. I didn't want to wake you after a tiring day at work." Caleb flexed his fingers.

"Can this wait until tomorrow, son? You could probably use a good night's sleep too." Eli shook Elizabeth's shoulder. "Come to bed, *fraa*."

"It can, but if you don't mind, I would really appreciate getting something off my chest."

Eli remembered how problems seemed immediate and crucial

when one was young. "Let me take your mother upstairs and then I'll come back down. Why don't you fix me another cup of tea? This one is cold."

Elizabeth staggered from the rocker. "Don't stay up too late, Caleb. You look as exhausted as we feel." She clung to Eli's arm as they limped stiffly from the room.

Ten minutes later Eli found Caleb on the back porch, gazing at a clear sky studded with stars. A steaming mug of chamomile tea sat next to his usual chair, along with a can of Coke next to the swing. "Nice night," he said, joining Caleb at the rail. "It'll be *gut* for sleeping. Time to get the heavier quilts out of the trunk."

His son turned from the awe-inspiring view and handed back his cell phone. "*Danki* for letting me use yours. And I think you're right. I've plugged mine in and will use it for construction purposes." Caleb sat down next to his can of soda. "I wanted to talk about my phone call."

Eli slumped into the chair, eager for his tea, not late-night chitchat. "I don't need to hear your business. I trust you."

"My call wasn't work related. I owed my friend, Pete Taylor, an apology for dropping off the planet after his and Michelle's visit here. That had to have been April, maybe even March, before their wedding. I never congratulated them on their marriage, despite everything Pete did for me in Cleveland. I've been a terrible friend."

Eli took a sip of tea, having burned his tongue too many times to count. "How is the young couple faring? Is Pete working steadily now that he has a wife to support?"

"Pete's job is secure and so is Michelle's, but I didn't call solely to express congratulations. I called to ask him for another favor—number 879, if anybody's counting." Caleb leaned back in his chair and released a hollow-sounding laugh.

Eli tried to concentrate despite his fatigue. "You'll soon join our church and accept our way of life. Your contact with the Taylors will be minimal, although they'll always be welcome here. What favor could you possibly need from them that your family can't provide for you?"

After a sip of Coke, his son launched into a convoluted story about Josie's former employer, Michelle Taylor's preacher in Lakewood, the lake at Mohican State Park, and the burdens of sin. When Caleb concluded, he sat staring into space for almost a full minute.

Eli rubbed his eyelids, confused. "Why on earth would you need to get baptized at a swimming hole when it will be part of our fall communion service? You'll invite the Holy Spirit into your heart when you join the church." Unwittingly Eli gripped the arms of his chair as though in danger of falling.

Caleb finished his soda and locked eyes with him. "I intend to get baptized twice. Although I know you probably wouldn't like the idea, I wanted to tell you anyway. The *Englisch* way will help me break free from my old life."

"Ridiculous." Eli punctuated his single-word summation with a stomp of his foot. "You left on *rumschpringe* to see how the rest of the world lived. You went to Cleveland, you realized it wasn't for you, and you came home. End of story. I'll admit you stayed longer than most during your running-around, but when you walked through our door on Christmas Eve you *broke clean from your past.* You are home with a family who loves you, Caleb. No one holds anything against you because you left. If a district member still snubs you that is their problem, not yours. You will answer only to God for your sins."

Caleb stared into darkness so long Eli thought their conversation might have ended. "I understand what you're saying and I respect your opinion, but I intend to take this step before committing to our faith."

"Then you are willful," snapped Eli. "No different from your insistence on using a Sawzall on that roof. As your bishop I forbid you from pursuing this nonsense."

Lifting his chin, Caleb turned to face him. "Who I used to be has driven a wedge between Josie and me. Not because she won't forgive me, but because I can't forgive myself. She suggested this idea, and I want to take her advice. Otherwise, she won't believe that I want our relationship to work."

His words were as soft as a cat's purr, but Eli wasn't moved by his son's eloquence. "Then Josie Yoder is behaving as willfully as you. *Make our relationship work*—that's how an *Englischer* talks. That's how an *Englischer* thinks. You two should forget this nonsense, finish your membership classes, and take the kneeling vow next month. You're making this complicated when it's really very simple: Submit, and give your life to God." Eli pushed himself to his feet, wearier than he thought possible. "You're welcome to consult the other district ministers on this matter if you like."

Caleb reached out to lend support as Eli crossed the porch. "No, I realize you're instructing me in accordance with our *Ordnung*. The other elders will offer the same advice. But I'm planning to do this soon, and follow through with my remaining classes. I invite you and *Mamm* to witness, but I understand if you choose not to come."

Shrugging off his son's hand, Eli braced himself against a post. "I can walk on my own accord; I'm no cripple. And I suggest you pray long and hard about jumping into a lake with a bunch of strangers." Exhaustion was rapidly turning him mean-spirited, not an enviable trait for a bishop.

"I won't be jumping. I will walk slowly with my eyes fixed on the future and the man I want to be. *Gut nacht, Daed*." Caleb pulled open the screen door and entered the kitchen. On the table the kerosene lamp threw off a pool of yellow light, its wick turned low.

Eli remained on the porch, reflecting on what had transpired. Just when he thought his son had turned the corner, Caleb pulled this stunt. Would he ever become a simple Plain man? And that Yoder gal must have rocks in her head or she wouldn't lead him down this path. But the bishop could no longer think straight. He was even too tired to pray.

Tonight, he would rest. Tomorrow he would bow his head and seek divine guidance for another baffling conundrum with his firstborn. Then he would do what had always served him well for the last twenty years: He would talk matters over with his *fraa*.

18

Clothed then in blood washed linen
How I'll sing Thy sovereign grace

 lizabeth punched the pillow a second time and pulled the covers tight beneath her chin. It was too early to get up and too chilly to do anything but bury her head and catch another forty winks. Digging the heavy quilt from the cedar chest had been a *gut* idea on the part of her *ehemann*. If this cold snap continued, she would have Caleb build a fire in the living room woodstove, besides the one in the kitchen. They'd already put that one to use weeks ago. Heat from the front room's stove would drift up to their bedroom through vents cut in the floor, while the kitchen's woodburner warmed her *kinners'* bedrooms. Elizabeth shifted again, looking for a comfortable position for her stiff back.

"What has you tossing and turning?" Eli's question floated through the air in the dark. Not a hint of dawn showed beneath the muslin curtains.

"I'm thinking this frost will put an end to my garden. And I haven't picked the last apples from our trees near the pasture fence."

"*Ach,* leave those for the birds. You've canned enough to make pies all winter long." Eli shifted closer beneath the covers.

"The temperature is another thorn in my foot. If it's this cold in October, what does this bode for January? My joints are already complaining about the dampness."

"What would my bride have me do?" he asked. "Pray for balmy weather for Wayne County this winter?"

She smiled at his affectionate moniker. "*Jah,* or buy us a nice retirement home someplace warm. I heard that Pinecraft, Florida, is mild year-round."

Eli snorted. "Big talker. I can't picture you moving that far from your children. At least, not until we get all four married—and Katie isn't even thirteen."

Elizabeth settled her head against his shoulder. "I can dream, can't I? Now go back to sleep. Caleb has been doing barn chores every morning. You have plenty of time before Jack picks you up for work."

"I don't need more sleep. What I need is advice from someone with a level head."

"That counts me out." Elizabeth pulled the covers over her head like a turtle into its shell and produced a very believable snore.

Eli yanked down the quilt. "You're my best available choice. Help me, *fraa*, before I do something wrong with Caleb. I need a *mamm's* point of view."

That got her attention. She boosted herself higher against the pillows. "Tell me what happened. You two have been getting along well for months. Is this about you not calling a doctor for Sarah? No one blames you, Eli—not Sarah and not Adam."

Eli struck a match to light the kerosene lamp next to their bed. The wick produced an amber glow that visibly warmed the room. "No, this isn't about Sarah. I thank God she's recovering nicely. This is about something our son brought up after you went to bed. I was so tired I couldn't see any logic to his idea. Now that I've slept and prayed on the matter, I still think it's a harebrained notion."

Elizabeth reached for his hand. "Let's go downstairs to the kitchen. Caleb is outside in the barn and the girls aren't up yet. We can talk while the coffee brews and keep our ears open for Sarah and Rebekah. I'll need caffeine if I'm to be any help at all."

Eli slung his legs out of bed. "I hope you bought plenty of Folgers. This might take more than a single pot."

Fifteen minutes later they were bundled in thick bathrobes at the table, sipping their first cup. Eli hadn't taken time to build a fire. "Tell me, *ehemann*. What's got you troubled?" she said.

Eli sighed and repeated last night's conversation with Caleb. "Can you make sense of this? Caleb wishes to get baptized twice—once in a river or pond with a bunch of *Englischers*, and a second time with the young people at our communion service." Glancing at the stairs, Eli lowered his voice. "Have you ever heard such gibberish? All the water in the Atlantic Ocean can't wash away that horrible tattoo. He needs to keep his sleeves down and forget about it." Eli hissed the words through his teeth, his vehemence revealing a man deeply distressed.

Elizabeth swallowed another mouthful of coffee and set her cup primly on the saucer. She had to choose her words carefully to be the voice of reason, even if she had no experience with the situation. "John baptized Jesus in the waters of a river. No cup of water had been poured over his head. Instead, the Jordan River washed away dust from the road because our Savior was sinless. If Caleb wants to be washed clean in the Mohican River or Killbuck Creek or in somebody's farm pond, what could it hurt?" She lifted the coffee carafe to refill both cups.

Eli stared, transfixed, as though she'd grown a third ear. "What would it hurt?" He repeated her question. "I am the bishop of our congregation, the man charged with upholding the *Ordnung* and maintaining the old ways that have served us for hundreds of years. When change comes to our district, it's after much prayer, many discussions among the ministers, and sometimes even a vote by the membership. Our son wants to casually throw the practices of another Christian sect into our worship. And you think it's a practical idea?"

Elizabeth twisted her paper napkin into a corded rope. "If I understood you correctly, Caleb doesn't wish to change our district's policies. This is something meant solely for him, to heal his shame."

Eli emitted a sound akin to a dog's bark. "Heal his shame, *bah*. That sounds like feeling sorry for yourself after you fell into the hog pen. When all you need to do is climb out and wash off." He picked up his mug and drank deeply.

"In his own way, isn't that what Caleb is trying to do? If he plans to join our church and start following our *Ordnung* at the next communion service, then I don't think you should judge him. Or try to prevent this."

"We're not to call attention to ourselves in this showy fashion. That is for the *Englisch* Christian believers." Eli opened his mouth to say more, but clamped his lips together instead. His expression, however, didn't soften.

"You asked for my advice, *ehemann,* and now I've given it to you. I believe you should tread carefully on thin ice."

"*Danki* for your opinion." It appeared to take great effort for the bishop to utter those four words. "Now if I can trouble you for a bowl of oatmeal, I need to get ready for work. Jack and the crew will arrive in thirty minutes."

"It would be my pleasure." Elizabeth patted his arm and set about her normal morning routine. But she didn't need to see his pinched frown or the sag of his shoulders to realize his disappointment. Eli had expected her to support his decision, not just as their bishop, but as her husband and head of the family. Parents often turned to each other for a united front when teenagers tested the limits of household rules. And in the past she would have gone along even if she didn't agree one hundred percent. For everyone's well-being, it was important that a child didn't divide and conquer.

But Caleb wasn't a child. He wasn't even a teenager anymore. He was a grown man who was suffering from his past mistakes. Caleb had approached his father as an adult and offered respect for Eli's dual roles in his life. His decision had been reached after months of struggle. And frankly, what would it hurt? Sometimes exceptions should be made to their *Ordnung,* exceptions that could restore a man's soul and bring peace to their household.

"Please, Lord, shine Your healing light on my son," she prayed. "And give Your loyal servant Eli wisdom and patience to deal with this crisis."

When Elizabeth opened her eyes, her basket of laundry still needed to be folded, a kettle of water was boiling away on the stove, and the saucepan of oats was just beginning to thicken. On the surface, everything was business as usual for the Beachys that morning. But something had changed—a shift on their family's axis. Whether or not Eli ever accepted Caleb's choices, she knew her son would find his true path in the Plain community. Of that, she was absolutely certain.

ॐ

On the last Saturday in October Josie hopped in her two-seater buggy pulled by their fastest Standardbred and arrived at the Beachy farm shortly after nine o'clock. She knew she would be early, but didn't wish to hang around her house any longer. One of her parents would try to talk her out of participating in today's momentous event.

Momentous for Caleb, and also for her.

Both *Mamm* and *Daed* hated the thought of Caleb going against district rules and their *Ordnung* in this fashion. When Josie admitted the idea had been hers, their expressions rivaled the time they'd witnessed a monkey manning the reins of an elephant while wearing a red top hat. After the elder Yoders recovered their wits, they took turns making doom-and-gloom predictions that could stem from Caleb's rash actions. *Daed* concluded that if this led to a delay in joining the church for another year, their hands would be tied. After all, Caleb's father was the bishop. *Mamm* sat wringing her hands in her lap all throughout breakfast. "I had such high hopes," she had muttered more than once.

Josie nodded with proper respect and deference and then packed the cooler with her special four-bean salad, along with a roaster of fried chicken. She'd orchestrated a covered dish picnic after Caleb's baptism, just like the Wilsons had for their congregation. With no clue as to how many people would brave censure to show up, it had been difficult to decide upon a logical amount of food. Sarah assured her that baked beans would arrive at the park even if she didn't. Angela Wilson promised to make potato salad and another pan of chicken wings. She also volunteered use of her chest freezer for leftovers, in case the number of guests was fewer than ten.

Let the Lord work out the details. Josie repeated what she'd seen on a calendar page all the way to the Beachys. By the time she knocked timidly on their back door she had full faith in the words, even if her parents didn't.

Elizabeth separated the curtains and gaped at her. "Why are you here so early, Josie? Caleb didn't expect you for another hour. He's still in the shower."

"I was eager to get started," Josie called as the curtains dropped in place.

A moment later Elizabeth yanked open the door. "Why are you standing there instead of coming inside? It's chilly today. Let's hope the sun shows its face this afternoon."

"*Nein*, I'm content to wait for Cal out here." Josie pointed at the porch swing.

"Don't be foolish. The bishop is at our neighbors' if that's why you're hiding." Elizabeth's brows knitted together to form one.

Josie stepped across the threshold and headed to the closest chair. As usual, something sugary with cinnamon and nutmeg scented the air, whetting her appetite. She spied a tray of muffins on the stove. Blessedly, Elizabeth carried her basket of ironing into the front room, leaving Josie alone with her thoughts. For what seemed like hours she listened to running water, the tick-tock of the wall clock, and the occasional honk of migrating geese beyond the windows. With flagging courage, Josie pondered her *daed*'s dire warning and wondered if she had indeed lost her mind as *Mamm* suggested. But when Caleb exited the bathroom a short time later, dressed in black pants, *mustfa* vest, and white shirt, her anxiety vanished.

"*Guder mariye, liewi*," he said.

It wasn't his expression of surprise, followed by unabashed joy. It wasn't the tender endearment used with his normal greeting. It was his face full of hope that allowed her to relax. Gone were the dark circles beneath his eyes and deep creases around his mouth. Caleb looked like a content man for the first time since his return home.

"Good morning, my love." Her matching reply was in English.

"Has it warmed up any?" Caleb brushed a kiss across her forehead on his way to the stove.

"Not a single degree, but at least the rain barrel wasn't coated with ice when I left this morning."

"I'm relieved to hear that." Caleb poured two mugs of coffee, added plenty of milk and sugar to hers, and sipped his black. "It would have

been nice if your idea had come to you in July rather than October."
He stated this matter-of-factly without a trace of discouragement in
his voice.

"*Jah*, I agree. But this will prove you're a man of convictions." She
grinned over the rim of her mug. "Are you ready?"

"As much as I'll ever be. Will Michelle's preacher need to go into
the cold water too?"

"Of course. He can't very well baptize from a rowboat. Angela said
he'll wade in waist-deep. You, on the other hand, will get completely
wet."

Caleb reflected for a moment and then glanced at the wall clock,
which seemed not to move. "I packed extra clothes as Pete instructed
so I can change, plus a couple of towels. He's bringing me a pair of flip
flops so I won't walk on the squishy bottom. I have my own Bible, but
I guess the minister will bring his. I've studied the questions he sent
in the mail and prepared what I will say to each one. I'm as ready as I
ever will be. Thank you, Josie." He spoke in English, not their familiar
Deutsch, perhaps in keeping with today's service.

"You can thank me later, after you're warm and dry."

Caleb tipped his head back and drained his coffee. "Why don't we
fill a thermos and set off? We don't have to rush if the others won't arrive
until one o'clock, but I thought we could make a few stops at our favorite places. I'd like to talk to you along the way."

Josie felt a frisson of apprehension as she closed the door behind
them. Her unease continued until Caleb pulled the buggy off the road
at a lovely vista. "What did you want to talk about? I told you everything I know about the *English* service."

"I believe I understand about today. What I'm curious about is the
rest of our lives. Would you like me to build a house on your *daed*'s
farm, or add a *dawdi haus* onto this one? Maybe you'd like a small
house in Fredericksburg. You could watch the bicyclists coming and
going nowhere in particular."

"But always in a hurry." Josie tightened her cape around her
shoulders.

"So what I really want to know is do you love me, Josie Yoder? Are you willing to marry and spend the rest of your life with me? Because I surely do love you."

"Do you think we'll still be allowed to marry after today?"

"I do. God would never keep two perfectly suited people apart."

"In that case, I'll marry you. And yes, I love you, but you already know that."

Caleb leaned over and kissed her softly on the lips. "Yes, but it sure feels good to hear the words on a day like this."

She laughed—an oft-repeated response during their drive to Pleasant Hill Lake in the nearby park. For some reason, her mood improved with each passing mile. When they pulled into Mohican State Park, filled with the promise of newly laid plans, Josie pivoted toward him on the seat. "Are you getting nervous?"

"I would be lying if I said no." Caleb cast a glance in her direction.

"*Gut,* because if you weren't nervous, a person might think you're not taking this seriously."

"No chance of anyone getting that misconception." Caleb applied the brake and brought the buggy to a stop. "Three cars are here. I guess that makes sense—the Wilsons, Pete and Michelle's, and the preacher's."

"*Jah,* but look over there." Josie pointed toward a grassy, open field where at least a dozen buggies were lined up. With heads bent, horses nibbled on tall grass to pass the time.

Caleb blinked and stared, as though his eyes were deceiving him. "Who do you suppose those belong to?"

"At this distance, all black buggies look the same, but I did invite a few people." She shielded her eyes and squinted. "I wasn't sure if anyone would show up."

Caleb's eyes bugged from his face. "You sent invitations?"

"Most were verbal invites, but yes. Angela Wilson said it was commonplace for people to celebrate your new beginning. I fixed a picnic lunch for later. It's in the cooler under the blanket. We can't expect people to attend a festive occasion without serving a meal; that would be un-American." Josie hopped out while Caleb continued to stare at the assemblage along the sandy beach. "Are you just going to sit there? Or are you going ahead with our plan?"

He broke from his trance. "Get back in. We'll park with the other buggies."

After parking at the end of the row, they walked hand in hand toward a group of smiling faces: the minister, Angela and Justin Wilson, Pete and Michelle Taylor, as expected. But several members of the Beachy family also approached while Caleb was still twenty paces away.

Sarah hurried to his side. "At least the sun came out. You won't be nearly as cold," she said.

"I'm praying that you don't catch pneumonia." Adam Troyer slapped him on the back.

"Caleb, look who picked me up at Country Pleasures so I wouldn't be late?" Rebekah asked a rhetorical question since James Weaver stood at her side with Katie on the other. "He hired a driver for the day."

Josie gave Caleb a nudge with her elbow. "When did you become so shy?" she whispered in his ear.

"Hi, James. Thanks for bringing my *schwestern*." Caleb reached out to his friend.

"Hello, partner." Albert stepped forward from behind Sarah. "Tobias and Josiah insisted on coming once they heard lunch would be served." Albert snickered, while the other Sidleys ducked their heads.

"For whatever the reason, thanks for showing up." Caleb shook their hands in succession.

Josie spotted Jessie and Laura off by themselves, so she waved them forward. But before she had a chance to talk to her sisters, the honk of a horn drew her attention.

Jack and Bob climbed out of a pickup and sprinted toward the group. "Are we too late? Have we missed it?" called Bob.

"Nope, I'm still dry, aren't I?" Caleb called to them. Beaming with pleasure, he introduced the carpenters to the rest of the group.

But his greatest joy had been obstructed by a huge "No Fishing" sign. Eli and Elizabeth stood on the bank of the lake, elbow to elbow, huddled together for warmth. Josie spotted them first and inclined her head in their direction. "I don't believe it." Caleb spoke softly so that only she could hear.

"Miracles happen, even in Fredericksburg in October," said Josie. "Go pinch your *daed*, make sure he's real."

"Oh, he's real all right. I'd recognize him anywhere. *Danki*, Josie." Caleb squeezed her hand and strode toward the evangelical minister. While Josie watched, Caleb introduced the two preachers and allowed them a few minutes to get acquainted. Then the *Englisch* minister called everyone to the bank of the lake and stated the purpose of today's gathering. He read several passages of Scripture and asked Caleb a series of questions. Then the preacher and Caleb waded into the water several yards from shore. The bishop craned his neck and arched on tiptoes so as not to miss anything while Caleb's *mamm* shivered in empathy for him. Before twenty witnesses, the minister leaned Caleb back and dunked him under very cold water, baptizing him in the name of the Father, Son, and Holy Ghost. Caleb accepted the Lord and pledged to live as a Christian until his death.

With her sisters by her side, Josie swallowed down the lump in her throat, willing herself not to cry. After all, wasn't this a joyous occasion? Caleb had taken the first step of his new life…a life that included her.

❧

On the day he was to join the Amish church, Caleb rose at his usual time to milk the cows and feed the livestock. He showered and dressed in his black pants, coat, vest, and white shirt, no different from any other preaching Sunday. While eating his bowl of cereal and drinking a glass of milk, he thought about the qualities that would be expected for the rest of his days: resignation, calmness of mind, tranquility, detachment, unselfishness, and inner surrender. He would lose his sense of self, his uniqueness, and join a community where no man or woman was more special than the next. The needs of one became the responsibility of all, where any personal suffering from the past would simply not be tolerated. Caleb was ready for this day. He looked forward to a resolute walk, not with assurance, but with hope.

Fortunately, the Beachys didn't have a long ride because their hosts, the Yoders, lived on the next road. Since they carried several hampers of food for lunch, Caleb drove his mother and sisters instead of taking the path. Eli had already left for an early meeting with the elders. When they arrived, people were already filing into the outbuilding. A spirited feeling of anticipation filled the crisp air.

Caleb waited with the seven young men about to join the church. The eight young women waited inside the house for the service to begin. At the appointed time, they filed in and took seats in the first row on both sides. After the opening hymn and Bible reading, the bishop called them forward to kneel and take their vows. One at a time, his father confirmed each new member. He placed his cupped hands above their heads while the deacon filled his hands from a pitcher. As the water ran through Eli's fingers, the young men and women were baptized, bound to the Amish faith for the rest of their lives. The bishop welcomed each male member with a kiss and asked if he would be willing to serve as clergy if chosen by lot. Elizabeth welcomed each female to the district with a kiss of her own.

When his turn came, Caleb took his vows without misgivings. This time there were no outsiders as witnesses, only the people who would remain part of his life until they were separated by death. The new members returned to their respective sides of the room and the service continued with songs, Scripture, and sermons. Finally, the bishop and ministers washed everyone's feet in preparation for communion.

The service lasted far longer than the usual three hours. At some point, people might have grown weary or hungry or thirsty. But for Caleb, those sensations came and went without notice. When he finally strolled from the barn, the cool air revitalized him. He saw Sarah with her beloved Adam under a tree, their heads bent in conversation no one else would be privy to. Caleb felt a surge of pride when he spotted Albert in a cluster by the hog pen. His friend had decided to come back to preaching. Across the barnyard, Katie chased after a calico, determined to make a pet out of a barn cat. Rebekah stood in a group of teenagers that, not surprisingly, included James Weaver.

But it was the sight of Josie helping her *grossmammi* to the house that sent his spirits soaring. Now that they were baptized, nothing stood in the way of the announcement of their engagement. When Josie exited the kitchen, minus her *grossmammi*, Caleb was ready. "Say, Miss Yoder, do you have plans for the rest of the afternoon? There's something I'd like to show you."

She gaped at him. "Then why are you standing around? Get in line to eat. As soon as the men go through the line, the women can eat. Go, because I am starving." When he turned away, she placed both hands on his back and shoved.

"My, you really are pushy for a little gal," he said over his shoulder.

"You have no clue how assertive hunger makes me."

He hurried to the table of sandwiches and drinks set up on the porch. Josie was right—the sooner they ate, the sooner they could leave the Yoder farm. Caleb wanted to take a long walk with his green-eyed, five foot fireball before it grew dark. His parents' *Englisch* neighbor had agreed to sell him five acres. The hilly, tree-lined parcel wasn't suitable for farming, but Caleb had no need of flat land other than a quarter-acre garden plot. Since the parcel was landlocked with only a twenty-five foot wide easement, the real estate taxes would remain low. Sounded like the perfect homesite for an Amish carpenter turned small businessman and his successful beekeeping *fraa*.

Caleb gobbled a ham and cheese sandwich, drank a mug of hot cocoa, and wrapped his second sandwich in a piece of foil. But by the time he looked for Josie, she was already headed in his direction.

"If you've got something to show me, let's go." She wiped her mouth with her apron. "Before *Mamm* spots me and makes me help clean up. I have decades to be a dutiful daughter and wife, but not much time left to be somebody's fiancée." Josie hooted. "I love that fancy French word."

Caleb smiled and took her hand. "Did you get anything to eat? I thought you were starved. Most of the ladies are still in line."

"Laura said she would help *Grossmammi*, so I grabbed a sandwich from a tray in the kitchen and filled my apron pockets with cookies." She pressed her index finger to her lips for secrecy. "Since I don't know where we're going, we might need provisions."

"Not far, I promise."

When they reached the back path behind her house, she lifted one eyebrow. "We're heading to your house? I thought you had something to show me."

"I do, but we'll walk. *Mamm* and my sisters will take the buggy home before dark." Caleb offered his elbow.

Josie looped her arm through his and fell in step. At first she chattered away like a magpie on a telephone wire, repeating the news she'd heard in the kitchen. But after she'd been scratched by thorny bushes, tripped over hidden roots in the path, and stubbed her toe twice, Josie tugged her hand free. "We seem to be going in circles. Where on earth are you taking me? Can't we rest for a while in the old mill? No one will see us, and I'm sure they wouldn't mind if they did." She rubbed a bloody scratch on her arm.

"Speaking of the old gristmill"—Caleb lifted her chin to capture her attention—"who do you suppose owns that historic building?"

"I don't know. Maybe the Alexanders?"

"Nope."

Josie pursed her lips, peering up at him. "Do your parents?"

"No, not the Eli Beachy family." Caleb crossed his arms over his vest.

"Then who?" She stomped her foot with waning patience.

"You and I do—the Caleb Beachy family. At least we will after the title transfer. We've just walked the property line of our new homesite."

Josie studied him carefully. "You're teasing me, right?"

"I would never joke about something so important. What do you think? Could you tolerate a view of the old water wheel instead of the bike path?"

Her initial comment became lost in the folds of his coat as she hugged his waist tightly. "You bought the old mill?" she asked.

"I did. I thought Albert and I could fix it up after we finish building our house. Wouldn't it make a lovely spot for year-round picnics once we replace the roof?"

"I never took you for such a romantic man." Josie laid her head against his chest.

Caleb rubbed her back. "I've got all kinds of surprises in store, Miss Yoder. You just hang on to your *kapp* strings."

19

Come, my Lord, no longer tarry,
Take my ransomed soul away;
Send thine angels now to carry
Me to realms of endless day.

DECEMBER

When Eli entered his house that afternoon, he thought he had wandered into Troyer's Market in Berlin on a Saturday in July. His *fraa*, Rebekah, and Katie were flying from the oven, to the sink, to the counter, and back again like bees preparing the hive for winter. Sarah was rolling out dough and filling fluted pans with crusts for the next batch of pies. She glanced up and smiled, her face dusted with flour.

"Home from the Sidleys' already, *Daed*?" she asked.

"Already? I left right after breakfast, and now it's almost four o'clock." Eli surveyed his normally tidy kitchen with amazement.

"Nearly *four*?" Elizabeth squawked as though suddenly awakened by an alarm clock. "Where did the afternoon go?"

"Same place it goes every day."

"I haven't even thought about dinner." Elizabeth dropped her apple corer into the bowl of peels.

"What is all this?" Eli flourished his hand in several directions.

His wife blinked. "Have you forgotten that both your son and daughter are getting married on Thursday?" She counted using her fingers. "That's only five days from now. We've invited over three hundred people who will all show up hungry."

Eli winked at Sarah. "I do recall you mentioning that, but you'll have plenty of help from Margaret Yoder and her daughters, not to mention the entire Troyer clan."

"*Ach*, Eli, we're in charge of desserts. We'll worry about the rest of the food after the Sabbath." Elizabeth pressed a hand to her forehead, leaving behind a smudge of flour.

"Just make sure you don't collapse before the wedding." He hung up his hat and coat.

"I told *Mamm* to slow down, but she won't listen to me." Sarah shook her head. "She makes me sit while working, then takes the lion's share for herself."

"You still don't have your strength back." Elizabeth hurried to the refrigerator. "I'd better get that chicken cut up and into the stewpot."

The bishop crept up behind her. "That sounds like something our clever girls can handle without supervision. You're coming with me to the front room and putting your feet up. I would like to tell you about my trip to the Sidleys'." Eli waited until she'd washed her hands; then he dragged her from the room. "Katie, bring your *mamm* a cup of tea after it steeps."

Surprisingly, Elizabeth didn't argue. Once they were seated with an afghan covering her legs, she turned toward him. "How was your visit? I presume there's no buckshot for me to extract?"

"John's old shotgun was nowhere in sight and I have Caleb to thank for that." He rested his feet on the stool. "The farm looks *gut*. Manure has been spread and tilled under and the fields are readied for winter. The men of our district are to thank for that."

"What about the house?"

"You won't even recognize the place. New roof, new windows, fresh coat of white paint, fences repaired, even another porch. And the inside? They now have hot and cold running water, plus an extra woodburner in the front room. All walls have been painted too. No snakes, no hornets, and no mice wandering in and out as they please."

"But no gratitude from John Sidley, I would reckon." Elizabeth slanted a wry glance.

Eli leaned his head back. "We are to serve our fellow man without the expectation of gratitude or favors in return."

"I know that's what Scripture says, but an occasional *danki* would be nice."

"Then you'll be pleased the Sidley sons voiced plenty of appreciation about Caleb's work on the house. Elijah went on and on about hot water in the shower. He's been taking *three* per week lately."

"Not every day? He's a farmer."

"Change comes at its own pace, *fraa*. Plus Elijah leaves his chore coat and boots on the porch instead of tracking mud into the kitchen. He said the new window glass keeps his bedroom so warm he stopped sleeping in his clothes and hat."

Elizabeth rolled her eyes. "*Gut* to hear, *ehemann*. What about the other boys?"

"Tobias has pickled or smoked into jerky enough venison to last through the winter, according to his estimates. He stored the potatoes, carrots, and root vegetables from the district ladies where they won't mold or be eaten by critters."

Elizabeth nodded approval as Katie handed her a cup of tea. "Who does the cooking in a household of four men?"

"Tobias. He enjoys cooking and has mastered soup, stew, chili, and scrambled eggs. But he hasn't gotten the hang of baking yet. He says the oven burns everything at the drop of a hat."

"I'll tell Caleb to explain the knobs on the stove again. In the meantime let's not accept any supper invites for a year…or two."

"You can be so picky at times, *fraa*. What's wrong with squirrel stew and burnt cornbread?" Eli chuckled good-naturedly.

"What about Albert? Did you see him as well?" She sipped her tea, inhaling the steam as though it was a healing medicinal vapor.

"*Jah,* he loves working with Caleb and is proud of his new skills with hammer and saw. I know pride is a sin, but I didn't tamp down his enthusiasm. This might be his first joys of accomplishment. Albert even looks better—clean-shaven and scrubbed down."

"Maybe he's in the market for a wife." Elizabeth lifted her eyebrows.

"That's so like you—always the matchmaker. If you set your mind to it, you'll marry off every one of those boys."

"Elijah could be my greatest challenge thus far," she murmured more to herself than him.

"Wait until you see him on Thursday. Since he showers regularly and no longer keeps a pet snake, your task should be easy as pie."

"I'm glad Albert will stand up for Caleb, along with James."

"Albert had a new suit of clothes made by a district widow just for the occasion. I thought our son might ask Pete Taylor, but he said it would be easier with Amish attendants. Pete and Michelle are coming to the feast afterward."

"It's not a feast, just a wedding dinner." Elizabeth leaned her head back and closed her eyes.

"If I know you and Margaret Yoder, it will be a feast."

His wife sat still for so long he thought she'd dozed off. Then she opened one honey brown eye. "What about John Sidley? Did you speak to him as well, or did he hide in the attic until you drove down the lane?"

Eli stretched his neck from one side to the other. "I talked to him. He was lying on a sheet on the couch. At least the quilt covering him was clean. He began our conversation by calling me a 'nosy do-gooder.' Then he said if I'm expecting payment for all the construction materials, I have another think coming."

"Sounds like the renovations haven't improved his attitude."

"*Nein*, and he had nothing nice to say about his sons either." Eli sighed with the weariness of the elderly even though he wasn't yet fifty. "I suppose not all those who fall wish to be helped back to the path."

She reached out to pat his arm. "At least you tried."

"I got him talking about Emma a bit. He still misses his *fraa* after all these years. I said she wouldn't like seeing him in such poor shape, health-wise."

"That was a dangerous thing to say, knowing John's history of violent outbursts."

"Maybe so, but he took it well. John said he can't stand being so helpless and dependent for his needs. He would rather do without care than be a burden for his sons."

"His sons are *gut* boys. I'm sure they don't mind."

"In the end, John agreed to let a visiting nurse come two or three times a week. I think he needs to see a doctor for his cough, but we'll take things one step at a time. I will arrange for one to stop out when I can be there too." Eli closed his eyes, his empty belly adding to his weariness.

"Do you think John is seriously ill?"

Eli considered before replying. "I do. You could almost hear death rattling around in his chest. I prayed for him all the way home, and I shall continue to do so in the coming days. May the Lord have mercy."

Elizabeth struggled to her feet. "I'll pray for him as well. Now, let's see if the girls started cooking that chicken. I'm getting hungry."

Eli rose too and reached out to support her arm. "I almost forgot the best part of my visit today. While I was hitching my horse to come home, Albert came outside to speak to me. Perhaps he didn't wish his father to overhear."

She halted in the doorway. "You've got my undivided attention."

"Albert said they would attend preaching services regularly from now on. And next year, he and Tobias plan to take membership classes and get baptized. Elijah is still too young." As he reached the doorway, she wrapped both arms around his waist and hugged him. After all these years, affection still made him blush.

"That must have made your day, *ehemann.*"

"It did indeed. I almost cried. How would that look for a bishop— to be crying in middle of a cold rain?"

"It would make you look human—something I've suspected for years." Elizabeth squeezed him again before scampering off to check on her *dochdern.*

"I'll thank you to keep that information under your *kapp,*" he called, but it was too late. His *fraa* was already busy barking orders regarding supper, giving Eli time to thank God for His extraordinary gifts on a rather ordinary Saturday.

❧

"Caleb? Are you in there?"

Usually it was one of his sisters knocking on the bathroom door, eager for their turn. None of the Beachy females had ever been known for their patience. But on the day of his marriage, no less, the voice was decidedly male.

"I'm shaving," he called through the solid oak door. "I'll be out in a few minutes."

"It's Adam Troyer. I need a word with you and it can't wait." It sounded as though his face was pressed against the wood.

Caleb set down his razor, the job only half finished. But since he was dressed except for his starched white shirt, he took pity on his almost-brother-in-law and swept open the door. After all, it was Adam's wedding day too. "What's the matter? Getting nervous and need some advice from someone about to meet the same fate?"

The worried bridegroom stepped inside the bathroom and closed the door behind him. "I apologize for my rudeness, but I would like you to talk to your sister."

"Which of them have annoyed you past your boiling point?" Caleb picked up the razor to finish what he started.

"Be serious, please. It's Sarah. She insists on getting married today."

If he hadn't been using a dull disposable, he might have nicked his throat. "*Jah*, that's what people do on their wedding day. Since the invitations have been sent, folks will start showing up within the hour. Sarah and my family have been cooking, cleaning, and baking all week." Caleb regarded Adam for signs of sudden insanity.

"Just take a good look at Sarah and tell me what you think. She is as colorless as rainwater and seems like she would blow over in a stiff breeze. I doubt she's been following the doctor's orders of rest, rest, and more rest. We should never have allowed your father to publish our engagement. It was too soon after the hospital released her."

Caleb concentrated on shaving his upper lip and then rinsed his face in cool tap water. "But the announcement has been made and today is the day. She doesn't feel sick, does she?" He slapped Adam's back for encouragement.

"She says no, but I don't think she would tell us if her leg was broken. She'd just limp her way through the ceremony and reception. Everybody here has come for both couples, so the wedding food won't go to waste. You and Josie can enjoy all the attention. And folks can come back when Sarah is one hundred percent recovered."

Caleb dried his face and turned to give Adam his full attention. The man looked like he hadn't slept in days. "Sit down on that stool before you fall down. You're the one who might need a doctor before today is done." Once Adam complied, Caleb continued, "Why on earth wouldn't Sarah admit she felt poorly if that was the case?"

"Because she doesn't want me to doubt her love. She's afraid I'll accuse her of purposefully stalling our marriage." Adam braced his elbows on his knees.

"That might not be the stupidest thing I ever heard, but it's in the top ten."

"You don't know the whole story. I've been pestering Sarah to marry me for well over a year, before she went looking for you in Cleveland. I've been demanding, manipulative, and an all-around lousy beau." Adam gazed out the window where his *bruders* were carrying additional benches into the Beachy outbuilding.

"Sarah doesn't begrudge your bad behavior, much like Josie with mine. I know for a fact she's downright fond of you." Caleb shrugged into his fresh white shirt.

"*Jah,* she loves me. That's why she'll go ahead with this against her better judgment. You're not the only one who's a changed man, Cal. I want to wait until she's strong enough to enjoy herself at our wedding. I've become a patient man at long last."

Adam spoke with such sincerity Caleb didn't dare smile. "I'm happy to hear it, but let's not get ahead of ourselves. You go outside and help with the benches while I talk to my *schwester*. Just don't get dirty. I'll judge for myself if Sarah is too sick to take her vows."

After Adam left, Caleb buttoned his *mustfa* vest and gazed into the mirror, reflecting for a moment on what lay before him. What will it be like to move into their new house next spring? Would he miss the constant commotion of living with three siblings? It might be a long six months at the Yoders, but he would endure far worse to be with Josie. And considering the temperament and energy level of his bride, she would certainly guarantee an un-boring life. Shaking off his daydream, he sprinted upstairs to his sisters' bedroom.

Sarah was sitting on her bed receiving last-minute instructions from their *mamm*. Rebekah and Katie were lined up on the opposite bed, equally attentive. Caleb knocked on the wood molding even though her door was open. "Could I have a word with Sarah?" He spoke to the room at large.

"Katie and I are her attendants. Doesn't this concern us too?" asked Rebekah, taking her duties very seriously. Katie nodded in agreement.

"No, this is a personal matter that won't take long. You'll soon be back to work tending the bride."

His mother smiled on her way out; his siblings' expressions were far less jubilant.

Sarah held out a hand to him. "Come in. I trust this must be important."

By the time Caleb crossed the room, he'd completed his assessment. Adam was right. Sarah looked even thinner than she had in the hospital. Why hadn't he noticed how frail she had become? Was he that self-absorbed? "Your betrothed sent me up to check on you, to make certain you're strong enough to enjoy the festivities."

"I'm fit as a fiddle. That Adam always finds something to worry about." She pinned the traditional black *kapp* carefully over her hair. It would be replaced with the white *kapp* of a matron after the marriage service.

"You are by no means fit. I've never seen you so skinny. Adam is worried about you and for good reason. You came to Cleveland to intervene on my behalf. I'm here to do the same for you, although I didn't have to travel so far." He sat down on the bed beside her. "Adam thinks you two should wait until you're completely well. The new house will still be there; your friends can come back, and your pretty blue dress might fit better if you gained a few pounds."

Sarah smacked him on the arm with her hairbrush. "Stop swelling my head with flattery."

"He loves you, Sarah. And he knows you love him. It's no big deal to wait until February or March."

Her brown eyes widened and filled with tears. "You listen to me very carefully, big *bruder*. I might be skinny, but I'm strong enough to take my vows. *This* is my wedding day, and I have no intention of waiting another week, let alone another three months. Adam might have mastered patience during our courtship, but mine is in short supply lately." She rose to her feet with dignity. "Go downstairs and make yourself useful. I love you and appreciate your concern, but I am fine. Wild horses couldn't stop me from getting married today. So if Adam Troyer is getting cold feet, he'd better warm them at the woodstove. Or come up with something a whole lot better than this." Sarah buzzed a kiss across Caleb's cheek and pointed at the door. "Now go. I've got a few prayers to say before the service starts."

❧

Josie rode to the Beachy house that morning with her parents and her two sisters. Her *bruders* would walk the back path around the mill so the buggy wouldn't be overly crowded.

Not *the* mill, but her mill. Hers and Caleb's.

Trying to get her mind around that notion was difficult. Almost as hard as imagining that this was her wedding day. She had always known Sarah would take her vows before Christmas and that she would be at her side, but as her attendant, not a fellow bride. If someone had suggested a year ago she would marry Caleb Beachy, she would have laughed in their face.

God worked in mysterious ways.

Caleb had returned from Cleveland an *Englischer* and had stayed that way for quite some time. Her beloved had become a Plain man at last. She could never underestimate the power of love…or the power of the Lord.

"What are you thinking about?" Seated on Josie's right, Laura nudged her in the ribs. "All the practical gifts you'll soon be unwrapping?"

Jessie leaned forward on their bench. "I'll bet she's thinking about the sweets she'll pig out on later," she said. "Once she's married, she won't need to keep her skinny figure."

"Nature has a way of taking care of a gal's figure soon after most weddings." Laura offered sage wisdom like a seasoned matron, while Josie stared out the window.

Margaret swiveled around on the front seat. "If we can't reflect on the solemnity of the occasion, perhaps you two can leave your *schwester* to her private thoughts."

That put a cork into her two attendants, at least until they arrived at the Beachy's. They were early, yet plenty of buggies were already lined up in the closely mown pasture. Women had come to help prepare the wedding feast. Josie stepped out into a December morning and reached for a hamper of cold dishes from the back. Today she and Sarah would officially become sisters. She had always considered her best friend that way. Now they would be joined together as assuredly as she and Caleb. Inhaling a deep breath of crisp air, Josie hurried toward the Beachy kitchen.

"Don't get dirty," *Mamm* called. "Go find Sarah; you two can amuse yourselves while we prepare the meal for later."

Josie waved her hand, delivered the basket to Elizabeth, and went in search of her friend. She found Sarah sitting in her room by the window. Her eyes were shut, but her lips were moving. Josie stood stock-still until Sarah's eyes fluttered open and spotted her in the doorway. "Last-minute prayers for strength," she said.

"How are you feeling?" Josie stepped into the room.

"*Gut,* so don't start fretting. Adam and Caleb have been more worried than two old *grossmammis*. I feel fine, but it will be a long day." Her brown eyes sparkled with anticipation.

"Okay. I've got a plan." Josie plopped down opposite her. "After the noon meal, after we've greeted our guests and opened any last-minute wedding presents, we slip away for an hour and take a nap." She slapped the quilt on Rebekah's neatly made bed. "Everyone will be busy playing games and gossiping, so we probably won't be missed."

"Sneak away from Adam and Caleb?" Sarah's puzzlement furled her brow.

"No, we tell our husbands we need to rest for the evening. Then you tell your *schwestern*, and I'll tell mine too. They will be happy to take turns standing guard so we're not disturbed. Laura and Jessie both want more to do, and I'll bet Katie and Rebekah feel the same. They can show people our gifts in the living room if anyone starts asking too many questions."

Sarah tipped her head to the side. "I never knew you to take a nap in all the years I've known you. You're doing this for my sake, *jah*?"

"Yes and no. You might need it more, but I want to keep going strong into the wee hours. After the evening meal, everyone who's not over the hill will sing and visit until midnight."

"Over the hill? How you talk. My *bruder* has rubbed off on you. But since you've certainly rubbed off on him, I suppose it's only fair. *Danki*, Josie, for bringing Caleb back from a very dark place."

Josie felt a blush climb her neck. "You're the one who found him in Cleveland and convinced him to come home. I only agreed to court him."

"Caleb never would have stayed if not for you. I'll be forever grateful." Sarah leaned over to kiss Josie's forehead.

"Look what I got out of the bargain—a man who thinks I'm pretty and funny. He even laughs at my jokes."

"You two are a match made in heaven. Let's go downstairs and help our *mamms*. I can't wait to get this show on the road."

An hour later the two couples sat on the living room sofa for the *Abroth*—a final dose of admonition and encouragement dispensed by Eli. The rest of their families, their attendants, and three hundred wedding guests were already worshipping in the Beachy outbuilding under the leadership of a minster. After the bishop was certain they understood what would be expected of them, the four of them entered the barn where they sang hymns and prayed, similar to any other preaching Sunday.

Seated beside Sarah on the women's side, Josie fidgeted on the hard bench. Feeling too warm in the crowded barn, alternating with shivers and raised goosebumps when the wind blew through gaps in the walls, Josie wanted this portion of the day behind her. Across the room, pale-as-milk Caleb looked equally nervous. Sarah and Adam, however, seemed to be contemplating the service fully at ease. Apparently a long engagement bestowed serenity on brides and grooms.

Finally Bishop Beachy approached the front with prayer book in hand. He opened the main sermon with readings from the book of First Corinthians. Josie shifted uncomfortably as he issued instructions for husbands and wives of all ages. Would she be able to live up to biblical standards for godly wives? Or would her foolishness and penchant to take matters lightly disappoint her new husband? Sarah would do just fine. Always a cool head on that tall pair of shoulders. Adam could rest assured his home would be well managed once Sarah's vitality returned.

As though drawn by the scent of something sweet in the oven, Josie lifted her gaze to lock eyes with Caleb across the room. He was smiling like he knew how everything would turn out forty, fifty, or sixty years down the road. She exhaled slowly and just like that, Josie relaxed. Caleb knew *exactly* what kind of wife he was getting.

Toward the end of his sermon, the bishop summoned the two couples, along with their attendants, to stand before him. They spoke their vows in clear, distinctive voices so that even the back rows could hear, and Eli declared them man and wife. They shared no kisses, nor had they marched down the center aisle dragging long trains of lace behind them. Nevertheless, when Josie and Sarah returned to their seats they wore the white *kapps* of matrons.

Josie and Caleb, Sarah and Adam—married at long last.

As they filed out into cold December air, Laura wrapped a wool shawl around Josie's shoulders while James produced a heavy coat for Caleb. They remained outdoors for forty or fifty minutes, accepting best wishes from those who came from near and far to share their special day. Josie never noticed the stiff wind or even the feathery flakes of snow that fell like confetti across the fields. With Caleb by her side, she was warmed by the eternal flame of love.

As they finished greeting their guests, Elizabeth Beachy and Margaret Yoder marched toward them side by side. "All right, my brides and grooms," said Elizabeth. "We have moved around the benches and set out the luncheon feast. It's time to take your seats so we can start feeding people."

"And don't look at me when you see your wedding cake." Margaret leaned close to Josie and clucked her tongue. "That extravaganza was Angela Wilson's doing. What was she thinking? That money could have been put to a much better use," she muttered under her breath on their way inside.

"It'll be fine, I'm sure." Josie spotted her former employer standing with her husband, daughter, and infant son along the wall. Angela lifted her hand in a friendly wave.

Caleb guided her to the two corner tables loaded with desserts especially for the wedding party. On one table stood an enormous, multiple-tiered confection with rosettes, twisted ropes of icing, fresh flowers embedded in the white frosting, and a plastic couple standing beneath a bower of real miniature roses.

"What do you think?" asked Caleb, his expression benign.

Josie glanced over at Sarah's double layer spice sheet cake with sour cream frosting and then back at Cinderella's castle. "It's beautiful! As long as the cake is chocolate under all that frosting, I'm happy as a clam."

Caleb checked over his shoulder and then stuck his finger knuckle-deep into the bottom layer. When he removed his finger, chocolate cake crumbs coated the tip. "We're in luck. And a clam never looked at pretty as you, Mrs. Beachy." He leaned his face close to hers.

Josie expected a chaste kiss or buzz on the cheek, but she received a swipe of frosting across her upper lip. "Yum." She licked away the stickiness. "Are you happy, Cal?" She turned her face up to his.

"Like I never have been before." He snaked an arm around her waist. "Let's grab a plate of beef and ham so we can start on those goodies. Looks like my sister plans to gain back all her weight in one day."

Sarah held a walnut tart in one hand and an oversized Snicker-doodle cookie in the other, nibbling both on her way to the buffet.

Josie reached for Caleb's arm. "Let's let Adam and Sarah get in line first. I want to thank Angela for her lovely creation. I've decided not everything needs to be Plain for this gal."

Caleb took hold of her hand as they walked toward the *Englisch-ers*. "I have a feeling much of our life will be *anything* but Plain married to you." He kissed the backs of her fingers tenderly. "And that's fine with me."

JOSIE'S SECRET RECIPE FOUR-BEAN SALAD

Salad
 1 can green beans
 1 can yellow wax beans
 1 can kidney beans
 1 can garbanzo beans
 1 cup chopped celery
 1 cup chopped carrots
 1 cup chopped peppers (green, red, yellow, or combination)
 ½ cup chopped red onion
 1 cup chopped black olives (optional)

Dressing
 2 cups olive oil
 1⅓ cups cider vinegar
 2 cups sugar
 2½ tsp. Old Bay seasoning
 2 tsp. prepared mustard
 1 tsp. celery seed
 1 tsp. Hungarian paprika
 1 Tbsp. chopped fresh parsley

Combine all salad ingredients in large bowl. For dressing, heat oil and vinegar together, stirring in sugar and seasonings. Heat only until sugar is completely dissolved and seasonings are blended. Do not boil. Let cool and add *only* enough dressing to lightly coat salad. Chill in refrigerator several hours or overnight.

Before serving, drain off any runny dressing and add fresh parsley (1 or 2 tablespoons, or to taste). Store excess dressing in a sealed jar in the refrigerator to use as needed. Shake well before using. This can be used on coleslaw and lettuce or spinach salad too.

I never make this recipe the same way twice, so play around with the quantities or types of peppers to suit your taste.

ROSIE'S FAVORITE BREAKFAST CASSEROLE
By Rosanna Coblentz

2 Tbsp. butter
4 cups hash browns
Lawry's seasoned salt
18 eggs
1½ cups milk, divided
½ tsp. salt
2 lbs. bulk sausage
1 can mushroom soup
2 cups shredded cheddar

Preheat oven to 350°. Melt butter in skillet. Add hash browns and season with Lawry's seasoned salt to taste. Cook until brown and layer into bottom of 9x13 pan. Set aside. In large bowl, beat eggs, ¼ cup milk, and salt. Pour into skillet and scramble. Layer eggs over hash browns in pan.

Sauté sausage in skillet until brown. Add a small amount of Lawry's salt while sautéing. Layer half the sausage over the scrambled eggs. To the remaining half of cooked sausage add the mushroom soup and remaining 1¼ cups milk. Heat, stirring occasionally, until just beginning to bubble. Pour sausage gravy over sausage.

Bake until bubbly—about 30 to 40 minutes. Sprinkle cheese over top and continue to bake until melted and beginning to brown, 5 to 10 minutes longer.

This recipe can be prepared the day before and refrigerated overnight. You'll need to add a little extra baking time.

APPLE BETTY BARS
By Rosanna Coblentz

Crust
- 1 cup butter, softened
- 1 cup brown sugar, packed
- 2 cups flour
- 2½ cups quick rolled oats, divided
- 1 tsp. baking powder
- 1 tsp. baking soda
- ⅛ tsp. salt

Filling
- ½ cup white sugar
- ½ cup brown sugar (packed)
- 2 Tbsp. fruit pectin (such as Sure-Jell)
- 4 egg yolks
- 2 cups sour cream
- 2 cups coarsely chopped apples, such as Golden Delicious

Preheat oven to 350°. For crust, cream butter and brown sugar in large bowl. Beat in flour, 2 cups oats, baking powder, baking soda, and salt. Mixture will be crumbly. Remove 1½ cups of mixture and stir in remaining ½ cup oats. Set aside. Pat remaining crumbs into the bottom of a 9x13 pan and bake for 15 minutes.

While pan is in the oven, make the filling. Mix together sugar, brown sugar, and Sure-Jell. Beat in egg yolks and sour cream. Stir in chopped apples. Pour mixture into a saucepan and cook over medium heat, stirring constantly, 5 to 8 minutes, or until bubbling.

Pour filling over crust and sprinkle reserved crumb mixture over top. Bake 15 minutes longer. Let cool and cut into bars.

This recipe is also good made with raisins or fresh-cut rhubarb.

Discussion Questions

1. Caleb is a loner when he returns home. How does that conflict with the Amish lifestyle?

2. Why does Eli have almost as much difficulty adjusting to Caleb's return as his son?

3. Caleb butts heads with his father on the job site on more than one occasion. How does Eli's dual role as his father and his bishop add to the difficulties?

4. Why does Eli choose to keep some separation between his *Englisch* and Amish employees?

5. Caleb's first outing with other Amish young people in Shreve almost ends in disaster. How and why does he react differently from James and Adam?

6. Why would Josie's parents frown on her courting Caleb if his past history is to be forgotten?

7. What lies at the root of the problems between Rebekah and Sarah? How is this universal within most families?

8. The labor strike in Ashland becomes the proverbial straw that breaks the camel's back. How does this prove to be a blessing in disguise for Caleb?

9. The sad situation at the Sidley farm is atypical of Amish households in many ways. Explain.

10. Josie can deal with the residual effects of Caleb's years living as an *Englischer*, but what eventually causes their breakup?

11. How does working with Albert change Caleb's life? How does his intervention affect each of the Sidleys?

12. Why was Sarah reluctant to admit to anyone just how ill she was?

13. Josie and Caleb believe a normal Amish baptism won't be sufficient to cleanse Caleb of his sins. What does this say about their understanding of baptism? What is it that truly washes away our sins? (See Hebrews 10:10-14.)

14. Why would Eli object to Caleb's decision regarding baptism?

15. Describe how the pathway to faith was so difficult for Caleb.

**Read the Beginning of Caleb and Sarah's Story
in *Sarah's Christmas Miracle***

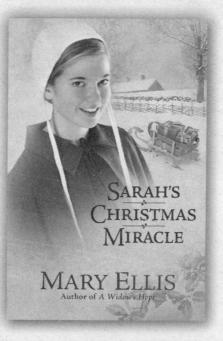

From the bestselling author of *A Widow's Hope* and *Never Far from Home* comes an Amish novella that will add joy to the Christmas season.

Sarah Beachy has plenty to be joyous about as autumn leaves start to fall. She loves her job at the *Englisch* bed-and-breakfast where she cooks and refreshes rooms between guests. She has a serious beau, and everyone expects an engagement soon. Why, then, would she jeopardize everything by suddenly deciding to take a trip to Cleveland to track down a brother who left the Order years ago?

Her family's faith in God is put to the test as the holiest night of the year approaches and Sarah remains far away. Sarah's mother, Elizabeth, has been missing her son for such a long time...will she lose her daughter to the *Englisch* world as well? Or will the Beachy family receive an unexpected Christmas miracle?

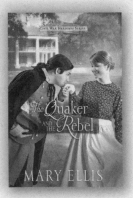

Mary Ellis fans will want to watch for her new book, *The Quaker and the Rebel*, the first title in her Civil War Heroines series of books telling the stories of brave women in difficult times and the men who love them.

Emily Harrison's life has been turned upside down. At the beginning of the Civil War, she bravely attempted to continue her parents' work as conductors in the Underground Railroad until their Ohio farm was sold in foreclosure. Now alone, she accepts a position as a governess with a doctor's family in slave-holding Virginia. Perhaps she can continue her rescue efforts from there.

Alexander Hunt is the doctor's handsome nephew. While he does not deny a growing attraction to his uncle's newest employee, he cannot take time to pursue Emily. Alex is not at all what he seems—rich, spoiled, and indolent. He is the elusive Gray Wraith, a Quaker leader of Rebel partisans. A man of the shadows, he carries no firearm and wholeheartedly believes in Emily's antislavery convictions.

The path before Alex and Emily is complicated and sometimes life threatening. The war brings betrayal, entrapment, and danger to both of them. Amid their growing feelings for each other, can they find faith in God amid the challenges they face and trust in the possibility for a bright future together?

❧